STILL HERE

STILL HERE

A Novel

LARA VAPNYAR

London/New York

Copyright © 2016 by Lara Vapnyar

All rights reserved.
Published in the United States by Hogarth, an imprint of the
Crown Publishing Group, a division of Penguin Random House LLC, New York.
crownpublishing.com

HOGARTH is a trademark of the Random House Group Limited, and
the H colophon is a trademark of Penguin Random House LLC.

Photo of Afghan hound used as Facebook icon on pages 289 and 290 is sourced
from http://a-z-animals.com/animals/afghan-hound/pictures/4329/,
"Afghan Hound XXXIII Dogs Show in Ustron, Poland," File owner: Lilly M.
Licensed under a Creative Commons Attribution-Share Alike 3.0 Unported
License, http://creativecommons.org/licenses/by-sa/3.0/deed.en.

Library of Congress Cataloging-in-Publication Data
Names: Vapnyar, Lara, author.
Title: Still here : a novel / Lara Vapnyar.
Description: First edition. | New York : Hogarth, [2016]
Identifiers: LCCN 2015040138
Subjects: LCSH: Russians—New York (State)—New York—Fiction. |
Immigrants—New York (State)—New York—Fiction.
Classification: LCC PS3622.A68 S75 2016 | DDC 813/.6—dc23 LC record
available at http://lccn.loc.gov/2015040138

ISBN 978-1-101-90552-4
eBook ISBN 978-1-101-90553-1

Printed in the United States of America

Book design: Lauren Dong
Jacket design: Michael Morris
Jacket photographs: (*New York City*) Win-Initiative/Getty Images; (*floor molding*) Jon Boyes/Getty Images; (*floor*) bgblue/Getty Images

10 9 8 7 6 5 4 3 2 1

First Edition

STILL HERE

Chapter 1

VIRTUAL GRAVE

PROMISE ME YOU WON'T CALL IT 'VIRTUAL GRAVE,'" Vica said as they turned onto the West Side Highway.

"You were the one who hated 'The Voice from the Grave'!" Sergey said.

"'The Voice from the Grave' is even worse. We can't afford a name that's a downer."

"Well, the entire idea is about death. And death happens to be a downer," Sergey said.

They had been discussing it the entire time in the car, all the way from their home on Staten Island to Vadik's new apartment in Morningside Heights, and Vica was getting tired.

"You're not getting it, are you?" she asked. "Death is a downer. But your app is about fighting death. That's why you should be talking about immortality, not death. And don't mention your Fyodorov either. Nobody's ever heard of him."

"He was the most original philosopher of the nineteenth century!"

"Nobody thinks so except for you!"

Sergey groaned and squeezed the steering wheel tighter.

He'd been steadily losing his looks for the last year or two. He used to be the handsomest guy in their circle. He had looked like a French movie star, like what's-his-name—the guy from the Truffaut films. Now his angular features had become unsteady and incomplete, as if worn down by constant discontent, and even his wiry frame had become kind of unwired and clouded with fat. Vica had been watching the demise of his former splendor with mixed feelings. There were times when she felt sorry for him. There were times when she gloated. But mostly she felt cheated.

"How about calling it 'No to Death' or 'No, Death, No'?" she asked.

"No, death, what?" Sergey started to laugh. His laugh was throaty and coarse and sounded a lot like a cough, a very bad cough. And it seemed to sputter resigned disapproval, as if he were trying to say that he found her disgusting and stupid, but that he was used to her and almost okay with it.

Vica hated his laugh so much that she wanted to kick him, but instead she turned away from him and fell silent.

She wished Vadik's place weren't so far away. But then everything was far from Staten Island. Regina lived in the most beautiful part of Tribeca. It would take her twenty minutes by taxi to get to Vadik's. Vica wondered if Regina was already there.

They had all been friends in Russia. All four of them: Sergey and Vadik, then Regina, then Vica. Sergey and Vadik had met when they were sixteen and had had a hotly competitive friendship ever since. Vica didn't quite understand their relationship but felt envious just the same, because she had never had anything like that with anybody. Regina had been Sergey's girlfriend all through graduate school. Then Sergey left her for Vica, but Regina didn't disappear from their group, because she had developed an intimate, completely unnatural friendship with Vadik. How can you have a platonic relationship with a man, Vica often wondered—especially a man like Vadik?

They'd all wanted to leave the country. Vadik, Sergey, and Regina had applied to several graduate schools in the United States. They were all smart—with Vadik the most flexible, Regina the most reflective, and Vica the most diligent, but Sergey was probably the smartest. He had gotten his Ph.D. in linguistics when he was twenty-four. And Sergey was the only one who had gotten accepted to an American graduate school, New York School of Business. This wasn't exactly what he wanted, because he had been hoping to continue to study linguistics. But it was the only graduate program that offered him a free ride, and everybody said that NYSB was a great school. He and Vica had just gotten married, and they were going to America! Such amazing luck!

"Doesn't it feel like we're entering the afterlife?" Sergey had asked Vica on the plane to New York. "We're leaving our lives behind and plunging into the unknown."

Vica had had two years of her Moscow medical school left at the time, but they couldn't stay and wait until she graduated. The idea had been that Vica would support them while Sergey was in school, and then after he found a good job, she would go to an American medical school to finish her studies. It was an American education that mattered anyway. For a while it was working out as planned. Vica received her license as an ultrasound technician, found a job at Bing Ruskin Cancer Center, which was the number one cancer center in the United States, and whatever was number one in the United States was clearly number one in the entire world as well. Sergey studied hard, got high grades, graduated with honors. Even the surprise pregnancy didn't derail things. Vica had the baby, just as Sergey entered the job market. But who would have thought that he'd turn out to be such a loser at finding, and especially keeping, jobs? He had the mind of a scholar, not of a businessman. It was genetic. Both his parents and three of his grandparents were college professors. Five years ago, Sergey asked Vica if he could possibly go back to school to get his American Ph.D. so he could pursue an academic career. She'd been supporting him all those years, and now he wanted to spend more time studying? She wanted to smack him on the head, but all she said was "Excuse me?" And he said, "Forget it." Now she kind of regretted it. He could have been more successful as an academic.

By the time Vadik made it to the United States (via an invitation to work as a computer programmer for a prestigious company in New Jersey), Sergey had been fired from yet another job at a bank and Vica had just realized that there was no chance that she would ever go back to school. Especially since they now had a child to support. Two children. "I have two children," Vica loved to say, meaning both her son and her husband. And then two years ago Regina married the insanely rich Bob and moved to the United States as if to rub her newfound wealth in their faces. Bob had developed a supersuccessful start-up designing new mobile apps. It seemed like all around them people were developing Internet start-ups, building new applications, creating successful businesses out of thin air, getting rich overnight, just like that. Their Facebook pages were crowded with photos taken in the Alps, at Mexican all-inclusives, on African safaris, at their brand-new country houses. "Why not just post a pic of your bank account?" Vica complained to Sergey.

Bob's company was called DigiSly. He'd already made millions. He'd been clever enough to find a unique niche and create apps designed to serve middle-aged people's needs. One of the most popular DigiSly apps was called LoveDirect and it was designed to help grandmothers deal with their electronic picture frames. With Love-Direct, children and grandchildren sent photos from their phones directly to their grandmothers' frames, the new images popping up automatically. All of Bob's ideas were like that—unpretentious, practical, banal.

Regina had helped Vadik get a job at Bob's company, and now he too made some serious bucks. Other people were getting rich off apps too. People they knew. Ordinary people like them, immigrants like them. Angela, Vica's friend from medical school, had just launched a very successful app that allowed people to compare the side effects of various medications so that they could choose the least harmful one to take. Sergey's old classmate Marik had created an app that would randomly insert smiley faces into your e-mails and texts, making you appear to be a warmer, more upbeat person.

Stupid, right? But guess what? The app became superpopular. All of Vadik's IT friends were bursting with different app ideas. So why couldn't it happen for her and Sergey? Well, they didn't work in the IT business, but they were surrounded by people who did. You didn't have to be a computer programmer to come up with a viable idea. You just had to be smart. And Sergey wasn't just smart, he had a spectacular mind. Wasn't he repeatedly called a genius by their friends—and not always with irony? Didn't they joke at the university that for Sergey brilliant ideas came as easily as farts?

The problem was that Sergey was incapable of coming up with a simple idea, and the most obvious apps were the ones that were really taking off. Sergey's mind was perpetually mired in existential shit.

"What about an online game that helps you find your soul mate?" he offered once. "Players are offered pairs to choose from: Godard or Truffaut, Tolstoy or Dostoevsky, Chicken or Steak, Pro-Life or Pro-Choice. Hundreds of pairs. And after you're done, you get to know the person with the matching results. Could be location based. You're riding a bus and you can find out who else prefers Tolstoy to Dostoevsky on that same bus." Or his other idea, also location based, called "Touch me!" It was an app that would provide immediate physical contact to people who needed it. You could press a button and find somebody in the vicinity who wouldn't mind holding your hand or patting you on the shoulder.

"No, Sergey, no! Nobody needs that shit!" Vica would tell him again and again.

She did like his Virtual Grave idea though. It was existential too, even kind of morbid, but it was also practical. She believed in it. If only they could persuade Bob to take on the idea along with Sergey, who would be essential to developing it. Bob's middle-aged clientele had to be interested in death. All they needed was a clever pitching strategy.

Vica turned to Sergey, who was still squeezing the steering wheel as if his life depended on it.

"Make sure it doesn't sound like a pitch, okay?" she said. "Because if Bob catches even a whiff of a pitch he will shut you down. You have to be subtle and stealthy. We're coming to see Vadik's apartment, and we'll talk about his apartment, and then when Bob is happy and drunk, you'll just mention it, okay? Not to Bob, but to everybody. And don't wait until Bob gets so drunk that he misses it. Okay?"

"Why don't I just shout 'Nodeathno'! Would that be subtle enough?" Sergey asked and then burst out laughing.

This time Vica did hit him.

They parked too close to the curb. The right front tire was up on the pavement, but Sergey shot Vica such a look that she decided to keep silent. It was a shock to come out of the air-conditioned car into the fierce July heat. It was past seven, but it was still unbearably stuffy. Staten Island was just as hot, but at least there an occasional ocean breeze made it possible to breathe.

Vadik's street was a narrow one, with crooked five-story buildings clinging to one another, flimsy trees with listless branches looking parched, and piles of garbage bags exuding all kinds of rotting smells, fruit and fish and diapers all together. Unlike the other buildings on the street, Vadik's looked empty and new, seemingly out of place, as if it had been put there by mistake.

"It has a terrace! I love it!" Vadik had told them.

"I'll give him two months to start hating it," Sergey whispered to Vica.

Vadik had moved to New York eight years ago, but this was his sixth housewarming party.

The problem wasn't that Vadik couldn't find a suitable place to live, but that he couldn't figure out what kind of place would be suitable for him. For most people, the choice of apartment was determined by their financial situation, social status, and personality. But for immigrants it was more challenging. They couldn't figure out what their social status was, their financial future was murky, and relying on one's personality seemed too frivolous. Most immigrants just picked a ready-made "house in the suburbs/ski trip every year" lifestyle. That was what Vica and Sergey had done by moving all the way out to Staten Island, where there was space for a family and a little more room in the budget.

Not Vadik though. He decided to let his personality guide him, which turned out to be problematic. "Vadik shed his old personality when he left Russia, and the new one hasn't grown in yet," Sergey said after Vadik's fourth housewarming. "What he has now is a set of borrowed personalities that he changes on a whim."

"You're just jealous," she replied.

But that wasn't true. It was Vica who was jealous of Vadik. Jealous of Regina too. Jealous of their money, of their freedom, but most of all of the boundless opportunities the future still held for them.

"You're here! You're here! You're here! The boy-genius and our perpetually angry little lynx!"

Vadik squeezed both of them in a hug. Sergey was just a little bit taller than Vica, but Vadik was much taller. He was wearing an apron over skinny jeans and a new expensive cologne. A lot of people found Vadik handsome. He had the straw-colored hair, prominent cheekbones, large mouth, and typical Russian nose that started unimpressively but gained in heft and complexity at the tip. Vica wasn't sure if that qualified as handsome to her. One thing was clear though, Vadik shouldn't have shaved his clumpy beard. He had that beard on and off. When he had it, Vica would pull on it and complain about how ugly it looked. But when he shaved it off, she found herself missing it. She thought if he still had the beard, that "angry little lynx" comment would have sounded nicer and funnier. Another thing was that Vadik was too tall and burly for an apron, and too Russian-looking for skinny jeans. The jeans must have been Sejun's idea. Vadik and Sejun had recently met through the Hello, Love! dating app. According to Vadik, Sejun was "exciting and complex."

"I'll give it two more months, three at the most. Then he'll dump her," Vica said to Sergey.

"I think she'll dump him," Sergey replied.

"Where's Sejun?" Vica asked Vadik.

"She's back in Palo Alto. I don't want to jinx anything . . . but there's been talk about her moving here. I'm keeping my fingers crossed."

"We all are," Sergey said, and Vica kicked him a little. They all secretly joked about the fact that Vadik couldn't keep a girlfriend for more than three months. He claimed that he had found and lost the love of his life on his first day in New York. They didn't really believe him. What was more likely was that his love problems had to do with his quest to find his own personality. He couldn't possibly know what kind of a woman he needed before he decided what kind of a man he wanted to be.

That was another thing that made Vica jealous of Vadik. He was free to make bad choices. He could do something and then immediately undo it. She was stuck with what she had. Forever. She had been so eager to jump into that "forever" when Sergey asked her to marry him. Now the word made her head spin with horror.

"How's Eric?" Vadik asked.

"Good, fine," Vica answered. "He's in the Poconos with Sergey's mom."

She was always surprised when Vadik asked about their son. Most of the time he seemed to forget about Eric's existence. Regina was the same way. Vadik had a biological child in Russia. He had donated his sperm to a couple who had had trouble conceiving, and he knew that the wife had gotten pregnant, but he never even bothered to ask if they had a boy or a girl.

"Don't just stand there—come in, explore!" Vadik said, and prodded Vica in the back.

The living room was pretty unimpressive: large and dark. Very little furniture. No dining table, no chairs. Just a coffee table next to a skinny leather couch, two leather puffs, and a large flat-screen clipped to a bare wall.

"Nice! It has a futuristic-lab vibe," Sergey said.

"Two bedrooms?" Vica asked.

"One," Vadik said, "but enormous. With a terrace! And there are two bathrooms—one right off the kitchen. The kitchen is quite something here! Let me show you."

"Whoa!" Sergey said.

The kitchen was narrow and frightening, lined with gray floor-to-ceiling cabinets and chrome equipment. There was a huge marble counter with the stove in the middle of it that jutted right at them.

"What's this about?" Sergey asked, tugging on Vadik's apron and pointing at the gleaming collection of pots and pans.

"Exploring molecular cuisine," Vadik said.

"Uh-huh," Sergey said.

"I bought an immersion cooker and this amazing new app to go with it. It's called KitchenDude. It tells me what to do. After I put the food in the cooker, I get texts that inform me about its progress. Like right now I have osso buco in there, and I'll get a text when it's ready."

Vica sighed. Another maddeningly banal app.

"What did you call it? Bossa nova?" Sergey asked.

"Osso buco!" Vica corrected him. "I can't believe you don't know about this dish. It's mentioned in every American TV series."

Something buzzed with an alarming intensity.

"The bossa nova ringing you?" Sergey asked.

"Osso buco!" Vica hissed.

"No, our friends are ringing me," Vadik said and rushed to open the door.

Regina raised both her arms to hug Vadik, a frosted bottle of champagne in each hand. Back in Russia, Regina had been a famous translator of North American literature. She'd even won a bunch of important prizes, as had her mother, who was even more famous. Both Sergey and Vadik mentioned the two women's "magical touch." Vica wasn't persuaded. She had picked up Regina's translation of *The Handmaid's Tale* and wasn't impressed at all. She then read *Howards End* in translation by Regina's mother and didn't love

it either. The books were boring, but to be fair, perhaps that was
Atwood's and Forster's fault, not Regina's or her mother's.

When Regina was younger, people had often commented that
she was a dead ringer for Julia Roberts. Vica always found that ridiculous. Regina did have a long nose and a big mouth, that was
true, but she had never been pretty. She had always been clumsy
and unkempt, and not very hygienic. Now that she was a rich man's
wife, she had managed to clean up a bit, but she seemed to wear her
newfound wealth like a thin layer over her former subpar self. Her
monstrously crooked toes showed through her Manolo sandals and
her long Nicole Miller dress clung to her deeply flawed body. Bad
posture, pouches of fat. With all that money and free time, Vica
thought, Regina had an obligation to take better care of her body.

Bob was different. Bob was so neatly packed into his clothes that
they appeared to have been drawn on him. He had the solid frame
of a former football player and a shaved head that gleamed under
Vadik's fluorescent lights. His face was impenetrable, like a marble
egg. He was ten years older than Regina. Which would make him
what? Fifty? Regina said that Bob wasn't "really" rich. Not at all.
What he had was moderate success, and he would never become a
billionaire. He was too old—the field belonged to the young guys.
In fact, Bob would have laughed if he knew that Vica considered
him rich. Yeah, yeah, yeah, Vica thought.

Still, Regina fascinated Vica. She often wished that they could
be closer. Back in Moscow, it was Vica who thwarted all of Regina's
attempts at friendship. Ever since Sergey had dumped Regina to be
with Vica, Vica had been suspicious of her, had expected Regina
to get back at her, to harm her in some way. If Vica was in her
place, she wouldn't have accepted defeat with such calm. "But she is
not like you," Sergey would tell her, "Regina is not like you at all."
Then when Regina came to stay with them after her mother died,
Vica felt so sorry for her that she offered Regina all the warmth she
could summon. But Regina appeared to be thoroughly indifferent.
And when she married Bob and came to live in the United States,

she was cold and standoffish to Vica. Vica started to suspect that Regina felt that being friends with Vica was beneath her. She must have felt that way. Vica worked as an ultrasound technician and struggled to keep her family afloat, while Regina had a Ph.D. and knew all those languages and lived in Tribeca.

Vica watched how Bob inched past them and planted himself on the couch. She couldn't read his expression. Vica had lived in this country for many years now, but she still didn't understand Americans. Especially American men. She had a vague understanding of women, because she'd watched every season of *Sex and the City* three times over. But a man like Bob—what made him tick?

"Young people," Regina told her once. "He hates that they're running the tech business."

"What else?"

"What else? Death. Death makes him tick. He's scared of death."

"Isn't that true of everybody?" Vica asked.

"No. When I think of death, I just get depressed. But Bob's been gearing up to fight it."

"How?" Vica asked.

"Well, for one thing, he's obsessed with preventive measures."

Vica had made a mental note to remember that.

"Vica!" Regina cooed, reluctantly making an attempt to hug Vica but not quite doing it. Regina's eyes had recently developed a strange glazed look as if she had trouble focusing. People thought she was perpetually stoned, but Vica knew that the glaze came from watching TV shows for eight to twelve hours a day. Regina didn't have children and she didn't have to work for a living. She would wake up in her enormous Tribeca loft, make herself a pot of coffee, and spend the day on the couch watching *Frasier, Seinfeld,* and *Cheers* reruns plus all the new shows that popped up on the screen. Their apartment had one of the best views in the city, but Regina preferred to keep the blinds closed to avoid the glare on her TV screen.

"When I think about what it does to my brain," Regina once said to Vica, "I imagine a melting ice cream cone, all gooey and dripping. It's terrifying. The other night I struggled to read a Lydia Davis story. She used to be my favorite writer. There were just one hundred and sixteen words in the story. I spent two hours reading it and I couldn't finish it!"

Vica often wondered if Regina remembered that she owed her good fortune to her. Regina met Bob two years ago when she came to spend a week with Vica and Sergey. Vica had designed a very tight cultural program for them to follow, but then one evening, when she and Regina were going to see a Broadway show, both Sergey and Eric came down with the flu, so Vica had to stay at home. She made Regina go alone. "Make sure you sell the extra ticket!" she told her again and again. Regina sold the extra ticket to Bob. Six months later he asked her to marry him. Asked Regina! Regina, with her crooked toes and her ill-fitting bras. Some people were just lucky like that.

Sergey sat down next to Bob.

"So, Bob," he said. "How's business?"

"Can't complain. What about you?"

"Funny you should ask. I've been working on something really amazing."

Vica tensed and frowned at Sergey. Now was not the time! He had no idea how to be subtle. Last year at Regina's birthday, Sergey had cornered Bob in the kitchen and started whispering in his shaky drunken English, spitting into Bob's ear and into the bowl of Regina's homemade gazpacho that Bob was holding in his hands. "Bob, listen. Listen, Bob. Bob! We need an app that would provide immediate physical contact to people who need it. Like a touch or a hug. Real touch. The opposite of virtual! Like when you're feeling lonely and you're, let's say, in Starbucks or at the mall, and you press a button and find somebody in the immediate vicinity—in the same Starbucks or in the same stupid Macy's—who wouldn't mind holding your hand or patting you on the shoulder. Do you get it, Bob? Bob?" And Bob had winced, then shrugged and tried to squeeze past Sergey or at least to move the bowl away from Sergey's face.

Finally he had shaken his head and said, "You immigrants think of apps as this new gold rush."

"Yes, we do," Sergey had said. "What is so wrong about that?"

"Oh, my poor friend." Bob had smirked.

The mere memory made Vica shudder. Now she grabbed Sergey by his sleeve and dragged him away.

They all drank champagne on the terrace.

The door to the terrace was in the bedroom, so they had to walk along the long hall and then through the bedroom past Vadik's unmade bed. Vica found his crumpled mismatched sheets stirringly indecent.

Outside, they leaned over the railing and pretended to admire the view. Vadik's apartment was on the fourth floor, so there wasn't much to see. It was still very hot, but now there was a warm breeze that felt more like a jet coming out of a hair dryer than a refreshing one.

"Can I make a toast?" Bob asked.

"Sure, man," Vadik said.

Look at him sucking up to his boss, Vica thought.

"So you're all what, thirty-eight, thirty-nine now, right?" Bob asked them.

"Yep," Vadik agreed.

"Hey, I'm thirty-five!" Vica said, but Bob ignored her.

"That's a crazy age," he continued with the hint of a smirk. "Kind of like puberty for adults. When you're forty, you're branded as what you really are, no wiggle room after that—you gotta accept the facts. People do a lot of crazy shit right before they turn forty."

But I still have a little wiggle room, right? Vica thought.

"You know what I did between thirty-nine and forty?" Bob asked. "I divorced my wife, sold my house, quit my corporate job, started DigiSly, and ran for office."

"I didn't know you ran for office," Vadik said. "Which office?"

"Doesn't matter. It didn't work out," Bob said. "My point is, let's drink to Vadik, and to all of you and to your pivotal time in life!"

They cheered and drank.

I'm younger. I must have at least some wiggle room! Vica thought. She took a sip of her champagne and the bubbles got into her nose. She snorted, then choked and started to cough.

Vadik pounded her on the back.

"Better?" he asked. She nodded.

His expensive cologne had worn off and now he had his dear familiar smell of briny pickles. She remembered that smell ever since she and Vadik had dated in college, and also from the miserable day five years ago when they'd spent two hours kissing on the couch in her house on Staten Island. She'd reached for him, but he'd jerked away and the buckle of his belt scratched her right cheek. It had even drawn a little blood. Vadik acted as if he had long forgotten those two hours. One hour and forty minutes to be exact. He was right. It was wiser to forget. It was always wiser to forget, to let go, to not expect too much, to not demand too much from life.

"Vicusha, you demand too much. That's your problem," her mother used to say to her all the time. She worked as a nurse in a small town on the Azov Sea. She had a quiet drunkard of a husband, a dog, and a crooked apple tree in her backyard. She didn't demand more. Vica's two sisters didn't demand anything either. One was older than Vica by fourteen years and the other by twelve. She had always thought of them as her mean, dumb aunts rather than as sisters.

But how could you help but want things, demand things? Especially if there were so many riches around you and life was so shockingly short? There was so little time to make the most of it! Vica spent her working hours performing sonograms, peering at the computer screen, where the signs of disease lurked in the gray mess of inner organs. "Relax, relax," Vica would say while moving her slippery stick over somebody's stomach or chest. Everything would seem to be fine on the outside and yet on the screen there would be a jagged dark spot, or a white speck, or a luminous stain. And then she would see a bunch of printouts on the desk. Like a bunch of postcards from Death.

"That's good champagne!" Sergey said.

Bob grinned.

"Bobik loves it!" Regina said and kissed Bob on the ear, which was a weird way to show affection. Bobik was the number one name for a dog in Russia. Vica wondered if Bob knew that. But how could he know that? His only knowledge of Russia came from the words of his wife, who told him that she came from a famous and very cultured Russian family. Her great-grandfather was a renowned artist, her grandparents were persecuted under Stalin, her mother once went on a date with Brodsky. All of that was true to a certain degree, just not entirely true. Vica couldn't disprove the story about Brodsky, but she knew for a fact that the artist great-grandfather couldn't have been that famous. Otherwise, he would have been mentioned in the Soviet encyclopedia, and he wasn't—Vica had checked.

Vica had once told Sergey that she knew why Bob married Regina. It was really simple. After he had gotten rich, he had developed an old-fashioned American desire to invest in some old-country culture and a philanthropic cause. Regina seemed to provide him with both.

"You're so mean!" Sergey had said.

A shrill persistent ringing came from the vicinity of Vadik's crotch.

"Bossa nova?" Sergey asked.

"Osso buco!" Vica corrected once more.

"Sejun!" Vadik said and answered his phone quickly. His face immediately broke into a bright idiotic smile. He whispered something into the phone, then pressed it to his ear, then whispered something again.

"Guys, say hi to Sejun," he said, turning the phone toward them.

A fuzzy but obviously pretty woman whose face filled the entire screen said: "Hi." She sounded rather indifferent.

They all greeted her.

Vadik turned the phone away from them and whispered something to the screen. Sejun whispered something back. They kept whispering until the tone of their voices changed from intimate to mildly annoyed to angry, and their whispering turned into hissing.

"I'm switching to the iPad," Vadik said, "better image there."

He went into the bedroom, dropped the phone on the bed, picked up the iPad, and dialed.

A larger, prettier Sejun appeared on the iPad screen.

"What now?" she asked.

Vadik headed toward the bathroom.

"Hey, where are you carrying me?" she protested. "You know I don't like it when you move me around!"

"I have to show you my new shower curtain!" Vadik carried Sejun into the bathroom and closed the door behind him.

"He didn't show us the curtain," Regina said, yawning.

"I'm pretty sure he's gonna show her something else," Sergey said.

Regina sighed, but Bob started to laugh like crazy. Disgusting, Vica thought.

Something buzzed again. The sound was coming from the phone on Vadik's bed. Sergey rushed toward the bedroom.

"Don't answer it," Vica said, "it's private!"

"What if it's a text from osso buco?" Sergey said, checking the number.

"Osso buco!" Vica said, even though this time Sergey was right and there was no need to correct him.

"The caller ID says 'KitchenDude.' What do I do?"

"Just open the message!" Vica said.

"Okay. It says: 'Your food is ready, dude.'"

"Did it say 'dude'?" Bob asked.

"It did! It said 'dude'!"

Vica snatched the phone from Sergey and headed toward the bathroom.

"Hey, don't!" Sergey said. "Don't disturb them!"

But Vica was already pounding on the bathroom door.

"What?" Vadik asked.

"What do we do about the osso buco?"

"Take care of it! Check the app!"

Vadik's kitchen did have a futuristic-lab feel. To Vica, it looked positively scary. There were all kinds of gadgets, all of them high-tech, gleaming, and enormous.

The stove was empty, as was the pressure cooker, as was a strange machine to the right of the pressure cooker. The only thing that seemed alive and working was a square plastic box that looked like an oversize microwave with a cockpitlike panel on it. Was that the immersion cooker? The red light on top of it was blinking.

Vica tried to open it to check on what was inside, but she couldn't find any part that would detach from the rest of it.

"I can't open it!" she yelled.

"Easy," Bob said.

Vica turned away from the immersion cooker to face Bob. He was standing in the doorway with a full glass of champagne in his hand. He came closer and handed it to Vica. The glass had the imprint of Bob's fingers on it. Vica took it and sipped.

"Drink up," Bob said.

She did. There was something about Bob that made her listen to him. His eyes were blue. Very small. Very bright. Slightly bloodshot. He was standing too close to her. She could feel the heat emanating from his body through his expensive shirt. She took a step back but the counter was behind her.

"You're a very delicate woman, Vica. Very delicate. Very unusual. You're a very special woman, Vica. You know that?"

Vica felt dizzy. Nobody had ever called her delicate. Nobody saw that in her. Why the fuck couldn't they see it? She was delicate!

Bob moved closer. If he continued to move forward, he would crush her against Vadik's counter.

She was overcome by the intense smell of meat. She couldn't decide if it was emanating from the immersion cooker or from Bob.

She was about to faint when she heard voices in the living room. Sergey and Regina must have come back from the terrace.

"Osso buco," she said. "What do we do about the osso buco, Bob?"

He chuckled. "Don't worry about the osso buco," he said, briskly stepping away from her. "I'll take care of it."

Vica hurried into the guest bathroom. It was tiny and dark, not nearly as nice as the bathroom adjacent to the bedroom. The memories of Bob's smell, Bob's heat, and Bob's desire for her were so intense that she had trouble peeing. How strange that they had met so many times before and he never seemed to notice her. Well, he noticed her now. Would he want to have an affair with her? He must! She peered at her reflection in the mirror. She had a tight curvy body ("curvy" didn't mean fat, did it? She wasn't fat), full lips, catlike eyes. Vica blew a wisp of reddish hair off her face, admiring the gentle slope of her forehead. Her eyelids were a bit too heavy, but that gave her a "bedroom eyes" effect—she'd read about that in *Cosmo*. Bob simply had to fall in love with her! They would meet in posh hotels that had bathrobes and slippers and little pillows on the bed. They would have dinners in the best restaurants that served butter in little silver dishes. She would finally try foie gras and chocolate soufflé, and maybe even have one of those omakase meals at a Japanese place. And he would buy her that La Perla slip she'd seen in the window of a shop on West Broadway. And then Bob would leave Regina and marry her. She deserved somebody like Bob so much more than Regina! She could pretend to be cultured just as well as Regina could. She could even invent a grandfather who had perished under Stalin's regime and a grandmother who had dated Stravinsky or Balanchine. Bob was getting tired of Regina anyway. Who wouldn't? Would it be too much to ask Bob to pay for her graduate school? Definitely not! But what about Eric? Oh, Eric would be fine. Bob would pay for a private school and take him skiing in the Italian Alps. They usually skied in the Poconos, and Eric complained about how icy and crowded the slopes were. He would like the Italian Alps so much better. And then tennis camp for the summer. Somewhere beautiful instead of that shitty camp in the Catskills where the kids spent their time playing videogames in a dingy clubhouse. What about Sergey, though? She imagined him all alone in their moldy basement littered with Eric's old toys and discarded household items. Sitting in his favorite chair in the dark, his face wet, his shoulders trembling. A rush of affection for Sergey cut through her like a sharp pain. Vica washed her hands, splashed some water onto her neck, and went out of the bathroom.

It had gotten darker outside, and the living room was now bathed in the soft light of the floor lamp. Vadik wasn't back yet, and Bob must have been still busy with the osso buco. Sergey and Regina were alone in the room. Taking dishes out of the cabinet and setting them on the coffee table. Talking. The coziness of the scene made Vica so sick that she considered going back into the bathroom.

IN THE LIGHT of Vadik's lamp, Regina did look a little bit like Julia Roberts. Except, of course, for the toes. But then who knew what kind of toes Julia Roberts had.

"I also enjoy *Frasier,*" Sergey was saying. "It's kind, you know? A kind show about kind people. Sometimes that's what you want. A little bit of kindness."

"Yes, I know exactly what you mean. It's soothing."

Vica wiped her damp forehead with her sleeve.

"Excuse me!" Bob said, squeezing past her with a huge plate in his hands. "The osso buco is here. Now where is our host?"

And just then Vadik came out from the bathroom with his iPad.

They ate dinner balancing the heavy plates on their knees. Vica, Regina, and Sergey were sitting on the couch, and Vadik and Bob were on the two large leather puffs across from them. There wasn't any place to put the wineglasses, so they kept them on the floor by their feet.

Vadik insisted that Sejun should join them for the meal, so he propped the iPad in the middle of the coffee table right next to the platter with the osso buco.

"Isn't it insanely hot in New York?" Sejun asked.

"It is!" Sergey rushed to confirm.

"And you're eating roasted meat?" Sejun asked.

"The A/C is on full blast," Vadik said.

After they were finished, Vadik cleared the plates and brought out large bowls of salad. "Kale and peach," he announced.

Vica found the salad disgusting. The kale was so tough that it felt like she was chewing on the sleeve of a leather jacket, and the peaches were overripe and slimy. And anyway, what an idea to serve salad after the meat! She kept throwing glances in Bob's direction, but he behaved as if he had forgotten all about their encounter. Oh well, she thought, fuck you, Bob. His face acquired that tranquil pinkish hue, which signified that he might be just drunk enough and ready for the pitch. Vica shot a look at Sergey, but his attention was apparently focused on removing a piece of kale from between his teeth.

"Where is Sejun?" Bob asked. "I don't see her." He tapped on the screen and called for her as if she were hiding. "Sejun?" Vadik called.

Sejun sighed with a little too much exasperation and said that she was going to the library.

"It's ten p.m.!" Vadik protested.

"It's seven here," Sejun said, "and I'm kind of tired of watching you guys eat."

"Sejun!" Vadik said, but the screen went blank.

Vadik put the iPad back on the table. He was visibly upset.

"I love your apartment, Vadik!" Regina said, attempting to change the subject. "It's a little strange, you know, but maybe that's why it fits you so well."

Bob nodded in agreement, then drained yet another wineglass. One more drink and he would become unpitchable. Vica wanted to tap Sergey on the shoulder, but she couldn't reach across Regina.

"She's right, man," Sergey said, turning to Vadik. "Really cool place. It's not that big, but you can actually breathe in here. It's the suburbs that make you suffocate."

Vadik stared into his glass for a long time, then sighed. "Did you know that I wanted to kill myself, when I lived out in Jersey?"

Not the bike story again, Vica thought. She had heard it three or four times before. As had Sergey. As had Regina. But they all looked at Vadik attentively. Even Bob did.

"Yeah, that's right. I wanted to kill myself. It happened eight years ago when I first came here. I lived in Carteret first, then in Avenel. Avenel had Mom's Diner. Carteret had a view of the Staten Island dump. In Avenel, I rented a two-bedroom. I had just come from Istanbul and I had a two-bedroom there, so I thought that that was what I wanted. But in Istanbul, I had furniture, and here there were three enormous rooms, perfectly empty. I put the bed in the master bedroom. I put the TV and the exercise bike in the living room, but there was nothing left for the second bedroom. The emptiness scared me. I tried to avoid it, but I kept wandering in. So I decided to put the exercise bike in the middle of the second bedroom. It looked small in all that empty space. I got on it and started pushing the pedals. I was pushing and pushing, but then I caught my reflection in one of the windows. I was perched on that bike, pushing the pedals, inside of that huge white box. I looked like a lab rat strapped to some piece of equipment. I got off the bike, went to the bathroom, and grabbed a bottle of Tazepam. I didn't know how many pills I'd need to kill myself. Ten? Twenty? Thirty just to be sure? I unscrewed the bottle and there were three. Just three. I remember thinking how pathetic that was. Well, I took those three and went to sleep. I slept for fourteen hours. When I woke up, I packed up my things—a suitcase, a computer bag, and two boxes of books—and escaped to the city."

Regina started either sniffling or snickering, as she always did at the end of this story.

"What's Tazepam?" Bob asked.

"Russian tranquilizer," Sergey explained.

"Can you get it here?"

"I don't know. It's kind of like Xanax but deadlier."

"So how many do you need to off yourself?" Bob asked.

"Still no idea," Vadik said. "I wish there was an app that helped you commit suicide. Just, you know, help you find the easiest and most rational way to do it."

"Suicide Buddy?" Sergey asked. They all laughed.

Now, now was the perfect moment to bring up Sergey's idea! Vica thought. But Sergey being Sergey, he wasn't getting it.

Vica reached around Regina's back and prodded Sergey with her fork. He didn't budge. She prodded him harder. He glared at her. She knew exactly what he was thinking: that she was a coldhearted bitch to try to pitch their idea right after the suicide story. But she didn't care what he thought.

"Bob," she said.

Bob raised his eyes to her. His eyes were now the same color as his face. Red. Forget about their encounter in the kitchen, he looked as if he'd have trouble remembering who she was. She hoped he wasn't past lucidity.

"Bob!"

"Yeah?"

"Speaking of death . . ."

"Yeah?"

"Sergey has the most amazing idea for an app."

They all stared at her as if she were drunk. She was tipsy, but she didn't care. She didn't care about being subtle either. She would just pitch the idea head-on. And she would pitch it right to Bob.

"This new app, Bob. It would allow you to fight death."

Bob stretched and screwed up his face while making an honest effort to understand. "To fight death?" he asked.

Sergey cleared his throat. They all turned to look at him.

"Well, not exactly, of course, but it would allow you to keep your online presence after you die," Sergey said, "to remain immortal in a virtual reality. You see, the idea that inspired me comes from a nineteenth-century Russian philosopher, Nikolai Fyodorov."

No, not Fyodorov! Vica thought. But then she looked around and saw that Bob was listening with great interest.

"Fyodorov's main idea was the resurrection of the fathers. He thought that it was the duty of every son to resurrect his father."

"Huh," Bob said. "My shrink thinks just the opposite. 'Bury your father' is what he tells me. Bury your father, free yourself of his grip, or you'll never become your own man."

"Well, not so in Fyodorov's opinion. He thought that the problem with modern man was that he had lost connection to his ancestors. Fyodorov thought that mortality was conquerable, and it was also necessary to conquer, because mortality was the source of all the evil among men. I mean, why be good if you're going to die anyway? Fyodorov argued that the struggle against mortality should become the common cause for all humans, regardless of their ethnicity or social status. Science was advancing in such a fast and powerful way that it would soon be possible to make human life infinite and to revive the dead. Fyodorov thought that eventually we could collect and synthesize the molecular material of the dead. He actually predicted cloning."

Sergey was gaining confidence as he spoke. He had such an impressive voice—slightly scratchy, but deep and commanding. Vica had forgotten how much she had always loved his voice. Even his English had improved. He still had a strong accent, but it was the accent of a confident man.

"What year was this?" Bob asked.

"The 1880s," Sergey said.

"That's pretty amazing," Bob said.

"But Fyodorov thought that the genetic or physical restoration of a person wasn't enough. It was also necessary to give the revived person his old personality. Fyodorov explored the theory of 'radial images' that may contain the personalities of the people and survive after death, but he had a very vague idea of how to preserve or extract those images."

" 'Radial images'?" Bob asked.

"I think he meant the soul," Vadik said.

"Yes, the soul," Sergey said. "The soul that is supposed to be immortal by definition, but it's really not. Because where does it go after we die?"

"Right," Bob said.

Vica saw that his eyes were beginning to glaze over and that he was looking for a bottle of wine. She peered at Sergey, trying to communicate: "Get off Fyodorov!" He wasn't looking at her.

"And that was Fyodorov's problem. How do you go about preserving something if you don't know how to find it?"

"Right," Bob said again.

"But now we know where to find it."

"We do?"

"We do. It's in your online presence. Your e-mail. Your Twitter. Your Facebook. Your Instagram or whatever. That's where people now share their innermost feelings and thoughts, whatever they find funny or memorable or simply worthy in any way. Our online presence is where the essence of a person is nowadays."

"Right!" Bob said. The phrase *online presence* seemed to revive him a little.

"And that's where my app comes in."

Sergey listed the basics of Virtual Grave. "I created a linguistic algorithm that would allow you to preserve and re-create a virtual voice of a deceased person from all of the texts he had created online while he was alive. It's not that hard to run the entire flow of somebody's speech through a program and come up with semantic and syntactic patterns as well as the behavorial patterns determined by people's online personalities. Suppose your loved one suddenly died. You would be able to connect Virtual Grave to her social media accounts, run the app, and re-create her voice. Then you would be able to ask her questions. No, the answers aren't expected to be meaningful—this is not spiritualism. But we don't need meaningful advice from dead people anyway. It's the contact that matters, the illusion that they are still present somewhere, watching over us, if only virtually."

All those words Vica had heard so many times in the recent weeks now sounded different. More poetic, more powerful.

Vica imagined Eric trying to get that moment of contact with her or Sergey and felt a lump in her throat. She had to make an effort to fight back tears. Even Vadik seemed moved. It was only Regina who couldn't help but snicker. That bitch, Vica thought.

A loud sniffle came as if from under the coffee table.

"Sejun!" Vadik said. "I thought you'd left."

The iPad screen had long gone black, and Vica had completely forgotten about her.

"Sejun," Vadik said and tapped on the screen.

A glowing pixelated shape of Sejun's face emerged from the darkness. Her eyes were moist as if she was about to cry.

"That is beautiful, guys. That is a beautiful, beautiful app," Sejun said.

Bob's was the only expression that was hard to read. He sat there staring at Sergey as if frozen. Then he rose from the couch, walked up to Sergey, and punched him on the shoulder.

"I love the way you think, man! Love it. Love it. Love it. It makes me sick that the whole tech business is in the hands of those young kids. What do they know about life? What do they care about death? What can they possibly create if they don't know and don't care? It's only natural that they come up with dumb toys."

Bob plopped back onto the couch that bent obediently to his shape. "Oh, how I love it . . ." He moaned again.

Vica reclined in her seat and closed her eyes. It was done. Bob was hooked. She could hear her heart thumping in drunken excitement. The image of their bright, bright future branched out in her mind and kept growing, past those omakase meals, five-star resorts in the Italian Alps, VIP beaches in the Caribbean, and their own Tribeca loft, and finally to a really good graduate school and her newfound happiness and amazing sex with the wonderful, talented, magnificent Sergey.

"I'm concerned about one thing though," Bob said.

Vica opened her eyes and stared at Bob. His intoxication seemed to have subsided. His expression was sharp, even severe.

"I do like your idea, man," Bob said. "I fucking love it! But it won't take. Not in the North American market at least. You see, Americans deal with mortality either by enforcing their Christian beliefs or by ignoring it. We don't like to think about death. We prefer to think about more uplifting things, like prolonging life or making it better. That's the way it is. Sorry, man." He sighed and reached under the table for another bottle.

"Vadik, tell your friend not to be upset," Sejun said from the darkness of the screen.

"He'll live," Vadik said.

Was that it? Did Bob mean it was over? Vica thought. Over? Just like that? No, it couldn't be over!

"No!" she screamed. "Our app is not about death! It's about immortality, not death. Immortality. Sergey, tell Bob about immortality. Immortality is uplifting. Sergey, tell this to Bob! Tell Bob! Tell him!"

She jerked her foot and kicked Regina's wineglass on the floor. The wine spilled all over Vadik's newly waxed floor. They all threw their napkins over the puddle, and Vadik stomped on the pile of napkins with his foot as if trying to extinguish a fire. They all seemed to be avoiding looking at her. Sergey too. Especially Sergey.

"Sergey!" she screamed.

"You know what app would be really cool?" he said without looking at anybody in particular. "An app where you could press a button and turn somebody's volume down. Like you do with the TV, only with a real live person. Imagine a dinner party and everybody's talking, but there is this one person that you just wish would shut up. So you point your device at that person—you can do it under the table discreetly—and lower her volume. Everybody else can hear her fine, and you can hear everybody else but her. Now wouldn't that be a dream?"

They all started to laugh. Not at the same time though. Vadik was the first with his series of chuckles. Then Bob with his hoarse hooting. Then Regina joined in, but with her it was not one hundred percent clear if she was laughing or crying. But Sejun was definitely laughing and her laugh was the happiest. "I'm sorry," she kept saying, "it's just so funny. Too funny. I want that app."

Vica hated their laughter right away; she recognized it as disgusting, but it took her a moment to realize that they were all looking at her and laughing at her.

She turned away from them, stepped over the bunched-up napkins, and walked toward Vadik's bedroom.

"No, no, don't," she heard Sergey say, "she'll be fine. She just needs to be alone for a minute."

Do I? she wondered, stepping onto the terrace. Do I need to be alone?

The air had become significantly cooler. Vica was holding on to the last remnants of her drunkenness to keep herself warmer and less sad. She was lost. They all were. So thoroughly lost. Why couldn't anybody think of an app for that? To help one find one's way in life? She didn't care about immortality. Fuck immortality! What she cared about was this short meager life that they had to live. Why couldn't they think of an app to make it easier?

Vica looked out at the roofs of other buildings. They boasted tangled wires and broken tarps. Some had water towers, perched on clumsy legs. Others had chimneys clustered together yet bending away from one another like dysfunctional families. Yes, exactly like dysfunctional families. It was the sight of the chimneys that made her cry.

Chapter 2

HELLO, LOVE!

BEFORE SEJUN THERE WAS RACHEL II, AND BEFORE
Rachel II there was the sane Sofia, and before the sane Sofia
there was Catherine Jenkins, and before Catherine Jenkins
there was Tania. Vadik had met all of them through Hello, Love!

Tania had used the face of Saga Norén as her profile picture.
Saga Norén was a Swedish detective with Asperger's from the Danish series *Broen*. Vadik didn't really like Tania, but he loved *Broen*
and *Broen*'s quirky heroine, so every time he saw Tania, he imagined
that he was really seeing Saga Norén.

Millie, Fosca, Teresa, the insane Sofia. He had met them on another dating site Match4U because the vastly superior Hello, Love!
hadn't been available yet. Match4U made it very difficult to read
the insanity level of a person based on his or her profile. The insane
Sofia had turned out to be a freelance doll-maker. She made tiny
scary dolls with eyelashes and fingernails and silky pubic hair. Who
would've thought that three-inch dolls with pubic hair were even
possible? "Touch it, Vadik!" Sofia would insist. "Stroke it. See how
soft it is?"

Or take DJ Toma, for example, who Vadik had also met on
Match4U. DJ Toma said that she used to own the largest PR firm in
all of western Siberia but had to flee Russia because of political per-
secution. When Vadik met her, she was working as a cleaning lady

during the day and deejaying in an East Village club at night. In her spare time she was trying to set up a business selling ancient Siberian potions. In the four months that Toma lived in Vadik's apartment in the Bronx, she managed to fill the entire fridge with different potions in labeled jars. The labels read: DIVINE INSPIRATION, GRACE, LOVE, HEALTHY HEART, STOMACH PROBLEMS, and A LOT OF MONEY. Sergey had been particularly interested in the last two. He kept asking Vadik if they worked. "I guess they do," Vadik said. "I guess they do." One day, while Vadik was at work, Toma poured most of her potions down the toilet, packed her things (and a few of Vadik's things), and left. She wrote Vadik a note in which she said that she was going to Peru to find out if San Pedro was all that different from LSD. She'd bought a package trip that included a week of San Pedro tastings at the house of a real shaman. Vadik hadn't heard from her since. There was a rumor that she had overdosed and died. But there was also another rumor that she had become the shaman's manager and helped him expand his client base.

There was Barbara, the New Age–y masseuse. Before Barbara (but actually during) there was Abby. Then Barbara found out about Abby and Abby found out about Barbara, and Vadik was alone again.

Who else was there? Jesse, his headhunter. Dana, the woman who worked in the next cubicle at Morgan Stanley—he'd sworn off dating his coworkers after Dana. Vica. Yep, his former girlfriend now his best friend's wife, Vica. That was the one encounter he was trying very hard to forget. Nothing had happened, he'd managed to stop himself at the very last moment, but he still squirmed with shame for months afterward. He felt awful guilt toward Sergey—he could only hope that Sergey would never know—but he also felt revulsion because the encounter with Vica had made him regress into his Russian past. He had come here to start his life anew, not to rehash his old romances.

Before Vica there was Sue, a waitress at Mom's Diner in Avenel, New Jersey. Before Sue there was Angie, another waitress at Mom's.

Sue had a faded tattoo of a kitten on her shoulder. Vadik couldn't remember a single detail about Angie.

"I'm sick of this mess," Vadik confessed to Regina right after his breakup with Abby. Via Skype, because Regina was still in Russia back then.

"Of course you are," Regina said, "dating is exhausting. You know what is the most exhausting for me?"

"What?"

"Getting my hopes up. It's as if I needed enormous physical strength to get them up, like a weight lifter or something."

Vadik's friendship with Regina started out awkwardly, when Vica left him for Sergey—then Regina's boyfriend. A few days after the breakup, Regina asked him to come and pick up some of the things Sergey had left at her apartment. Vadik wondered if she was interested in him. He wasn't really attracted to her—she had this weird stale smell that he found off-putting—but he was definitely curious. But when he got to her apartment, Regina was so shaky and sad that trying to have sex with her seemed obnoxious. They got to talking instead. Neither of them would say anything bad about Vica or Sergey—that would have been tacky, but they couldn't resist talking about Fyodorov, Sergey's obsession, and confessing to each other how much they hated his philosophy. Gradually they had become each other's confidants/therapists/dating mentors. After Vadik left Russia, they would talk on Skype two to three times a week.

"I need to be tied down. I can't go on like this!" Vadik said to Regina via the screen.

"Just pick a girl and marry her," Regina said. She was about to get married to Bob and was feeling very enthusiastic about marriage.

Vadik was dating Rachel II then, a social worker studying for her master's. When Rachel II was a young girl, she'd had a passionate relationship with horses. She kept the photograph of her pet horse, Billie, on her desk.

Rachel II and Vadik broke up because she walked in on him

making fun of Billie to Regina. At first Vadik denied it. He was speaking in Russian, so why would Rachel even think that? But wasn't he holding up the picture of Billie and laughing? Rachel asked. And wasn't that ugly Russian woman on the screen hooting in response? Vadik had to admit his fault.

The sad thing was that Regina actually thought that Rachel II was the best fit for Vadik. She was the most grounded of the lot.

Vica disagreed. Vica thought that the sane Sofia was the best fit. She said that it was a good thing that Sofia was quite a bit older than Vadik, because that would make her more forgiving. The sane Sofia taught comparative literature at SUNY New Paltz. She had a club membership to swim the lap lane in Lake Minnewaska, situated about ten miles away from campus. Sofia listed that membership as one of the six things she couldn't live without on her Hello, Love! profile. She kept urging Vadik to get a membership too. "There is a rope right in the middle of the lake," Vadik told Sergey, "and they're just swimming along the rope, back and forth, back and forth, like convicts." Vadik and Sofia broke up because Vadik refused to see the beauty of lap swimming in a natural body of water.

Sergey's top choice for Vadik was Sejun. He couldn't believe you could meet a girl like that through online dating. Vadik met up with Vica, Sergey, and Regina soon after his latest housewarming party, and since the subject of the failure of Sergey's pitch was too painful, they were discussing Sejun. Sergey said that Sejun was remarkably pretty for such a smart girl. Vica said that first of all that was an incredibly sexist remark and that she didn't find Sejun all that pretty. Regina started to laugh.

"Oh, yes, she is very pretty," Sergey said. "The problem is that she is way out of Vadik's league."

"Why is she out of his league?" Vica asked. "He makes quite a bit of money, doesn't he?"

"Right," Sergey said.

"Hey, guys," Vadik said. "I'm sitting right here!"

But they continued to argue, not paying any attention to Vadik, as if his own opinion didn't matter.

"I think I'm still in love with Rachel I," Vadik said. Regina stopped laughing. And all of them looked away as if he had said something intensely embarrassing.

Vadik met Rachel I on his very first day in the United States.

He arrived in New York on a Saturday morning in the middle of winter. It was snowing pretty hard that day. Vadik woke up as the plane started its descent into JFK. He rushed to open the shade on the window, hoping to catch a glimpse of that famous Manhattan skyline. He couldn't see anything but the murky white mess. It was still thrilling. He could not see the contours of the buildings, but he could sense them right there, right underneath the plane, hidden by the clouds. He felt a familiar surge of excitement, the excitement that had buoyed him for months, ever since he'd gotten that coveted H1-B visa that allowed him to work in the U.S. for three years. He had spent two year in Istanbul and had grown sick of the place. He had celebrated his thirtieth birthday there, but the new decade began in the new country for him. Every now and then he would open his passport and stroke the thin paper of the visa as if it were something alive.

The announcement came through with the usual crackle. The flight attendant said that it was snowing rather hard and that they might not land in JFK after all, that the plane might be rerouted to Philadelphia. No, no, no! Vadik thought. Landing in Philadelphia would certainly ruin his plans. He was starting work on Monday, as a computer programmer in the corporate offices of EarthlyFoods in Avenel, New Jersey. He was to live in Avenel too, in an apartment provided by corporate housing. Sergey was meeting him at JFK. He was supposed to take Vadik to his and Vica's house on Staten Island and then drive him to Avenel on Sunday. But Vadik hoped to ask Sergey to take him straight into the city so that he could spend the entire Saturday exploring. He knew exactly what he wanted to do.

He wanted to walk the streets without direction, just follow his intuition wherever it might lead him. He wanted to walk like that for
hours, then find a bohemian-looking bar, where he would spend the
rest of the day with a glass of wine and a book, like a true New York
intellectual. And he would wear his tweed jacket. Vadik had put the
jacket on before boarding the plane, because he hadn't wanted to
put it in the suitcase where it might get wrinkled. He had spent a lot
of time choosing the book to read in that bar. Something French?
Sartre's *Nausea*? Gilles Deleuze's *Cinema I*? And no, this wasn't sickeningly pretentious. Vadik wasn't doing it to make an impression
on other people. He did want to be seen as a charismatic tweeded
intellectual, but it was more important to him to be seen as such in
his own eyes.

Vadik looked out the window again. It seemed like they were
suspended in the clouds. Vadik closed his eyes and concentrated on
willing the plane to land at JFK. He imagined the hard body of
the plane pushing through the sticky mass of clouds, emerging in a
clean empty space between sky and ground, and then sliding down
in one bold determined move until its wheels touched the runway.
The cabin erupted in applause, and for a second Vadik thought that
the applause was meant for him.

"Can you take me to the city?" Vadik asked Sergey as soon as
they finished hugging.

"To the city? Now?" Sergey asked with a degree of puzzlement
that suggested that the city was very far away. That there was some
existential impossibility to getting there.

"Now. Yeah," Vadik said.

"But Vica is waiting with all the food. She'll be disappointed."

The horror in Sergey's eyes showed how much trouble Vica's disappointment would bring to him.

So they went to Staten Island. Drove on the JFK Expressway followed by the long stretch of Belt Parkway, past the gray jellied mass
of the ocean, across the foggy Verrazano Bridge, and finally down

the endless Hylan Boulevard with its depressing storefronts. All that while Sergey sang along to his favorite Leonard Cohen CD.

Back at the university Sergey used to be a star. He was really handsome—everybody said that his sharp, taut features made him look like a French movie star; he was the smartest and most talented (professors used to quote him in classes); he played guitar; and he could sing, badly but still. He could have any girl he wanted. Hell, he'd snatched Vica right from under Vadik's nose.

Anyway, Sergey was still handsome. It was his singing that made him look unbearably ugly. The scrunching of his nose whenever he had to draw out a lyric. The furrowing of his forehead whenever he had trouble pronouncing the words. The pained expression on his face during the especially emotional moments. And the singing itself. It wasn't just that Sergey sang out of tune or that he sang with a gooey Russian accent—although that bothered Vadik too. The main problem was that Sergey's voice, which completely drowned out Cohen's baritone, was plaintive and childlike.

> *Baby, I've been waiting,*
> *I've been waiting night and day.*

Sergey sounded pathetic! Vadik couldn't help but feel squeamish pity for him. He felt anger too, mostly because "Waiting for the Miracle" was his favorite song and Sergey's singing was ruining it for him. Vadik saw a finger of Sergey's leather glove sticking out from the glove compartment. He felt like yanking the glove out and stuffing it into his friend's mouth.

He hadn't been looking forward to being at Sergey's place, but now he couldn't wait to arrive. Apparently, Vica couldn't wait for their arrival either. She rushed out of the door as soon as she heard the car and ran down the driveway barefoot, leaving footprints on the thin layer of fresh snow. Her hug was sticky and tight, and somewhat embarrassing. Vadik struggled to free himself. She looked great though, in those snug jeans and even snugger sweater, with her short curly hair cut in some new fancy way. "Vica, you look amazing," Vadik said.

"It's my teeth," she said, scowling at him. "See, I finally fixed my teeth!" Vadik had no idea what she was talking about. "I used to have crooked teeth in college. Don't you remember?"

And then he remembered. She used to smile with her mouth closed and would cover it with her hand when she laughed. When Vadik first met her, at a college party, he thought that she covered her mouth because she was shy. He found this habit intensely endearing even after he discovered that Vica wasn't shy at all.

Vica led Vadik upstairs on a tour of the house. All that Vadik noticed was that the furniture was brown and the walls were painted yellow. "We're giving you this exercise bike," Vica said, pointing to a bulky apparatus in the corner of the bedroom. "It's like new. I gave it to Sergey for his birthday, but he seems to hate it." Vica showed Vadik where he would be sleeping. Then she took him to meet Eric. There was a four-year-old person, small, sulky, and looking like a chubby version of Sergey. He was sitting on the floor of his tiny bedroom with a Game Boy in his hands. His fingers pressed buttons with such intensity, as if his life depended on it. "Hi," Vadik said. Eric looked at him and said "Hello." It hadn't occurred to Vadik to bring Eric a gift—a toy or something—and now he felt awkward. He had no idea how to talk to a child. "So, Eric," he asked, "what do you like to do?"

"I like to kill," Eric said and went back to pressing buttons.

The rest of the morning and the entire afternoon were spent in their roomy kitchen with a distant view of a playground and a cemetery outside. "They told us that this house had a view of the park," Sergey explained. "It was summer, so we couldn't see the graves behind all those leafy trees—"

Vica interrupted him. "But we can let Eric play across the street by himself, because, you know, we can see him from the window."

Vadik pictured sad little Eric on a deserted playground, rocking in the swings facing the graves. Then he remembered to admire the house.

"Yep, this was the right choice," Sergey said without conviction.

Vica told him that Sergey's grandmother had died and that Sergey's father had sold her apartment and sent the money to Sergey for the down payment. Now they were struggling to pay a huge mortgage every month, but still, it had been the right move to buy a house. Because that was how it worked here, Sergey added. Everybody we knew kept telling us that. You rented in the cheaper parts of Brooklyn for a while, then you bought a house in the suburbs or on Staten Island, then you sold that house and bought a bigger, better house, then when you grew old you left that house to your kids and moved into a retirement community. Sergey's tone was a dark mix of hatred and resignation, which made Vadik uneasy and even frightened him a little. He tried to imagine a happier Eric, all grown up, driving his parents to the retirement community so that he could take possession of their house.

Vadik made a few attempts to steer the conversation away from real estate. In his e-mails, Sergey had always asked about their university friends, so Vadik now tried to tell him that Marik was still working on his genealogy dissertation, but that Alina had quit hers and was busy making an animated Nabokov game, and Kuzmin—remember that shithead—was involved in some business with Abramovich. Abramovich, you know, the man who owns half of Europe including the Chelsea soccer club? But then Vica stepped on his foot and shook her head. Apparently, she thought that this line of conversation would be upsetting to Sergey. "He misses our old life too much," she had confided to Vadik during the tour of the house. She switched the subject to Vadik's long-term plans, but that filled him with panic. He didn't know if he wanted to go to school. He didn't know if he wanted to get married. He didn't know if he wanted to stay in the United States for good. He had no idea. He just wanted to lead the life of an American for a while, whatever that meant. He failed to explain his view to Vica. Even Sergey didn't seem to get it.

They drank vodka and ate cold cuts, pickles, and salads that Sergey had bought in the only Russian grocery store on Staten Island called MyEurope. Beet salad, carrot salad, eggplant salad, mushroom salad, cheese salad, herring salad, and cabbage salad with the lovely name of Isolda. There was some bickering about that Isolda. Apparently, Vica had specifically asked Sergey to check the expiration date and he hadn't. "Look, all the other salads expire on the nineteenth, and this one expires on the sixteenth. Which was yesterday!" Vadik volunteered to eat the Isolda, because he claimed to have an iron stomach.

At some point Eric emerged from his room and demanded to be fed too.

"What do you want, chummy chums?" Sergey asked. Eric declined the salads but took a few pieces of salami off the plate and squeezed them in his hand. Vica took the salami away from him and put it on a piece of bread, then took a cucumber and a salad leaf out of the fridge, put all that on a plate, gave the plate to Eric, and sent him to the living room to watch TV. Now their conversation was interspersed with the screams and squeaks of cartoon animals interrupted by the happy voices of children praising a certain brand of cereal or juice. After a while Eric complained of a stomachache. Vica took him upstairs promising to be right back.

Vadik grabbed Sergey by a sleeve and pleaded, "Serega, please, take me to the subway or something. I'm dying here. I need to get to the city!"

Sergey studied his watch, then listened to Vica's and Eric's muffled voices upstairs. "There is no subway here. The ferry is far away. I'll take you to the express bus. It goes straight into midtown."

The MetroCards were upstairs and Sergey didn't want to chance it with Vica, so he took a jar with quarters from the windowsill and counted out the exact change (forty quarters) for the ride to Manhattan and back and gave it to Vadik. Vadik loved the weight of the coins in his pockets. It made him feel as if he were doing something illicit. Running away with stolen gold.

They were almost out the door when Vadik remembered his book. *Cinema I* was in his suitcase upstairs. "Can I borrow a book?" he asked.

"All my good books are upstairs," Sergey said. "Here we keep garage sale books."

Vadik rushed to the shelves. There were used DVDs of *Bambi* and *The Lion King* and used copies of *A Complete Idiot's Guide to Home Repair, A Complete Idiot's Guide to Mortgage, Eat Healthy!,* and *Hell Is Other People: The Anthology of 20th-Century French Philosophy.* He grabbed *Hell Is Other People* and hurried to the door.

They made it to the bus stop a second after the bus pulled away. They had to rush to intercept it at the next stop. And then Vadik was in, dropping his coins one by one as the bus was pulling away. Going to the city.

The jetlag and vodka made him fall asleep, and by the time he woke up, they were approaching the last stop. Central Park South and Sixth Avenue. It had gotten dark and chilly, and the sidewalks were covered with melting slush, but none of that mattered to Vadik. He was finally here. He'd made it. It was snowing ever so slightly, and all that light pollution colored the sky yellow. The skyscrapers hovered above his head, as if suspended in a yellow fog. Vadik had no idea where to go from there. The park looked deserted, so he decided to head down Sixth Avenue, into the thick of the city. He walked along the wet sidewalk looking up, crossing whenever the light switched to green, stepping right into puddles of slush. He turned right or left whenever he felt like it, whenever he liked the sight of the side street. Soon he had no idea in which direction he was going. He didn't care. He was taking everything in, the buildings, the storefronts, the limos and yellow cabs, the people. There were so many people. Alive, energetic, determined, all in a rush to get to places. Women. Beautiful women. Some of them looked at him. Some even smiled. He felt very tall. He felt gigantic. He felt as if his head were on the same level as those breathtaking Times Square billboards. Everything seemed within reach. Hell, he felt as if he could just snap that huge steaming cup of noodles off the top of the building. He felt as if he were consuming the city, eating it up. It was his city. He had finally found it.

Vadik walked for hours. He stopped only when he noticed that his shoes were soaked through to his socks. There was a brightly lit diner a few feet away. Vadik decided to go there. The diner was nothing like the elegant Greenwich Village bar he'd imagined, but he decided that he liked it better. Plus he didn't feel like drinking wine or beer. He ordered a cup of tea with lemon and a piece of cheesecake, because he remembered Sergey mentioning that cheesecake was the ultimate American food. He liked the place. It was nice, homey, with American pop songs quietly playing in the background. There were almost no people in that diner except for an elderly couple at the counter eating soup, an unkempt, possibly homeless guy fiddling with the jukebox in the corner, and a girl in a bulky checkered coat sitting across the aisle from Vadik. The girl had a runny nose. She kept wiping it with a napkin and making sniffling sounds like a rabbit. Her nose was swollen and red, and he could hardly see her eyes behind her dark bangs, but he liked that her hair was done in two short braids. She had a clear mug filled with a cloudy brown liquid in front of her. Vadik wondered what it was. She raised her eyes for a second and he saw that they were small and amber-brown and very pretty. Vadik wanted to smile at her, but she lowered her gaze before he had a chance. She was reading a book. Vadik decided it was time to get out his. He opened it in the middle, took a long sip of his tea, and plunged into reading.

He couldn't understand a single word. Or rather all he understood was single words. He tried to concentrate, but he found it impossible because his mind was still busy thinking about that runny-nosed girl. Vadik took a bite out of his cheesecake and found it disgustingly sweet. He leafed through the rest of the book and discovered that about fifty pages were missing. When he finally raised his eyes, he saw that the girl was looking at him. He smiled and asked if he could join her. Normally, he would be too shy to do that, but just then he felt as if he was fueled by some strange happy confidence that helped him do whatever he wanted.

"What is it in your cup?" he asked after he settled in her booth.

"Cider with rum," she said.

Vadik asked the waiter to bring another cider with rum for him. He liked it very much.

The girl's name was Rachel. Vadik introduced himself and asked if she lived in the city. She said that she was from Michigan and that she had moved here a couple of months ago to go to graduate school. He said that he'd only arrived this morning.

She smiled and said, "Welcome."

Days, weeks, months, even years later, whenever Vadik thought of their first conversation (and he thought of it a lot), he would marvel at how easy it had been. His English was pretty good—he had spoken a lot of English while he worked in London, and even in Istanbul—but his conversations were never that effortless. He would struggle to find the right word, he would confuse tenses and articles, he would pronounce the words wrong. But in that diner with Rachel, he talked as if he was inspired. Not once did she ask him to repeat something because she didn't understand.

The track changed to Cohen's "I'm Your Man." Vadik laughed. Cohen seemed to be following him throughout the entire day.

"I love this song!" he said.

"Really?" Rachel asked. She seemed to tense.

"What?" Vadik said.

"Oh, it's nothing."

"No," Vadik insisted, "please tell me."

"I actually hate this song," Rachel said.

"Hate this song? Why?" Vadik asked. "The guy is offering himself to a girl. He's pouring his heart out."

Rachel tried to soften her words with an apologetic smile, but she couldn't help but say what she had on her mind. "Oh, he's pouring his heart out, is that right?" she said. "Look, this is typical precoital manipulation. He's offering her the world, but that's only until she gives herself to him. Do you understand?"

"I understand what you mean, but I disagree. The guy is expressing what he feels at the moment. He might not feel the same way afterward, but that doesn't mean he is not sincere in that precise moment."

Rachel shook her head with such force that her braids came undone and the fine wisps of light brown hair flew up and down. "Leonard Cohen is a misogynist."

"Myso . . . gynist?" Vadik asked. The word sounded vaguely familiar, but he wasn't sure what it meant.

"Antifeminist," Rachel explained.

"I don't understand," Vadik said. "Cohen? Antifeminist? Doesn't he idolize women?"

"Yes!" Rachel said. "That's precisely my point. He idolizes women, but he doesn't view them as equals. They're these sacred sexual objects for him. Something to idolize and discard, or, better yet, discard first and idolize later."

Rachel took another sip of her cider and asked, "Do you know the song 'Waiting for the Miracle'?"

"Of course, it's my favorite!" Vadik said.

"Well, I find the lyrics offensive."

Rachel looked at Vadik intently. "See what's going on here? We have a man up there, having these existential thoughts, talking to God, expecting to experience divine grace, and the woman is down below. Literally beneath him! Waiting stupidly. And for what? For him to marry her?"

Vadik shook his head.

Rachel was about to say something else, but she stopped herself. She looked embarrassed.

"So what are you studying in your graduate school?" Vadik asked. "North American misogynists?"

"No, actually, English romantics."

What luck! Vadik thought. He had been given the perfect opportunity to steer the conversation away from tricky Cohen and toward something that would allow him to shine. He said that he knew the entire "The Rime of the Ancient Mariner" by heart. In Russian. Rachel smiled and asked him to recite it. He did. Rachel loved it. She said that it sounded amazing in Russian, even though she couldn't help but laugh a couple of times.

The waiter came up to them just as Vadik belted out the last line. He asked if they wanted anything else. Vadik realized that this was the fourth or fifth time the waiter had asked them that. It was time to leave.

"I'll walk you home," Vadik said, and Rachel nodded and smiled.

The color of the sky had changed to gloomy indigo, and it had gotten really cold. The slush on the sidewalks had turned into cakey ice. Vadik offered Rachel his hand, and they started to walk like that: holding hands, but at a distance from each other. It was only outside that Vadik noticed that he was much taller than Rachel. Her head was level with his shoulders.

She asked him where he was staying. He told her Staten Island. The answer seemed to horrify her.

"Staten Island?" she said. "But it's so late! How are you going to get there?"

And then she cleared her throat and offered him the option to stay at her place. Vadik squeezed her hand tighter.

It's New York, he thought. It's New York that makes everything so easy.

They walked down a large avenue, then turned onto some smaller street, then onto another small street. Vadik loved Rachel's street. The dark trees. And the cheerful details on the stone facades. And the piles of hardened snow gleaming under the streetlamps.

They entered one of the buildings and walked up the creaky stairs to Rachel's fifth-floor one-bedroom. Rachel walked ahead of him. The stairs were carpeted. The railings were carved. Vadik's heart was beating like crazy.

But once they were inside the apartment, the easy feeling was gone. Rachel took her boots and coat off but kept the scarf on. And she moved nervously around the apartment as if she were the one who was there for the first time. Vadik felt that he needed to do or say something that would make her relax, but he had no idea what.

"Do you want some tea?" Rachel asked, rebraiding her hair. She seemed grateful when he agreed. She disappeared into the kitchen, still in her scarf. Her apartment was small and dark, with art posters on the walls. Vadik recognized only one painting, Memling's *Portrait of a Young Woman.* He had never liked it that much. Since this was the first real American home Vadik had seen, he couldn't tell how much of the decor was typical and how much of it revealed Rachel's personality.

He sat down on her small couch and took off his shoes.

His socks were soaking wet. These were the socks that he had put on yesterday morning in Regina's Moscow apartment, where Vadik had to spend a week between Istanbul and New York. He stared at his feet for a while, stunned by this realization, then he removed the socks and stuffed them in the pockets of his jacket. He heard a clatter of dishes in the kitchen and the occasional traffic sounds outside, but other than that it was stiflingly silent in the apartment. There was a small CD rack by the couch, but Vadik didn't recognize any of the albums. It occurred to him that Sergey and Vica would worry if he didn't come home. He asked Rachel if he could make a call. "Of course!" she said from the kitchen. Vadik dialed the number, praying that it would be Sergey who answered. It was. Vadik said in Russian that he was spending the night in the city. With a girl. An American girl. He had to listen to Sergey's stunned silence for what seemed like an eternity. "Okay, see you tomorrow," Sergey finally said.

Rachel emerged from the kitchen at last, carrying a tray with two mugs on it, some packages of very bad tea, and a little plate with strange grayish cookies. She sat down across from Vadik on a footstool and put one of the tea bags into her mug.

She glanced at Vadik's bare feet and they seemed to embarrass her.

Vadik took her hand in his. Her fingers were thin and startlingly warm.

"More English poetry in Russian?" he asked.

She smiled and nodded.

Vadik recited a strange medley of Shakespeare, Keats, and Ezra Pound, finishing with "The King's Breakfast" by A. A. Milne. Rachel was especially delighted with Milne.

He asked her to recite some of her favorites. She said that she couldn't. That there were two things she simply couldn't do in the presence of somebody else: recite poetry and dance. Her confession touched Vadik so much that he wanted to squeeze her in a mad hug. He reached and pulled on one of her braids instead.

She was shy in bed, shy and a little awkward. She squirmed when he attempted to go down on her. "It might take a while," she warned him. "I'm difficult that way."

But Rachel wasn't difficult. She was the opposite of difficult. This was the simplest, purest, and happiest sexual encounter he had ever had. And most likely would ever have, as Vadik tended to think of it now.

Memories of that night kept haunting him for months, for years afterward. At first, they were purely sexual—he would remember Rachel's smell and feel this jolt of desire that made him light-headed. She smelled of something fresh and green, like a slice of cucumber or some really good lettuce. But as the weeks passed, his memories turned more and more nostalgic. He would evoke a certain thing that Rachel said, her facial expression, her tone of voice. The image that Vadik loved the most was of her braids flying up and down when she delivered her ridiculous critique of "I'm Your Man."

He'd been trying to find her. He came to the city and tried to retrace his steps from Central Park. He searched online forums for scholars of English romantic poetry. He browsed through dating profiles. Once he discovered Missed Connections on Craigslist he started posting ads about Rachel. In fact, it became a habit of his. Every time he met a new woman, he would post a new Missed Connections ad about Rachel.

"Isn't that unfair to the new girl? Doesn't that make your new relationship doomed from the start?" Regina wondered.

"I think you simply invented your great love for Rachel to justify your failures with other women," Sergey said.

"Forget about Rachel!" Vica insisted. "There is a good chance that she would have turned out anorexic, or bipolar, or just plain boring!"

All of them could've been right in a way. And yet Vadik couldn't stop longing for Rachel. He could barely remember what she looked like anymore, but in the compact reality of his memory, Rachel remained perfect. There were times when Vadik tried to banish those memories because they were too painful. And there were times when Vadik felt numb and he would desperately try to conjure Rachel because pain was better than numbness. Once, in Avenel, as he sat perched on his exercise bike, in his empty white room, pushing and pushing on those dusty pedals, he said Rachel's name out loud and felt nothing. Or rather he felt a palpable nothing, weightless and glutinous at the same time. He felt as if he were about to simultaneously float away and drown. He had never felt worse. It was then that he got off his bike and went to take the Tazepam.

That morning at Rachel's apartment, Vadik woke at dawn. Rachel was still asleep, lying on her stomach, her face buried in the pillow, her mouth half-open. Vadik felt rested—he was still on Moscow time. He got up, pulled on his underpants, his sweater and jeans, and went to the bathroom. Everything in the apartment seemed smaller and shabbier in the morning. So much clutter in the bathroom. So many unnecessary things. Two blow dryers. Six different shampoo bottles. More clutter in the kitchen. Pots and pans peeking from the tops of the cabinets. Three ceramic cats. A ceramic dog. A ceramic chicken! Vadik went into the kitchen and looked out the long narrow window, but the view of the city was blocked by the stained brown wall of an apartment building across the street. He considered putting the kettle on and making some tea. He thought he would just sit there with his tea and read one of Rachel's books until she woke up. But he suddenly found himself dreading that moment. Eventually he would have to leave. He would explain that he was going to live in Avenel. She would want to exchange numbers. He didn't have a phone yet. Would he have to give her his e-mail? He had such a stupid e-mail address. Biggguy@gmail.com (with an extra "g" between big and guy). Rachel would hate how misogynistic that sounded. She hated Leonard Cohen! How could anybody hate Cohen? Anyway, she would ask when they would see each other again. He would have to promise to see her when? Next Friday? And then what? They would have to see each other every weekend? Vadik found the idea oppressive. This was only his second morning in the Land of the Free and he was about to be bound by some weekly routine. His new life was about to begin. He needed to be unbound.

He walked back into the living room and surveyed the scene. There was a notebook and a pen on the mantel. He tore out a page and pondered what to write. English poetry would have been great, but he didn't know any poetry in English. And Cohen clearly was a bad idea. "You're beautiful," he finally wrote and put the paper in the middle of the table. Then he picked up his jacket and sat down on the sofa to put on his socks. They were still wet. He squirmed at the touch of damp cloth against his feet. Then he put on his shoes.

It was so cold outside that it seemed like his damp feet were turning to ice. Vadik knew—Sergey had explained it to him—that the X1 bus to Staten Island stopped every few blocks on Broadway. He had no idea how to get to Broadway though, and he had no idea where he was. He waved down a taxi and asked the driver to drop him off at the closest point on Broadway. It took them five minutes or so. He got out of the cab, bought himself a cup of coffee in a deli, and walked down Broadway until he saw an X1 stop. He wasn't sure if the buses even ran that early. But the bus came within five minutes. Vadik was two quarters short of the exact fare, but the driver let him ride anyway. The bus was well heated and empty, and for some time Vadik just sat slumped in his seat enjoying the warmth. It was only on some overpass over Brooklyn that Vadik remembered that he had left *Hell Is Other People* at the diner. He had no idea where that diner was. He would never be able to find it again. He would never be able to go back there. Vadik felt a surge of panic and regret, so bad that it made his heart ache.

Chapter 3

EAT'N'WATCH

MORE OFTEN THAN NOT REGINA WOKE UP TO THE sound of Bob's alarm.

This morning the sound was sharper than usual. Bob must have changed it the night before.

Regina moved closer to him and squeezed her fingers over his stiff dick without opening her eyes. There was nothing sexual about that move. Neither of them was aroused. Bob's stiff dick in the morning was a simple fact of married life. Regina was thirty-nine, but before marrying Bob two years ago she had never lived with a man for longer than a month. And here was her man, a man of the house, a large and strong human being in possession of a penis.

Regina buried her face into Bob's armpit. Bob smelled especially nice in the mornings. Less like a squeaky-clean American, more like a man.

Regina enjoyed the simple facts of married life more than anything else. She couldn't have children. Bob didn't need children (he had a grown daughter from his first marriage). They would have to just enjoy each other for the rest of their lives. That is, if they stayed together for the rest of their lives. But so far it looked like they would.

Their bedroom was huge, square, and perfectly dark. ("Wow, those are some blinds!" their friends said.) There was no light even on the brightest mornings except for the soft glow of Bob's iPad screen. That was the first thing that Bob did every morning—checked his messages and the news.

"Did you sleep well?" Bob asked.

"Yes, Bobik, pretty well."

She called him Bobik, and Bobs, and Bobcat, Bobbety Bob, and Bobbety Cat. This was another thing that she loved about her marriage—to be so close to someone that even his name felt like it belonged to her.

"Did you sleep well?"

"More or less. My shoulder's acting up again."

"Do you want me to put the ointment on?"

"Yes, please."

Regina took her hand off Bob's dick, which had become significantly softer, and groped for the ointment on the nightstand.

She squeezed out a cold slippery dollop and began to smear it a little above Bob's right shoulder. His shoulder was freckled and substantial like the rest of him. The sharp sweetish smell of the alcohol in the ointment made her gag, but she continued to rub it in with tender force. This was her husband and she was eager to take care of him. Sometimes Regina wondered if it would feel any different if she actually loved Bob. She doubted that it would.

"Thank you, sweetie," Bob said and climbed out of the bed. Regina wiped her hand with a tissue and stared at him as he did his morning stretches. All that square bulk. All those muscles gained on exercise machines. Even on his butt. She hadn't known people had muscles in their butts. Her own butt was all skin and bones with some lumpy fat, as was the rest of her body. She didn't like to be seen naked. She slept in her old gym shorts and a stretched-out tank top. Regina looked in the wall mirror and winced at her reflection. She wondered if her new hairdo with the part in the middle made her look like an Afghan hound. It did, didn't it?

She was tall and long-limbed though. Bob got a kick out of how tall she was. Tall, long-legged, imperfect, and Russian. Ph.D. in linguistics, fluent in four languages, but missing two teeth. (The missing teeth were in the back of her mouth. This was not a big deal.) Regina suspected that Bob got a kick out of the strangeness of his choice as well.

Regina sat up in bed to watch Bob doing push-ups, her favorite part of his routine. Five, six, seven. Muscles bulge, relax, bulge. Then he went to take a shower and Regina lay back down and closed her eyes.

She remembered the thrill of meeting Bob for the first time. At the doors of a theater on Forty-third Street. She stood leaning against the door, squeezing that extra ticket in her hand. "Make sure you sell that ticket," Vica had said. But nobody was asking for tickets, and Regina couldn't just assault strangers and offer it to them. She hadn't wanted to see that show in the first place. She'd always hated musicals. She was sad. She was hungry and cold. But it was Vica's firm belief that no visit to New York City could be considered a success if a visitor didn't get to see a Broadway show. It was a great show too, she insisted, *Billy Elliot*. Vica had procured the tickets using her boss's member discount. They were forty dollars each. Regina felt guilty—Vadik had paid for her plane ticket, but it was Vica and Sergey who housed and fed her and spent a lot of money to entertain her, even though it didn't look like they were very well off themselves.

The show was about to begin. Nobody wanted her ticket. Regina was cold and tired and filled with mixed feelings toward Vica. She had twenty dollars in her purse. She decided to just tell Vica that she sold the ticket for twenty dollars instead of forty and go in alone. Vica would be angry, but there was no way Regina could sell that ticket. She was about to enter the theater when a bulky bald man tapped her on the arm.

"Are you selling that ticket?" he asked. She nodded. He paid for the ticket and led her in.

He said that he'd seen *Billy Elliot* before, with his clients, but he liked it so much that he was excited to see it again. He seemed genuinely moved when Billy sang that ridiculous song about how it was "inner electricity" or something that made him dance. There were tears in Bob's eyes. Normally, a song like that would have made Regina gag, but she found Bob's emotional reaction to it exotic and wonderful and intensely American. All through their after-theater dinner, Regina tried to decipher Bob. He seemed to be stranger to her than all those foreign writers and artists she'd met at the translator residencies that she used to attend. Writers and artists belonged to a unified, easy-to-understand social group. They'd read the same books, were familiar with more or less the same art and music, had similar personality traits. Bob was different. Bob was unlike anybody she'd met. Regina didn't have any choice but to try to understand him through the classic American novels she'd read. His father's family came from the South. Faulkner? He was a self-made man. Gatsby? He dabbled in politics. Willie Stark? He had a tumultuous relationship with his ex-wife. Philip Roth? Then, by the time they ordered dessert, Bob said that Regina reminded him of Lara from *Doctor Zhivago*. And Regina realized that Bob was doing the same thing—trying to decipher her through the Russian novels he knew. Well, maybe Bob was referring to the American movie rather than the Russian novel, but Regina was delighted anyway. She said that her grandfather used to be friends with Pasternak and was impressed by how impressed Bob was. They spent the remainder of her visit together, and at the end of it, as they were saying good-bye to each other at the airport, Bob told Regina that she was precisely the kind of woman he'd always hoped to meet. And it was smooth sailing ever since. The initial sexual enthusiasm might have waned, but respect and affection were still there.

Bob was back in the room, but Regina was reluctant to open her eyes. She just lay there taking in the sounds of Bob dressing: opening and closing the drawers, rustling his clothes, grunting a little as he put on his socks. Then he leaned in to kiss her; even the smell of him was clean and energetic.

"Bye, honey," Regina said, opening her eyes a little.

"Aren't you going to get up?" Bob asked.

"Soon," she said.

Regina heard the resolute bang of the door and closed her eyes again.

ACTUALLY, THERE WERE a couple of annoying things about Bob. For example, he couldn't help but flirt with other women when he was drunk. "Please don't take it seriously!" Bob's daughter, Becky, said to Regina once, noticing her discomfort. "Dad's embarrassing, but he means well. He flirts with women out of politeness rather than anything else. My uncles are like that too. Even Grandpa used to be the same way."

Well, she could live with that. Another surprising problem was Bob's jealousy. Completely unfounded! She would occasionally catch him browsing through her e-mails and text messages, but every time he would apologize so profusely that she couldn't help but forgive him. There was the mitigating fact of Bob's ex-wife's betrayal. Apparently, she had been cheating on him with his various colleagues for years. Another reason why Regina was so quick to forgive him for snooping was that she secretly found his jealousy flattering. Nobody had ever been jealous of her before!

But what upset her the most was Bob's need to do the "right thing" no matter what or, rather, his belief that there was one single "right thing" to do in every situation. Vadik, who considered himself the expert in all things American, told her that this was a common belief here.

Vadik told her that the major difference between Russians and Americans was that Americans believed that they were in charge of their lives, that they could control them. Not just that but that it was their responsibility to control their lives as much as they could. They would try to fight to the very end against all sense, because they considered letting go irresponsible.

Another thing was that Americans didn't believe in luck as much as Russians did. They believed in hard work and fair play. They believed in rules. That life had certain rules, and if you followed them and did everything right, you were protected. They said things like "life ain't fair," but they secretly believed that people brought the unfairness of life on themselves.

Vadik had told her that Bob once asked him why some very stupid apps succeeded and others didn't. "Pure luck?" Vadik asked.

"No, my friend, no way!" Bob said. "The success comes from a combination of hard work and smart strategy."

When genetic testing for all kinds of diseases became all the rage, Bob put a lot of pressure on Regina to take the test. "Why do I need the test?" Regina protested. "I can't have children, remember?"

"But what if you carry a gene for a disease that needs to be found and treated early?" he said. "Getting tested is the right thing to do, Regina."

Well, Bob's obsession with genetics was really annoying too.

He and Becky had recently ordered an online test from this hot new genomics company, Dancing Drosophilae, to look for their distant relatives and found thousands of them. Queen Elizabeth I was listed as one of their ancestors. Becky thought it was hilarious and she even started referring to Queen Elizabeth as Grandma Liz, but Bob was secretly proud of this fact. He ordered two very thick biographies on Amazon—Henry's and Grandma Liz's—and spent a lot of time reading them and looking at the pictures. Regina once caught him staring at himself in the mirror while studying Holbein's portrait of Henry VIII. She found it silly but endearing.

Most of Bob's extended family thought that his lifestyle in New York was too frivolous and his business too silly, so they kept offering him idiotic app ideas to mock him. Last Thanksgiving Bob's brother, Chuck, had suggested that Bob create an app for people who were bored on the toilet and wanted to chat or play chess with somebody who was also on the toilet and bored. Little did Chuck know that a company called Brainstorm Commandos already had an app like that in development and was calling it Can Companion. Regina had been terrified of meeting Bob's extended family, but it turned out to be okay. Since Bob's parents were dead, everybody gathered at the huge house of Bob's older sister Brenda in Fort Collins, Colorado. Everyone was very welcoming to Regina, and none of them seemed put off by her quietness. Cousin Willie had a foreign wife too—Thai in his case—and she didn't talk much either. Nor were they particularly curious about Russia save for an occasional drunken question about politics: "Now, how about that Putin? Flying with cranes, poisoning his enemies! Some guy, huh?" Some of the men made occasional drunken attempts to flirt with her: "You're a very special woman, Regina! Very special, very delicate." Other than that, Bob's family mostly left Regina in peace. She would sit there at the table enjoying exotic American food like mashed yams with marshmallows and studying Bob's relatives in search of common genetic traits. All those prominent cheekbones, all those heavy jaws. Bob always said how much he hated Thanksgivings with his family. Still, Regina thought, it must be reassuring to be surrounded by people who shared so much of your genetic makeup. And he had a daughter, who looked just like him and who was the closest person in the world to him. Closer than Regina could ever hope to be.

Becky was twenty-six years old, a Williams graduate now enrolled in the NYU Tisch film school. She lived in a sprawling decrepit house in Bushwick, which she shared with her best friend, Martha, and a team of Polish construction workers who had come to renovate the house six months ago and stayed. The house was bought with Bob's money. It was bought at a bargain price, because it was part of a group of houses meant for low-income people, and Becky, with her annual income of $12,000, easily qualified. Vica was close to having a heart attack when Regina told her about this. Even Vadik was outraged. Bob was the only one who didn't see anything wrong with the arrangement. "She's an artist trying to survive," he said.

Regina had expected Becky to be spoiled and obnoxious, but she was surprised to find that she wasn't that at all. If anything, she was too nice. "The innocence of privilege," Vadik had said. He had asked Becky out once, but she answered with a very firm no. Becky was really welcoming with Regina though. She kept hugging her and saying how pleased she was to finally see her dad so happy. She was squarely built, like Bob, but she had softer, warmer features, and her hugs were forceful and affectionate at the same time. She was very impressed with Regina's work and even more impressed with the roster of artist residencies Regina had attended. She was ecstatic when she saw *Infinite Jest* on Regina's shelf. "It's my favorite too!" She was awestruck by Regina's *samizdat* books. "Those are incredibly important artifacts!"

When they first met, Becky showered her with questions. Regina made an effort to answer them all, but lately she couldn't help but notice that when she talked, Becky's enthusiasm for her seemed to be waning. "Regina is nice but a bit standoffish," she overheard her saying to Bob recently.

"Why would she think that?" Regina asked Vadik, and Vadik, so proud of his expertise, rushed to explain. "So she asked you all these questions and you gave her detailed, honest answers?"

Regina confirmed.

"Did you ask her questions in return?"

"No! What would I ask a perfect stranger? And I was too busy answering."

"There you go. You were supposed to skip the answers—Americans don't really care about them—and ask her questions in return."

"Wouldn't that be rude?" Regina asked.

"No!" Vadik said. "Quite the opposite! Giving long answers is rude and arrogant."

The next time Regina saw Becky she used some of Vadik's strategy and found that it worked better. There wasn't any real warmth between Becky and her but rather a solid goodwill. She could live with that.

The clock read 10:00 A.M. It was time to get up. Or not. What difference would it make if she slept just a little bit more? Regina turned onto her stomach and buried her face in the pillow.

She dreamed that she and Bob had a baby. The baby was tiny, the size of a medium carrot. It appeared to be healthy though. "Do you think it's all right?" she asked Bob. He laughed. "Of course it's all right, it's our baby, Regina!" "But why is it so tiny? Are babies supposed to be this tiny? Did your daughter used to be this tiny?" Bob laughed again. "Heck if I remember, Regina." Then she tried to pick the tiny baby up, but it kept slipping right out of her fingers and falling onto the floor.

Regina woke up in shock. This was not the first time that she'd had a dream about some sort of weird or disfigured baby. Every time it happened, her heart was beating so hard that it took her ten minutes or so to calm down.

Regina showered and walked out of the bathroom. There was a whole day in front of her. The problem was that she had no idea how to fill it.

In Russia, her days had belonged to her job. She would tackle the most challenging projects. In fact, the more difficult the translation was, the more she loved it. But she had abandoned her work when her mother got sick. Taking care of her seemed to have eaten up all of Regina's time, energy, and spirit. She would let the assignments pile up and then look at them and cry, because it was futile to hope to ever complete them, and the whole idea of work seemed pointless in the face of her mother's impending death. Her favorite editor, Inga, who used to be the closest to a friend that Regina had in Russia after Vadik, Sergey, and Vica moved away, was very understanding. She kept offering to help, but Regina was too drained and depressed to sustain a relationship that required even a minimum amount of energy. Then after her mother died, Inga kept asking if Regina was going back to work, and Regina kept being evasive and vague until she finally called Inga and said that she was getting married and moving to the U.S., and that, no, she wouldn't be returning. Even on the phone she could hear how shocked and offended Inga was.

When she married Bob, there was a chance that her editors would have let her work remotely, but she was so eager to be done with her Russian life that she broke all ties with them.

Regina started missing her job about three months after the move. She would have these violently real dreams about working on a manuscript, about missing a deadline. She would wake up and experience relief at first, because she hadn't actually missed a deadline, but then feel disappointment.

She wrote to Inga and said that she wouldn't mind an assignment.

"Don't be a pig, Regina. There are people who actually need money," Inga replied. The meanness of her reply told Regina just how hurt Inga still was.

Bob tried to interest her in politics, but all his efforts failed. Regina subscribed to Tolstoy's point of view that particular candidates or even political parties didn't matter, that historical process was shaped by the collective will of all people and not one single politician could possibly change anything.

"Okay," Bob said, "we'll let a nineteenth-century Russian writer guide you in matters of contemporary U.S. politics." He then suggested that she "take up" something else. But the expression "take up" disgusted her. "Taking up" meant doing something fanciful rather than serious. There were wives in Bob's circle of friends who had given up their jobs after marriage and now "taken up" photography or art or writing. Some of them were deeply engaged in motherhood, so they didn't have the time to "take up" things; what they did instead was "dabble." Regina had been a professional woman all her life—the thought of "dabbling" made her stomach turn. She would rather spend her time reading books than "dabbling" in anything.

But what frightened Regina was that she had stopped reading. In Russia, she used to read voraciously, both in English and Russian, but here she hadn't yet finished a single book. Their entire den was crammed with unread books.

Today will be different. I'll definitely read a book today, Regina thought. I'll make coffee and start reading.

There were no traces of Bob in the kitchen. He didn't like having breakfast at home. He usually bought some seriously enhanced smoothie on the way to his office and drank it there while listening to his assistant's report.

Regina put the kettle on, sat down on the edge of the windowsill, and reached for her iPhone to check her messages while the water boiled. A confirmation for her ticket to Moscow made her squirm. The two-year anniversary of her mother's death was approaching, and Aunt Masha—not her actual aunt, but her mother's best friend—insisted that Regina come and visit the grave. Regina had missed the one-year anniversary because she had been sick. This time she didn't have any excuse. She had gone ahead and bought the ticket for early November.

The next e-mail was from Aunt Masha. She was overjoyed that Regina was coming to Moscow! They would go to the cemetery together and then have a meal in Olga's honor. She insisted that Regina stay with her during her visit. "It's unthinkable," she wrote, "for you to stay at a hotel in Moscow, like a tourist in your own city!" Regina groaned. It was hard enough to go to visit the grave, but to stay with Aunt Masha would be unbearable. Ever since Regina's mother had died, Aunt Masha wouldn't leave her alone. Even though Regina lived in America now, and was married to a kind, wonderful, and very rich man, Aunt Masha felt that her duty was to watch over Regina and take care of her. She would write her very detailed letters and ask embarrassingly personal questions about Regina's new life. She would ask if Regina had found work, if she was happy with her new life in general, if she was happy with Bob, if she was in love with him. Did Bob have any children? Was he a good father? Did he want more children? Was he sad that Regina couldn't have children? Would he consider adoption? Aunt Masha wasn't subtle, no. She worked as a math teacher at an orphanage, and sometimes she would even go so far as to send Regina pictures of younger orphanage kids. Mostly babies, an occasional toddler. All had pleading expressions in their eyes, or was Regina just imagining that? She had to be firm and told Aunt Masha that adoption was out of the question, that the subject of children was painful and uncomfortable to her, and if Aunt Masha wanted to keep in touch with Regina she had to stop badgering her. The pictures and the questions did stop after that. Yet something told Regina that they hadn't stopped for good. Aunt Masha often brought kids from the orphanage home. They would stay with her for days and sometimes even weeks. Regina could only hope that Aunt Masha's apartment wouldn't be teeming with adorable little orphans by the time she arrived.

The next e-mail was from a former classmate Alexey Kuzmin, who claimed that he was Abramovich's business partner. He said that he lived in New Jersey now and wanted to get together. Kuzmin had been the sleaziest, most obnoxious guy in their entire grade. They had never been friendly; in fact, Regina didn't think they had ever talked while they were in school. It was clear that he had heard that she was married to Bob and was now trying to get to him through her. Regina switched off her Gmail and turned to Facebook. Facebook was easy: a perfect stranger named Anita Lapshin who wanted Regina to like the page "Anita Lapshin." Regina hesitated but didn't "like" the page. She did "like" Vica's photo of a smiling Eric though, just so Vica wouldn't get mad. Vadik identified Regina's social media personality as "the lurker," because she rarely posted anything herself and almost never commented or liked. There was something unsavory in that description, as if she was spying on people, but she had to admit that Vadik was right. She thought of the drama unraveling in her friends' social media as something like a TV series she could watch without participating. The idea of commenting and liking was foreign to her as well. Or perhaps she simply didn't have the skill of responding to something that wasn't addressed to her personally but released into the wild for everybody's attention. Now, Vica was "the affirmer": she "liked" everything and posted all these uplifting photos of their family trips, of Eric smeared with ice cream or pasta sauce, and especially of colorful breakfasts. Sergey was—she forgot what it was called. Sergey never posted anything himself, but he would often butt in on his friends' discussions with an especially lengthy intellectual comment and then comment on his own comment, sometimes days later. Vadik himself thrived on social media, because it allowed him to try all those different personalities. He was witty on Twitter, charming on Facebook, philosophical on his Tumblr. When Regina shared Vadik's social media ideas with Bob, Bob just shook his head. "Why are you making such a big deal out of this? Social media is meant for communication, it's not supposed to be creative, definitely not supposed to be soul shaping." Bob and Becky were model social media citizens. Their posts were not too frequent and not too long; they liked generously and commented sparingly; they radiated personal warmth and promoted their work in moderation.

There was a Facebook message from Vadik. He wanted her to help him interpret Sejun's sudden idea to look for a job in New York so that she and Vadik could live together. Regina was so tired of interpreting Vadik's love life! "But you're so levelheaded," he would say. Which meant what? Cerebral, coldhearted, incapable of love herself?

When Vica dumped Vadik for Sergey and Sergey dumped Regina for Vica, some people were hoping that Regina would take up with Vadik. The problem was that they weren't attracted to each other. Well, Vadik definitely wasn't. Everyone said he was still pining for Vica. It would have been disastrous for Regina. To be with another man who preferred Vica to her? No, thank you! So, yes, a romantic relationship between her and Vadik was out of the question, especially now that she had Bob, but Regina couldn't help but hate it when Vadik came to her with his love puzzles.

Her relationship with Sergey and Vica was more complicated. After her breakup with Sergey back in Russia, Regina had never expected to become friends with him and Vica. She found herself forced into this friendship because she was friends with Vadik, and Vica and Sergey and Vadik kind of came as a package. And here, in New York, she didn't really know anyone and couldn't afford to refuse friends. She was especially starved for female company. Becky was there and Becky was smart and nice, but she belonged to a different generation and she was Bob's family—you couldn't be completely open with your husband's daughter. So Regina did try to become better friends with Vica, but each of her attempts was met with spiky resistance on Vica's part. And every time the four of them met, Vica kept darting sneaky inquisitive stares at Regina, clearly worried that she still loved Sergey. Sergey seemed to wonder the same thing. She didn't love him! More than that, she now doubted that she ever had. But the worst thing about Vica and Sergey was that they constantly tried to push yet another of their stupid app ideas on Bob. They tried to exploit him, and she felt exploited as well. Regina cringed every time Vica made allusions to her frivolous lifestyle while complaining about her job, and her awful commute from Staten Island, and all those chores she had to do, and the fact that she basically had two children—Erik and Sergey. Was Vica trying to guilt her into helping them? That would be so unfair. Still, Regina couldn't help but feel guilty because of the simple fact that Vica and Sergey had to struggle financially and she didn't. Sergey kept asking her if it was possible to change Bob's mind about Virtual Grave. No, she told him, it was not possible. And even if it was, Regina wouldn't have lifted a finger to try. She hated the idea of

Virtual Grave. Death was an ugly, stupid, terrifying joke. There was nothing, absolutely nothing, you could do to make it more meaningful, or more beautiful, or easier to stomach. The only way to deal with it was to ignore it for as long as you could.

The water started to boil. Regina put coffee into her French press, poured the hot water, stirred, let it it brew for a little while, and pressed down on the plunger. She poured herself a cup and carried it out to the terrace. To unlock the terrace door, Regina needed both hands, so she had to balance the cup against her stomach. Some coffee splashed—onto her stomach.

And then she was outside and blinded by all the light from the sky and the river, the boats, and the pretty disarray of buildings in New Jersey. The weather was perfect too—cool and delicious with an early September breeze.

"Did you even dream of living like this?" her father had asked when he visited. They were standing on her terrace together. He was short, shorter than Regina, thin wisps of his gray hair fluttering against his bald crown. He used to be a writer. "His very first short story was published in *Novyj Mir*!" Aunt Masha told Regina. When Regina was five years old, he went to Canada and decided to stay there, basically abandoning his wife and child. Now he lived in Montreal and taught Russian literature.

"A simple Russian girl like yourself. And look at you now—the queen of Manhattan."

His words made Regina gag. She was neither simple nor Russian (she had Jewish, Polish, and a smidgen of French blood in her veins), and she definitely was not the queen of Manhattan. She was tired of explaining to people that Bob wasn't that rich. When the news of the Occupy Wall Street protests reached Regina's father, he called to ask if Bob was in the "one percent." He was. Regina's father couldn't be prouder. He wasn't nearly as excited when Regina told him about her latest translator's prize. It was her father who had given Regina her stupid embarrassing name. He must have been hoping that she would eventually become a queen. Regina had never been very fond of her father, and now she couldn't forgive him for the simple fact of his being alive, when her mother was dead.

She sat down on one of their pretty metallic chairs and took the first sip. The seat was still wet from yesterday's rain, but she decided that she didn't care. The huge letters on the other bank of the river spelled the word *Lackawanna*. She didn't know what that meant, but the word fascinated her. She took another sip. The coffee hadn't come out that well, but at least it was still hot and bitter. It was her mother who had taught Regina to drink black coffee: "Black coffee tastes like a punishment that makes you strong."

Regina wasn't nearly as talented a translator as her mother had been. She did her job well, but she couldn't boast of any special gift. Her mother's special gift was humor. She could find the smallest grain of humor in the novel and push it just a tiny bit more, so that it became suppler, brighter, but didn't lose its subtlety. Regina had read the entire oeuvre by George Eliot in her mother's translation, chuckling and grinning and sometimes even laughing like crazy. She was deeply disappointed when she read the novels in the original English. She found them to be rather moralistic and dull.

Not only was her mother a brilliant translator, she also seemed to have had a personal relationship with each of her dead authors. She would read all of their biographies, diaries, correspondence. She would call them by their first names and talk about them as if they were family members. "Did you know what Charlotte's father did when she died? Charlotte Brontë?" she would ask at breakfast while stirring the kasha in her bowl. "He cut up her letters and sold the pieces to her grieving fans so that he could make more money!" And then hours later, when they were sitting at their adjacent desks working, she would cry out: "The bastard!" "Who are you talking about, Mom?" Regina would ask. Her mother would answer, "Charlotte's father, who else!"

They'd lived in a one-bedroom flat on Lyalin Lane in Moscow. The kitchen was dark and moldy, and there were always pigeons on the window ledge, peeking in, tapping on the window. Her favorite room was the living room. At noon there was always a thick ray of sunlight coming from the locked balcony door into the middle of the room. When Regina was little, she loved to run into that ray and freeze there so that she could catch the sparkling specks of dust that flew around her like snowflakes.

There was the old sofa in the back, where her mother loved to sit with little Regina and show her family heirlooms. Photographs, letters, various old trinkets. Regina's favorite objects were the buttons. They were kept in a large tin box, and what a treat it had been to open the lid—she had to push it really hard, as it sometimes would get stuck and then she would have to pry it with a butter knife—and plunge both her hands into a smorgasbord of shapes, textures, and colors. And then as Regina arranged and rearranged the buttons on the table—by size, by color, in ornaments, in artistic disarray—her mother would look at them and say: "Oh, I remember that one! It's from my old blue jersey dress." Or "This golden one is from your grandfather's uniform." That sofa was where Regina slept and where she spent long hours crying for Sergey. She cried so much that the wallpaper next to her pillow became damp and warped. It was her mother who nursed Regina through the heartbreak. She didn't pester Regina with questions; didn't say anything bad about Sergey; didn't pressure Regina to confront Sergey, to get back at Vica, or to have a rebound, like all her friends did. She just took Regina on walks and fed her and gave her books to read, but other than that she let her be. She offered just one piece of advice: "Don't show him how much you're hurting. It won't help and it will make you feel even worse." And so Regina didn't. She distanced herself from Sergey and Vica as much as she could, and whenever they met by chance, she went to great pains to keep it normal. And it did help. The effort it took her to pretend to be free of sorrow distracted her from her actual sorrow.

Regina learned to live in her work, to become submerged in her texts. There were days when she worked for twelve or even fourteen hours, until her vision started to get blurry and her butt would get numb and achy, pressing into a chair for so long that it felt like a frozen piece of meat. Perhaps this was the reason she had become so successful. Offers of teaching jobs followed and invitations to participate in panels and writers' residencies. Writers' residencies were the only places where she could have something resembling a love life.

She'd been to the French Villa Mont-Noir six times, where she drank bottomless glasses of free Bordeaux and had affairs with three different French writers.

She'd been to Swiss Maison d'écrivains at the Château de Lavigny four times, where she napped in the haunted library, ate excellent soups, and had an affair with a sweet German writer suffering from performance anxiety.

She'd visited Hawthornden International Retreat for Writers in Scotland twice, where she ate oatmeal for breakfast and had sex only once (her second time there), with Ben, an American translator of Russian literature who liked everything Russian and dressed like a character from Turgenev. They exchanged letters for months afterward, mostly helping each other with puzzling cultural references. Elephant tea? he would ask. What does it mean? And Regina would explain that the author was referring to the Soviet brand of Indian tea with an elephant on the label.

There were also Bellagio Center and Bogliasco Foundation in Italy. At Bellagio she ate and drank so much that she fell asleep as soon as her body made contact with the bed. Her lover, a warty and passionate Polish artist, complained about it. He told her that he was in love with her, then confessed that he was engaged to be married.

What a pain it was to return to Moscow after these trips. To step out from Sheremetyevo International into the darkness and the cold, shivering in her light Italian raincoat. To walk down smelly alleyways, stepping over puddles, her heart skipping a beat whenever she saw a suspicious stranger. Regina would feel depressed for weeks

STILL HERE · 67

after she returned. Sometimes she would be depressed for a period of time that was longer than her term at a residency.

Still, there was something worse than the cold and gloominess of her surroundings. Back in Russia, Regina seemed to lose her sex appeal. Instantaneously and irreversibly, as if she were stripped of a precious layer of attractiveness by Sheremetyevo customs officers. Whatever it was about her that had seemed exotic and wonderful to her foreign lovers was thoroughly unexciting to Russian men. Regina had had occasional short-lived reationships with Russians, but outside those writers' residencies, she mostly led a monastic existence. Sometimes her foreign affairs continued in the form of intense epistolary relationships, but those either bored or distressed her. The Polish artist kept sending her long passionate e-mails, but Regina couldn't help imagining him pressing the Send button, closing his laptop, and then going to bed to snuggle next to his wife. It wasn't the sex, but the snuggling that made her insanely jealous. Going to sleep next to a warm familiar body, opening her eyes in the morning to see a dear familiar face.

Being an introvert, she didn't have that many friends either, almost nobody since Sergey and Vica and then Vadik left for the U.S. Her mother was the only person who kept Regina from feeling hopelessly lonely. She did enjoy their long walks together, drinking tea in their tiny kitchen, gossiping about long-dead writers as if they were acquaintances.

Regina and her mother had had only two disagreements in all of their life together. The first one was over Regina's abortion. Regina had gotten pregnant on her last trip to Villa Mont-Noir. She had just turned thirty at the time. The father was a mediocre French writer who had a wife and three children at home. Regina's mother was vehemently against the abortion. She developed this fantasy of them bringing up the baby together, being a tight little unit, no need for men. But it was precisely this idea of the baby tying her to her mother forever that scared Regina. If she had the baby she would never be able to get married or even to leave. Their life together was comfy, but Regina hoped that she could lead a different life someday, a freer, more independent one. Plus, she doubted she would make a good mother. "Are you even capable of truly loving another human being?" the Polish artist asked her once. She wasn't sure she was. She had been deeply hurt when Sergey left her for Vica, but she wondered if it wasn't her wounded pride that had caused most of the pain.

Regina went ahead and had the abortion. It didn't go well. There were complications that rendered her unable to have children. The surgery following the procedure left her with lingering pain that grew so intense at times that she felt as if the baby was being yanked out of her again and again. As for the emotional side of it, Regina didn't suffer that much. She had to admit to herself that she was a little relieved. Not everybody was meant to have a child. It was her mother who was devastated, not Regina.

The second disagreement happened when a university in Berlin offered Regina a two-year teaching appointment. She was beside herself with joy. She pictured her time in Germany in minute detail. She would improve her German, impress her students and colleagues, go to concerts and gallery openings, meet interesting people, eat warm apple strudel in a little café at the Tiergarten in the company of a European academic who would find what Russian men saw as homeliness mysterious and alluring. As for her mother, Regina didn't really see a problem. They would visit each other often. With the salary that the university offered her, they would certainly be able to afford travel. But her mother didn't share Regina's enthusiasm. She said that if Regina wanted to teach, she should look for a position in Moscow. She would have a much better standing there. Regina was adamant. Her mother had cried for three days and then she started to get sick. She would complain of the lingering pain in her abdomen, digestive symptoms, fatigue, arthritis-like aches in her knees. She even lost some weight. She said that she had actually had those symptoms for a while, she just hadn't wanted to worry Regina. Regina was sure that her mother was doing it on purpose. Well, not exactly faking the symptoms, but bringing them on herself, because she didn't want to let Regina go. There were some ugly scenes between them. A lot of words were said that made Regina squirm for months afterward. Then there were doctors' appointments. Tests. Waiting for the results. Regina was impatient for proof that her mother was healthy as a horse so she could go ahead and accept the Berlin offer. Then the results came back. Advanced and aggressive cancer. What really broke Regina's heart was the expression on her mother's face the morning they got the news. She looked ashamed, apologetic, horrified for Regina. "I didn't mean to do this to you," she said. She did mean to try to make Regina stay, but not like that.

She died three months later. Aunt Masha and some of her mother's other friends would come to help, and there was a hired nurse who came twice a week, but it was Regina who stayed with her mother most of the time, who had to witness the rapid transformation of her large, strong mother into a withered corpse. "At least she didn't suffer," her mother's friends kept telling Regina. It's true, she didn't suffer—thanks to their decision to forgo debilitating and largely useless treatment, and the morphine that Regina managed to buy after selling most of her great-grandfather's paintings, but still the horror of witnessing her mother being erased as a human being was indescribable.

Years earlier, Regina translated an American bestseller *Dealing with Death*. Chapter one was titled "Stages of Dying." The encroachment of death was described in a series of detailed steps that seemed to be ridiculously specific.

Two to three weeks before death the patient will take to his/her bed and spend most of the time sleeping.

One to two weeks before death the patient will lose his/her appetite and become disoriented.

One to two days before death, his/her eyes will become glazed.

A few hours before death the body temperature will drop and the skin of the knees, feet, and hands will become a mottled bluish-purple.

It can't be like this, Regina had thought back when she was laboring over the sentences. It can't possibly be the same for everybody!

But apparently it was like that. And it was the same for everybody. Regina's mother took to her bed three weeks before she died. "Regina, can I sleep for a little while longer?" she would ask with the pleading expression of a young child. Two weeks before she died she stopped eating. "Oh, yes, this soup is very good, can I finish it later?" Shortly after that the confusion set in. "How do you tell time? Take this clock, what are you supposed to do with the numbers? Add them up?" And then: "Are you my mother? But you are!"

She would refer to Regina as her mother more and more often, the closer to death she got.

"Mama, where were you?"

"I just went to the bathroom."

"But I wanted you. I cried—that's how much I wanted you!"

Is this the only experience of motherhood I'm going to get? Regina thought as she turned away to hide her tears. She tried to feel maternal as she stroked the warm fluff on her mother's head; as she held her hand, shriveled and cold like an autumn leaf; as she whispered "It's okay." She couldn't. She didn't feel like a mother; she felt like a child instead, a frightened, abandoned child.

On the day of her death, her mother's eyes lost focus and filmed over. Then her feet and hands became a mottled bluish-purple. Then she died.

She hit all the marks described in that book.

There was something insulting, something demeaning, about the universality of death. Regina's mother, who had always refused to follow the rules and live her life like everybody else, couldn't escape dying exactly like everybody else. Regina plunged into depression and anger. Or, rather, she wallowed in anger while she had the strength and sank into depression when the anger exhausted her.

Her mother's old friends took care of the funeral and tried to take care of Regina as well, but she couldn't bear their attention. Aunt Masha was especially persistent. Regina had to tell her she was going to visit her father in Canada and she said the same thing to her editor Inga, to avoid their visits and calls. The truth was that she didn't even tell her father. She didn't tell her friends either. She had mentioned that her mother was sick, but she didn't tell them how serious it was. And when her mother died, Regina simply couldn't bear making that phone call. "Vadik, my mom died." "Sergey, my mom died." "Vica, my mom died." The mere thought of dialing a number and saying those words out loud made her shudder with revulsion. How could you possibly express the horror of what had happened in those three ordinary words? Regina abandoned her work, ignored her e-mails, didn't answer the phone, and just stayed on the sofa crying until she fell asleep. She barely ate. She'd lost eighteen pounds by the time Vadik knocked on her door about six weeks after the funeral. He had a connection in Moscow on his way back to New York from Minsk, where he was interviewing some Belarusian programmers, and he had tried to contact Regina, but since she wasn't answering her phone or e-mails, he'd come to her place. She was so weak from hunger and exhaustion that she could barely make it to the door. "Vadik," Regina said when she opened the door, "my mom died," and folded over sobbing. Vadik canceled his plans, changed his return ticket, and stayed in her apartment for about a week, and then he insisted that she visit all of them in New York. He even offered to pay for her ticket and help with the visa.

Regina told all of this to Bob during the period of insatiable intimacy they had in the first couple of months of their relationship. They were cuddled against each other on the huge sofa in Bob's apartment. They had been talking for hours; it had gotten late and the room had gone dark, but they didn't bother to get up and turn on the lights.

"I still don't know what it was," Regina said. "Did she subconsciously want to punish me for trying to get away? Or was this a gift of freedom? She knew how much I needed freedom, but she understood that she wouldn't be able to give it to me while she was alive. So she had to die."

"Or maybe it was neither," Bob said, stroking her hair. "She could've died because it was her time. People die. They don't do it on purpose, and they don't do it for somebody else."

The *swoosh* that Bob's fingers made when they went over her ears reminded her of the sound of the sea. It was amazingly soothing.

Bob said that Regina's mother was actually very lucky to have died like that, at home, in her own bed, in the presence of her daughter. Most people he knew died in hospitals, hooked to machines, surrounded by strangers, rendered speechless by trach tubes—no last words there. When his father was dying, Bob's older brother, Chuck, kept screaming at the doctors to "do everything," to "use every fucking heroic measure!" They broke two of his father's ribs performing CPR. Bob told her, "You can't imagine how much he suffered." Later, he recounted all that to his shrink, and the shrink sighed and said, "Yep. Death is not what it used to be."

Bob had never loved his father that much, but his death devastated him. The man had been a driving force behind Bob's many endeavors. The family legend was that when Bob's father saw Bob for the first time in the hospital, he had winced and said, "He's nothing like Chuck!" Chuck was already the best and the biggest student in his kindergarten class. He could count to one hundred and kick the ball far into the bushes. Bob's shrink told him that in a way this made Bob's life easier, because if you're born as a disappointment there's no crippling pressure to succeed. Perhaps he was right. Bob's biggest aspiration was not to succeed but to live his life in a completely different way. Bob went to an East Coast university, moved to New York, aligned himself with liberal politics, entered the IT field, and married a difficult woman.

"I mean my first wife, honey," he explained to Regina, "she was a real piece of work." And Regina felt momentarily jealous. Was she less challenging, less interesting than Bob's ex?

"So when my father died, I felt lost, perfectly empty, as if my life was stripped of purpose. I felt as if I had been living my life for my father, even if my main goal was to defy him. I think I felt depressed for about a year.

"When my mom died, it was different. I loved her more, and the pain of losing her was way, way more intense. Once, something reminded me of her smell—she had a very particular smell, clean and dry like freshly sawed wood—and I started to cry like a baby. She was very reserved. Loved to read more than anything else. Actually, you remind me of her a little bit."

That's alarming, Regina thought, but the tenderness of Bob's tone reassured her.

"My mom wasn't a very warm person. I don't think she ever kissed us unless we were sick. I used to believe that her kisses were a legitimate medical solution. Once I had a fever in school and the nurse gave me some aspirin, then later asked me if I was feeling better. And I said, 'No! My mother didn't kiss me!'"

"Bob, honey!" Regina said.

"Yes, I was very sad when my mother died, but I wasn't devastated. It wasn't as if my life stopped, which was how I felt when my father died. But the real horror reached me a few months after her death. I was at a dinner party with my old friends. Everyone's in their late forties just like me. And then it hit me that I was the only person in the room with both parents dead. There was nobody between me and death anymore. No protective layers. I was next in line. I've never felt more scared or exposed."

Bob had slid down and was lying on the sofa with his head in Regina's lap. Regina leaned down to kiss him and her hair fell over his face as if to shield him from the horror, to create that protective layer he was seeking. She felt an affection for Bob swelling inside her, pushing against her rib cage, hurting her.

That memory never failed to move her. "Bob, sweetheart," Regina said out loud, looking in the direction of the Hudson.

A baby's cooing broke into Regina's reverie.

"Now look at the nice lady! Is that a nice lady? Yes, it is! Yes, it is! Let's wave to her."

Regina turned to her right. On the next terrace over, there was a woman with a baby in her arms. Theirs would be the perfect neighborhood if it wasn't for all the kids. Everybody seemed to come there to have a child. The woman was swinging the baby's little hand so it would appear that the baby was waving to Regina. Regina gave the baby and the mother a Soviet-style young pioneer salute, picked up her empty cup, and headed inside.

Regina closed the balcony door behind her and walked over to the bookshelves. They had a whole wall of built-in shelves—Bob had installed them as a wedding gift to Regina, to house the books she'd brought from Russia. Old editions of Russian poetry, her mother's translations, all the European classics, Soviet relics—like a *samizdat* copy of Solzhenitsyn. But there were also several shelves devoted to the American books she'd been meaning to read ever since she moved to the U.S. The novel *Infinite Jest* had the most handled cover, because this was the book she'd made the most attempts to read. Every time Regina opened it, she would be knocked out by its sheer brilliance. And the language! Reading *Infinite Jest* was such a powerful experience for Regina that she couldn't read more than a few pages without stopping to take a rest. A long rest. More often than not, Regina wouldn't resume reading it for months. But that book wasn't the only one that presented a problem. There were shorter, less draining books on her shelf that didn't fare much better. Claire Messud's *The Emperor's Children*. Joseph O'Neill's *Netherland*. Back in Russia she would have finished novels like these in a couple of days. She traced her fingers over their worn-out spines, pulled out *Infinite Jest,* and sat down on the sofa trying to summon the energy to start reading. The energy refused to be summoned. Regina remembered that she hadn't had breakfast yet. Breakfast should help! she thought, leaving the book on the sofa and walking into the kitchen.

She wouldn't eat a big, distracting breakfast. She wasn't even hungry. She would just drink some more coffee—enough to give her the necessary energy for reading—and reward herself with food after she had finished a certain number of pages. She made herself a fresh pot of coffee. The coffee was good. In fact, it was so good that it would be a shame to consume it quickly. Regina put the coffee on a tray and carried it to the living room. She placed the tray on the coffee table, sat down on the couch, and clicked on the remote. Now what would be the perfect show to watch while drinking coffee? She knew where to get her answer. She had an app, this secret piece of joy that she had hidden from Bob on her phone. The problem was that the idea for the app had been Bob's young assistant's. He had pitched it to Bob and Bob had rejected it on the spot. More than that, Bob had laughed at it. Well, the assistant had gone ahead and pitched it to somebody else, who had developed it, and the app had became incredibly successful. Bob was still reeling. "I've misjudged the American consumer," he liked to complain. "We are even lazier and more stupid than we think we are."

Bob's assistant had called his app "Dinner and a Movie," but the company that developed it renamed it "Eat'n'Watch," because they thought that "Dinner and a Movie" was too outdated and too limiting. Why not watch a movie while eating breakfast or lunch? "My thoughts exactly," Regina had confessed to Vadik once.

You picked a movie or a TV program on Eat'n'Watch, then it suggested the best food to eat while watching it and helped you order it from a neighborhood restaurant. The app saved and studied your preferences too, so that after a few months of working together, it seemed to know you better than you knew yourself. And sometimes even better than you wanted to know yourself, thought

Regina. Eat'n'Watch asked you to rate the shows and the food, but it never actually based its suggestions on your rating system. The algorithm was based solely on the frequency of your ordering a certain item or on the time you spent enjoying it. Eat'n'Watch got you what you truly liked, not what you wanted to think that you liked. For example, Regina would give five-star ratings to Bergman and Rohmer and healthy salads, but based on the frequency of her orders, Eat'n'Watch knew that she really liked pizza, hamburgers, the greasiest items on Chinese menus, and American TV series like *Seinfeld, Friends,* and *Cheers.*

"How about the TV series *Blameless,* about a mousy wife and mother secretly running a chain of adult-only resorts (Season 1, Episode 1), and the Lumberjack Special from Just Food on Leonard Street?" Eat'n'Watch was asking her now.

That shit and the Lumberjack? Really? Why do you think of me so meanly? Regina thought. She wasn't even planning to have a big breakfast, yet the second the suggestion was made she realized that this was exactly what she wanted—some fast-paced, juicy, and brainless show, accompanied by a deliciously satisfying amount of sugar, salt, and fat.

She pressed the Okay button. That's how effortless it was. All she needed to do was to turn on her TV and wait for the delivery person.

The problem was that Regina could never synchronize the time it took her to watch an episode with the time it took her to consume food. By the time episode one of *Blameless* ended, she still had one pancake, two strips of bacon, and some home fries left. She could just eat them in dumb silence like an animal, like a stupid zombie, or she could do the more civilized thing and turn on episode two. Regina chose to do the latter. Episode two was even better than the first episode, because that was when those blonde PTA bitches started to suspect that the main character was involved in something clandestine. Imagine Regina's disappointment when she reached for a bacon strip in the middle of a very important scene and found out that there was none left. She clicked Pause. It was unthinkable to watch this shit for the sake of watching it. Or, rather, it was impossible to enjoy it without food. Regina thought of those Pavlovian dogs that started to salivate when they heard a bell, because they were used to hearing the bell right before the scientists brought them food. Physiological reflexes—blah blah blah. It was the same with her. Regina was so used to watching TV while eating, and eating while watching TV, that her mouth wouldn't salivate unless there was something on the screen, and her brain wouldn't accept video and audio stimulation unless she was eating. Eat'n'Watch had a solution—an excellent Cobb salad from Parsley, just around the corner. Regina sighed, added some extra blue cheese to her order, and pressed Okay.

She fell asleep in the middle of season three of *Blameless* and slept until six forty-five, when a phone call from Bob woke her up.

"I got held up," Bob said, "but I'll be home in ten minutes."

Regina got off the sofa and surveyed the scene. The smell of kimchi permeated the room. There were crumbs on her bare legs and a gob of blue cheese was stuck in her hair. The coffee table was littered with plastic containers and dirty napkins. There were four huge plastic bags on the floor: Just Food, Parsley, Muriel's Sweets, and Happy Wok. *Infinite Jest,* which had somehow ended up on the floor by the sofa, was stained with soy sauce. Regina was disgusted with herself. She felt sad and angry. She picked up the largest bag, which happened to be from Happy Wok, scooped all the trash along with the other bags into it, and pushed it down the garbage chute. Then she shoved *Infinite Jest* back onto the shelf, opened the balcony door to air out the room, removed her stained clothes and threw them into the laundry bin, and rushed into the shower.

Chapter 4

STILL HERE

ERGEY HAD DOZED OFF ON THE LOWER DECK OF THE ferry and woke just as they were passing the Statue of Liberty. He wiped a trickle of drool from the corner of his mouth and stood up. The moldy-green figure was looming on his left, the skyscrapers moving closer, getting bigger, sturdier. The cloudy sky, the gray waves. Everything so solid and stern. Sergey dreaded going to the office. The rumors of huge layoffs at Langley Miles had been circulating for a while, but yesterday they actually announced that a large group of employees would be "let go" this week. He had good reason to worry that he would be fired today. His position as a business analyst was insignificant enough, and he had been hired not that long ago. He knew that the newest employees were usually the first to get cut.

Some of Sergey's friends who worked at other places were happy to lose their jobs. The generous severance packages they received made it feel like a paid vacation. They would gather together for "unemployment brunches" and discuss their upcoming trips to Iceland, Peru, or other exotic locations. Vadik usually used the time and money granted by unemployment to go someplace new, find a new girl, and move into a new apartment. He would complain about his vagabond life, but it was hard not to envy him. Actually, Sergey would have enjoyed some free time so he could work on his linguistic algorithms for Virtual Grave. That fiasco with Bob had showed him that he wouldn't be able to sell Virtual Grave as a mere idea; what he needed was a working prototype. But that would require some serious time and effort, and Vica would never let him devote himself to working on the app full-time. She treated each of his unemployment periods like a disease from which he should be cured as soon as possible. Every time he lost his job—he always had more or less the same junior position in various investment banks—she made sure that he spent every second of every day looking for a new one.

Sergey took his smartphone out of his pocket and opened Facebook. In his fourteen years in this country he hadn't made a single American friend. Even most of his Facebook "friends" were Russians. He rarely posted anything himself, but he read his friends' posts avidly, often with masochistic pleasure. They published books, founded literary magazines, fought against the regime, participated in antigovernment protests on Bolotnaya Square. One of his friends, a left-wing journalist, had been severely beaten by pro-Putin thugs. Sergey caught himself envying even him. They seemed to have real lives, lives pulsating with excitement and meaning. They had lives he could have had if he'd stayed in Russia. Why, why, on earth had he been so sure that he'd make it here?

Sergey shivered from the wind. It was an unusually cold day for early October. He tied his scarf tighter but didn't move away from the railing. A few years ago, a Staten Island ferry just like this one had crashed into a pier. Sergey wasn't on it, but he'd read about the accident. The pier ripped into the ferry's side and tore into the main deck, where many of the passengers were gathering, about to disembark, just like they were now. Sergey imagined that a similar accident was about to happen. He imagined the mangled metal, the blood, the screams. He imagined himself flattened against the ferry's inner wall. Dead. Free of responsibilities. Free of judgment. Free to relax. He imagined Vica's grief with some satisfaction—they were barely talking after he had "brutally humiliated" her at

Vadik's housewarming. In the three months since then, the atmosphere at home had turned so hostile that Sergey felt that right now his death was the only thing that would warm Vica to him. But the idea of Eric being fatherless, unprotected, lost, made Sergey sick to his stomach. That was one of the main points of Virtual Grave for him, to provide some posthumous guidance or even encouragement to a person's loved ones.

Sergey's father died six years ago. A heart attack. He'd complained of chest pain and was dead a couple of hours later. He died in their large Moscow apartment, not in bed, but on the couch, Sergey's mother told him. On the very same couch where they used to watch TV together. Sergey had watched the evening news with his dad ever since he was five. He could barely understand what was going on on the screen, but the fact that he watched the news—along with the heft of their couch, its scratchy surface against the backs of his knees, its funky smell, his father's warmth next to him, his father's disgruntled sighs in reaction to the news, which Sergey sometimes imitated—made Sergey feel mature, important, special. Other kids watched *Good Night, Kiddies!* Sergey watched the evening news.

Sergey had been in New York when his father died. He got the news by phone. He and Vica left Eric with a neighbor and flew to Moscow for the funeral. Sergey saw his father's body in the coffin and the coffin enter the chute of the crematorium oven, then held the urn with his father's ashes in his hands. They flew back to New York two days after the funeral. When they got out of the taxi in the driveway of their Staten Island house, Sergey checked the mailbox. There was a heap of slightly soggy mail—they couldn't get the mailbox door to close all the way—and in the midst of bills, statements, and all the "fantastic offers," there was a letter from his father. Sergey checked the date—his father must have mailed it a few days before he died. Sergey waved away an angry Vica, stepped over their suitcases in the driveway, and went straight into the house and down to the basement to read the letter. It turned out to be a very ordinary letter. Sergey kept in touch with his mother via weekly phone calls, but his father disliked talking on the phone. When he did call, usually just to wish Sergey a happy birthday, there would be long pauses between his sentences, so long that Sergey would start to worry that the connection had been lost. "Dad?" Sergey would say, and his dad would sigh and answer, "Still here." They preferred writing letters once a month. Sergey's father was a retired math professor who detested a flowery style of writing, so his letters were always dry and to the point. He mostly listed the significant events of that month without bothering to describe them in detail.

Went fishing with Grisha Belik. He caught two large pikes.
I caught one medium-size pike and one small catfish.
The weather was good. They raised train fares once again.
It used to be 18 rubles. Now it's 22. Went to the concert hall
with your mother. The program was good. All Beethoven . . .

The letter went on like this for the entire two pages and ended with the usual "Kiss you, Papa." Sergey pored over it again and again, trying to find something between the lines, to decode some secret meaning, some last piece of advice. Was there any significance that the concert was all Beethoven? Or that the pike was medium-size and the catfish was small? No, there wasn't. No significance whatsoever. It was the fact that the letter was written in his father's voice that made the experience of reading it so powerful for Sergey. His father was gone, dead, yet his voice remained alive and unchanged: dry, skeptical, vaguely ironic. Sergey stayed in the basement reading every line over and over again, until Vica came down and smothered him with her warm damp hug.

Sergey happened to be between jobs at the time. He spent the weeks following his father's death in the basement, rereading Fyodorov. He had always admired Fyodorov, but he had never found his works so relevant before. How should a grieving son conquer his despair? The lowest of the low would be to ignore his own looming mortality and lose himself in animal lust, to go binge-fucking until death was imminent. The best and most moral thing to do was to set to work on resurrecting the father. Not many people understood the importance of this aspect of Fyodorov's philosophy.

Vica didn't. "Digging for molecules in the dirt to bring your dead father back to life? With your sand pail and your little shovel? That sounds like stupid sci-fi for children."

Regina didn't get it either. "Resurrection of the fathers? What about the mothers?" The simple answer was that Fyodorov deemed women impure and worthless, but Sergey chose to keep that to himself. Fyodorov's opinion of women clearly sprang from some deep personal trauma, and Sergey didn't want it to discredit his philosophy.

Even Vadik never really got Fyodorov. "Wouldn't you end up wasting your own life if you devoted all your efforts to resurrecting somebody else's?"

No, Sergey tried to explain, not at all! Constant pursuit of immediate gratification was what made you waste your life. Concentrating your endeavors on restoring the essence of timeless humanity was going to give you much greater satisfaction than the fleeting pleasures of sex.

It was back then that Sergey had the first inkling of Virtual Grave. Fyodorov might have predicted genetic cloning, but he couldn't have envisioned digital archiving. Atoms and molecules weren't needed to resurrect the essence of people; words were enough. Words recorded in digital documents. E-mails, chats, texts, tweets. If you could just gather and process the textual artifacts produced by a certain person in one place and then sift through them looking for distinctive patterns, you could create a linguistic portrait of that person, which was equal to restoring his or her essence or, in other words, his or her soul. And once you did that, you could enable the restored essence of that person to communicate with his or her loved ones, to provide much-needed guidance and support. He even managed to impress Vica when he explained this idea to her.

"Virtual voice," she repeated with that familiar hungry glow in her eyes. "A powerful illusion. An extremely marketable illusion."

The deafening whistle that signaled the ferry's imminent arrival made Sergey jump. He walked across the crowded deck closer to the exit as the ferry made its uneasy way to the pier, screeching, groaning, bumping into the scruffy wooden boards. The ferry workers lowered the walkway onto the deck, and Sergey started to squeeze toward the exit along with the other sleepy, hungry, and cranky commuters.

He was almost sure that today would be his last day at Langley Miles. His recent evaluations had been pretty bad.

"Sergey needs to be more proactive and take more ownership of the projects he leads," one said.

"Sergey needs to demonstrate improvement in human relations."

"Sergey needs to react to criticism in more constructive ways."

Back in Russia, when he first got that letter of acceptance from New York School of Business, Sergey imagined his future in a completely different way. He would sit in his roomy office alone, bending over his massive desk, reading, thinking, coming up with brilliant financial strategies. None of his fantasies had involved junior positions, difficult bosses, cubicles, bathroom passes, corporate parties, corporate birthdays, corporate community days, corporate baby showers, networking, adjusting, catering, fitting in. Failing to fit in.

His first disappointment was that New York School of Business wasn't actually a very good school. His friends who'd praised it must have had New York University's Stern School of Business in mind. He quickly discovered that great companies weren't particularly eager to employ NYSB graduates.

Still, since Sergey had graduated at the top of his class, he did manage to find a decent first job. He worked as a financial analyst for Gray Bank. It was far from the job of his dreams, but it was a start. He worked there for two years and his evaluations had been consistently good. He used to make fun of them to Vica, and even quoted the most ridiculous passages in e-mails to Regina and Vadik, but he was secretly proud of them.

"Sergey initiates good conceptual ideas with practical applications."

"Makes inventive and resourceful decisions."

"Is competent. Is clear-thinking. Is vigorous."

"Possesses a personal magnetism."

That last one made both Vadik and Regina crack up. Does your boss have a crush on you? Vadik had asked.

Sergey's career was destined to get better and better. He was offered another job with a much better salary and benefits, at a much larger bank than Gray. He and Vica decided that after he had worked there for a full year, they would be able to afford for Vica to quit her job and go to graduate school.

The problem was that Sergey's new boss proved to be insane. "He looks like a demented squirrel," Sergey complained to Vadik and Regina, making them laugh. "He does!" he insisted. "He has these rodent teeth and vacant little eyes." Vica failed to appreciate this comparison. She really hated Sergey's being so negative about his boss. It wouldn't help him succeed, she said. But it was hard not to be negative. The guy kept piling the most boring, humiliating work on Sergey and making him the office scapegoat. The worst was his patronizing contempt. If Sergey asked him to clarify this or that, he would stare at him with his beady black eyes for ten seconds or so and say, "Didn't they teach you that at business school?" And if he had to ask Sergey a question, he would pretend that he couldn't understand the answer because of Sergey's English. "Excuse me?" he would say, or "Say that again," or just shake his head.

"Sergey demonstrates fine professional expertise, but he could use some improvement in his verbal skills," he wrote in an evaluation.

"What if he really doesn't understand you?" Vica asked. "Your English is not that great." Well, yes, Sergey knew that his English was far from perfect, but he strongly believed that his brilliance and wit should compensate for that. Sergey loved to watch interviews with European luminaries on PBS. They too spoke with strong accents and made occasional grammatical mistakes, but these imperfections weren't seen as a handicap, but rather as a sign of superiority. They spoke the English of European intellectuals. And they sounded just like Sergey. Sergey got really mad when Vica burst out laughing when he shared that sentiment with her. That was when they had their first really big fight. Vica refused to understand why Sergey had to quit that job. "I hate my job too, so what?" she said.

"I'll find a new job in no time," Sergey told her. And he did. He found a new job within two weeks. The salary was almost as good as his last job, but the workload was lighter, and the boss was a nice, really nice, man. Kind of pale and sickly looking with these dark circles under his eyes, but nice. When, after two months, the decision was made to let Sergey go, his boss actually bothered to explain his reasons. It was not Sergey's fault, this was just a wave of layoffs. It happened. "Yeah, right," Vica said, when Sergey repeated that to her. She threw the cake he brought to appease her directly into the garbage bin. She kicked his computer bag with her foot. She yelled at Eric to get the hell out and go play outside. Sergey thought she was rather unreasonably angry. He promised to find a new job, a better job, within weeks. He'd done it once, he could do it again. Sergey did find something, but then the financial crisis hit and he lost it almost immediately.

It all went downhill from there. His enthusiasm faltered. His panic grew. His insecurities bloomed. His résumé became stained with longer and longer periods of unemployment. Each of the jobs he managed to find seemed to be a little bit worse than his last one, and the effort required to find them was greater and greater. There were fewer and fewer graduates from good schools among his co-workers, more and more immigrants like him.

"So what is it you do there exactly?" Regina asked when he got the job at Langley Miles. How he hated when people asked him that!

"I perform daily reconciliation of interest rate derivatives positions," he said to Regina.

"What does that mean?" she asked.

"Do you really want to know or do you just want to rub it in about how senseless my job is?"

"Sorry," she said.

No, his job at Langley Miles wasn't great, and still Sergey wouldn't have gotten it at all if not for Vadik's help—Vadik used to work there as a programmer before he accepted Bob's offer. Vadik had come to the United States years later than Sergey, and now Vadik was helping him. Still, the worst was Vica's attitude. She reacted to his work problems as if they were entirely his fault, as if he had done something to get fired on purpose, to spite her, to punish her, to make her life harder. Sergey's body couldn't handle the relentless disappointment either—he developed gastritis and a host of sexual problems. Vica took the latter as a personal affront.

His evaluations were getting increasingly critical, and Sergey found he was reacting to them with more and more pain. He knew them all by heart, he couldn't help it. They seemed to attack everything about him from his technical skills to his character, merging in his mind into sickening poems of judgment.

> *Lacks skills, spirit, drive.*
> *Lacks goals.*
> *Lacks control.*
> *Fails to aspire.*
> *Fails to evolve.*
> *Fails to progress.*

Apparently, he was failing not just professionally but on some basic human level.

He imagined that people were displeased with him everywhere. He would get embarrassed if it took him more than two seconds to produce his credit card to a cashier; he would be mortified if somebody asked him for directions and he didn't know the answer. When he ordered in restaurants, he imagined that waiters made fun of his imperfect English. He constantly saw dissatisfaction in Vica's eyes, more dissatisfaction that she actually felt, and far more than she meant to express. Even Eric. . . . Didn't he look annoyed when Sergey failed to assemble his toy robot? Didn't he sound sarcastic when he said "Yeah, Dad, the instructions must be wrong." Until just a couple of years ago, his son used to sit at the top of the living room stairs waiting eagerly for Sergey to come home from work. "Daddy's here!" he would yell when Sergey opened the door. He would slide down the stairs and jump into Sergey's arms. When Eric was born, Sergey had been hoping that his boy would grow up to be somebody who could understand him, become his true friend. There were moments when Sergey still hoped that was possible. Most of the time, though, he would look at Eric and imagine his son judging him as a father, listing his failures, mocking his weaknesses. He couldn't understand why these evaluations plagued him to such a degree. Perhaps it was a personality flaw that he couldn't "react to criticism in a more constructive way."

In his youth, he was accustomed to being admired, adored, praised, showered with applause, starting when he was four or five. Every single time his parents hosted a party, his father would bring little Sergey into the room and ask him to sing. And Sergey didn't disappoint. His musical ear might not have been perfect, but he had a strong, ringing voice and plenty of confidence. His father encouraged him to forgo stupid children's songs and go straight for romances and even arias from famous operas. His biggest hits were "La donna è mobile" and Lensky's aria from *Eugene Onegin*. He didn't understand any of the words, but it didn't matter. He took enormous, almost sensual pleasure in producing the sounds, in the musical reverberations that seemed to run down his body. And there were adoring stares all around. Smiles of delight, murmurs of appreciation. This was how Sergey's addiction to praise started. He'd stopped singing for an audience when he hit puberty, but he'd had ample gratification from other sources throughout his entire life, up until the last few years. Excellent grades in school and college, becoming the youngest person with a Ph.D. he knew, acceptance to an American business school, great friends, the love of intelligent, discerning Regina, the admiration of Regina's brilliant mother. Regina's mother used to give him English lessons. Lots of people of his generation dreamed of emigrating, so English lessons were essential. Regina and her mother lived in a tiny one-bedroom apartment crowded with antique furniture and paintings. And books, so many books—old, new, foreign, neatly typed manuscripts, disheveled hand-written drafts. The apartment looked unlike any other place Sergey had ever seen. It seemed to radiate waves of a bookish culture that inspired awe and admiration. Regina's mother was a large woman with a horsey face. She wore pants and had a man's haircut. Regina looked a lot like her except that she wore her hair in a long braid and was very shy. Regina's mother conducted the lessons in their sunny kitchen, and there was always a plate of crumbly cookies on the table. English had always intimidated Sergey, and Regina's mother often insisted that he take a break and eat a cookie. As he ate, she would ask Sergey questions about his dreams, about books, about his general opinion of life. He loved answering her questions, and it took him a while to notice that they were talking in English. Regina's mother was amazing. More than once Sergey caught himself wishing that his mother, Mira, was more like her. Sometimes, as he studied, Regina would often appear in the kitchen and sit on the edge of the windowsill, her long braid hanging over her left shoulder and her very long legs stretching all the way to the kitchen table. "I love this boy!" Regina's mother would say, addressing Regina but looking at Sergey. "He's read everything!" And Regina would smile and flip her braid. When Sergey and Regina started to date, everybody thought they were a perfect match. Except that he wasn't in love with her. He had never been in love with her, but he didn't know that until he met Vica. Vadik brought Vica to Regina's place so that he could impress her with his cool Muscovite friends. Vica walked in, took off her enormous fur hat, and looked around the apartment with her hungry, disapproving eyes. Her short reddish hair was damp with sweat and her upturned nose was glistening. She took in every object one by one. The antique furniture. The paintings. The china. Regina. Sergey. And he was gone. He started on a rant about some stupid scientific concept that interested him at the time (he couldn't remember what it was now) and he couldn't stop. Vica listened to his words with such fervent attention! She would lean forward and nod, and even gasp when he said something especially striking. Sergey had never experienced that before. Regina listened to him with interest, but her interest was patient rather than passionate. He went on for a crazy long time, but he couldn't bring himself to stop. It was getting embarrassing, and he was afraid that Regina, or Vadik, or especially Vica would think that something was wrong with him.

When Vica and Vadik left, he couldn't stop thinking about her. He didn't think he would see her again, because Vadik never kept his girlfriends for a long time, which was probably for the best, and yet he kept fantasizing about her. Then a week later he saw her in Lenin's library by pure chance. She had come to research her paper on Pavlov. He sat next to her in the reading room while she studied, then they went to get ice cream and ended up walking around Moscow for hours. By the end of the night, it became impossible to imagine that they wouldn't be together.

Vica broke up with Vadik right away, and Sergey was relieved to know that Vadik wasn't too mad at him. If anything he seemed amused. "You and a girl like Vica, huh! Good luck!" He seemed to gloat a little bit too, because Sergey's remarkably uncomplicated love life was becoming bumpy just like his.

The hardest part of it was telling Regina. It was the thought of disappointing her mother that horrified him the most. For some reason Sergey imagined that the breakup scene would involve all three of them. They would be sitting in the kitchen, just like they had during English lessons, their cups on the table with a dirty spoon, a half-eaten cookie, a crust of bread. And then Sergey would deliver his news and disrupt the harmony. He imagined that Regina would run out of the kitchen in tears, but her mother would stay. She wouldn't say anything, she'd just stare at Sergey for a very long time. Vadik unwittingly spared him from that. He had no idea that Sergey hadn't yet told Regina when he talked to her. She called Sergey right after to say that he disgusted her and that she never wanted to see him again. "Disgusted"—that was what she said, and the word bothered him for a long time after that. But he was with Vica, and he felt that no amount of pain or guilt could ruin his happiness. It was like this: He would wake up in the morning, go out onto the street to get to work or to the university, and find the world saturated with Vica. The trees, the sidewalks, the honking cars, the heavy buses were all somehow about Vica. The image of her seemed to bounce off every single thing and go straight to Sergey, making him impatient to see her. He'd never wanted anyone as much as he wanted Vica, nor had anybody wanted him as much as she did. She kept telling him how she loved his taste, how she missed his smell, how he could have her anytime, anytime at all—"even if I'm asleep, you can just wake me up. I won't get mad, I promise. Always, anytime!" She was greedy and loud, but she was also fragile— something that very few people saw in her. She had this capacity to feel more intensely than other people he knew—both joy and grief. There was something raw about the way Vica experienced the world, something that always moved him, and he had always felt the need to protect her, to hug her, to shield her from the pain of living.

Hug her! Sergey thought with bitterness now. It had been a long time since Vica let him touch her. In the past couple of weeks, there were days when she wouldn't even look at him.

He walked across Whitehall Street toward Broad Street. The skyscrapers there formed solid walls and blocked the view, making

Sergey feel as if he were at the bottom of a gigantic water well. When they first came to the U.S., Sergey was thrilled by skyscrapers. He would stop in the middle of a street, throw back his head, and stare at the tops of buildings that floated in the sky against light, sluggish clouds. He would stand like that with an aching neck, marveling at how something so amazing, so impossible could exist right here, within reach, constructed by mere humans. But after 9/11 their splendor was suddenly gone; they looked vulnerable, exposed, just like the residents of the city who seemed to lose their confidence overnight. He and Vica were at home when the planes hit the towers. He had no classes that day and Vica had a late shift. They still lived in Brooklyn then. He was sitting in their falling-apart armchair that they had picked up off the sidewalk and hauled four flights up to their apartment. Sitting as if frozen, staring at the TV screen without really seeing the images. While Vica—Vica couldn't sit still. She was darting back and forth between the TV and the kitchen, where she was cooking something red and messy (borscht? tomato sauce?)—her apron had disgusting red stains all over it. She was constantly on the phone with her mother, screaming at her that she should calm down. Then she got this idea into her head that people buried under the towers were still alive. Their bodies were smashed, but they were still breathing. She took her apron off and threw it to the floor and was crouching by their entrance trying to untangle the shoelaces on her sneakers. She had medical training! She could help! She could! And Sergey had to stand up and walk over to her, then crouch before her, take her by the shoulders, and tell her that there couldn't be any survivors, that those people were dead. Dead, do you understand this, dead! And there was absolutely nothing either he or Vica could do about it. Then he walked back to the armchair. He needed to process his grief in peace. They had lived through the tumult of the 1990s in Russia and arrived here, in the land of stability and permanence and well-being, where if you played by the rules, a bright future was basically guaranteed. And here they were, with stability blown up just like that. Sergey couldn't imagine what the future held for them anymore, couldn't count on everyone playing by the rules. This was probably the only time when he found himself on the same wavelength with Americans. They felt the same thing, they were like him, he was like them. This was his country. Sergey had felt like that for a long time, all the while the trauma of 9/11 had been fresh. Then the grief faded, and he became a stranger again. Now, when Sergey looked at the city, he found it hostile rather than vulnerable, threatening and boring at the same time.

It was eerily quiet at the office. Sergey arrived fifteen minutes early, but most of his colleagues were already at their desks. Their computers were on, but nobody seemed to be working. Their fingers didn't run across the keyboards, their eyes didn't move over the pages. They sat staring at their screens as if paralyzed. Sergey felt nauseous with panic. He nodded at Anil and the heavily pregnant Lisi, but Anil looked away and Lisi barely smiled. There was a half-dead helium balloon under Lisi's desk. A sad relic from her recent baby shower.

His coworkers started to disappear around ten o'clock. Every time Sergey raised his head, there would be another empty desk. And yet he couldn't catch the act of disappearance itself. Not until it happened to the man who sat in the next cube. His name was Mehdi. He was a thin man in his fifties with large expressive eyes that reminded Sergey of those of a sad cartoon animal. At eleven fifteen a pretty young woman appeared in the narrow space between their two cubicles. She wore a pencil skirt and a thin yellow cardigan that looked so soft and inviting that Sergey longed to touch it. Mehdi tensed but didn't turn around, as if he thought that ignoring the woman could make her go away. She tapped him on the shoulder. He stood up, moved his chair away, and followed her down the hall, all without raising his eyes. All his things were still in the cubicle: a scarf on the floor, a glass teacup with some tea in it, countless photographs of his family. Dark-haired, white-teethed—a good-looking bunch of people. Sergey was especially taken by a large photo of a young woman that stood right next to Mehdi's computer. The woman was in her late twenties; she must be Mehdi's daughter. She wasn't that beautiful and she wasn't smiling, but there was something warm in her expression, some unwarranted, undeserved kindness. She was looking away from the camera, but Sergey desperately wanted her to look at him, to see him, to have some of that warmth directed at him. He was still staring at the photo when he felt the tap on his own shoulder. There she was—the woman in the yellow cardigan. Sergey walked after her down the hall, his eyes following the pendulum-like rocking of her buttocks. She led him into the smaller conference room and disappeared. There they were: the grave David, the grave Brian, and a tense middle-aged woman from HR fingering a thick stack of papers. Sergey could barely understand what they were saying, but it didn't matter, because it was only a few minutes before he was walking toward the exit squeezing those papers in his hands. The woman in the yellow cardigan was nowhere in sight. He no longer deserved her. Instead, there were two bulky security guys who escorted Sergey out of the building.

Once outside, Sergey was assaulted by a burst of wind so strong that it seemed to be attacking him from all directions. What was the point of skyscrapers if they couldn't even shield people from the weather? Sergey checked the time and started to walk toward the ferry. When he turned onto Pearl Street, he slipped on a piece of a hamburger on the pavement and barely kept his balance.

His phone started to vibrate. Vica. She must've sensed that he had been fired. The thought of answering it and talking to her right now made him sick.

He passed an express bus stop. There was just one person waiting there, a sullen-looking man in his sixties wearing a thick sweatshirt with the hood down and work boots splattered with white paint. But then, of course, it was only twelve fifteen, too early for the commuter crowd. Sergey wondered if the guy had gotten laid off as well.

Sergey made it to the ferry just as the glass doors of the terminal were closing. He was completely alone on the left side of the deck.

He could see the Verrazano Bridge in the distance, thin and fragile like a spiderweb.

He grabbed the railing and stared straight ahead, imagining himself in charge of the ferry.

Sergey strengthened his grip and steered it forward. The waves were thick but not too unruly. The important thing was to keep the ferry steady. It was a challenging task, trying to make it safely between all those barges and yachts and erratic speedboats. He managed to turn the ferry to the right toward the Statue of Liberty, when he noticed an enormous cruise ship right in front of them surging at full speed. In a split second, Sergey calculated the approximate speed of the cruise ship, its distance, and the angle at which it was going and decided that a collision could be avoided if he could steer his ferry to the left. He turned his head to see what was on the left side. There was a long, slow red barge, but it was far away enough. And the coast guard boat was getting pretty damn close. He should have given the signal to alert the coast guard boat to his intentions. But that was something he couldn't do. He had no power over signals. Only over the ferry. So he adjusted his grip again and took a very slight turn to the left. And then straight, then to the right again. The cruise ship was rushing right at them. Could it be that he had miscalculated the speed and a collision was inevitable? He felt like closing his eyes, but he knew that he couldn't. He had to stay in control. Strong grip. Steady course. Stare forward. Ignore the cruise ship. Ignore the boat. Forward through the wind. He made it!

A couple of tourists in yellow rain ponchos over their thick parkas walked on the deck, saw Sergey, and smiled at him. He became aware that he was still gripping the railing. He let go, and walked toward a bench. He had been holding on so hard that his fingers were stiff and white.

Once again the whistle that signaled the ferry's arrival came too soon. Sergey disembarked, walked to the parking lot, unlocked his car, and climbed in. He started the car, then hesitated. This was Tuesday, the day when Vica worked nights. She would be at home now. Snug in the armchair like a big lazy cat, her feet in warm socks on top of an electric heater. Watching TV. Her first reaction on seeing him would be annoyance at being interrupted. Then the true meaning of his coming home early would dawn on her and her face would take on an expression of woozy disappointment. He could deal with her anger, with her screaming, with her kicking things, but he couldn't deal with her disappointment. He couldn't possibly go home yet.

Sergey suddenly had an idea. There was that strange place he'd accidentally discovered a couple of months ago. He'd been driving home from the mall—he'd had to pick up some last-minute supplies for Eric's school project—and it was late. The usual route was closed due to road repairs, so he had to drive down some unknown, unmarked road. He soon saw that he had lost his way but continued to drive. He found himself on top of a hill overlooking the ocean and the glittering Verrazano. The road was narrow with charming villas on both sides half hidden in their lush gardens. The view reminded Sergey of the Mediterranean villages he and Vica had visited on their European tour five years ago. He had liked it so much that he'd saved the location in his GPS under favorites. He decided to drive there now. He would park the car, walk down the hill, explore the neighboring streets, find out if the place would hold its charm in the daylight. Sergey turned on the GPS, found the coordinates, and pressed Go.

"Turn right on Victory Boulevard," the GPS commanded Sergey, and Sergey told him to go to hell. First of all, he didn't want to take Victory Boulevard—with the road repairs going on now, traffic would be awful. Another reason was that Sergey couldn't stand this GPS person (default American male)—he reminded him of his boss David's voice, brimming with overconfidence and extra *r*'s. The name of the street came out as "Victorrrr Ry Boulevarrrd." Sergey switched to the American female, but she proved to be everything that he hated about American females. She was too righteous, too optimistic, too enthusiastic. She reminded him of their tennis instructor. That had been Vica's idea—to make them all, including little Eric, learn how to play tennis, because she thought it was a necessary step on the way to becoming true middle-class Americans. Their instructor kept yelling "Good job!" when one of them hit a ball; "Good try!" if one of them missed. Her pointless praise made Sergey feel like an idiot. He switched off the American female and decided to try the Russians. There was no Russian male option, and the female sounded mean and controlling. She expected him to do whatever she told him, and there were really nasty gloating notes in her *"Pereschityvayu!"* when she was recalculating the route. That nastiness was all too familiar. Sergey hurried to switch her off. He didn't speak any other languages, but he didn't really need to know them to understand directions. All the GPS said was "turn left," "turn right," and "recalculating."

The Italian man was dripping passion—he sounded too much for Sergey's taste.

The German man sounded disappointed.

The French woman sounded haughty and patronizing.

The Chinese woman was too harsh.

The Japanese woman was too playful; she seemed to be on the verge of giggling at all times. Sergey enjoyed it for a while, but then he started to doubt if she was sincere.

The Icelandic woman, however, was perfect.

She said: *"Snúa til vinstri."* She said: *"Snúa til hægri."* And when she attempted to recalculate the route, she simply said: *"Reikna."* It must have meant "recalculate." She sounded both respectful and firm. She sounded as if she were aware of Sergey's limitations but didn't mind them at all. He could miss a turn, miss a turn again, miss a turn twenty times in a row—she wouldn't be angry, annoyed, or disappointed. So what if he kept missing turns? There was still plenty about him to admire and appreciate. There was still plenty to love. The tone of her voice was perfect, the melodic notes magnificent. The way she rolled her *r*'s and softened her *l*'s made Sergey feel butterflies in his stomach. And the word *reikna* made Sergey's heart melt. He drove to the northern part of the Staten Island Greenbelt, found a deserted parking lot, and kept circling and circling it for the sake of hearing *"Reikna"* again and again. The parking lot was covered by last year's brown leaves. They made whooshing sounds under the wheels of the car. There were tall trees all around him, mostly bare but still beautiful, gracefully crisscrossing patches of blue sky.

"Reikna," the woman said.

"Yes," Sergey answered.

He imagined her walking toward him wearing one of his dress shirts and nothing else. He couldn't see her face, but he saw that she had a full bush, like Vica used to have before she started doing Brazilian waxes. Thick brown hair with a golden tint. Just like Vica's.

"Reikna," the woman said.

"Yes," Sergey answered.

His right hand rested on the steering wheel while his left hand reached into his pants.

"Reikna," the woman said.

"Yes," Sergey answered and squeezed his cock tighter.

"Reikna."

"Yes."

"Reikna."

"Yes," Sergey said reaching for a tissue.

"Reikna!"

"Yes! Yes! Yes! Yes! Fuck!"

It took Sergey a long time to catch his breath. When he finally got ahold of himself and pressed the gas, he heard that word again: *"Reikna."* This time it annoyed and even embarrassed him. "Quiet," he said to the woman, and turned the GPS off. He was driving uphill with the Verrazano looming far in the distance. He felt good. He felt energized. He felt better than he'd had in months.

" 'Is competent. Is clear thinking. Is vigorous,' " he recited aloud, then added a few more.

"Lacks nothing.

"Fails at nothing.

"Is brilliant. Is persistent. Is strong."

Sergey made a sharp right turn and headed in the direction of home.

Chapter 5

#KNOWTHYSELF

NEXT CUSTOMER!" SAID THE PALE, PIMPLY BOY WITH the blue hair, and Vadik obediently unloaded his purchases onto the cashier's belt of HippoMart. When he first moved there, Vadik misread the name of the store and thought it was called HipMart. "How fitting! Even groceries are hip here," he said to Vica, Sergey, and Regina.

Organic ground chicken, maitake mushrooms, a small container of coconut rice, a pack of mâche salad, eggs, Icelandic yogurt, Intelligentsia coffee, a thin wedge of Gruyère, a smallish bunch of broccoli, three bars of Ritter Sport chocolate, a six-pack of local IPA, ultra-strength toilet paper, a pack of condoms, and a package of dishwashing sponges. Wait, where was the package of sponges? Nowhere. He'd forgotten to pick it up. It was too late to run back and get it, especially since that ghoulish boy didn't seem too happy to be helping Vadik to begin with. He looked at Vadik's items with a patronizing smile, as if he had a way of knowing that all of them had been forced on Vadik either by other people or by circumstances. That he had switched to Intelligentsia coffee because of Sejun's insistence; that he didn't really like broccoli but kept eating it, because broccoli was on the list of the ten healthiest foods; that he didn't need his toilet paper to be ultra-strength; and that he longed to be in an exclusive intimate relationship that didn't require condoms. He composed a Tumblr post in his head: "I used to think that stocking up on condoms was a sign of virility, now I think it's a sign of loneliness."

The cashier cleared his throat. Vadik looked up.

"Eighty dollars and seventy-five cents," the boy hissed. Vadik swiped his credit card, picked up the plump shopping bag, and headed for the door.

All the passersby crowding Bedford Avenue on Saturday at midday were young and dainty, both men and women. Vadik felt bulky and old. He was thirty-nine years old, over six feet tall, and one hundred and ninety-five pounds. He didn't fit in here at all. And not just in his physical dimensions.

Here in Williamsburg, Vadik often felt as if he had wandered into the wrong theater by mistake and had to sit there watching some stupid play that he didn't understand and didn't want to watch, then finally realizing that he was sitting not in the audience but on the stage and was expected to act his part. The sensation of being onstage was even stronger at home. His new apartment was situated on the first floor with all of the windows looking out over the busy street, with its constant traffic of cars, bikes, and pedestrians. He felt like he was being watched even when the blinds were drawn.

He decided that he didn't have the strength to go home yet and entered a small expensive coffee place on the corner of Bedford and Fifth. Vadik ordered an espresso and sat down at a table away from the window, with his bag by his feet—veggies, condoms, ground chicken, and all.

Williamsburg had been Sejun's choice. She had announced her decision to move in with him in August. Vadik was overjoyed, even though the circumstances of the announcement were a little strange. In the weeks leading to her decision, they were getting more and more distant—Vadik had prepared himself for the imminent breakup. But then Sejun asked him to come visit her in Palo Alto. "I'll come in a few weeks," Vadik said. "No, come now! Come this weekend!" she insisted. That last-minute ticket was outrageously expensive, but it was worth it. Sejun was unusually affectionate to Vadik. She kept snuggling against him, crying and laughing, cooing over him and praising him, and telling him how he was so much better than all the other jerks out there. At the end of his short stay, she announced that she was done with California, that she would be looking for a job in New York, and that they would be living together. Vadik was so happy that he picked her up, squeezed her in a hug, and spun her around the room so hard that she hit her shoulder against her garage-sale antique armoire. It was only when he was on the plane back to New York that her behavior started to seem suspicious.

"Sounds fishy!" Vica said, adding to his unease. Regina agreed. But Sergey was all "Sejun's coming!"

Vadik half expected her to call him the next day and say that she had changed her mind. She did call him very early the next morning—it must have been 6 A.M. in California—and his heart dropped, but she just wanted to tell him that she had sent out her résumé to several promising places in New York.

She found a job in no time, at some hip start-up in Brooklyn. They asked if she could relocate in two months. She said yes. "*Ura!*" Vadik screamed into his iPad. He immediately imagined all the wonderful dishes he would cook in his immersion cooker for her, all the wine that they would drink on his beautiful terrace, and all those interesting stimulating things they would do in his enormous bedroom. But when he shared some of his fantasies with Sejun—fantasies that included cooking and fantasies that didn't—she said: "No! Your apartment is too far from Brooklyn, you need to find a new one."

Vadik went silent. He thought about the deposit he would lose if he moved out of his current place and all the other costs of moving again so soon, but then he thought that he should be ashamed of worrying about such things on the verge of this life-changing event.

"Hello?" Sejun said.

"Yes?" Vadik answered.

"What do you think about Williamsburg?"

Vadik didn't know much about Williamsburg, but he figured that if Sejun thought it was a cool place, there was no reason he wouldn't be happy there.

Over the next few days, Sejun picked out a few places on Street-Easy and asked Vadik to go there with his iPad so that she could check them out via Skype.

"Okay, now move it forward so that I can see inside that closet. Oh, wow, that's huge! I'm not in love with the bathroom tile though. Ask the landlord if we're allowed to change it."

The apartment Sejun finally approved was a large two-bedroom ("We need a second bedroom in case my parents come to visit from Seoul"). It was on the first floor, but Sejun said she didn't mind. The rent was a little higher than Vadik'd expected, but he thought that with two salaries they could certainly manage it. The next step was to pick out the furniture. Sejun allowed Vadik to keep his immersion cooker, but not much else. Most of his things were either sold or ended up in Vica and Sergey's house on Staten Island. Sejun then furnished all the rooms via her iPhone using an app called Stuff Me! All Vadik had to do was receive the furniture when it was delivered and connect Sejun with the delivery guys so that she could explain where exactly she wanted it.

Two weeks before she was supposed to arrive, Vadik vacated his old place in Morningside Heights and moved into the new one.

"Show me all the rooms again," Sejun demanded on his first night there. "I want to see how they look with a person there."

It was then that Vadik noticed the first signs of trouble. Once Sejun saw the pictures of the apartment "with a person there," she didn't seem to love it as much as before.

"Shit, you're too tall for that chair," she said.

"You can use it then," Vadik said.

"No, no," she said, "I ordered it specifically for you. I won't be comfortable in that chair. Oh, and please don't lean on the table—it's delicate."

"It seems like she likes everything about our apartment except for me in it," Vadik complained to his friends. Sergey laughed. Vica said, "Imagine that!" Regina was the only one to reassure Vadik, but even she didn't sound too convinced.

A few days before Sejun's arrival date, Vadik called to ask her for her flight number—he wanted to meet her at the airport.

There was a long pause and then Sejun said that she hadn't bought the ticket yet.

Vadik almost dropped his phone. "But you have to start work in less than a week!"

Sejun explained that she was waiting for a cheaper last-minute rate.

"I'm fucked, right?" Vadik asked Regina.

"I'm afraid so," she said.

After that conversation, it became really hard to reach Sejun. She refused to pick up the phone and ignored Vadik's texts. Her final communication came in the form of an e-mail with a huge video attached. Vadik read the text of the e-mail while lying on the Danish Modern bed she had ordered, so low that it seemed like a continuation of the sidewalk outside. If Vadik opened the blinds, there would be strangers' legs on the same level as his head, marching back and forth and all over him. Sejun explained that they couldn't possibly live together. How they didn't match at all but were simply drawn together out of loneliness, and how terribly sorry she was for making him move. "It's a really nice apartment though, I'm sure you'll grow to love it."

Then Vadik opened the attachment. It was an electronic collage of their best moments together. A tasteful and moving collection of their photographs, with snippets from their e-mails dancing on the screen to Cohen's "Dance Me to the End of Love," hiding, fading, suddenly coming into focus and ultimately merging into a large "I AM SORRY!"

Cohen! What a nice touch! Vadik thought before smashing his iPad to pieces against the footboard of his Danish bed.

This new place was the seventh apartment he had had since he moved to the U.S. Seventh! He knew that his friends made fun of this fact, but he had never thought it was ridiculous. He had tried out different places and he had enough courage to admit that they were wrong and move. He used to think it was admirable. A lot of people hated their lives, but just a few were able to admit it, and even fewer to make a change. And how on earth were you supposed to figure out what worked for you if you hadn't tried and discarded the things that didn't work? Weren't you defined by what you were not? Wasn't it Sartre who said that? Vadik took a sip of his espresso and googled the quote, confirming the words did belong to Sartre, but the sentence was a little different. "You are what you are not and are not what you are." The second half made the entire sentence pretentious and senseless. Vadik decided to tweet just the first part and typed: "You are what you are not. #KnowThyself." That sounded too serious. He changed the hashtag to #KnowThyselfie.

His phone buzzed just as he was posting the tweet. "Where are you? I'm hungry," the text read.

Vadik sighed, left a generous tip on the table, and hurried home.

When he opened the door, he found Sergey in his usual position: sprawled on the settee by the window with his old laptop propped against his chest. Comfortable, contented. His dainty frame made him fit Sejun's furniture better than Vadik. Sergey even enjoyed the fact that the apartment was on the first floor. He insisted that they leave the blinds up, because that way he felt "in the middle of the racket."

"Hi, there!" Sergey said.

"Hi," Vadik said, trying hard not to wince. Seeing Sergey first thing when Vadik entered his apartment was getting harder and harder to tolerate.

When Sergey appeared on Vadik's doorstep three weeks ago, Vadik had no choice but to take him in. He was even a little excited. Vica threw Sergey out! No, he didn't gloat that Vica and Sergey had finally broken up, he was excited because something huge had hap-

pened, some major event that would inevitably change their lives—
his and Regina's too. Of course Vadik welcomed the distraction
from the prickly humiliation of his breakup with Sejun.

So he had led Sergey into the living room, brought him a shot of
vodka and a huge mug of green tea, and listened to the stuttering
account of what had happened.

Vica wasn't shocked or angry when Sergey told her he'd been
fired. Her expression was that of deep revulsion. She said that she
knew it would happen. She asked if he understood how selfish it was
of him to keep losing his job. Yes, she thought it was his fault. He
acted like a child. He was ridiculous. What grown man would insist
on drinking a glass of milk before bed? She said that he would never
ever accomplish anything with the apps either. He was delusional
about his genius. He was incredibly, sickeningly pretentious and
some foolish people took this for intelligence. She used to be one of
them. She was duped into admiring him. But now she was positive
that not only was he not a genius, he wasn't even very smart. He had
loser genes. He was pathetic. She was sick of him. The thought of
touching him made her shudder with disgust.

Sergey sat in Vadik's elegant chair, rocking back and forth, his
hands on his knees, staring straight ahead as if his life were a sad,
incomprehensible movie playing out on the invisible screen in front
of him.

"Do you have your things?" Vadik asked.

Sergey nodded and reached for a yellow plastic bag with MY-
EUROPE on it. There were several crumpled pairs of white briefs, an
odd number of cheap socks, a falling-apart volume of Fyodorov's
writings, and a two-quart carton of milk. "I stopped in a deli on the
way," Sergey explained to Vadik. "I wasn't sure if you had any milk."
That carton of milk in a plastic bag made Vadik choke up.

Sergey had been Vadik's best friend for more than twenty years
now. They first met when they were sixteen. Sergey and his parents came to spend two weeks at the Black Sea resort town where
Vadik lived. Vadik's aunt was their landlady. Vadik was immediately

impressed by Sergey's looks, his knowledge of American music and French philosophy, and his cool Muscovite airs. But Vadik managed to impress Sergey too. Vadik knew a lot of poetry by heart and he had already had sex with a girl. Her name was Nina. She made Vadik so crazy that he kissed her on the butt once. "Did you really kiss her butt?" Sergey asked. Vadik confirmed that he had. "I would never do that," Sergey said. "Yes, you would, when you're in love," Vadik said. They spent hours talking about sex, and love, and death, and poetry, and the meaning of life.

They must have made a very funny pair. Sergey, short, trim, and Jewish-looking, and Vadik, blond, burly, and big, humming Leonard Cohen songs, reciting Mandelstam and Sartre, strolling along the beach together, Vadik's footprints noticeably larger than Sergey's.

They solidified their friendship when Vadik came to Moscow to study mathematics at the same university where Sergey was studying linguistics, and sustained it through all the calamities of their lives. But it was there in the United States that they grew especially close, taking turns navigating each other through the intricacies of American life.

"STAY AS LONG as you want," Vadik had said to Sergey. "Make yourself at home."

And Sergey did.

It was amazing how fast he recovered. He had been thoroughly miserable for the first couple of days, but then one morning he woke up, made some Intelligentsia coffee (overbrewing it and splashing it all over Vadik's white counter), and announced that he felt much better. He actually felt better than he had in months, possibly in years. After Vadik left for work, Sergey took the car, drove to Staten Island, picked up his clothes, drove back to Williamsburg, and spent the day exploring the neighborhood. When Vadik came home, Sergey told him that he had walked all the way to the Brooklyn Bridge and crossed into Manhattan and back.

"Did you know that if you go to the top of the bridge and stick out your open hand, you can see the entire downtown fit onto your palm?"

Vadik did know that. That was exactly how he felt when he first came to New York. Gigantic, omnipotent, bursting with energy. That was so many years ago.

The next morning Sergey announced to Vadik that he simply wasn't a corporate nine-to-five guy. It had been a huge mistake for him to have spent so much time trying to fit in when it was impossible. Vica was too narrow-minded to see that. Virtual Grave was a brilliant idea, but trying to approach a developer with the mere idea for an app was an idiotic move. What he need was a working prototype so that he could ask investors for money and oversee the development himself. And now he had all the time in the world to build the prototype!

He wanted to tell Vadik more about his plan, but Vadik, being a "corporate, nine-to-five guy," had to leave for the office. Sergey's words stung precisely because lately Vadik had begun to doubt that he had made the right choice of profession. Back in Russia he used to enjoy programming. It was cool, it was exciting, it gave him a small adrenaline rush whenever he came up with some clever solution to a problem or wrote especially elegant lines of code. But more important, the job gave him the freedom to look for a perfect lifestyle. Programmers were needed everywhere—he could change companies, locations, even countries. The work was hard, the hours were long, but the money was pretty good, really good, in fact. Especially the money he made at DigiSly. The money allowed him to travel, to dress well, and to try out expensive hobbies like tennis, skiing, skydiving, or molecular cooking. But lately the senselessness of working so much was starting to dawn on him. He had to work for eight to ten hours every weekday and often on weekends too. It took him a couple more hours simply to unwind after work. So what time did that leave him to actually enjoy his life? A few hours every day and a bit more on weekends? It was ridiculous that he had to work so hard for a mere couple of hours of enjoyment, yet he could have lived with that if enjoyment was still there. But there was less and less of it, and whatever pleasure he experienced was becoming increasingly meager and forced.

So yes, it was hard not to envy Sergey, who plunged into his new life with youthful abandon. The first thing he did was to sign up on Coursera for several classes on new discoveries in linguistic patterns, web design, and user experience. Then he created a detailed schedule for his work over the next few weeks. He would wake up at six, make his awful coffee—spilling it on the counter every single time—and go for a run. Then he would buy and eat a bagel, and study for exactly four hours. At twelve thirty he would put on Vadik's gym shorts—which looked ridiculously big on him—and do a hundred jumping jacks and fifty push-ups. "Draw the blinds when you do it," Vadik told him. "Why?" Sergey asked. "I like it when people watch me." Then he would make himself a sandwich, consume it at the tiny side table by the window, and put in four more hours of work. Then he would wait for Vadik to come home and make dinner, after which he would sometimes persuade Vadik to go out with him. He spent most of his weekends on Staten Island with Eric. He arranged it with his mother so that he could pick Eric up and drop him off without having to see Vica. He didn't talk about her either. He would tense if Vadik mentioned her, and he never ever mentioned her himself.

Vica talked about Sergey all the time.

The first time she called Vadik was five minutes after Sergey arrived at his place.

"Is he there?" she asked. Her voice was thick with snot and tears.

"Yes," Vadik said.

"Is he okay?"

"More or less."

"Okay," she said and hung up.

She called Vadik often.

"I just want to make sure he is okay," she always said.

But Vadik sensed that there was some other motivation behind those calls. He was expecting her to ask him out or something like that, and the prospect was both frightening and intensely unpleasant. He still remembered the stickiness of her hug, the hunger in her eyes, when he first arrived in the country. As if she had been waiting for him, as if she had been hoping that he could fix whatever was wrong with her life. And then those two stupid hours on her couch five years ago and the feeling of shame afterward. Now that Vica was practically single, there was no stopping her. He would have to reject her, but he had no idea how to do that without hurting her. He desperately needed to talk to Regina, but Regina was reluctant to discuss their friends with him. "I don't think I should meddle," she told him. "I used to be Sergey's girlfriend, remember? All of this is really awkward."

Still, it was unfair that the entire burden of dealing with Vica and Sergey fell to Vadik. It was Regina's duty to share some of that!

"What's for eats?" Sergey asked, not raising his eyes from the screen.

"Chicken and broccoli."

"Broccoli again? I think we should vary our lunches a little. Well, it doesn't really matter, I guess, as long as we're eating healthy. Did you remember the toilet paper?"

"Yep."

"Ultra-strength?"

"Yes, ultra-strength!"

Vadik added the need for ultra-strength toilet paper to his mental list of things he couldn't stand about Sergey.

The list also included:

Sergey's inability to close cabinets after he opened them.

Sergey's socks strewn all over the apartment.

Sergey's habit of wearing Vadik's socks, because he could never find his own.

Sergey's bite marks left on wedges of cheese in the fridge.

A collection of dirty glasses was building up by Sergey's bed. Every night he would put a glass of milk by the bed to drink during the night, but he never put the empty glass into the dishwasher in the morning; he would just take another glass the next night. So dirty glasses accumulated by the bed, a few cloudy with a milky film, others boasting some thick yogurtlike substance at the bottom or dried-up mold on the sides.

But the worst was Sergey's singing on the toilet:

"Dance me to your beauty with a flaming violin."

Vadik would groan and think: Burning violin, you idiot! Burning! Not flaming.

And there was also the question of money. In the three weeks that Sergey had spent at Vadik's, he had yet to offer to pay for rent or groceries. It seemed as if contributing money had simply never occurred to him.

Vadik turned on the immersion cooker to preheat, washed the broccoli, and broke through the wrapper on the ground chicken container. Shortly after his breakup with Sejun, he invented this dish that was delicious, soothing, and easy to make. "Soothing?" Regina had asked. "Why do you need soothing food?"

"For my broken heart," Vadik said.

"Your heart is not broken!"

It was incredible how all his friends denied him the ability to experience genuine heartbreak. None of them cared about his breakup with Sejun. None of them took his suicide attempt seriously. None of them even pretended to believe that what he had had with Rachel I was love. There were times when he doubted it himself, yes, but he never let himself doubt it for long, because the loss of Rachel was the only thing that gave his life in America a hint of tragic beauty. Without it, all that had happened to him in all those years was a stupid farce. A ceaselessly spinning carousel of crazy women. He would hop on and hop off, hop on and hop off, and there was no end to it.

The immersion cooker announced its readiness with a series of happy beeps. Vadik mixed chopped broccoli florets with ground chicken, added minced garlic and ginger, poured over some soy sauce, and put the green-gray mass into the cooker.

"How much longer? I barely had any breakfast today," Sergey yelled from the living room.

"Eight minutes, forty-three seconds," Vadik said.

"Good!" Sergey said. "I think we should go out tonight."

"Aren't you going to Staten Island?"

"No. Eric's on a school trip to Washington."

The bathroom door opened and closed, and a few seconds afterward Vadik could hear Sergey's flawed rendition of a Cohen song filter down the hallway.

Vadik went into the living room and sat down on Sejun's squeaky loveseat. He had counted on Sergey's being on Staten Island tonight because Vica had finally asked him out after all. She'd called and said that she really needed to talk to him, and suggested a nice place for dinner. Hole in the Woods. Right off Union Square, so it was convenient for both of them. She said that Saturday at six would work best for her, because she was doing a weekend shift until five thirty. Vadik had no interest in dating Vica, and he was fully prepared to turn her down, but he couldn't possibly tell Sergey that he was meeting her. And if he just told him that he was going into Manhattan, Sergey would definitely want to go with him.

A series of loud beeps broke his reverie. There were two messages on his phone: "Your food is ready, dude" and "Seriously, dude." Vadik made himself stand up and went into the kitchen. The chicken and broccoli looked gray and pathetic, and smelled like burned garlic.

They ate it anyway.

After lunch Sergey went back to work and Vadik tried to read some Sartre.

"If you are lonely when you're alone, you are in bad company." Vadik wondered if he should tweet it or post it on Tumblr. He decided to tweet it. And a few minutes later this: "Like all dreamers, I mistook disenchantment for truth." #KnowThyselfie now seemed stupid, so Vadik changed it back to #KnowThyself.

Around five, Sergey knocked on his door. To be fair, he always knocked.

"I'm done for the day. What time are we going out?"

Vadik cleared his throat and looked away.

"I have a date tonight."

"Nice! With who?"

"Just this girl I met online."

Sergey shrugged. "I could never understand online dating."

"And why is that?" Vadik asked.

"It's just so rational, so unromantic."

"And what is romantic in your opinion?"

"A sudden meeting, a thunderbolt kind of thing."

"Like what you had with Vica?" Vadik didn't want to be mean, but he couldn't help it.

Sergey tensed. "Yes, or like what you had with Rachel," he said and left the room.

But an hour later, they were fine again, and Sergey said that he'd walk Vadik to the subway and then go for a long stroll around the neighborhood.

And so they walked to the subway, a grumpy Vadik and Sergey, delighted with everything—strange angles of buildings, graffiti, window displays, girls with funny hair, girls with funny shoes on, girls in funny shorts over funny tights—"I don't even want to talk to them. I'm just happy that they are in such near proximity.

"Would you look at that graffiti!" Sergey exclaimed, pointing to the crumbling wall of a building across the street.

Vadik squinted, but all he could see was the green and yellow muddle of lines. Looks like vomit, he thought.

"I think these are aliens invading the earth," Sergey said. "Reminds me of Bruegel's *The Triumph of Death*."

It was probably Sergey's enthusiasm that annoyed Vadik the most. His ability to enjoy the same things that depressed Vadik proved that there was nothing wrong with Vadik's surroundings, but that, instead, there was something wrong with Vadik himself.

"Look at it, it's really good!" Sergey insisted.

"I can't see," Vadik said.

"I'm worried about your eyesight. You should seriously check it out."

Was it just Vadik, or was Sergey starting to sound like a wife?

It was such a relief to finally reach the subway and part ways.

He had to prepare himself to reject Vica though. He hadn't heard about Hole in the Woods before, but the name sounded peculiar, and he imagined that it would be dark and romantic and they would be sitting in a booth, and at some point she would touch his hand. Would it be rude if he moved his hand away? Would she take the hint or continue with her advances? Wouldn't it be better if he told her right away that they couldn't possibly be a couple? He thought about it all the way to the Union Square stop.

He couldn't find the damn place. He checked Fourteenth Street and Seventeenth Street, the east side and the west side. The restaurant wasn't there. He even asked a few passersby—nobody had heard of it. He thought for a second that it was some stupid prank. He felt like a fool. Then he got a text from Vica. "Where are you? I'm already in." "I can't find it," he texted back. "It's right off the south side of the square." He walked back to the south side. There wasn't a single restaurant there. Just Burlington Coat Factory, Forever 21, and the huge Whole Foods.

Then it dawned on him. Whole Foods! That was what Vica had said. She didn't mean to meet him in a dark romantic place. She meant the fucking salad bar at fucking Whole Foods.

He saw her right away, standing at the counter with a little paper container in her hand, dressed in a nondescript pantsuit and looking wan in the harsh fluorescent lights. She didn't appear to be happy or excited to see Vadik. "Hi," Vadik said, leaning in to hug her. She had the sad smell of a medical facility hanging about her, drowning out her perfume.

"Are you coming straight from work?"

"Yes, I signed up for a weekend shift since Eric's not here. Grab some food. I'm starving."

There was a pile of dry spinach leaves in her container and a large pile of shrimp that she must have picked out of the big vat of paella.

"Are you still eating according to your formula?" Vadik asked.

It took her a moment to understand what he meant. She forced a smile.

"Yes, kind of."

Eight years before, when Vadik first arrived in the U.S., Vica shared a few personal survival rules with him, just as he did for Regina six years later. One of Vica's tips was about choosing food in a salad bar.

"If you want to get the best value, pick the items that cost the most and weigh the least. Don't pick a piece of meat that has a bone in it, like a chicken drumstick, bones give it extra weight. Don't drown your salad in dressing, it's both heavy and unhealthy; skip the gravy; pick the shrimp out of the pasta dish; pick the octopus out of the octopus and chickpea salad; leave the carrots and potatoes in the stew."

Vadik quickly put some salad into his container and followed Vica to the cashier.

They picked a table by the window overlooking the square. It seemed squashed by the surrounding buildings.

"Don't you just love Whole Foods?" Vica said. "So many choices and the best salad bar in the city!"

Vadik saw that she hadn't intended to offer herself to him. In fact, it was clear that the thought of offering herself to him hadn't even occurred to Vica. He felt relieved, but a little bit annoyed too. The idea of dating Vica suddenly seemed filled with irresistible narrative logic. A guy makes a clean break from his past, goes away, explores another country, has adventures, overcomes setbacks, only to make a full circle and return to the woman he loved in his previous life. He imagined telling all this to Regina and seeing her approving nods, her admiring smile. "Yes, Vadik, of course! That's how it's supposed to be."

But the woman he loved in the past wasn't even looking at him. Vica kept piercing spinach leaves with her fork as if she wanted to see how much she could pick up in one go.

"So tell me honestly now. How is he?" she asked.

Just last night Sergey had confided to Vadik that he was able to envision his future for the first time in years. Before, every time he tried to picture it, he felt as if he had opened a door and there was nothing but dark stinky smog outside. Now, he could see some vague but cheerful shapes.

Vadik couldn't bring himself to tell this to Vica. He sighed and looked away.

"That bad, huh?" Vica said.

She put her fork on the table and ran her fingertips over the tines.

"It was the right thing to do, right?" she asked. "It's been hell for the last few months. You have no idea. He would walk in the door and I would immediately start fuming, because he didn't shut the door well enough, or he slammed it too hard, or he didn't put his boots in the right place. Or, you know, I would look into his eyes, and his expression would be so harsh, as if he couldn't stand the sight of me. And I would get so angry, so angry that I would try to do something to make him hate me even more."

She kept talking, picking up her salad with her fork, putting it back, looking up at Vadik as if begging him for support. She seemed to want some reassurance that she hadn't made a horrible mistake. She looked thinner and younger in her distress. Less like American Vica, more like the Vica he remembered from their days in Russia.

He had never been nostalgic for the past before, but now he found himself missing not just that Vica but his college days, his time in Moscow.

Vadik felt like reaching for Vica's hand and pressing it to his face, to his lips. He imagined the tart taste of her skin. He looked away, afraid that she would read his mind.

They ate in silence for a minute or two. Then Vica said, "Okay, so I need your advice."

Vadik nodded.

"I keep thinking of Virtual Grave."

"Uh-huh," Vadik said.

"You see, Sergey is a quitter. I'm not."

Vadik didn't have the heart to tell her that Sergey was actually working on the app like crazy, because it would reveal that he wasn't pining for her all that much.

"Bob turned us down, because the idea was too morbid," Vica said, "just as I'd predicted. I'd always wanted to make it more optimistic and upbeat. I actually had some great ideas. It was Sergey who wouldn't budge. So I'm going to try to rework it. It doesn't even need to be an actual app, just a service for people concerned with their online legacy. I was thinking of writing a business proposal and then maybe approaching some people at work. But it has to be more palatable. No more Fyodorov! What do you think?"

"Oh, yes, absolutely," Vadik said. "No more Fyodorov!"

He wondered if he was wrong to encourage her about Virtual Grave, especially since he knew that Sergey was working on it too. The fact was that neither Vica nor Sergey had a chance to succeed. So what was the harm in their trying? If anything, it would distract Vica from her pain.

Vica smiled. She still had that tense closemouthed smile, a leftover from the era of crooked teeth. Vadik had forgotten how much he had always liked that smile.

"Do you want to go listen to some music?" Vadik asked after

they scraped the last of their salads off the bottom of their Whole Foods containers. "There are some excellent venues around here."

"No," Vica said, "I have a bottle of sauvignon blanc waiting for me in the fridge. I'm going to drink the entire bottle as I browse through Hello, Love! I've been looking forward to doing that for ages!"

Vadik squirmed. The idea of Vica on Hello, Love! seemed offensive to him. Disgusting. Unbearable.

"What's wrong?" Vica asked.

"Nothing. Just something in my teeth," Vadik said.

When Vadik hugged her before they parted, he was overcome by that smell again. The sharp, chemical, merciless smell.

The smell haunted him all the way back to Williamsburg and for hours after that. It was barely nine when he got home, but he went to bed right away.

He woke up around eleven with a dull headache and exasperation over a wasted Saturday.

He sat up in bed and called for Sergey. There was no answer. He walked into Sergey's room, but he wasn't there. This was unusual, because Sergey started his day at six and didn't like to stay up past ten thirty. He dialed his number, but there was no answer. Should I worry? Vadik wondered, then decided that he shouldn't. Not yet.

He went to the living room, plopped onto the couch, turned on Netflix, and browsed for a long time until he found what he wanted to watch. *Doctor Who,* the series with David Tennant. Vadik was on episode six of season three when he heard some commotion at the door. Did he forget the key again? Vadik thought and went to open the door.

There was Sergey leaning against the wall kissing a girl. When Vadik opened the door, the girl moved her face away from Sergey's mouth and said, "Hello." She was small, with large, widely set brown eyes, a pale face, and long dark hair highlighted with yellow. Her smile exuded unwarranted friendliness.

"Hi," Vadik said and stared at Sergey.

"Rachel, meet Vadik. Vadik, meet Rachel," Sergey said. He looked a little scared and a little embarrassed.

Rachel #3, Vadik thought, even though for Sergey it was Rachel #1.

"Pleasure!" Vadik said.

"Likewise!"

Then they all fell silent. Sergey was the one to break it.

"I've had a very nice time, Rachel," Sergey said. "I'll call you soon."

She looked a bit disappointed.

"I'm going out of town for a while. But call. Sure, call. Or, you know, message me on Facebook."

"Sure," Sergey said, and he and Vadik went into the apartment.

"Here, I brought some food for you," Sergey said and handed Vadik a large paper bag. Then he went into the bedroom and closed the door behind him.

The paper bag had the words FETTE SAU BARBECUE on it. Inside there were three pork ribs, half a pickle, and a chicken drumstick with neat round teeth marks on it.

Vadik turned the TV back on and bit into the chewed-on drumstick, marveling at the degree of his discontent.

Chapter 6

BURY YOUR MOTHER

O N HER SIXTH DAY IN MOSCOW, REGINA WOKE UP AT six A.M. There was a message on her iPhone. "Good morning, honey. How are you? Love, Bob." She texted back: "Everything's fine with me. I miss you. I love you very much."

She tried to go back to sleep, but the sticky anxiety she felt about the task she had to accomplish today wouldn't let her.

Her flight back to New York was scheduled to depart in thirty-six hours, but she hadn't seen Aunt Masha yet or visited her mother's grave. "I will definitely do it today," she would say to herself every morning, and late every night while she undressed to go to bed, she would say to herself: "I will definitely go tomorrow."

Regina didn't feel like going to the theater or visiting any of her favorite museums either; what she did was wander around Moscow neighborhoods all day, then return to her hotel room, order dinner, and eat it while watching old Russian movies. She talked to Bob on Skype every night, but these conversations were so tame and boring compared to what they used to do when she was still living in Russia. Back then they used Skype for sex. She thought of the thrill of seeing their bodies on-screen. They both appeared to be longer, softer, more mysterious. The best part for her was watching Bob hold his breath while she unbuttoned her blouse.

And now it was more like "How's the food?" "Is it really cold over there?" "Is the traffic as insane as it used to be?" Bob said that he missed her, but he was also too engrossed in his business to seem convincing. He had come up with an idea for an app that allowed you to find people with similar genomes in any crowd. He thought it had the existential value of breaking the void of loneliness, of making strangers feel connected. There were actually tears in his eyes when he first described the idea to Regina. He'd been talking to Dancing Drosophilae for a long time, but now it seemed like they were ready to sign the deal with DigiSly.

"That's exciting, honey!" Regina said, even though she didn't really understand Bob's obsession with genetics or his pride in his supposedly Tudor lineage. Last night though, while they talked on Skype, Regina opened an image of Holbein's *Henry VIII* and looked for similarities. She thought she could see some. If you mentally erased Henry's beard, you could see that both Henry and Bob had thin lips, sharp eyes, and a perfect oval face. The padded shoulders of Henry's royal costume actually reminded her of Bob's old football uniform.

Regina's phone buzzed, announcing another text message. This one was from United, reminding her to check in for her upcoming flight back to New York. Today would have to be the day to visit both Aunt Masha and the cemetery. She couldn't possibly postpone it any longer. What she could do was try to start the day as late as possible.

Regina turned on the TV, but everything on the screen struck her as demanding and loud. There was none of that sweet pampering that American TV provided to its viewers. Russian TV aimed to goad its customers rather than soothe them.

There was nothing to do except get dressed and go downstairs to the restaurant.

The Sheraton breakfast was a buffet boasting bizarrely international offerings—miso soup and croissants vied for guests' attention with porridge and blini with red caviar. The few patrons in the room were all grave-looking Russian businessmen. One of them raised his eyes at Regina, winced, and looked away. She was reminded once again of how utterly unattractive she was to Russian men. Regina heaped her plate with a little bit of everything and went to her table. She had forgotten how unbearably boring chewing your food was unless you did it while watching TV.

She reached for her iPad. There was a long e-mail from Sergey. The first since he and Vica had split up. Sergey apologized for avoiding her, explained that he'd needed some time to sort things out. The detailed analysis of what went wrong in his marriage to Vica followed. He started with a long paragraph meant to convey that Regina had always been the only person who truly understood him, then switched to an in-depth analysis of Vica's person. Regina didn't have the patience to read the entire thing; she skimmed through the long descriptions of Vica's materialistic passions and obsession with power and prowess in most of its forms—physical, sexual, financial, although not spiritual. She was very smart. Really smart. She wasn't well read, no, but she had this incredible ability to grasp the most complex ideas better than anybody he knew. And it would be wrong to say that she had an emotional intelligence rather than an intellectual one. Emotional intelligence was what Vica lacked. If anything, she was emotionally obtuse. She didn't understand him at all. Sergey ended with an admission that marrying Vica had been a mistake. That he had been blinded. Blinded by what, Regina wondered, Vica's "obsessive sexual prowess"? Which Regina apparently lacked. She half expected Sergey to conclude by admitting that he should have married the spiritual but bland Regina instead. He didn't. Regina wasn't sure if that made her depressed or relieved.

The next e-mail was from Vadik. He wrote that there was some crazy shit happening with Sergey and he was getting plenty sick of him, and it was time she took him off his hands.

"No, thank you," she wrote and put her phone back into her purse.

Regina left most of her food uneaten, checked out of the hotel, left her luggage with the concierge, and went out on Tverskaya

Street. She decided to visit the cemetery first, then go to Aunt Masha's and spend the night with her. Regina checked her watch—she didn't have to go right this minute. There was still time for a little walk.

Early November always brought her favorite weather. The trees stood bare and the air stung her cheeks, but it wasn't bitingly cold yet, and the sun shone bright and strong, creating a dry, aching clarity that usually came a couple of weeks before the first snow. Moscow had barely changed in the two years that she had been gone, and for some reason Regina found herself reluctant to look up and savor the view. Nor did she want to look into the eyes of the passersby, because the newly increased level of anger and discontentment in the Muscovites' expressions frightened her. She just walked and walked, circling, zigzagging, shortcutting, thrilled by the fact that she never made a wrong turn. She knew Moscow so well that its maps seemed to be imprinted in her footsteps.

Regina walked to the Moscow River, strolled a long stretch of the embankment, then turned away from water toward the city center. She didn't realize how tired she was until she reached Chistye Prudy. She had been avoiding this area on her previous walks, but there she was—just a few feet away from her former home. Regina sat down on the bench facing the lake and stretched her legs. They ached and throbbed and all but hummed some unhappy tune. The water in front of her looked fake as if there were no depth to it, just a thin layer of mirrored glass. She had sat in this very spot so many times before. She made an effort to bring up the most intense memories of her past so that she could feel an exquisite pain followed by the inevitable release.

Here she was in her dad's lap when she was three or four, waving to the ducks . . . the pleasure of his strong grip, his hand pressing into her ribs. With her mom when she was five or six and her legs were so short that she couldn't bend her knees—her legs clad in thick winter boots stuck out at a ninety-degree angle. Her mother reciting a poem about snow: how the falling snow put everything in turmoil, and it was as if the sky itself came down like an old man in his patched-up winter coat. Regina's face was smeared with smelly kids' cream that protected from the frost, and her forehead itched under her woolen hat. She remembered that sensation so well, but she couldn't remember how her mother looked as she read the poem. All she saw in her mind's eye was her mother's emaciated body and glassy eyes as she lay dying. As a teenager Regina would come to the bench by herself. She would sit here with a book, hopelessly homely, but desperately hopeful. Princess Maria from *War and Peace* was her favorite heroine. So ugly, so serious, so pious, yet she dreamed of carnal love. Princess Maria did find it at the end, with a good, solid, if a little dumb man. Sergey was anything but dumb. Regina smiled, recalling the many times when they had sat in this very spot, and Sergey wouldn't shut up about Fyodorov while she willed him to kiss her. And when he finally did, she found his kisses too wet and kind of disappointing. As was her makeshift nostalgic therapy. The images in her mind were feeble and loose, incapable of producing enough intensity to result in catharsis.

Regina got up off the bench and walked toward her old building on Lyalin Lane. When she moved to the United States, she had asked Aunt Masha to sell the old apartment and what remained of the furniture and donate the money to an orphanage. But Vadik told her she was crazy. "What if it doesn't work out with Bob?" So Regina put the money into her bank account.

Their old street looked statelier than Regina remembered, and cleaner, too clean. Most of the buildings were painted soft pastel colors. One of the buildings had a hotel sign on it. A taxi stopped and a young, well-dressed couple got out and walked toward the entrance dragging their bright suitcases, the wheels rapping against the pavement. It was as if whatever messy marks her and her mother's lives had made there were now removed, cleaned away, painted over. Regina didn't feel like seeing her building anymore. And it

was time to go to visit the cemetery anyway. Aunt Masha had insisted that they go together, but Regina said no. She had to visit her
mother's grave by herself.

She considered a cab, but the thought of sitting in endless traffic jams was unbearable. She walked to the subway station. At the
entrance there were a couple of kiosks selling fast food and Regina
bought a little meat pie and ate it right there by the kiosk even
though she was still full after breakfast. The cemetery, Nicolo-
Arkhangelskoye, was situated in one of the newer developments at
the far end of Moscow. It was Aunt Masha's choice, because Regina
had refused to have anything to do with the funeral arrangements.
She had been drugged out of her mind during the funeral—she
could barely remember the ceremony or the place—so this would be
like visiting her mother's grave for the very first time.

The subway ride took forever and then Regina had to take a bus
to get to the cemetery. After the first few stops the bus emptied out,
with most of the passengers getting off at the treeless new residential
complex. White and blue buildings, pristine malls, large empty lots
with some construction equipment on them. The cemetery was the
last stop on the route. The few remaining passengers on the bus
were all women, sullen, withdrawn, resigned. Dutiful daughters,
wives, possibly mothers. Most of them were clutching bouquets. Regina had forgotten about flowers. She wondered if it was necessary.
You were supposed to either plant or put flowers on the grave, but
why? As a remedy for your guilt? To make the grave a nicer place
to visit? As a tradition you didn't question? As a simple means to
feel less horrible? Or was this part of some complicated ritual that
allowed you a fleeting moment of contact with the departed? Regina hoped that they sold flowers by the cemetery gates. It would be
crazy not to. But of course they didn't. There was a long stone fence
connecting the main entrance with the gates reserved for funeral
corteges. Not a single flower in sight. "Is there a flower shop inside?"
Regina asked one of the women. She glowered at Regina and shook
her head. "You should've thought about flowers before you boarded

the bus," another woman said. She was proudly carrying a bouquet of imported roses. A younger woman tapped Regina on the shoulder: "Take a few of mine." She had a large bunch of pale carnations. Regina thanked her and took three. "Take some more," the woman said with a grin. "I'm sure Misha won't mind." Regina took a few more. She felt light-headed and empty as she went through the gates. Once inside, she saw a vast field—she estimated that it was half the size of Central Park. She didn't remember the grounds being so big. Stone slabs rose like crops in neat endless rows. Regina took out a piece of paper where she had written down the section and lot number and went to consult the map. The map was mounted right on the fence next to hundreds of flyers advertising various services: people offered to fix your loved one's gravestone, to take care of your grave, to say a prayer in church, to bring flowers and send you timed photographs of those flowers to assure you that they were fresh. The largest flyer warned that the fee for decorating the grave with pine branches didn't include the cost of branches. And to the right of it was a handwritten sign that asked: "Are you heartbroken because you haven't visited your loved ones' graves in a while? Do you feel so guilty that you can't breathe?" And then it reassured: "Now you don't have to!!! GrieveForYou will take care of everything." Regina felt a sudden bout of nausea and hurried away from the fence into the depths of the cemetery. She found her mother's grave sooner than she'd expected; there it was in the far left corner, exactly as promised on the map. She had expected to be overwhelmed, but what shocked her was how little she actually felt. There was a black granite slab with her mother's name on it. There was her picture on an oval ceramic plate. None of that stirred Regina. None of that made her feel closer to her mother. If her spirit still existed in some form, it certainly wasn't there. Regina kneeled by the headstone and put her flowers on the little shelf attached to it. "Hey!" called an old woman a few feet away from her. "Put your flowers in the soil, as if you were planting them; they will keep longer like that." Regina dug a little hole in the ground with her bare hands—the soil was cakey and cold and somehow revolting. She planted her dead carnations and secured them in a little mound of soil. They looked ridiculous standing up. "But they will keep longer," Regina said to herself, wondering what was the point of them keeping longer. She stared at her mother's photograph. Her mother was looking away from the camera, as if she was avoiding Regina. People were supposed to talk to the dead. Regina had no idea what to say. She cleared her throat, terrified that she would sound fake. "Mamochka," she whispered, "everything's fine with me. I miss you. I love you very much."

It was only on the way back—she chose to take a taxi this time— that it hit her that these were the exact words she had texted to Bob this morning. She pressed her forehead to the cold glass of the window and started to cry, not from grief but from shame and emptiness.

Regina asked the driver to take her to the hotel to pick up her luggage and then to Aunt Masha's.

"That's your address?" the driver asked, pulling up to the long, moldy, barely lit nine-story building. He sounded doubtful. "Yes," Regina said. She remembered the building well. When she was a child, Regina's mother would take her to visit Aunt Masha every week or so. Regina was encouraged to call her "aunt" even though they weren't related, and Regina was used to referring to the neighborhood as the Aunt's place. "Are we going all the way to the Aunt's stop today?" she would ask.

The driver helped her to unload her bags and swiftly drove away. Aunt Masha had told her the downstairs entrance code, but Regina had trouble entering the right combination in the dark. The elevator was all scratched and dented, and there was a stench coming from the garbage chute. She hadn't expected the building to become so decrepit. Aunt Masha, who took a long time to open the door, looked decrepit as well, older than she was supposed to look. She wore a turtleneck and loose corduroy pants as she always did, but she seemed somehow smaller. Her white hair was shorter and thinner, with patches of pink scalp shining through. "Reginochka!" she exclaimed, pressing her skinny little body into Regina's, her thin fingers digging into Regina's back, her sharp chin poking into her shoulder, enveloping her in the smell of the cheap strawberry soap that Regina's mother used to buy all the time. She immediately felt the lump in her throat and the urge to escape. At least her nightmare proved to be wrong, and the apartment wasn't teeming with orphans.

"You look well!" Aunt Masha said.

"Thank you, so do you."

"No, I mean it," Aunt Masha said, leading Regina toward the kitchen. "I've always thought that you looked like Virginia Woolf. But your mother didn't see it at all."

"People used to tell me that I looked like Julia Roberts."

"What, like *Pretty Woman*? No! Virginia Woolf. Definitely Virginia Woolf."

Regina followed Aunt Masha to the kitchen, where the tea had already been served. Aunt Masha had never been a fan of elegant meals. There was a greasy aluminum teakettle on the table, a whole loaf of bread, some butter in a chipped teacup, sliced cheese on a saucer, and a one-liter jar of pickled mushrooms. A little girl was sitting on one of the old square stools. She slid down and scampered past them out of the kitchen.

Oh, no! Regina thought.

"That's Nastya. From the orphanage," Aunt Masha said.

Regina nodded.

Aunt Masha took out two little shot glasses from the cupboard and a bottle of vodka from the fridge. "Let's drink to Olga," she said, pouring half a shot for each of them.

They took a few sips, then ate a mushroom each.

Another idiotic tradition, Regina thought. To eat and drink in memory of the departed. There was something gross about it. As if they were taunting the dead person. Hey, you're dead and gone, but life goes on, and look how well we're all eating.

"How was the cemetery?" Masha asked.

"Good," Regina said. An empty answer to an empty question.

"I visit the grave often," Masha said, "keep it tidy."

She took a slice of bread and spread some butter on it, topped it with a slice of cheese, and handed it to Regina. "So, tell me about your life," she said as soon as Regina took the first bite. "Are you content? Is he a good man?"

Regina smiled, noting the word *content*. Aunt Masha didn't believe in marital happiness, only in contentedness. She felt grateful for that phrasing. She did feel content.

"I am. He is a wonderful man."

"He doesn't mind that you're Russian, does he?"

"No, not at all."

"So you think he understands you?"

Regina nodded. Aunt Masha had always been very direct, but she hadn't expected a barrage of personal questions of such calculated precision. It sounded as if Aunt Masha had prepared the questions in advance and was reading them off a list.

"You wrote that he has a daughter?"

"A grown daughter from a previous marriage. He's very fond of her."

"Good! So he doesn't mind that you can't?"

"No, he doesn't," Regina said, and rushed to change the subject. "These mushrooms are very good. Did you can them yourself?"

"Nastya helped. She picked most of them, and she helped me clean them. Nastya, come here!"

Regina turned and saw that the little girl was peeking at them from behind the large cabinet in the hallway. She ran away as soon as she caught Regina's stare. Gawky, unpretty, in a dress that was too small for her. Regina didn't have a chance to get a better look.

"How's Sergey? Do you see him?" Aunt Masha asked. She never bothered with small talk. Always went right for the subjects that really interested her, no matter how awkward they were.

Regina told her about Sergey's marital troubles. Aunt Masha seemed surprised.

"I've always thought that pushy girl was a perfect fit for him," she said.

"And I wasn't?"

"No, you weren't. And he wasn't a right fit for you. I would tell this to Olga again and again, but she wouldn't listen to me. She never listened to me."

Oh, just leave my mom alone, Regina thought, but she couldn't help but ask: "Why didn't you think Sergey was the right fit for me?"

"He's too weak and too much of a dreamer. You need a manlier man."

Vadik? Regina thought and was immediately ashamed. Why Vadik, when she had Bob? Bob was a manly man, whatever that meant. A wholesome man. Vadik was anything but wholesome.

"It was Olga who brought Sergey and you together. I remember how she called me all excited and said that her new student was perfect for you. She used to really rule your life, you know."

"No, she didn't," Regina said, helping herself to more mushrooms.

"Oh, yes, she did. Up until she died. I bet she still does in a way. I saw your piece on translation in the last year's issue of *Foreign Literature*. You could've written about your wonderful career, but you chose to rehash Olga's old works."

"That was the idea; they'd asked me to write about my mother."

"Right," Aunt Masha said. "And how's your work? Anything exciting?"

Regina was getting very angry, but she didn't have enough courage to tell this old woman to stop pestering her. To just stop!

Aunt Masha drained her glass and poured herself another. Poured some more for Regina too. Her face became flushed and she looked younger and feistier, more like the Aunt Masha Regina remembered.

"Do you remember your back exercises?" she asked Regina. "You had to do your homework with a broom handle fixed behind your elbows to keep your back straight. I would visit and see you grimacing in pain, trying to lean over so that you could see your textbook better."

There was a curling wisp of hair growing out of the right side of Aunt Masha's damp chin. Regina found it especially hateful.

"I had scoliosis! Those exercises were important."

"No, you didn't have scoliosis. All you had was bad posture. A perfectly normal posture for somebody who preferred spending her days on a couch with a book rather than playing sports. Your dad had the same one. How's he doing by the way?"

Grateful for the change in subject, Regina told her whatever she knew of her father's life in Canada. Aunt Masha asked for more details. Regina realized that she didn't know that much.

"How often do you speak to him?"

"He calls me once a month," Regina said. She neglected to add that she rarely picked up the phone.

"Poor man," Aunt Masha said and drained another glass.

Regina didn't touch hers.

That poor man abandoned his wife and child! And Aunt Masha knew this. She had been Regina's mother's closest friend at the time. She had been her closest friend ever since college. Why had she decided to unleash this hateful attack on Regina's mother? Who had died? Who had died!

"He was an enormously talented writer, your father was."

"Yeah, a great writer who never published a book."

"Do you know why he didn't?"

Regina could guess where this was going. The evil Olga wouldn't let him.

"Olga was really jealous of his talent."

Yep, Regina thought. She wished she had enough courage to just stand up and leave. But she realized that it wasn't only politeness that stopped her. She had a perverse desire to hear the rest of this bullshit. To hear how far Aunt Masha would go.

"Because Olga, even though brilliant as a translator, had never been really creative. She couldn't stand Grigory's success. So whatever praise he would get from his early publications in magazines, she would squash him with her 'kindly' discouragement. And she always maintained that she had to be honest with him because she loved him, because she was the only one who truly cared."

"You know, if he really were so talented, a little honesty from his wife wouldn't have ruined his career."

"He was not a strong man. No, he wasn't. And look at you. Always in your mother's shadow. They asked you to write a piece, and what topic did you choose? Mommy dearest!"

Regina felt a quiet movement behind her back. Nastya had walked into the kitchen and was standing by the fridge. Her light blue woolen dress had some dark (chocolate?) stains around the collar.

"Nastya, come in, sit down," Aunt Masha said, and this time Nastya came closer and climbed on a smaller stool across the table from Regina. Aunt Masha gave her a piece of bread with butter and cheese, and Nastya took a big bite and started to chew.

She was an unusually homely child, with pale unhealthy skin, a big nose, and mousy hair.

"How old is she?" Regina asked.

"Why are you asking me? Ask her."

Regina had always hated talking to children. She wasn't that good at talking to adults either, but it was conversing with children that made her sweat. She could never find the right tone. She did her best to sound neutral, but it came out as either too cheerful or too cross.

"How old are you, Nastya?" she asked. Too cross.

Nastya didn't say anything. Just stared at Regina intently, making energetic movements with her jaws.

"She knows that she's not supposed to talk while chewing."

Nastya made an audible gulp to swallow the bread mass in her mouth and then said that she was five.

"She is five, but she can count to one hundred," Aunt Masha announced.

"I forget nineteen and forty-seven," Nastya said and took another bite. There was something about her that made Regina uncomfortable. They made a nice pair, Aunt Masha and Nastya—Baba Yaga and her creepy little helper. Regina had planned to stay with Aunt Masha the whole day before her flight the next night, but now she saw that she wouldn't be able to stand it. She would stay the night, then go straight to the city center and spend the whole of tomorrow just wandering the streets.

After they cleared the table, Aunt Masha made Regina a bed on the couch in the large living room and took Nastya to the other room that served as their bedroom. It was 10:00 P.M., only 2:00 P.M. New York time. "Do you mind if I watch TV?" Regina asked.

"The TV's not working," Aunt Masha said. "It broke a few months ago, and I decided not to fix it. Do you want a book? Come, pick a book."

"I have a book," Regina said and settled on the couch with her iPad. She had downloaded several books for her trip, but she found that she couldn't concentrate on them any better than when she read printed books. It was actually worse. That thing on the bottom of the page that showed the progress of her reading just wouldn't move past "1%." This made it harder to pretend that she was reading and not just staring at the sentences. She lay on scratchy sheets with the iPad propped on her chest, its screen dark, listening to the sounds that came from Aunt Masha's room. They went to brush their teeth, then each of them peed and flushed the toilet. Then there were soft sounds of Aunt Masha reading a story to Nastya, Nastya's giggling. It was hard to imagine what Nastya looked like when she giggled. Then it was quiet. Regina turned the iPad back on, but she still couldn't focus. She made a few futile attempts to find a Wi-Fi signal. She badly needed to watch something. She couldn't understand why she hadn't downloaded any movies before she left. Regina got off the couch and walked to the bookshelves hoping to find an easier and more entertaining book. She noticed a framed picture of herself on the wall. She was about fourteen in it. Awkward, unsmiling. That was the age when she did those back exercises. Every day for more than a year. She had a vivid image of herself doing homework with that broom between her elbows. The terrible pain just below her shoulder blades. Biting her lips, willing herself to ignore the pain and focus on her studies. It never occurred to her to question the wisdom of that daily torture. Other kids wore braces. She had perfect teeth, but an imperfect spine—she wore a broom. And what was that nonsense about her dad? Could it be that he really was talented? It had never occurred to her to read any of his stories and judge for herself.

Another train passed by. The whole apartment seemed to shake. This was unbearable.

She heard a soft tapping on the wall of the doorway. There was Aunt Masha in her long white nightgown. Ghostlike in the dark. "Reginochka," she said, her voice trembling. "Are you asleep?"

"No," Regina said.

Aunt Masha walked up to her and sat on the edge of the sofa. "Reginochka, please forgive me," and she started to cry.

Regina sat down next to her, horrified. "No, Aunt Masha, no," she said, stroking her bony shoulder.

"Reginochka, I'm such a fool. I shouldn't have said all those things about Olga. It's just that I felt I had so much to tell you. And I kept rehearsing it all these years. And now you came, but we have so little time to spend together that I had to sort through all those things and pick the important ones. I felt rushed and it came out as cold and awful. I hurt your feelings. Please, please, forgive me!"

Regina nodded.

"You know how much I loved Olga. You must know that!"

"I know," Regina said.

"Do you?" Aunt Masha asked. "Do you really?"

"Yes, yes, of course I do. She loved you too."

"She did. I know she did. But she would never admit it. Not as she lay dying. Olga Zhilinskaya—always straight as an arrow."

Aunt Masha started to sob again and left the room.

Regina went to the bathroom and found some Tazepam on the shelf. She took a pill and went back to the couch. She was out in about five minutes.

She was awakened by a quiet rustling sound. She opened her eyes and saw Nastya sitting at the table with a big children's book, the sun streaming through the windows. It was hard to tell if she was reading it or just looking at the pictures.

"Good morning," Regina said. Her head felt unbearably heavy, as if somebody had put a huge sack of potatoes on top of it. That Tazepam was a killer.

"Good morning," Nastya answered and flipped another page.

"What are you reading?"

"Buratino."

"Do you like it?"

"I don't know how to read yet," Nastya said. "I'm looking at the pictures. There is a boy with a long nose who looks like Pinocchio from the movie."

Regina was about to explain that Buratino was in fact the Russian version of Pinocchio, shamelessly stolen by Alexey Tolstoy, but decided not to.

"I used to like Buratino too. In fact, it was the first book I read by myself."

Nastya was unimpressed. Regina wondered if it was more appropriate to leave the child alone or to continue talking to her.

"Bring it over, I'll read it to you," she said.

Nastya carefully climbed off the chair, walked to the couch, and sat down in the corner. Regina took the book from her, placed it on her lap, and opened the book to the first page. The inscription in black ink sprang at her: "To Reginochka, on the day when she stops being a Little Puppytail and becomes a schoolgirl." It was her book! It was the book her mother had given her.

"Oh, my God!" Regina exclaimed.

"Shh!" Nastya said.

Little Puppytail was her pet name all the way through babyhood and preschool.

"This is my book! My mom gave it to me when I was your age," Regina whispered.

"Masha gave me this book," Nastya said and started to cry. Regina released her grip on the book, but it was too late.

"Of course, it's yours now. Of course! It's just that it used to be mine. But that was a long time ago. Hundreds of years ago."

Nastya took the book away from her and retreated into the bedroom. There was a long silence, followed by quiet voices, and then puffy-faced, disheveled Masha appeared in the doorway.

"Fighting with a little girl over a book? Seriously, Regina?"

Regina was mortified. "It was a misunderstanding."

But Masha smiled and said that she was just kidding.

"I'm making farina for breakfast. Do you like farina?"

Regina said that she did.

Nobody talked much over breakfast. Masha looked tired and Nastya was still sulking, and Regina kept adding spoonful after spoonful of cherry jam into her bland kasha.

Regina was about to say that she was leaving when Aunt Masha asked if she could watch Nastya for an hour or so, while Masha went to a doctor's appointment. Regina had a quick paranoid thought that this was a setup, that Masha would just disappear and Regina would be stuck with taking care of the girl forever. But that would be ridiculous, wouldn't it? And so far Aunt Masha hadn't even mentioned the subject of adoption. She must have finally accepted Regina's objections.

"There is a suitcase with a few of Olga's things under my bed," Aunt Masha said before she left. "Look through them. You might want to take something."

Aunt Masha's room was long and narrow, with a door opening onto the small glassed-in balcony, filled with some old boxes, burlap sacks, and dusty jars. All the furniture was put in two rows lining the walls. Bookcases on the right side. Masha's rickety desk, her narrow brass bed, and a small couch that must have served as a bed for Nastya on the left. In the little corner by the door, there were a kid-size table and chair, a toy piano, a tiny makeshift doll-house, and a few easy-to-reach bookshelves. Most of the books there used to belong to Regina, but she knew better than to comment on it, especially since Nastya was crouched by the shelves with a defiant expression. She seemed to be prepared to guard her belongings. Regina noticed that she had moved her little table so that it now blocked access to her corner.

"Nastya," Regina called, but she turned away from her.

Fine, Regina thought.

She reached under Masha's bed and dragged the large leather suitcase out. When she opened it, the smell of mothballs was so strong that her head started to hurt.

"It smells like rats," Nastya said.

There was her mother's old fur hat on top. Faded to gray now, but still fluffy. Regina pressed it to her face, trying to ignore the smell.

It was really soft, achingly soft.

She buried her face into the fur and moaned. "Mama."

"Is that your mama's hat?" Nastya said. She was standing right next to her.

"Yes, it used to be my mom's hat," Regina said. "She died."

Nastya furrowed her forehead and looked at Regina intently.

Was she not supposed to say that to a child? She wasn't! Clearly she wasn't. Perhaps Nastya didn't know what "died" meant. How could she possibly know that? But it turned out that she did.

"I know," Nastya said, "Masha told me. She is in the grave. My mama is in the grave too."

Regina reached out her beret-clad hand to Nastya. "Do you want to pet it? It's soft like a kitten."

Nastya edged over, touched the beret with the tips of her fingers.

"No, like a bunny," she said. "We had a bunny, where I lived before. It got sick and then it got dead."

"Do you want to see what else is in there?" Regina asked, pointing to the suitcase.

Nastya nodded and knelt on the floor next to Regina. "What is that?" she asked, pointing at the round tin box buried between two sweaters.

"Let's look," Regina said.

Nastya took the box and tugged on the lid. It wouldn't budge. This was an old blue and white tin box with the golden letters BE-LUGA CAVIAR. Something jingled inside.

"Pirate coins!" Nastya said.

Regina couldn't open it either. She got a knife from the kitchen and hooked it under the edge of the lid. The lid gave in and jumped off the box and onto the floor.

"Ah!" Nastya cried as if she had discovered a much better treasure than either diamonds or gold coins. "Buttons!!!"

Nastya climbed off her chair, took the box from Regina, and set it on the floor. She then sat cross-legged down next to the box with her back very straight. Her thin greasy hair was done in a braid, so short that it stuck out on the back of her head. Her neck was long and skinny and not very clean, with a hollow in the middle that made her look especially fragile.

Was that how I had looked to my mother when I sat and played with those same buttons? Regina wondered. She sat down next to Nastya and stroked her thin shoulders.

That was what Aunt Masha saw when she came back from her appointment. The two of them sitting on the floor together playing with buttons. She couldn't have been more pleased.

"Let's go for a walk, girls," she said.

Regina looked at her watch. "Twenty minutes, and then I'm leaving."

"Suit yourself," Aunt Masha said.

Nastya had a virtuoso way of dressing. She sat down in the middle of the floor, pulled on her boots, stood up, and stomped on each foot to make them fit tighter. Then she put her knitted hat on, tied the strings, and made a neat bow, centrally located under her chin. The next step was to put on her coat, which had a system to it too. She pulled on the ends of her sweater sleeves, squeezed them in her fists, and only then started pushing her arms through the sleeves of her coat.

"Good, Nastya, good," Aunt Masha said. "You don't want your sleeves all bunched up inside your coat."

In a few seconds Nastya was all buttoned up and standing by the door, holding her sand pail, her slightly battered Barbie, and an assortment of sand tools.

In the daylight, the neighborhood looked even worse. The entrance of the building was half blocked by the overflowing garbage bin, and there were three stray dogs picking at the garbage without much hope in their eyes. One of the dogs growled at them. Nastya grabbed onto Regina's thigh, hurting her.

"Regina, take her hand!" Aunt Masha ordered.

Regina was amazed at how light Nastya's hand turned out to be. Warm, weightless fingers, so thin that Regina was afraid that she'd accidentally squeeze them too hard. She realized that she had never led anyone by the hand before. She marveled at how much intuitive precision was required to make this simple action work. You had to communicate direction by the tiniest pressure of your fingers, and you were entirely responsible for the person you led.

They crossed the street and walked to the neglected playground, with a couple of rusty swings, a broken seesaw, a sandbox, and a strange contraption that looked like a huge rotating birdcage. There were two small children in it, and another older child was pushing the thing counterclockwise, producing a horrible screech. Nastya let go of Regina's hand and ran toward the sandbox.

Aunt Masha went to sit down on the bench; Regina joined her. It was strange how she could still feel the warmth of Nastya's fingers in her palm. One of the stray dogs ran up to them, and Aunt Masha reached into her purse, took out a piece of bread with cheese, and fed it to the dog. Then she stroked its grateful muzzle, and the dog lay down and curled at her feet.

"Are you sure you have to leave tonight?" Aunt Masha asked.

"Yes, I have my ticket."

"I really hoped you'd spend more time with us."

"Well, I need to get back," Regina said.

Aunt Masha took a large handkerchief out of her pocket, blew her nose, and folded it back into her pocket.

"Then we will have to talk now," she announced. There was an ominous note in her voice and Regina didn't like it one bit.

She turned to Regina and took her hand. "Regina, I want you to adopt Nastya."

Yes, up until that day Regina had been expecting something like this. But as her time in Moscow was coming to an end, she'd stupidly allowed herself to relax. She'd allowed herself to think that the danger was past and Aunt Masha wouldn't bring up the subject of adoption.

Regina was shocked and she reacted as she always did when shocked. She started to laugh. Right there on that stupid old rusty playground she was shaking with an idiotic, sputtering, unstoppable laughter.

Aunt Masha chose to ignore the laughter and proceeded with Nastya's story.

"She was sent to our orphanage about a year ago. Her mom died in a car crash. No dad. No relatives. Apparently her mom was an orphan too. A young girl, she was only twenty-two when she died. And Nastya was in a bad shape. Sobbing all the time. Refusing to eat, refusing to talk. Then there were these fights with other kids. Nastya didn't get along with them. The teachers complained that she would bite other children. They nicknamed her Mad Dog."

There was that indecent sputtering laughter again. And again Aunt Masha chose to ignore it.

"There was talk of transferring her to an institution for mentally challenged children. You can imagine what happens to kids there. And I just knew that she was a perfectly normal kid, and a smart wonderful kid at that. I could see it in her eyes."

Regina still wasn't registering what any of this had to do with her. She sat there nodding, shaking her head from time to time, as if she were listening to a radio play.

"Look, I'm digging a grave for my Barbie," Nastya yelled from her sandbox.

"Good girl," Aunt Masha yelled back. "Dig her a big one.

"So I would take her aside," she continued, "and try to comfort her, play with her, read to her, and she started to respond to me. She got better. But then every time my shift would end, she would break down crying, and sometimes I would just bring her home with me. Our director didn't mind. Tatyana Ivanovna, you must have seen her at your mom's funeral. A nice woman. Not very bright, far from it, but with a heart. So I would just bring Nastya home, and then I would let her stay during vacations, and then gradually she just started to live with me unofficially."

"That sounds like an ideal situation for both of you," Regina said.

"No, Regina," Aunt Masha said, her voice turning low and grave. "The situation is not ideal. They won't let me legally adopt her, because I'm too old, so this whole arrangement is hanging on Tatyana Ivanovna's goodwill. What if she leaves? What if they take Nastya away from me? And then what if I drop dead tomorrow? Look what happened to Olga, and she was healthy as a horse her whole life! While I have high blood pressure, diabetes, kidney problems. Regina, you have to take her!"

Aunt Masha took Regina's hand and squeezed it so tightly that Regina cried out in pain because her wedding ring cut into the flesh of her little finger.

No, she wanted to scream. *No! No! No!*

It took enormous effort for her to answer in a normal voice. "No, Masha, I can't do this."

"And why the hell not?" Aunt Masha asked. She was getting flushed and angry again, and a little bit crazy. Regina remembered the violent fights she and her mother sometimes had. There was even that one time when Aunt Masha had slapped her mother across the face. She looked as if she was ready to slap Regina now.

"You're young, you're healthy," she said, "you're happily married. Your husband sounds like a kind, responsible man. You have plenty of money. So why don't you do a single unselfish thing in your life and save this little girl?"

Now it was Regina who felt like hitting Aunt Masha. "I can't," she said. "I simply can't."

"Tell me why."

Regina wanted to say that Bob wouldn't go for it. But that wasn't true. In fact, she was almost sure that Bob would welcome the idea. The problem was her and her alone, and Aunt Masha knew this. Then a thought of salvation occurred to her.

"Well, what about Dima Yakovlev's law? We are Americans so we can't adopt a Russian child."

This law was named after an adopted Russian boy who died in a parked car, left there by his adoptive American parents. The law imposed by Putin's government in 2012 prohibited American citizens from adopting Russian children. It was an ugly hypocritical law. It was designed to hurt Americans, but it actually robbed Russian orphans of their chance to have a decent future. When she first heard about it, Regina was infuriated. Now she felt almost grateful.

"I've thought about Dima Yakovlev's law," Masha said. "And there is a way to get around it. You're not an American citizen yet?"

"I have a green card."

"Yes. But do you still have your Russian passport?"

"I do," Regina said reluctantly.

"There you go. They can't refuse a Russian citizen, can they?

Especially one like you, who can afford a really large bribe. I happen to know just the person to bribe. And nobody needs to know that you're planning to live in the United States with the child."

Regina looked at Nastya squatting in the sandbox, building a sand mound with a focused expression on her face. She tried to imagine Nastya living in their Tribeca loft. They would have to outfit their guest bedroom as a room for a child. Buy the furniture, buy clothes, buy toys. She would have to learn how to care for a child. There were books on the subject. There were people to help her. Bob knew how to care for a child. Vica and Sergey knew. Nastya would go to school. She would go to doctors. She must have been deeply damaged—just look at her digging that grave—but there were child psychologists for that. All the little practicalities were doable. And yet there was something that made the whole thing impossible.

She could imagine taking care of Nastya and even doing it well, but she couldn't imagine loving her. A parental love was the craziest, the most incomprehensible of human emotions for her. You had to love somebody ferociously, absolutely, no matter what. Look at Vica and Sergey, who seemed to be competing for the worst parent award (both negligent, permissive, easily annoyed, preoccupied with themselves), and yet they were both crazy about their boy. And look at her mother, forcing her to wear a broom, with her fierce attempts to rule her love life, with her violent fight to keep Regina at her side. No matter how misguided, that was real love.

"I don't think I can love a child," Regina said. "I've known this for a long time. I don't have the capacity for that. And a child deserves to be loved fully and absolutely."

Aunt Masha's features seemed to soften. She reached out and stroked Regina's hand in the same way she'd stroked that stray dog.

"Look at it this way, Regina. Suppose you take Nastya and you can't love her the way a mother would. You would still take care of her, you just won't love her enough. She'd be fine, just slightly underloved. Now, compare this fate to the fate of somebody destined to spend a lifetime in a state-sponsored Russian orphanage."

As if on cue, Nastya smiled and waved at them with her little shovel.

"Listen," Aunt Masha said in the softest voice she was capable of. "You don't have to decide now. Think about it, talk to your husband. Spend some time with Nastya just to try it out. We won't tell her anything until you decide."

Regina felt a numb horror. A well-planned trap. A horrible, sticky, suffocating trap. If she refused, she would be saddled with a horrible guilt for the rest of her life. She hadn't done anything wrong and yet she would have to carry that guilt. And if she agreed . . . But she couldn't agree! She couldn't! And since the only impulse of a trapped person was to try to escape, that was what Regina did.

"I can't! You can't do this to me. It's unfair!" she screamed and stood up with such force that the stray dog under the bench jumped up in fear.

"Masha, what is it?" asked a scared Nastya from the sandbox.

"Let's go," Aunt Masha said. "Regina has to go to the airport."

They walked back to the apartment. This time it was Aunt Masha who was holding Nastya's hand. Regina packed her things in a hurry and picked up the suitcase with her mother's things.

"Good-bye," Nastya said, "come again."

Regina leaned down to kiss her on the top of her head, and Nastya's little braid brushed against her cheek.

"Good-bye, Nastya," she said. "Good-bye, Aunt Masha."

Aunt Masha nodded silently.

"Wait," Nastya said, "take your buttons."

"You can have them. I want you to have them."

Nastya smiled a happy, but slightly embarrassed smile, as if she had been given an undeserved treasure.

It took Regina forty minutes to find a cab, and when she did, she asked the driver to take her straight to Sheremetyevo. She thought she'd just wait the remaining few hours there in the airport. She had absolutely no desire to spend any more time in the city. She sat in a gleaming leather seat in the business-class lounge watching TV but not really seeing it. She dialed Bob's number, and when he answered it, his voice was so dear and so kind that she couldn't speak for a moment. She was gasping for breath.

"Baby, what is it? What's wrong? Baby, are you okay?" he kept asking her. It took her a few minutes to get ahold of herself and find her words.

"I'm fine," she finally said. "I just can't wait to come home."

Chapter 7

GIFTED AND TALENTED

WHEN ERIC WAS SIX MONTHS OLD, VICA HIT HIM across the face with an open palm.

She did it while she was changing his diaper. Vica put Eric down on the sofa bed—she didn't have a changing table. They had come to America only two years before, and Sergey had been in school the entire time, so they definitely couldn't afford any of the wonderful baby things that taunted Vica in store windows, mail-order catalogs, magazines, and movies. Sometimes, as she stared at yet another Victorian-lace layette or at an amazingly high-tech baby swing that had seven different modes of rocking, sang songs, did animal voices, and had shimmering lights, she couldn't help but think how different the whole experience of motherhood must be for women who could afford everything that they wanted for their children. Or the experience of babyhood. Was her Eric doomed to unhappiness for the rest of his life because she had failed to provide a changing table or Victorian layette for him?

Vica slipped a plastic bag under Eric's butt, unbuttoned his over-alls, pulled them up, so far up that the pant legs were sticking above his shoulders like angel's wings, and unfastened the diaper. She had developed back pain since childbirth, which made bending down torture, so she had mastered a way to change her baby with record speed and efficiency. Turn away, take a deep breath, hold it, unfasten the diaper, hold the baby's legs up with one hand (how wonderful that both ankles fit into one hand!), take dirty diaper off, put dirty diaper in the bin. Wipe, wipe, wipe. Wipes in the bin. Bin closed. Breathe! Breathe, but do not stop. Never stop between diapers, especially when changing a boy, or your face might be sprayed. Don't slow down until the new diaper is securely fastened. Sometimes, Vica actually got pleasure out of this process, a sense of pride and wonderment at how quickly and efficiently she could do it.

But this time there'd been an unexpected obstacle. The wipes got stuck in their cylindrical container. She yanked at the top one but only managed to tear off a tiny piece. Now she had to unscrew the lid of the container, and for that task she needed both hands. She had to let go of Eric's legs and, since she couldn't really hold her breath any longer, exhale and inhale. By the time she finally got the wipes out, this was what she saw: Eric's perfectly round face. His hand over his face. Shit squeezed in his tiny fist. Shit dripping through his fingers onto his pointy chin. Shit smeared over his mouth. Lips making smacking movements. The pensive expression on his face communicating his uncertainty as to whether he liked the taste or not.

The picture was wrong, disgusting, vile. Too wrong. Not just momentarily wrong, but monumentally wrong. It could be a reflection of everything that was wrong with her life. How they had moved from Moscow into this cold, dark, ugly, disgusting apartment in Brooklyn. How she couldn't finish medical school. How bad her back hurt. How she was rapidly losing her looks—at twenty-four! How Sergey didn't want her anymore. How it was a mistake to leave Russia and come here. How it was a huge, huge, enormous mistake! All of that came to her clearly in a split second. She didn't think—she reacted. She raised her hand and smacked it across Eric's face. The sensation of how small and soft his face was against her hand, soft and still and smeared with shit, told her that it had happened. She had just hit her six-month-old baby. And then the stunned and puzzled expression on his face, as if he couldn't believe where the pain had come from. Vica grabbed Eric, pressed him to her chest, and stayed like that, trembling. Only then did he start to cry. She pressed him harder and harder to her chest. She stroked his downy hair, she stroked the tiny hollow on his neck, she stroked his bare back and his bare butt—still dirty. She carried him to the sink and washed his face, his mouth, his bottom. She dried him off, carried him back to the sofa, put a clean diaper on, pulled his overalls down. And then he raised his arms up, reaching for her, asking that she take him. She cradled him in her arms and started to rock him, marveling at how quickly his distress changed to contentment, peace, and then sleep. He'd reached to her for comfort even though she'd been the one to hurt him. He didn't have a choice, he didn't have anybody except for her. She put him gently into his crib, then went to lock herself in the bathroom so that she could sob and wail as loudly as she needed to.

Even now, eleven years later, the memory of that incident made Vica wince in pain.

They were standing in line to get to the Castle, which loomed above them, leaning toward them from the horizon line. The school was actually called Sebastian Levy High School, but everybody called it the Castle. Vica wrapped her coat tighter and urged Eric to do the same. They moved slowly—a couple of steps, a pause, a couple of steps, a pause—in a long chain that stretched around the Castle's perimeter.

It seemed that the presence of the Castle made them even colder because it blocked the sun. Although to be perfectly honest, the sun wouldn't be much help either at eight twenty in the morning on a frigid November day. Anyway, it was hard to believe that this building was right in the middle of the Upper East Side, where endless streets stretched in all four directions, yellow cabs rushed by, and dog walkers walked whole packs of dogs.

"Are you cold?" she asked Eric. He shook his head. But he looked cold; he looked tired and a little morose. But then all the children in line looked a little morose. They all looked very young—younger than eleven. They had thin necks and funny ears: large, tiny, hairy, bent, stuck out, misshapen, glowing, red, dented by eyeglasses. About a fifth of these children would pass the test, be accepted into this school, and officially be regarded as "gifted and talented." The strangeness of their ears would be redeemed by their genius. The rest of them would just be regular children with funny ears. Vica hugged Eric and pulled his hat lower over his ears.

Vica had to take a day off for this. Sergey had offered to take Eric to the test, but she couldn't trust him with something that important. He might have been late, or he could have started saying stupid shit like "A good education is what matters, chum, but a good school doesn't necessarily mean a good education." How she hated it when Sergey called Eric "chum"!

Thinking of Sergey made her momentarily nauseous. Ever since they had separated Vica developed a disturbing habit of seeing strangers on the street and mistaking them for Sergey. She would feel a fleeting joy, followed by disappointment and then relief. She wasn't sure if she missed him though. She missed the Sergey who loved her. But that Sergey no longer existed. He wouldn't have behaved like he had if he loved her, wouldn't have made fun of her at Vadik's party, wouldn't have left without a fight. Hadn't he actually look relieved as he was leaving? So, no, she didn't miss him. It's just that there was this space in her body that her love for Sergey used to occupy. She imagined it as a concrete physical space, shaped like a mushroom. A huge mushroom, with the stem originating in the pit of her stomach and the cap swelling over her heart and pushing toward her throat. That space was now unoccupied, but not clean, not entirely empty. It was filled with random junk, like hurt, shame, and fear. Fear that she had made a terrible mistake.

Vica wished she could talk to somebody about it. Vadik had proved to be useless. He had neither confirmed nor disproved that she had been right to throw Sergey out. Regina? Vadik kept singing her praises about how wise she was, how full of empathy, how much she had helped him with his love problems throughout the years. But to ask Regina about Sergey? Regina, who must be gloating?

She talked to her mother.

"You're such a pathetic idiot!" Vica's mother yelled into the phone. Vica mumbled the same explanation she had attempted to give to Vadik: how it was getting unbearable, how both of them were on the verge of hating each other.

"Just tell me, how can this possibly be good for you?" her mother asked. "You'll be worse off financially, you'll have to work even more, and you'll be all alone. Any husband is better than no husband!"

Vica's father was that "any husband" : a quiet alcoholic who liked to sing and weep when drunk; he would sing and weep himself into oblivion until he fell asleep right at the table.

"I might meet somebody else," Vica said.

"Good luck with that!" her mother retorted before slamming down the receiver.

Still, Vica's worst fear was that the separation would affect Eric in some irreparable way. He seemed fine, but who knew what went on inside his head?

"Are you sure you're not cold?" she asked Eric again. He shook his head.

"Hey, look!" Vica said. "Those dogs are funny." A skinny girl of about sixteen was walking a pack of four dogs: a rottweiler, two golden retrievers, and a small furry dog of unknown breed. The small one must have been intimidated by its peers, so it was doing everything possible to keep apart from them, stretching the rope, making the walker stumble.

Eric looked at the dogs, then up at her with surprise, because this was something that his dad would say, not his mom. Sergey had a special bond with Eric over funny animals. He would always point them out to Eric, and Eric to him. He would send Sergey links to various photos: "Dad, look at that furry pig!" or YouTube videos: "That's a real live killer rabbit!" And Sergey would take him to countless zoos, natural history museums, and aquariums to look at dinosaur bones, Galápagos turtles, and thousand-year-old fish. Eric had developed this passion for weird animals when he was four or five. He didn't have many friends then. (Well, he hardly had any friends now. Just that fat freak Gavin.) It would break Vica's heart when she watched Eric approach a kid on a playground to show him his toy dinosaur and explain how it used to be the most dangerous predator some millions of years ago, and the kid would laugh at him and run off, or kick the toy out of his hands and then run off. She always encouraged him to do sports, to play with other kids, to be more sociable, more normal. And it would break her heart to watch Eric run up to Sergey after work and tell him about the amazing discovery he had made—that dinosaurs looked just like chickens or some such—and Sergey would listen to him, as if it was okay to be interested in all that shit!

"Yeah, funny," Eric said and turned away. He was clearly not in the mood for talking.

Vica decided to study the parents in the line. You could easily divide them into two categories: Susan Sontag types and Outer Borough types. Vica knew who Susan Sontag was from Vadik's Tumblr. He once posted her photograph with a quote: " 'The truth is balance, but the opposite of truth, which is unbalance, may not be a lie.' "

Here, in the Castle line, the Sontag types were all about fifty years old, wore no makeup, had various amounts of gray in their hair, and had roughly the same amount of intellectual flair. Their clothes looked elegant yet comfortable, a sure sign that they were very, very expensive. Some of the Sontags were beautiful, others were not; a lot of them were Asian; a few of them were men. The Outer Borough types wore puffy jackets and knitted hats. There were a few more men among them: the non-white men were wearing suits under their jackets and dressy shoes, while the white men were wearing jeans and work boots, unless they were Russian—then they were wearing the same clothes as the non-white Outer Borough men. The phrase "deep social divide" darted through Vica's mind, but she was too tired and sleepy to think it through or even to use it in a complete sentence. Vica herself wore a fuchsia-colored puffy jacket, but that didn't mean that she belonged with the Outer Borough types, and the fact that she lived on Staten Island didn't mean anything either. It wasn't her fault that she lived on Staten Island. Vica's personality was pure Manhattan. It's just that her financial situation wasn't.

Although to be perfectly honest, Vica didn't belong with the Sontag types either, not because she lacked the intellectual flair but because she was only thirty-five years old and didn't have any gray in her hair.

None of that mattered though. What mattered was that this was one of the best schools in the city—and possibly in the entire country—and the only truly democratic one. All you had to do was pass the test, and if you were smart enough to pass it, you were guaranteed a spectacular free education that led to Ivy League colleges, Ivy League graduate schools, and then unfailingly to superior lives. The problem was that admission wasn't as democratic as it seemed. Some parents could afford tutors who'd been shoving intelligence down their children's throats for years and other parents couldn't. Eden, Vica's boss at Bing Ruskin, had a son in this school. Vica had heard Eden bragging to her friend Dr. Jewell that they had spent fifteen thousand dollars for tutoring so that their son would pass the exam. "But just think how much we saved in private school tuition!" she'd said. The maddening thing was that Eden and her husband could afford the tuition. So by paying for a tutor they had robbed some equally smart poor kid of the opportunity to attend this school. That was unfair! That was so unfair! And Eden wasn't even aware of it.

Of course, if she and Sergey had enough money, she wouldn't hesitate to hire a tutor too. This would have put Eric at that same unfair advantage. It's just that Vica didn't find unfairness toward others quite as painful as unfairness toward herself.

Several years ago Eden threw a Memorial Day barbecue for all of the diagnostic radiology employees at her beautiful farm near Princeton (she had the farm in addition to her huge Manhattan apartment). Real farm—goats and all. Vica had been really looking forward to that picnic. She liked Eden. Eden was fairly young, beautiful, and worldly, and Vica really wanted to see her in a social setting; she even hoped that they could become friends. Why couldn't they? Eden was a doctor, just as Vica would have been, if she'd had the chance to finish medical school. And maybe Eric could become friends with Eden's sons.

Vica decided to create the most elegant hostess gift for Eden. She bought a beautiful wicker basket at Pier 1, fitted it with a blue and white linen towel, and filled it with the most perfect strawberries she could find in Staten Island's Stop & Shop.

She thought she looked amazing when she parked her car and stepped onto Eden's lawn. She was wearing a tight low-cut tank top, a jeans miniskirt, pink high-heeled sandals, and a straw hat with a wide pink band. The outfit, combined with her basket of strawberries, was the very picture of country chic. Then the first thing that Vica noticed was strawberry patches all over the place, thousands, millions of strawberries. Eden was very polite about it: "Strawberries—how lovely!" she said. "Ours are not ripe yet." The second thing that Vica noticed were the beige shorts and loose white T-shirts that everybody, including Eden, was wearing. Oh, yes, and baseball hats. "Nice hat!" Santiago, who operated their C-scan machine, said with a smirk. Vica took her straw hat off and put it on a bench by the house, next to her basket.

Eden took her mostly immigrant employees on a tour of the house, a beautiful house, decorated with all the antique country stuff—there was even a collection of old irons—abstract photographs done by Eden's husband, and abstract sculptures done by Eden's sons. The boys ran in after a soccer game, sweaty, out of breath, flushed, confident, happy—and Vica had thought that Eric could make friends with them! When the tour was almost over, Vica decided to make up for her faux pas with the clothes and the strawberries and pay some amazing compliment to the house. "Eden," she said, "your house looks just like Howards End." Eden answered her with a blank stare. "Howards End," Vica explained, "the house in Forster's novel." Blank stare again, followed by a kind smile. Vica knew that before switching to premed at Harvard Eden had been an English major. There was no way that she didn't know who Forster was. Vica had read the novel in Regina's translation, perhaps the novel had a different title in English. And then Vica got it. Eden didn't expect Vica to know Forster (Vica—a simple immigrant ultrasound technician), just like she didn't expect one of her goats to bleat "Fors-ter." Eden gave Vica a polite, uncomprehending, but approving, perfectly democratic smile specially designed for her immigrant employees—Russian, Jamaican, Filipino, or whatever else they happened to be.

To add insult to injury, by the time they emerged from the house, the largest goat had eaten all of Vica's strawberries and about half of her hat. Vica picked up her bag and the remains of her hat and decided to go home without waiting for the food.

Vica's other botched attempt to make a friend at work was with Christine, another radiology technician. Christine was older than Vica, but not by much. She was a tall woman with rolls of fat pushing against her scrubs in expected and unexpected places. Her skin was of a perfect chestnut color, and her hair, black with a touch of gray, was done in gleaming cornrows. It was Christine who made the first move, back when Vica started working at Bing Ruskin. She offered some friendly advice, which Vica gladly accepted. They started having lunch together and chatting whenever they had a chance. In addition to professional advice, Christine gave Vica a lot of pointers on child-rearing, pie baking, ordering swimsuits online (you had to order Speedo at least three sizes too large), and American ways in general. Christine's manner had always been good-natured and caring, if a little patronizing. "Oh, so you have your cool black friend now?" Vadik would tease. "Shut up, Vadik,"

Vica would answer. But then things changed. The problem was that Christine took Vica for a struggling immigrant single mother. There was a picture of Eric clipped to Vica's locker, but she never talked about Sergey. Then one day somebody mentioned a cousin applying for a job at Gray Bank, and Vica said that her husband worked there too. "Oh, yeah?" Christine asked. "What does he do?" "He's a financial analyst," Vica said. "Oh, yeah?" Christine said again, and just like that, the friendship was over. Christine's husband worked as a mechanic, Leslie's husband was a bus driver, Sheena's husband worked as a security guard there at Bing Ruskin, Rachel and John were divorced, Michael's wife held the exact same position as he did but at Weil Cornell, and the youngest technician Liliana was single—she was all about dates and parties and fun. Having a husband at Gray Bank instantly turned Vica into this fanciful white lady who chose this job for some bizarre reason. Vica remembered what Bob's daughter, Becky, said about about her job at McDonald's. She worked there when she was a junior in high school. Bob thought it was important for her to experience a "real job." She told them how the other employees hated her, how they all gathered to stare at her getting into Bob's new Volvo after work, and how the nicer she was to them, the more they hated her. So that was how Christine saw Vica now? A spoiled rich brat who didn't really have to earn her living, who took this job just for the experience? But who in her right mind would choose to work at a cancer hospital, at a job that was both physically and emotionally exhausting, while being exposed to continuous radiation? There were times when Vica felt the urge to explain to Christine how things really stood, to tell her about Sergey's employment history, about how stupid they had been to buy that insane house that was just a big rotting piece of shit, and about how lonely she felt in the U.S. with no relatives and no real friends, just Regina and Vadik, both of whom preferred Sergey to her. But then she would remember how Regina had tried to explain to them that she wasn't really that rich, and how ridiculous that had sounded. And then pride would get the better of her. Why did Vica have to justify herself to Christine? And so they were cordial but not friendly. Certainly not friendly enough to talk about something as personal as the separation.

"Mom," Eric said, "Mom! I'm cold."

Vica rubbed his back. While she was doing that she noticed that Eric's glasses were dirty. She gasped and yanked them off, scratching his ear in the process. "Mom!" he protested.

"Hey! You should have cleaned them before we left," Vica said.

She could just see how these stains on the lenses would jeopardize Eric's chances at the test. Misread equation, misinterpreted sentence, blurry expression, fatal mistake. And there was nothing to clean the glasses with. Nothing. Nothing at all. Vica unbuttoned her coat, breathed on the lenses, then wiped them with the hem of her sweater. Eric turned away, embarrassed but resigned. "Here," she said, setting the glasses back on his face. "Thanks," Eric said, but she thought she caught a note of sarcasm. When they were just outside of the door, she opened his backpack and did a quick check: pencils, papers, all in place. Pink slip squeezed in his hand.

"Don't drop the slip."

"Mom, I won't!"

Okay, he probably wouldn't drop the slip. But then another horrible thought slashed through Vica's mind. Last year, when she took him out of school on Staten Island to take a test for another school for the gifted and talented (although not quite as gifted and talented as children admitted to the Castle), Eric decided to venture to the bathroom in the middle of the exam. He couldn't find it and then, once he found it, he couldn't poop right away because he was too nervous, and by the time he got back, they were already collecting the tests. He left twenty answers blank. Twenty answers blank!

Vica reached out and tapped the Susan Sontag in front of her on the shoulder.

"Do you know if they let the kids go to the bathroom?"

"Excuse me?" Susan Sontag said.

Yes, Vica knew that she spoke with an accent, but it wasn't that bad, it wasn't like you couldn't understand her. Susan Sontag's daughter (her huge ears half hidden behind her pigtails) answered for her.

"They don't! Once you hand in your pink slip, that's it, you can't go anywhere! And there are no windows in the school. Not a single one! Look, not a single one!"

Susan Sontag shushed her daughter and glared at Vica as if she had just said something completely inappropriate, had brought up a subject that should never be brought up in front of children, like sex, death, or financial troubles.

"Make sure you use the bathroom before they take your pink slip," Vica said to Eric.

"Mom, please!"

He was already in, talking to a guard and showing her his pink slip, when Vica noticed that she'd forgotten to zip his backpack. It was too late for her to squeeze through the crowd of children and zip it, and even too late to yell her son's name. There he went, with the backpack gaping like a hippo's maw. Seeing Eric among strangers, separated from her, made Vica look at him through the eyes of a stranger, which never failed to overwhelm her with disappointment. He was not a lovely child. He was awkward. Slouchy. Pale skin sprinkled with large freckles, dull eyes, droopy cheeks. Fat. Not obese, no, and not exactly fat yet, but getting there. Soft, squashy. Helplessly soft.

Vica raised her hand to wave to her son, but he didn't turn to look. He followed the guard and disappeared into the depths of the Castle.

"What are you feeding him? He looks awful!" Vica's oldest sister had exclaimed after she saw Eric on Skype. Their mother often said the same thing. "Let him be," Vica's father said, but when did they ever listen to him.

Guilt mixed with anger balled up somewhere in Vica's stomach. It was her own fault. It was the general unhappiness of their family, her constant fights with Sergey, the never-ending tension, and now the separation that made Eric fat, that made him slump in front of the TV with junk food instead of doing sports. It was his sick relationship with Sergey's mother, who kept overfeeding and overpraising her grandson. Mira was a tiny, fussy, heavily made up, not very smart woman. They had arranged for her to move to the United States after Sergey's father died. Vica was hoping that Mira would sell her apartment in Moscow, but she left it to her spinster sister instead. "Maechka is so sick, she wouldn't have survived on her pension." She herself came penniless. Sergey and Vica made sure she was getting benefits, found her state-sponsored housing in Brooklyn. But Mira wasn't adjusting to her new life that well. She was a clingy mother and a clingier grandmother. She and Eric had some sort of crazy romance going. He badly needed to be admired and she badly needed to be needed. Once Vica overheard the following exchange:

"Now, who is the smartest? Who is the handsomest?"

"Okay, okay, Grandma. I guess I am."

It was creepy, Vica thought, but they both looked so pleased with each other. They would spend hours talking. Mira would tell him all about her life in Russia, about his genius grandfather, and about Sergey as a little boy. Eric shared some of the facts with Vica. "Did you know that Dad used to be really good at picking berries? They would go into the woods and he would fill his little basket in minutes. Grandma says I would be really good too."

What hurt Vica the most about this was that Eric didn't have any connection with her side of the family. Her mother was very much involved in bringing up Vica's sister's kids; she considered them her real grandchildren, and Eric was nothing but a stranger whose first language was English and couldn't speak her language very well. Vica would prep him and make him rehearse some Russian phrases before their monthly Skype calls, but Eric would invariably stutter and mix up his words. "I don't understand what you're saying!" Vica's mother would say. "Better go play and put your mom back on."

Other parents from the line were dispersing in all directions. Outer Boroughs were heading to nearby cafés, Susan Sontags were walking west, to their beautiful apartments just across the park. The time was now 8:35. She had to pick Eric up at 12:30. She'd taken the whole day off work, so she had all that time to herself. She was free to do what she wanted. Vica's plan was to have breakfast at Café Sabarsky. She had heard Eden mention that they had "hands down the best coffee in the city." Vadik said that it was a bit pricey but a truly elegant setting. She walked to Neue Galerie, entered the museum, and stopped at the door of Café Sabarsky and peeked in. The dark wood interior was both cozy and grand. Vica loved marble tabletops and chairs with a dent in it for your butt. She took the dent as a special sign of luxury. At this hour, the café was almost empty; an old man was sitting at a table by the window with a deliciously fresh newspaper spread above his coffee cup. She would take a table by the window too. She would just order a cup of coffee and a bread basket. She would butter one of the rolls, put it on her plate, take a selfie of herself enjoying "the best coffee in the city" in "a truly elegant setting," and post it on Facebook. Let them see! Let them see that she was perfectly fine about her separation, happy, in a good place. She wasn't sure who "they" were, however. Her sisters? They didn't really use Facebook, preferring the Russian social media site VKontakte. Her coworkers? Yeah, why not? Regina and Vadik? Definitely! Sergey himself? Sergey had never been a fan of social media—what an irony that he was so obsessed with that app!—but if he ever happened to browse and see her photo, Vica wanted to make sure that it would send the right message. Vica was about to enter the café when her eyes fell on the menu clipped to the door. Seven dollars for coffee. Eight dollars for a bread basket with jam. That would be eighteen dollars with tax and more than twenty dollars with tip. She could afford it, but twenty dollars for bread and coffee! When she could buy a bagel from a breakfast cart for just a dollar! No, that was ridiculous. Vica turned to leave, then hesitated.

What about her Facebook photo? Vica, smiling, relaxed, sipping her seven-dollar coffee as if it were perfectly natural? No, she decided, it wasn't worth it. She wouldn't be able to drink that coffee without constantly running the price through her head. So the picture would come out as anything but natural.

Vica walked back to Madison, went into a deli, and stood in line for a bagel and a sour-tasting coffee in a paper cup. There was a man a few feet away, standing with his back to Vica, perusing the yogurts on a shelf. Short, wiry, dark hair. Sergey! Vica thought for a second. Then the man turned, revealing that he was not.

It was only nine. Vica sat down at the one of the rickety plastic tables, reached into her bag, and pulled out a book she'd recently bought at Barnes & Noble. It was called *Mobile Apps for Dummies*.

She opened the book to the marked page:

> Step 1. Define the Goal of Your App. Before you go into details, you must clearly define the purpose and mission of your app. What is it going to do? What is its core appeal? What concrete problem is it going to solve, or what part of life is it going to make better?

"To fight death" she wrote in her notepad. That was kind of a larger goal. She needed to make it more practical, more plausible.

Vica had never been that interested in Sergey's idea of re-creating the virtual voice or even the virtual personality of the departed. What she wanted was an app that would allow people to keep some of their online presence after they died. She thought the app should be designed for people who were going to die (which was everybody!) rather than their relatives and friends. They would be able to preprogram the posts, messages, or tweets that would appear after they died. It was more like a virtual will. "Virtual Will"— now, there was a nice name, so much better than Virtual Grave. She had mentioned it to Sergey and he sounded interested. "But where would my algorithm come in, if people will be creating their own messages before they die?" he asked. "They can't possibly prewrite everything. Some of them have to be automatic!" He took some time to think it over and told her that he loved her idea. He thought it was great that Virtual Grave could work both ways as posthumous restoration and as "prehumous" preparation. He did love it! Yet, he chose to pitch only his part to Bob. He must have thought that her idea was too banal, too practical. It was practical, and that was what was so great about it.

So what would be her app's plausible goal?

To keep your social media alive after you die.

To keep your online presence after you die.

To control your online presence after you die.

To keep control over your social media after you die.

Vica liked the word *control*. One of the things that was so scary about dying, falling down, or even falling asleep was the loss of control.

Yes, *control* was a powerful word, and no, she wasn't so naive that she thought you could actually keep it. But you could keep some semblance of it. Or at least die thinking that you did.

Now, how exactly would the app work? Would it only allow for the timed premade posts or tweets or photos to appear after you died, or would it also allow you to "react" to the posts of others?

"Posthumous feedback?" she wrote.

It shouldn't be hard to program the app to give out random likes to the posts of loved ones. A "like" for every second thing posted by your child. Or for every third thing posted by your friends. People were always "liking" random things as it was. But that was easy enough. It would be far more interesting and challenging to program the app so that it made meaningful comments. Would it be possible for it to distinguish a post about something good from a post about something bad? So that it could comment either "Congratulations!" or "That sucks"? But what if it made a mistake? What if a son posted that he lost his job and got "Congratulations!" from his long-dead father? There had to be some neutral comments. "I'm with you," for example. That would work for almost everything. iPhones already had ready-made quick text options that substituted for genuine emotions. You didn't have to go to all that trouble and type in "I love you" or "I miss you"; all you had to do for the app was to make those quick responses automatic. So what you needed for Virtual Will was a robotlike program that would be activated after you died to post neutral comments to your loved ones' posts. It should be compatible to any of your social media platforms. Vica thought about the most common expressions people used in their posts, tweets, and comments. She reached for her phone and opened her Twitter app. Her favorite social media was Facebook, so she never tweeted anything herself, but she enjoyed looking at other people's tweets, even though she didn't follow that many of them. Vadik's tweet was at the top.

> vadim kalugin @kalugin · Nov 30
> **When in doubt choose the least probable scenario**
> **#Simulated Existence**
> 0 retweets 0 favorites

Zero retweets. Zero favorites. What did he expect with stupid shit like that? Still, Vica felt sorry for Vadik and marked his tweet as a favorite.

Then there were a couple of funny little tweets from Mindy Kaling, who she loved.

Vica soon forgot about her task and got carried away by the tweets themselves.

There was one from President Obama about climate change. Vica smiled. Not that she particularly cared about politics or the climate, but she got a kick out of the fact that you could follow the president on Twitter.

A tweet from Liliana in radiology. "Another busy day." Well, yes, Vica thought, this was a weekday, and their job was hard. Why did Liliana feel the need to tweet about that?

Santiago from interventional radiology retweeted a picture of a Japanese dog with a square hairdo. Now that was really funny and cute!

Vica skipped through another ten or twelve tweets until she stumbled on this one from Ethan Grail.

ethan grail @etgrail · Nov 30

At least people don't stop me on the street anymore.
#PerksOfDying

653 retweets 1.5K favorites

Vica sighed. She felt a surge of pity that was so sharp it burned her throat the way hot coffee did.

Ethan Grail was her favorite patient. He was an actor, a quite famous one, even though Vica had never seen any of his movies. He was only thirty-two years old with a terminal lung cancer diagnosis. Ethan was the source of endless gossip at the hospital. Liliana would show Vica clips from his films on YouTube. Christine claimed that he had just broken up with his costar. Like right before his diagnosis. She'd read it in *People* magazine. "Poor fucker," Santiago said.

Judging from the clips and the countless photos floating across the Internet, Ethan had been very handsome a mere six months ago. Now he was painfully thin and had the pallor of a dead man, with large eyes that seemed to retreat into his skull farther than would be bearable. No wonder people didn't recognize him anymore. Ethan would always chat with Vica while she did his sonograms (his therapy made him prone to thromboses, so he needed frequent tests), and he would often sneak across the hall to see her when he came for his weekly radiation treatments.

Her male patients often tried to flirt with her. One man said that she had "the body of Marilyn and the soul of Chekhov." A lot of men made the same joke that finally there was a woman who could see right through them. Vica usually just smiled back at them, but she couldn't help but feel disgusted. It was as if she was kneading dough all day, and the dough suddenly decided to flirt with her.

But Ethan Grail was different. She actually enjoyed chatting with him. Not because he was a celebrity, but because there was something morbidly irresistible in the way he liked to flaunt his impending death. Usually, patients were encouraged to view death as if it were a mean but conquerable enemy, something they were expected to fight against rather than accept. Ethan said that Vica was the only one among the hospital's personnel who didn't discourage his quips about death, didn't call his attitude defeatist. He said that he loved her accent. That there was some bluntness, some bitterness, some refreshing lack of optimism in the way she pronounced words.

Both Liliana and Christine thought that Ethan had a crush on Vica. "What if he dies and leaves Vica all his money in his will?" Liliana mused. Vica fantasized about that too. She hated herself for doing it, but she couldn't help herself.

Vica clicked on Ethan's name to read his recent tweets in succession.

ethan grail @etgrail · Oct 26

Seth MacFarlane's birthday today! Happy Birthday, man!

200 retweets 863 favorites

ethan grail @etgrail · Oct 20

Watched Hangover for the umpteenth time. I wish laughing wasn't so painful! #hatecancer

267 retweets 971 favorites

ethan grail @etgrail · Oct 13

Watched When Harry Met Sally with my mom. She broke down crying several times.

220 retweets 692 favorites

ethan grail @etgrail · Sep 15

Got another stent inserted today. Couldn't they
insert something that would make dying less scary?
#hatecancer

623 retweets 1.1K favorites

ethan grail @etgrail · Sep 13

Last night was pretty tough. #hatecancer

123 retweets 345 favorites

ethan grail @etgrail · Aug 09

Happy Birthday, Anna Kendrick! Love you! Miss you!

453 retweets 488 favorites

ethan grail @etgrail · Aug 08

Oolong orange blossom is now officially my favorite tea.
And, no, Aunt Hero, I still won't try jasmine.

143 retweets 547 favorites

ethan grail @etgrail · Aug 01

Started typing "FYI." Autocorrect changed it to "dying."
Smart beast!

945 retweets 1.6K favorites

Shit! Vica thought, pushing back tears. She couldn't afford to get
emotional over a patient. Everybody at work told her so. Some of
her colleagues offered tips on fighting back emotions. Christine said
that whenever she was about to feel weepy she would try to visualize
her bank statement. Liliana thought of sex. Santiago of the recent
soccer game's score. But it was Sergey, who had never worked with
dying people, who actually gave her the best advice. This was years
ago, when she'd just started working at Bing Ruskin and would
often come home sobbing. "Think of it as a movie or a TV show,"
he said. "When I was little I used to get really upset over sad scenes
in movies. And my dad once told me, 'Serezha, listen, these are not

real people. They will go home and change their clothes after this and go on with their lives. Lassie the dog is not really dead, she's an actress. She will go home and gnaw on her favorite bone.' It helped a lot, although it did ruin the magic of storytelling a little bit."

For the most part Sergey's protective strategy worked really well. This is not real, Vica would tell herself. This is just a TV series. *ER, Grey's Anatomy, House M.D.* The doctors are not real. The patients are not real. That sweet kid who died last month didn't really die; he was simply killed off by the writers, because some new show offered him a better role. It didn't work with Ethan though. Possibly because he really was an actor, it was harder for her to imagine him as a pretend actor. Ethan was real and he was going to die for real. Fairly soon too. She had heard that the doctors were giving him only about a year.

The last time Vica had a chat with Ethan was about two weeks ago.

"I know what you want to ask me," Ethan said.

He was staring at her intently, even aggressively. She had to look away. He couldn't have guessed that I had been thinking about his money, could he? Vica thought, her spine tensing.

"Go on, ask me. Ask me if I'm scared of dying."

"Are you scared?"

"Hell, yeah, I'm terrified. I'm not ready. It's funny, isn't it, how my docs devote so much effort to prolonging my life and none of it to preparing me for death. Which is coming no matter what! Couldn't they think of something to make dying just a little bit easier, a little bit less scary?"

Vica had no idea what to say to him. Her heart was breaking, but she was rebelling against having to feel it. She wasn't Ethan's girlfriend or his friend. She wasn't even his shrink or his doctor. She was a mere radiology technician, and she couldn't afford to feel that strongly about a patient!

"There are excellent hospice programs; they take care of emotional issues as well as physical ones," she said weakly.

Ethan looked stricken with disappointment. He must have expected something honest, crazy, Russian from her, but what he'd gotten was a generic reply à la Bing Ruskin.

She looked at his "FYI" tweet again and her eyes filled with tears. She had to tip her face up not to let them escape.

"Hi!" Somebody interrupted her thoughts.

Vica raised her eyes and saw that there was a smiling man sitting across from her.

"You were in that line at the Castle school, weren't you?"

Vica nodded. The man was white, wearing a puffy coat, jeans, and working boots. Speaking with a slight Eastern European accent. Polish? Serbian? In other words, he was a typical Outer Borough.

"I heard the questions are even tougher than usual this year," he said. "My Ginnie nearly had a panic attack this morning. And I told her, 'Honey, no school is worth whipping yourself into a frenzy like this.'"

Except for this school, Vica thought. This school was worth it. She wondered if Eric had been whipped into enough of a frenzy.

"Listen," the man said, "can I buy you another coffee or a pastry?"

He was nice-looking. In his forties. Probably divorced. Broad shoulders. Attractive crinkles around his blue eyes.

"I have an appointment," Vica said with an apologetic smile and got up to leave. She had no desire to have a conversation with an Outer Borough.

As she walked toward the park, she wondered if she had been too curt with the man. And no, she hadn't left because she was a snob and felt that she deserved better, or not only because of that, but mainly because she couldn't help but see all Outer Borough men as variations of Sergey. Or just variations on the type of Husband. A Husband knew her the way she didn't want to be known, at her worst, her ugliest, her most embarrassing. He had heard how she lied, and he had heard how she screamed in rage. He had seen her throw up, seen her with cracked nipples, seen her pick an uneaten sandwich from the garbage bin in his mother's kitchen—she swore that she put the sandwich right back, but he didn't see that. A Husband knew her and he didn't want her. He didn't even fight for her. This was definitely one of the reasons Vica didn't want to date Vadik. She couldn't be with another man who knew her well. She had been attracted to Vadik for such a long time, but now that she was actually free, the mere thought of dating him made her squirm.

What she needed was a Lover. A man who came from another world. A man who didn't know her. A man who would take her for somebody good, and bright, and exciting. Special. Delicate.

The thought of such a man made Vica giddy with desire. Ever since Sergey left, she was plagued by these random bouts of desire, unwelcome and unexpected. Her recurrent fantasy was of a man throwing her onto a bed, spreading her legs, and greedily licking her, lapping her up as a cat would a bowl of milk.

The last time she felt like that was when she first went to Moscow for the medical school entrance exams. She was seventeen. The heated subway car smelled of old leather and sweat. Some of that sweat was her own. Vica was wearing a short cotton dress. She was holding her large backpack on her lap, and there were imprints of the bag's buckles on her bare legs. She felt damp all over, and messy and disgusting. But still men looked at her. She couldn't help but feel their gazes running through her body like electrical currents. It was exhilarating.

And then, when she was accepted to the best medical school in the country (the only one from her hometown!) and went to Moscow to live, she felt overwhelmed with the buzz of a sexual current all over the city. She would walk down a Moscow street or stand in a crowded subway car and catch somebody's stare and her knees would grow weak. But she was a good girl, brought up by her strict mother, by all the books about great romantic love she had consumed while growing up, and so sex for the sake of sex was out of the question. She would only have sex for the sake of great love. Or, rather, she would have a great love for the sake of great sex.

Lovelovelove/sex/love/sex/love/sexsexsex was all she could think about, so it was surprising that she found a way to study and earn good grades. Vica did go out with a couple of guys, but she wouldn't let them go all the way, because she was sure that what she felt for them wasn't great love. Great love was supposed to make you crazy, set your world on fire, move the earth—all those clichés, though Vica didn't know they were clichés back then. She refused to go to all those empty dachas with these guys, and their parents' apartments, and their friends' dorm rooms, so instead, they ended their dates on the dark staircase of some building close to her dorm that smelled of cats and rotten potato peels. She let the guy press her against the mailboxes, or the staircase railing, or the garbage chute, or the warm spines of the radiator, and they kissed until it hurt. She would try to stop and remind herself that she wasn't supposed to have sex without love, and that love was nowhere near, but her will would fail her and she wouldn't be able to stop. So she let the guy sneak his hand under her sweater, and his finger inside her panties, and his dick pressed to the damp skin of her upper thigh, and she moaned and wriggled and sometimes even came—when it happened, she tried her best to conceal it from the guy. Then Vica said good-bye, walked up the stairs to her dorm room, and wiped the semen off her thighs, crying from shame but wanting more.

One of these guys was Vadik. They met at her classmate's party—Vadik was the classmate's older brother's friend. He was twenty-two, in grad school in the department of applied mathematics at the university. He was tall and handsome, smart and funny, and liked to recite poetry. He boasted that he knew Moscow better than anybody else, and he was eager to impress Vica by being a connoisseur of all the finer things the city could offer. He took her for walks along the little-known "secret" nooks like Kuskovo park or Simonov Monastery, he treated her to the best hot chocolate ever, he took her to see a double feature at a Truffaut retrospective. Then he took her back to her dorm and kissed her at the entrance. Vica tried very hard to will herself into falling in love with him. "I'm crazy about him, I'm crazy about him, I'm crazy about him," she kept repeating in her mind as if trying to hypnotize herself. She enjoyed kissing him, but the craziness wouldn't come.

On their sixth date, they had a fight. Vadik was from a small town too, but his attitude toward Moscow was startlingly different from Vica's. Vica thought that the city was exciting and tough and strange, very strange, and it was pointless to try to fit in or even understand it, but that eventually she would conquer it (she didn't know how—she had no idea what conquering the city even meant—she just knew that she had to do it). Vadik grew up thinking he didn't belong in his dumb hometown, but in sparklingly cultural Moscow he would fit right in. He said that his father was dead, his mother was sleeping around, and his older brother was a drug addict ("he sniffs glue and other shit"), and that he hated them and had nothing in common with them and nothing in common with his hometown. He was a true Muscovite at heart. Vica said that she got it how you could hate your parents and your hometown, but that wasn't enough to make anybody a real Muscovite. He was just fooling himself that he could fit in. To prove that Vica was wrong, Vadik took her to meet his "true Muscovite" friends, Sergey and Regina.

Vica's first reaction on entering Regina's apartment and meeting Regina and Sergey was that, yes, they were true Muscovites. She immediately grasped the vast difference between Vadik and them. Sergey and Regina didn't have to work at being Muscovites, didn't have to prove that to anybody, they just were. They were born into the world of privilege and they took it for granted. That was precisely what made them true Muscovites—the fact that they took it for granted! Vadik couldn't see it. He was proud to be a Muscovite, and that pride betrayed the fact that he wasn't. But while Regina with her forlorn gaze and sallow complexion didn't interest Vica in the least ("a fish asleep," she thought), she couldn't take her eyes off Sergey. She didn't think he was handsome, not at first. He was short, thin, with a head too big for his body and a nose too big for his face.

But then she noticed that Sergey resembled that actor in Truffaut's films she and Vadik had just seen (Jean-Jacques? Jean-Pierre something?) and saw what she initially perceived as flaws in a completely new light. Sergey was graceful, both his movements and his manner of talking were. Vica had never observed this quality in a man before, so she didn't recognize it right away, but once she did she found it deeply attractive. He was graceful and passionate. He said that he was spending most of the time at the Lenin library doing research for an article about the concept of singularity applied to linguistics. He talked about the idea of singularity at length, and he would close his eyes for a moment or two as if overwhelmed by the intensity of his insights. Vadik liked to talk about scientific concepts too, but he wasn't really passionate about them, he didn't have the ability to get consumed by them the way Sergey did. He couldn't possibly generate as much heat as Sergey did. She thought of the scientific fact that impressed her most when she was a child. "Inside the Earth, there is a hot glowing core," their teacher said, "and if not for that core, life on Earth wouldn't be possible." Vica kept thinking about that for a long time, kept touching the ground to check if it was even a little bit hot. That's what Sergey had, she thought that day at Regina's place, a hot glowing core.

But he was taken, Sergey was. By this slovenly boring Regina, who obviously took him for granted, the way she took everything in her life for granted. Her beautiful old apartment, her paintings, her famous mother. Vica was sure that it was Regina's mother who ensured her daughter's acceptance to the most prestigious university in Russia, while Vica had to claw her way to medical school. Did Regina even love Sergey? Did she even want him? Was she even capable of wanting something or somebody with the same passion as Vica? How was it fair that Regina had Sergey?

They had to leave early, because Vadik had to go to work (he worked nights at a programming center). Back at her dorm, Vica couldn't fall asleep for a very long time. She would get up and pace around the room, then go back to bed, then get up and pace around the room again, thinking and thinking and thinking about Sergey. She finally fell asleep, praying that the next day she would feel calmer and would be able to go on with her life undisturbed. But when she woke up, she felt lovesick, angry, and determined to act. She had a quick breakfast, took the subway to the Lenin library, and got a temporary pass to the collections. She spent the entire day there, just walking around, hoping to see Sergey. He wasn't there. He wasn't there the next day either. When she finally saw him on her fourth day at the library, by the bookshelves at the far corner of the reading room, she was so nervous that she wanted to hide.

"Vica!" he shouted from across the room, making the other library patrons frown and shush him.

Vica dumped Vadik the very next day, but it took the "supersensitive" Sergey another three weeks to break up with Regina.

It was then that Vica understood that you couldn't will or force love. Love was all about surrendering her will to a force that was larger than anything she had encountered. A point of no return just like the singularity. How impatient she and Sergey were to take possession of each other, to penetrate each other as deeply and absolutely as they could. How greedily they listened to each other's childhood stories, how greedily they studied each other's peculiarities, as greedily as they made love. How eager they were to take that journey to the United States, to explore another country, to embark on a never-ending adventure together.

And what a crushing disappointment it turned out to be. Their disgusting apartment in Brooklyn, Vica's surprise pregnancy, the botched delivery by an exhausted intern that resulted in a horrible infection for her. (Thank God the baby was okay!) Sergey's losing interest in sex with her. There were times when he couldn't even get it up for her. The boredom, the hopeless, bottomless boredom of their daily routine. At night, as Vica lay in bed alone (Sergey was studying) with a heat pack attached to her aching back, facing away from sleeping Eric in his crib and his stinky overflowing diaper pail, she began to fantasize about her former boyfriends and how she

would be so much better off with any of them. Especially Vadik.
He had large hands. Rough fingers. Large dick too. She didn't get
to see it, but she imagined it as large. Way larger than Sergey's. It
was such a mistake to leave Vadik for Sergey. If only she was granted
a chance to fix that horrible mistake. When Vadik announced that
he had found a job in New Jersey and was coming here to live, Vica
thought she would go crazy with anticipation.

Then Vadik arrived, only to fall in love with somebody else on
his very first day here. But still, Vica kept chasing him, up until they
finally got their sick, stupid, embarrassing two hours on the couch.

Vadik, Vica thought. He's been acting strange lately. He seemed
tense when they had that dinner at Whole Foods. Reluctant to discuss either Sergey or Virtual Grave. Was it because of his sense of
loyalty to Sergey? Ugh, what a mess.

Vica needed to pee. Her first thought was to go back to the deli
on Madison, but she didn't want to bump into that Outer Borough
man again. The Met was right there. She decided to pay a dollar for
a ticket and go look at the collections after she used their restroom.

She hadn't been to the Met in ages. You couldn't consider yourself a refined and cultured person if you hadn't been to the Met in
ages, could you? But then did New Yorkers even go there? Tourists
and art students went there, yes, but what about regular New Yorkers? Vica tried to think of the most cultured New Yorker she knew.
Regina? Regina wasn't a real New Yorker. Eden? No, Eden never
went there. Both Eden and her husband had graduated from Harvard, so they didn't have to go to the Met because they didn't need
to prove they were cultured.

Well, screw Eden and her husband. Vica would go to the Met,
not because she needed to prove that she was cultured, but because
she truly enjoyed art.

She bought her ticket for a pay-what-you-wish dollar and asked
the guard about the restrooms. He pointed to the Egyptian wing.
Vica walked briskly past all those mummies and gravestones. She
always hated the Egyptian wing, because it reminded her of a cem-

etery, which it essentially was. These people seemed to have devoted their entire lives to preparing for death. Such a waste. Such a stupid horrible waste, Vica thought as she peed and then washed her hands in the tomblike bathroom. But then weren't modern people even more stupid when they chose to simply ignore death? Ethan was right. Death was inevitable, enormous, and terrifying. Wouldn't it be wiser to make at least some effort to be prepared?

She proceeded to examine several mummies. It was hard to believe that all of them used to be real people. Thousands of years ago, but still. They ate, they slept, they peed. She tried to imagine herself as an Egyptian woman, caring for her child, pining for her husband, all the while wearing that interesting headdress and jewelry. That jade snake must have felt deliciously cold against the skin. Vica moved to look at a photo essay documenting the embalming process.

She read the caption. "Then the embalmers would turn the body facedown to allow the brain to ooze out through the nostrils."

The image of her own brain oozing through her nostrils made her feel suddenly sick. She rushed through all the rooms toward the exit, then ran down the steps and stopped to take a deep breath. Vica didn't know where to go; she just wanted to get away, away from the mass grave of the Egyptian wing, away from the museum.

She started to walk down the park's East Drive. Usually crowded, in this weather the drive was practically deserted. There were no bikers and just a couple of joggers. A thin man in a blue jogging suit and a white knitted hat passed Vica. Sergey! was Vica's ridiculous first thought. What is this white hat—I've never seen it before.

Then she took another look and saw that the man didn't resemble Sergey at all. This was the second time today she'd made that mistake. Vica wondered how much longer it would take to free her mind from Sergey.

She swerved in the direction of the boathouse and started to walk along the lake toward the Bethesda Fountain. The cold now flapped around her in waves, hitting her on the legs and the shoulders.

The clearing by the fountain was mostly deserted as well. Vica walked right up to the statue and peered into the angel's face. The expression was cold and strict rather than ethereal.

The last time they were here Sergey told Eric the story of the Angel of the Waters. How there was a fountain like this in Jerusalem and all the sick, blind, and crippled people were lying by the edge waiting for the angel. Every once in a while the angel would come and disturb the waters, and then the first person who got in would be cured.

"What do you mean 'the first one'?" Eric asked. "Only the first one?"

"That's how it worked. The person who got into the disturbed water first was cured."

"But that's so unfair! That means only the fastest and strongest could be cured."

"That's the whole point," Sergey said. He tried to tell Eric about this one paralyzed man who could never get to the water in time, so Jesus performed a miracle and cured him himself, but Eric wouldn't listen.

"Still unfair! The whole thing with the angel is a miracle, right? I don't get what's the point of a miracle if it's so unfair!"

Sergey tried to explain that the term *miracle* used to have a completely different meaning, then he got really annoyed and gave up.

Eric was a strange boy. The girls thought he was ugly and the boys thought he was a geek. Vica wouldn't have minded his being a geek, if he was a determined one, if he was reading a lot. He wasn't. He hardly read at all. But he was smart. He was! He liked to think things through. "I want to know exactly what I will feel when I die, that way I won't be that scared," he'd said to her once. And he was kind. He was. He was capable of empathy in a way few people were.

Getting into that school would put him among other children like him, smart and weird and sensitive, and he would finally fit in. Being in that school would show him the point of learning. He'd learn how to read analytically, he'd learn how to look at art, he'd learn why people read, he'd learn why people looked at art. He'd learn how you could find something true, intimate, and personal, in the most unimaginable of places, in Egyptian art made a thousand years ago. No, Vica didn't hope that this school would make him feel privileged and self-assured like Eden, like Eden's husband, like Eden's sons—nothing would. And she didn't hope that this school would make him happy. She knew that people who went to good schools had their insecurities and their little miseries and their own ugliness, but still, she believed that even their unhappiness was far more interesting. A school like that opened the whole world for you. If you were bound to be miserable, you could have a whole variety of options, you could choose your own misery, not have one forced on you.

Just last week, when they were walking along the beach on Staten Island, Vica thought she would try to explain all this to Eric. But how do you talk about these things with a child? The day was surprisingly mild, and the wind was strong but not cold. They were heading toward their favorite picnic spot by the salt marsh, but it happened to be high tide, so there wasn't as much dry land as usual. Vica started to walk down the mossy, crunchy path built by colonies of mussels. "Mom, you're hurting the mussels, can't you hear it?" Erik said. She stepped away, but then her feet started to get wet. Erik ran to the beach and hauled back a large log stuck in the bushes. He put it over the wet area so that Vica could use it as a little bridge. She smiled and bumped Erik on the shoulder. He bumped her back. She felt good, and she thought that she didn't have to explain anything to Eric, that he understood. In his own way, he understood her better than anybody else.

VICA HIT ERIC for the second time just outside the Castle school.

The other parents were crowded by the entrance, looking anxiously at the door, Susan Sontags and Outer Boroughs alike. They started to let the children out around twelve forty. The children were walking out in trickles of ten or twelve. Eric walked out alone. He didn't see her at first; he stood there turning his head to the right and to the left, scanning the faces of parents. She yelled out his name and waved. He waved back.

"I'm hot," he said. She touched the top of his head. His hair was a little damp.

"How was it?" Vica asked. "Tough questions?"

He nodded. He looked a little shell-shocked, but not upset. She would even say that he looked relieved. Vica took that as a good sign.

"Did you answer them all?"

He said, "Yeah."

"And what about the essay? What was the topic?"

He said, "It was okay, not too hard."

"But what was the topic?"

He sighed.

She said, "Okay, fine, I won't ask. Better not to ask, not to jinx it, right?"

He nodded. She smiled and kissed him on the top of his head. He thought that public kisses were embarrassing, but he made an exception for the ones on the top of his head.

"Okay, let's get out of here," she said.

They passed a hot dog cart. Eric looked at her. Normally, she wouldn't have allowed hot dogs from a street cart, but these smelled so good and she was so hungry, and she knew that Eric must be hungry as hell.

She bought two. Both with mustard and ketchup.

Eric was about to bite into his when she noticed that he wasn't wearing his hat.

"Where is your hat?"

He wrinkled his nose. "Oh, right!" he said. "I put it in my pocket."

He reached into his pocket and yanked the hat out, and a pink square fell and landed on the pavement. She bent to pick it up.

"Admission slip? What's it doing in your pocket? Admission slip? Didn't you have to give it to the people in there? Admission slip? Why do you still have it?"

She would have preferred to keep asking these questions to delay the answer, which she knew, which she had guessed right away.

"You didn't take the test, did you."

He hunched his shoulders and started to cry, the hot dog still in his hand. He was saying something to her, quickly, quietly. How he had spent the entire time hiding in the bathroom. How he didn't want to go to that school. How the Castle was creepy. How it had no windows. How these kids were weird. How they were geeks. How they had weird ears. How he didn't want to go to school with weird geeks with weird ears.

It stunned her how loud the sound of the slap was. He dropped the hot dog. They both watched how it landed on the sidewalk, a smash of ketchup, the frank out. People were staring at them, but she didn't care. She looked at Eric. There was a red mark on his cheek. She watched it brighten. She wanted to run away, to hide, to sob and wail as loudly as she could.

Vica gave Eric her hot dog. "Here," she said, her voice trembling.

He took the hot dog and raised his eyes to hers. She couldn't believe it, but there was pity in his eyes.

He broke off half and handed it to her.

She suddenly remembered something Eric had said to her when he was very young—five or six. She had walked into the bathroom as he stood by the sink brushing his teeth. They'd just had a big fight.

"Sometimes I don't love you," he'd said and spat into the sink— Vica remembered that—blue frothy spittle. "But even when I don't love you, I still love you more than I don't love you." He said that and went on rinsing. He was very small. He barely reached the sink.

It was his kindness that hurt the most.

Chapter 8

THE REST IS SILENCE?

I T ALL STARTED WITH A SKYPE CALL.

Sergey was working on Vadik's MacBook Air—he preferred it to his own old Toshiba, which had a crack in the screen from when he dropped it on the cement stairs of his Staten Island basement. It's been six weeks since he moved in with Vadik. Sergey was putting the finishing touches on his rough prototype for Virtual Grave. He had a storyboard and sample wireframes, and he was satisfied with them, even though what he had created was miles away from his original idea. What he really wanted was to resurrect the personality of a departed through the traces left in his or her social media. He thought of the drunken pitch he'd made at Vadik's housewarming in Morningside Heights: "Our online presence is where the essence of a person is nowadays." Sergey had never been a big fan of social media; he barely engaged in it himself, but he firmly believed that this was true for most people. But now that he had pored over tons of strangers' tweets, public posts, and messages in order to test his algorithm, he found social media disappointing. In fact, he was appalled by how overly intimate yet somehow impersonal most of the entries were. People shared their and their relatives' diagnoses, described how the illnesses progressed, posted pictures of their kids in hospital beds, wrote about their breakups in great detail, listed ingredients for their breakfasts and dinners, reported how their bodies reacted to said breakfasts and dinners, confessed that they were either "extremely happy" or "devastated" by political events that had nothing to do with them. The oversharing and overreacting felt insincere to him. As did the smoothness of the language people used. Sergey still believed that you could find the essence of a person on social media; the problem was that it was hidden, encoded in silences, in omissions, in typos, and was thoroughly impenetrable by his algorithm. Virtual Grave did a great job of distilling an online voice of the departed, but it failed at getting to his or her true voice.

Perhaps one day, Sergey thought as he picked up a dog-eared paperback of *Hamlet* lying facedown on his desk. *Hamlet* had been Vadik's idea. Lately, Vadik was acting as if he couldn't stand even the mention of Virtual Grave, but Sergey was so into it that he could talk about nothing else.

"It seems like all you're trying to do is give a voice to your dead dad, right?" Vadik said to Sergey. "Just so he could speak to you one more time. How Shakespearean of you! How Hamletian!"

Sergey had told Vadik about the letter he received from his father after his death and how much it meant to him. And Vadik was mocking it?

"Yes, it is Hamletian. I don't see anything wrong in it," he said to Vadik, barely controlling his anger. There was a much-used Penguin *Hamlet* among Vadik's books. Sergey had read it in Russian years ago, but this was the first time he was compelled to read it in English. Reading it in the original turned out to be harder than he'd expected, but he found the very shabbiness of the book encouraging—a lot of people had handled it, a lot of people had struggled through it, and a lot of people had made it to the end, so he could do it too.

And then there were footnotes and a glossary for difficult words. Well, he had to agree with Vadik. The scene with the ghost that had moved him so much in the Russian translation sounded kind of ridiculous in the original. "List, list, O, list!" and "Adieu, adieu,

adieu!" were making him chuckle rather than cry. But the last words of *Hamlet* overwhelmed Sergey with their unexpected power.

> *O, I die, Horatio!*
> *The potent poison quite o'ercrows my spirit.*
> *I cannot live to hear the news from England,*
> *But I do prophesy th'election lights*
> *On Fortinbras. He has my dying voice.*
> *So tell him, with th'occurrents, more and less,*
> *Which have solicited. The rest is silence.*

Sergey put the book down and closed his eyes.

"He has my dying voice. He has my dying voice. He has my dying voice." He repeated it in his head. What Hamlet probably meant was just his last will. As simple as that. And yet the very idea of granting somebody your "dying voice" made Sergey shiver with excitement. Or maybe it was hunger. It was noon and he'd been working since six. Sergey went to the kitchen, made himself a sandwich of stale bread with old cheese, heated up the dregs of his morning coffee, and went back to his (Vadik's) computer.

He minimized his Virtual Grave screen and maximized Gmail. There were three new messages. One from Amazon confirming the shipment of *Pitching in the Digital Age,* one from Rachel, the girl he'd met at Fette Sau, and the last from his mother. Rachel had been out of town and now she was back and hoping to see him. Sergey didn't like her that much, but he was lonely, and Rachel was nice, so he wrote: "Sure. I'd love to!"

He braced himself before opening his mother's e-mail. Mira, who had never liked Vica, was "heartbroken" by his separation from her. Sergey couldn't possibly tell her that Vica had thrown him out because "he had loser genes," so he had just said that they had realized that they couldn't live together anymore. Mira didn't buy it. She would offer up her own reasons, a new one each week—and refute each of them right away. Is it because of money? But it never is! Is it because you were bored with each other? But that's only natural! Was she interested in other partners? Were you? But who isn't! Every time the reason would be wrong, but also a little bit right in some twisted way that made Sergey sick. This time Mira's message came hidden in an attached article with the following highlighted passage: "Most middle-aged men experience decline of sexual desire and abilities. Some try to resolve the issue by getting a new sexual partner. The crucial thing to know is that getting a new sexual partner is utterly pointless, because this decline is inevitable and irreversible."

Sergey hit Delete with a resolute motion of his index finger, as if saying no to his inevitable decline.

A new message popped up. This one was from Vica. Seeing Vica's name in his in-box never failed to disrupt Sergey's peace. Actually, any mention of Vica did that to him. There were times (almost every day) when he couldn't resist and would browse through her Facebook page, which was filled with all these uplifting posts and happy photographs. None of that joy was sincere, he knew that, yet he couldn't help squirming in pain every time. There was nothing cheery about her e-mails, however. They were always short, always businesslike. She would inform him about Eric's awful grades, or discuss a change in his visitation schedule, or ask his approval for certain home repairs. She used to start her e-mails to him with some creative greeting. At various times in their marriage they were: Privetik Sergunya, Zdravstvuyj Seryj Volchische, Hi Graywolf, Hello Mr. Graywolf, Bonjour Monsieur Loup, and Hi Furry Pup. This time it was just Hi, which was somehow worse than no greeting at all. Sergey felt a sticky heaviness in his gut, the kind he'd usually get after eating a cheap hamburger or an especially bad pizza. The message was in English, in Vica's harsh and imperfect English. He felt that he didn't have the strength to read it through. He didn't have to anyway, the few words that he managed to grasp were enough: "mediator" "no need to prolong" "separation agreement." Sergey marked the message as unread. This made Vica's name even more prominent, dominating the other messages with its bold font. He paused and hit the Delete button. Now the message wasn't in his in-box at all, as if it hadn't yet arrived. It was that easy to return to the virtual past.

Sergey went back to *Hamlet.*

That ghost was kind of nasty, wasn't he? He got the precious chance to speak with his son some more, but instead of providing him with some valuable guidance or simply saying some words of affection, he said some cruel shit about Hamlet's mother and demanded that Hamlet destroy his life by settling his father's scores. Some people were probably better left dead.

And just then he heard a melodic ring. Skype's sweet little icon appeared on his screen, a smiling female face in the frame. "Sejun Ku is calling you," the icon insisted. If it had said "Sejun Ku is calling Vadim Kalugin," Sergey might have resisted the urge to pick up, but it said "calling you." He picked up.

"Vadik?" Sejun said.

"No, it's his friend Sergey," Sergey said and turned on the video.

"Oh, Sergey! I'm happy to see you again." Sejun's bright if a little fuzzy smile confirmed the sentiment.

Sergey told her that Vadik was at work.

"But today's Friday," Sejun said. "On Fridays he works from home."

"He quit that working from home thing about a month ago," Sergey said. "It's easier for him to concentrate when he is in his office."

Sejun said that she hated to work from an office. She was doing web design for a small start-up in Silicon Valley. The work was boring, but they let her work from home.

Small talk ensued that quickly grew in size and significance.

Sergey explained why he was living at Vadik's at the moment. He said that he had lost his job and his wife.

Sejun said how sorry she was to hear that. She asked if he was dating.

He said that he hadn't been, not that much, not really, but he had met a girl at a barbecue restaurant of all places.

Sejun said that she was taking a break from dating at the moment. Wasn't dating exhausting? she asked. Especially breakups. Having to admit that you didn't like someone anymore or perhaps had never liked him that much in the first place. Having to explain yourself, having to come up with an explanation. That was draining, wasn't it?

Sergey started to tell her what went wrong with him and Vica, but he thought he detected a bored sigh on Sejun's end. Did he sound whiny, pathetic, loserlike? Oh, yes, he did. He hurried to change the subject and said that he'd been working on his app full-time, and it was going really well. In fact, he was almost finished with the prototype.

"Virtual Grave? I loved that idea!" Sejun said. Sergey blushed with pleasure because she had remembered. He told her how the app was shaping up to be completely different from its original conception. He told her how exciting that was. He quoted Hamlet's dying words.

Sejun stretched on her sofa and sighed. She seemed to be entranced.

" 'The rest is silence'?" she repeated after Sergey.

" 'The rest is silence,' " he said.

"But does it have to be?"

"Excuse me?" he asked.

Sejun removed her glasses, jumped off her couch, and assumed a stage actress's pose (chin up, straight back, hands folded on the level of her pelvis).

"The rest is silence, but does it have to be?" she recited with great feeling.

Then she put her glasses back on and smiled at Sergey.

"You can use it for your sales pitch."

Sergey stared at her, incredulous.

"Trust me, they love that cutesy shit," Sejun said and started to laugh. Sergey joined her.

They talked for fifty-two more minutes until Sejun said that she had to do some work. Only then did Sergey remember to ask her why she called Vadik in the first place.

Her brother was going to visit New York in a month, Sejun said. She wondered if Vadik would let him stay at his place. "I guess not, since you're living there?" she asked, and Sergey said, "Why not, he can sleep on the couch!" Sejun thanked him and said that she'd think about it.

Then she pressed End Call and her face vanished from the screen with an impish beep.

Sergey stared at the empty Skype screen for a moment longer: "Call from Sejun Ku, duration 02:08." There it was, the proof that he hadn't dreamed up this encounter. Was his heart really beating that fast? He took his own pulse—yes, it was.

Then he went back to the desk and he typed it in 12-point Courier New:

```
"The rest is silence, but does it have to be?"
```

Throughout the day, Sergey debated if he should tell Vadik about Sejun's call. But when Vadik finally came home, he was in such a bad mood that Sergey decided to wait. Vadik barely looked at Sergey, and instead of cooking dinner for them, he fixed himself a ham sandwich—a slab of ham on a slice of bread—and plopped on the couch in front of the TV. He watched CNN for about an hour, then made himself another sandwich and put on *The Wolverine*. Sergey had always hated fantasy, but he decided to keep Vadik company. He made himself a sandwich too—he put a few slices of onion on his— and sat down in Sejun's whimsical embroidered chair that stood next to the sofa. He thought it would be nice to sit like this, watch a movie together, eat their sandwiches. But Vadik wouldn't even look at him, wouldn't even register his presence except to wince whenever Sergey took a crunchy bite. Sergey had to admit that he hadn't felt that comfortable or that welcome at Vadik's for a while. Vadik had taken him in with such eagerness and warmth, but Sergey hadn't expected anything less, because he would've done the same for Vadik. In fact, he had done the same for Vadik. All those times when Vadik would suddenly discover that he couldn't spend a second more in a particular apartment, or with a girl he was seeing, he would come and stay at Sergey's. Not for long, just a couple of days, a week at most, until he found something new. Sergey was always happy to house Vadik, and Vica was just as eager to welcome him. Too eager, in fact. There was one time when Sergey thought that something might have happened between them, but the thought was too scary and upsetting to take any further.

Now it felt as if Vadik was getting increasingly disappointed in his company. And there was the question of money. Sergey couldn't possibly offer him any. You don't offer money to your best friend when he takes you in. Plus, Vadik knew that Sergey was sending most of his unemployment checks to Vica so that she could pay the mortgage. Sergey did try to buy groceries at least. But Vadik just wouldn't accept that. His first week at Vadik's, Sergey went shopping and came back loaded with the food that he usually bought for Vica. Every single item annoyed the hell out of Vadik.

No, he didn't eat McIntosh apples. And yes, there was a huge difference between organic and nonorganic yogurt. And nobody in his right mind would buy meat loaded with antibiotics and hormones. And Starbucks coffee wasn't even drinkable!

So, yes, it was clear, Vadik didn't like his shopping for food. So Sergey stopped doing it. But then there was the issue of toilet paper. Sergey had asked Vadik to buy the ultra-strength kind. The same brand—it wasn't more expensive, just stronger. And it wasn't like there was something wrong with Sergey's ass that it required special treatment; ultra-strong was simply better. Vadik had grudgingly agreed. But the last time he went shopping, Vadik came home with twelve rolls of something called Tenderlicious, some new brand that literally dissolved in your fingers before you even brought it to your ass. "It was on sale" was all the explanation he offered.

And what about those few times when they went out together? Sergey would reach for his wallet, but Vadik would stop him and say that he would pay for the meal. It was as if the sight of Sergey's scratched credit card embarrassed him. The worst thing was that after the meal Vadik would barely talk to Sergey and hang around the apartment with the sulky expression of somebody who had just been manipulated into doing something he didn't want to do. Lately, he wore that expression pretty much all the time.

They'd barely watched an hour of *The Wolverine* when Vadik announced that he was tired and was going to bed. He turned the TV off and left the room without bothering to ask Sergey if he wanted to continue watching.

It was all Vadik's fault that Sergey didn't tell him about Sejun. He simply didn't give him the chance.

Two days later, Sergey called Sejun to ask a few questions about the design for his app. This time he called her from his own Skype account. Sejun told him that she loved the logic and organization of the frames but hated the visual presentation. "A graveyard with tiny ghosts peeking from behind the stones? Seriously?" She found it both creepy and boring, like Walmart Halloween decorations.

This embarrassed Sergey so much that his voice went higher. He tried to explain that he didn't mean for the ghosts to be in the actual design but thought they were okay for a proto. Sejun seemed to be touched by his embarrassment. She then offered a few simple solutions to make the visuals work and suggested a good website with graphic templates.

The next time Sergey called Sejun he asked her if Virtual Grave was a good name for his app.

She said that it was morbid but biting, and biting was the most important quality for the name. Her use of the word *biting* stirred Sergey so much that he blushed. She said that when his prototype was ready, she would introduce him to her investor friend.

The calls were becoming more frequent. They would start talking about the app but would inevitably swerve someplace else, someplace personal. Sejun asked Sergey how he'd come up with the idea. He told her about the posthumous letter from his father, how he had sat in the basement reading it over and over again, trying to find some last piece of advice. He saw Sejun remove her glasses and wipe her eyes with the corner of her sleeve.

She told him that her own father never, ever talked to her. He spoke to her, he said things to her, he asked questions, he gave instructions, but they never really "talked," not when she was a child and not now. It was as if he found the idea of a conversation with his daughter incomprehensible. She said that one of the reasons she decided to move to the United States was to escape this condescending attitude that Asian men displayed to women. She wanted a Western man so that he would treat her as an equal. But here she found that the Western men who wanted to date Asian women were attracted to the idea of their servility.

"But not Vadik though?" Sergey asked. Sejun looked away from the screen. Sergey was afraid that he had made a faux pas. He shouldn't have mentioned Vadik; he should've pretended to have forgotten the fact that Sejun used to be Vadik's girlfriend.

Then she looked up at Sergey. "No," she said, "with Vadik it was different."

He wasn't misogynistic at all. But he liked her because she was strange to him. Not exotic, but strange. He knew that he would never truly understand her or she him. And that was exactly what he wanted. To be able to project whatever he wanted on to her and to be able to imagine that in her eyes he was whatever he wanted to be at the moment. And she was so lonely and weak that she almost agreed to become that for him.

One morning Sergey was sick with flu and he called Sejun from bed.

"Are you in bed?" she asked.

"Yes," he said.

"I love that lattice headboard. I was the one who picked this bed, did you know that?"

Sergey started to cough.

"Oh, poor Sergey!" she said. "I wish I was there with you, I would give you some tea."

"No, you wouldn't. You wouldn't want to appear servile."

"That's true," Sejun said. "But I could sit down on the edge of your bed and stroke your hair."

"I would give anything to feel your hand on my forehead right now," Sergey said.

Sejun smiled. Her glasses slipped down her nose when she was staring down, and she pushed them back with her index finger. She was sitting cross-legged on her couch. He could see her entire body, so her laptop must have been away, on the coffee table. She was wearing a loose black T-shirt and some sort of lounge pants. No socks, no bra. He searched for her nipples lost in the folds of her T-shirt.

"I would've tapped my fingertips on your forehead," she said, "and then I would run them down your cheeks, all the way to your mouth."

Sergey suppressed the urge to moan. "And I would have caught your finger with my teeth and pressed on it ever so gently," he said.

That first time they had sex discreetly. Sejun brought her laptop closer so that everything below her neck was hidden from view. Sergey did the same. He tried to masturbate as quietly as possible. He was hoping that Sejun was masturbating too, but he couldn't be completely sure. They kept talking the entire time.

"Oh, fuck!" Sergey finally cried, making his computer screen shake.

Sejun laughed. "Did you come?" she asked.

"Yes," he said. "What about you?"

"Oh, I came a little while ago. I was just embarrassed to tell you."

Afterward, Sergey felt feverish but insanely happy.

He went to the bathroom and aimed a perfect pale gold current into Vadik's toilet.

"Is vigorous," he said to the pearly gray tiles above the toilet. "Is brilliant. Is persistent. Is strong."

Each time they became bolder and more intimate. They would put their computers farther away to have a full view of each other's bodies, and they would wear ear- and mouthpieces to hear each other better. Her breasts turned out to be smaller than he'd thought, her hips wider. He couldn't imagine anything sexier than Sejun wearing nothing but a mouthpiece and headphones. Everything about her was endlessly exciting. Sometimes, hours after their call was over, Sergey would see his headphones lying on the table where he'd left them and just the sight of them would get him hard. She told him how smart he was, how imaginative, how handsome. She said that he looked like that actor from Truffaut's films. What was his name? Jean-Pierre Léaud? She asked him if he liked Truffaut. He said that he did. He loved Truffaut, had always preferred him to Godard. She had too, she said. She had always hated Godard.

Sergey walked around in a dazed painful state, the rest of his concerns—Vica, Eric, Virtual Grave, unemployment, Rachel, Vadik, especially Vadik—concealed from him by the smog of panic and excitement. He managed to disregard the fact that Sejun used to be Vadik's girlfriend, that they had broken up a mere two months ago, and the morality of Skype-fucking her was questionable at best. Once after Sejun's call, Sergey stayed frozen on the couch for hours, the MacBook in his lap, not doing anything, just thinking, or rather daydreaming, clinging to the details of what had just happened, as if trying to catch them all and lock them up. He was roused from his reverie by an angry call from Rachel. Apparently, they had sched-uled a date and Sergey had forgotten about it. "What happened?

Are you sick?" Rachel kept asking him, but there was no concern in her voice, just fury. And it was easier to address her fury than her concern. He said that he had met someone else.

The next morning Sejun didn't answer his Skype call. He left her several messages. She didn't reply. Three days later Sergey sent her a text: "Are you okay? I'm worried." He got a reply the next day. She wrote that she was fine but feeling "weirded out" by their relationship. "Do you want us to stop?" he asked. This time she answered right away: "Yes!"

It was very difficult to work after that, very difficult to make himself focus, but Sergey knew that his work was actually his way to salvation, so he recommitted himself with even more intensity.

Then, about a week after their virtual affair ended, the time for retribution came. One night, as Sergey was perusing the contents of Vadik's nearly empty fridge, Vadik appeared in the kitchen doorway with the iPhone in his hands. He looked confused rather than angry, but Sergey had a panicky premonition that this was going to be about Sejun.

It was.

"Look," Vadik said. "It says here that I talked to Sejun on December 18. I didn't talk to her. Was it you?"

Vadik was clearly anticipating some sort of crazy explanation. There wasn't any.

"Yes, we talked," Sergey said. "She called to ask you if her brother could stay here. I'm sorry, I forgot to tell you."

"Her brother staying here? Staying with me? Or should I vacate my own apartment to accommodate him? That girl has some nerve!"

Sergey took out a wilted lettuce and a couple of tomatoes and cucumbers. "I'm making a salad, do you want some?"

Vadik nodded. He sat down on a flimsy bar stool that looked as if it were about to collapse and put his phone down.

Sergey took a cutting board out and started slicing tomatoes. Never an easy task, and especially difficult under Vadik's stare.

"You should halve the tomatoes first," Vadik said, "and better use a serrated knife."

Sergey found the serrated knife.

"Not the cucumbers though. Never use a serrated knife on cucumbers. But you still have to halve them."

Sergey answered him with a glare and Vadik went back to playing with his phone. He looked really stupid in that tiny kitchen, perched on that tiny chair. In his white sweater with his shock of blond hair, he looked like a huge dumb parrot in a cage. If there was one thing Sergey couldn't stand, it was somebody's presence while he was cooking. Vica would always leave the kitchen when he cooked. Not that he cooked that often. But he could make cucumber and tomato salad, and a spectacular omelet. His secret ingredients were leftover cold cuts from MyEurope. A prosciutto and salami combination worked the best. He would make it for Vica, and she would always ask for seconds and proclaim it the most delicious dish in the world. "Seriously," she would say, "we should enter your omelet in contests." Too bad Vadik didn't have any leftovers. Or any eggs. Sergey felt a momentary pang of longing for Vica, but then he thought of Sejun and felt a pang of longing for her too.

"No, no, that's rosemary-scented oil. It won't do. Use the big bottle."

Sergey put the rosemary-scented oil back and reached for the big bottle.

"Wait," Vadik said, and Sergey felt like throwing the big bottle at his head. "Wait. It says here that the duration of the call was two hours and eight minutes. You couldn't have been discussing Sejun's brother for two hours, could you?"

Sergey stopped mixing the salad. He knew that one way or the other Vadik would get to the bottom of this. And the bottom of this—the fact that he had had an affair with his best friend's ex-girlfriend—suddenly seemed pretty horrible, pretty disgusting. He used to tell himself that this was not about Vadik, that this was about him and Sejun, and Vadik had nothing to do with it. Now, for the first time, he realized that in Vadik's eyes it would be very much about him.

He cleared his throat and said that Sejun and he talked.

"What did you talk about? Did you talk about me?" Vadik asked.

This suggestion offended Sergey. How typical of Vadik to think that they would have nothing to discuss except himself—such an endlessly fascinating topic.

"We talked about my app," Sergey said.

Apparently this was a mistake.

"Oh, how nice! You talked about your fantastic, super-brilliant app! Your genius app! Sejun loved your idea, I remember that. She thought it was 'brave and defiant.'"

Vadik said the last three words in a high-pitched voice that was supposed to be an imitation of how Sejun talked, but in fact it didn't sound like her at all. He jumped off the stool and stood leaning on the kitchen counter, hovering over Sergey. He was seven inches taller than Sergey, but Sergey had never been so aware of it before.

"Well, I've always thought your idea was stupid," he said. "Stupid and sick. Like freeze-drying your dead pet. No, worse than that, like freeze-drying your dead pet and making it talk."

He paused and looked at Sergey, making sure that his words registered. They did.

"Nobody wants to hear from dead people, you hear me? Nobody! It's creepy, it's horrifying. It's unbearably painful, for godsakes! I mean, yes, it's true, we all talk to our loved ones in our minds. And, yes, we all wish that they would answer. A single word of affection, of acceptance. We all need that. But what you're trying to do is not that! What people will hear is not the voice of their loved one, but the bits and pieces of that voice, the heartless morsels, a cruel parody. Listening to that voice will only make their sense of loss more acute. The person that they loved is gone. Gone! Nothing will bring him back. Nothing. Nothing. Nothing. Not God, not Fyodorov, and certainly not your fucking app. I mean, how stupid must you be not to see that?"

Sergey looked away and tasted the salad. He'd put way too much oil in it. And what kind of food was salad anyway? It would only make them hungrier.

"The only app that could possibly make sense in the face of death would be one that would cancel your entire online presence. Cancel it! Erase all your messages, delete all your posts, get rid of every trace of you. Make sure nobody could revive you, or speak in your voice, or do any other shit. Now that's the app we need. Because that's the idea of death. Death brings an absolute end. And we all should just respect that."

Sergey made a motion to go out of the kitchen, but Vadik was blocking the way.

"But you know all that, don't you?" Vadik said with a gloating expression, as if he had discovered Sergey's dirty secret.

"You don't really want to 'revive' dead people à la Fyodorov— God, what a stupid fuck he was! You don't really want to reconstruct their speeches or their souls. You're just hanging on to the idea of this app because it's the last thing, the very last thing, that you believe can pull you out of the dump, right? Right? Because if not for this app, you're done. You're stuck with being a loser forever."

And Sergey just stood there, listening to Vadik's diatribe, looking into his bowl, eating the salad, forkful after slippery forkful. He could hear and understand Vadik's words, he felt them almost like physical blows, and yet they weren't truly reaching him. He felt as if he were in the middle of a very wrong scene, a scene that wasn't supposed to be happening. He remembered feeling like this once before. He was only five or six and it was a snow day. He went out of his apartment building dressed in snow boots, a winter coat, and a thick knitted hat, mittens, and whatever, and there were older boys waiting in ambush behind a row of snowdrifts armed with snowballs. Their attack was immediate and merciless. Vicious wads of pain hitting him on the neck, on the face, on the eyes. He remembered thinking that this was not supposed to happen. These were his friends. He knew their names. They played in the sandbox together. This was wrong! So wrong that it couldn't be happening. He didn't even turn away or cover his face. He just stood there waiting until this frightening scene would disappear or be changed into something else.

"And Sejun was impressed with your idea, wasn't she," Vadik said again. Sergey still didn't say anything, but Vadik continued.

"Of course she was. Did she tell you how brilliant you were? How she was smitten with your intellect? How she was in love with your brain? How arousing your brilliance was? How she was dying for this brilliant, brilliant man to fuck her? Skype-fuck if nothing else? Oh, Sejun used to love Skype-fucking! She even preferred it to the real thing."

Sergey put the bowl on the counter and looked at Vadik. A muscle or something must have shifted in his face and Vadik caught it. His expression immediately changed from vicious and mocking to helpless and almost scared.

"Huh, so you did, didn't you?" Vadik said. There was a pleading note in his voice now. As if he were begging Sergey not to answer. "On Skype?"

Sergey pushed Vadik away and walked toward the bedroom.

"That's pathetic!" Vadik yelled at his back. "Do you know how pathetic that is?"

It didn't take him long to pack his things. Vadik had barely given him any space in the closet, so most of his clean clothes were still in his duffel bag, and he kept the dirty ones in the plastic HippoMart bags under the bed—the red fat hippo stretched even fatter by his socks and underwear. Vadik employed a complicated sorting system in his laundry hamper, so Sergey preferred not to mess with it. He zipped up his duffel bag. Put his old laptop in his sturdy backpack, pondered whether he should take the paperback of *Hamlet*, decided that he should—after all, Vadik had never returned his copy of *Hell Is Other People: The Anthology of 20th-Century French Philosophy*. He threw the book into the backpack, picked up the hippo bags, and headed to the door.

Vadik was in the living room pacing, in sync with all those passersby in the window, his facial expression a complex mix of hatred, remorse, and fear, as if he were debating whether to hit Sergey or beg him to stay.

"You don't have to go, man," he said in a more or less controlled voice. "It's all perfectly understandable. I mean, who wouldn't try to fuck his best friend's woman, given the opportunity? We are not saints, neither of us."

Vadik was about to say something else, but he stopped himself.

Sergey was standing with his back to Vadik, his right hand on the door handle. The image of a wild-eyed, disheveled Vica with that strange scratch across her cheek tramped through his mind. His heart was beating so fast that it was becoming less and less possible to breathe. He thought that if Vadik followed through and admitted that he had fucked Vica in their house on Staten Island, his heart would collapse, he would go into cardiac arrest and die.

"Oh, come on, man," Vadik finally said, and Sergey opened the door and left.

He walked briskly down Bedford Avenue, away from Vadik, away from Vadik's words, toward the place where he parked his car. A few blocks away from there, he stopped and looked around. He had no idea where to go. Some tiny cold drops fell onto his face and hands. Sergey looked up and saw that it was either drizzling or snowing. He went into the coffee shop next door, ordered a large tea, pushed his bags under the table, and sat down.

He could go back to Staten Island. Vica would have no choice but to let him in. But that would be the Vica who had thrown him out, who wanted to "get it over with," and who might have fucked Vadik. He couldn't bear to see her.

There was his mother, who would be overjoyed to let Sergey into her one-bedroom in the projects and have him stay on her "Italian" sofa. She would feed him the foods that he used to love when he was five, like rice meatballs called *ezhiki* and sweet farmer's cheese, and make him watch some endless movie on her Russian TV channel, and after the movie was over she would plague him with talk of his inevitable decline until he felt the decline in his bones.

And there was Regina, who had reacted to the news of his separation from Vica with shocking coldness. Didn't want to meet for a drink, didn't bother to answer his long letter. Still, it was impossible to imagine that she would refuse to let him stay at her place for a couple of days. He thought she should be back from Russia by now. He imagined entering her and Bob's sparkling lobby with his bulging HippoMart bags, then Bob looking at him with squeamish pity. No, that was out of the question.

His mother was the only acceptable option. Sergey braced himself. It looked like a night of Russian TV and *ezhiki.*

"I'm fucking desperate, man!" cried out the man at the adjacent table. "I can't believe Natalie just bailed on me. Now I can't go."

He had a long silky beard that probably required very expensive shampoos. His friend had no facial hair himself, but he wore an "I Love Castro" T-shirt as if to compensate.

"What about your neighbor? She could watch your cat."

"My neighbor Helen? The one who called the police on me? Twice? My music was too loud? No, thank you! She would just poison the fuck out of him."

"Why don't you leave him with a pet care service?"

"Hey, why don't you leave your child with a child care service?"

"I would. Absolutely!"

"Well, I happen to love my cat. And you know how Goebbels is crazy, he loves the apartment, he loves his fucking cat tree, he won't be happy anywhere else. And he's arthritic, poor thing. He needs his pills."

So this man had to go on a trip, Sergey thought. But there was this arthritic cat, and he couldn't leave the cat anywhere else but in his apartment. And the catsitter had fallen through. This could be his chance!

"Hey," Sergey said after he cleared his throat, "sorry, I couldn't help but overhear. I happen to be really good with cats."

The bearded man turned to Sergey and looked him over, as if trying to determine his trustworthiness.

"I'm a financial analyst," Sergey said as proof of his reliability. "I work at Langley Miles."

The bearded man seemed duly impressed.

"My wife just threw me out and I need a place to stay."

"Ouch!" the beardless man said.

The bearded man tapped his fingers on the table surface. "We're talking about six months here. I got this composers' fellowship in Rome. You can't bail on me, because I'll be in Europe."

"Six months is perfect."

They continued to discuss details and logistics, but it was clear that the thing was going to work out.

Okay, Sergey thought, a sick cat named Goebbels. This could be interpreted either as yet another unfortunate complication in his already terribly confusing life or as divine intervention—a cat savior, a redeemer cat, a knight cat on a white horse.

Chapter 9

DANCING DROSOPHILAE

T HE FLIGHT BACK TO NEW YORK TOOK NINE HOURS
and fifty-five minutes, and that was exactly how long it took
Regina to get her bearings. By the time the plane was approaching the fuzzy rabbit-shaped Newfoundland, she felt together
enough to brush her teeth and comb her hair in the plane's lavatory.
She even thought about applying some makeup. By the time they
landed, she felt almost normal. She decided that she would write
Aunt Masha a letter in which she would calmly explain why she
couldn't possibly adopt a child, that while Aunt Masha had a right
to suggest it, she certainly didn't have a right to demand it from her.
Even if Regina eventually decided to adopt a child, it would have
to be her own decision. She couldn't be either pressured or rushed
into it. She mentally composed most of that letter while she stood in
the long line at passport control. She was almost finished when the
young officer stamped her papers and welcomed her back to New
York. The last sentence came to her in the cab. "And even though
adoption is out of the question, I want you to know that Nastya can
count on our help." Yep, that was the solution. Regina would send
them money. She was sure that Bob wouldn't mind. That would
certainly make her feel less shitty. Regina wanted to send the e-mail
right away but decided that typing it all out on her phone would be
bothersome. She'd send it as soon as she got home. So as soon as she

got there, she dropped her bags at the front door and went straight to her computer. "Your message has been sent," Gmail informed her, and Regina felt instant relief. She took off her clothes, went to shower, fell onto her bed all clean and wrapped in two large towels, and slept. She woke up just as Bob entered the apartment after work. They ordered a square gourmet pizza and had a quiet dinner together, or rather it was Bob who was having dinner, while Regina just nibbled on his uneaten crusts. She was still jet-lagged and deaf in one ear after the flight, so Bob's voice sounded as if it were coming from far away. He told her that she had towel marks all over her neck and the left side of her face. He said it was charming. She smiled. Then he asked her a question she couldn't hear. "What?" she asked.

"How was your trip?" Bob asked, shaking his head because it was a pretty obvious question.

She sighed. They had Skyped every day, so there wasn't much she could add to that except of course to tell him about Nastya.

"Exhausting," she said. Bob saw that she was too tired to talk and started telling her about Dancing Drosophilae in more detail—they were definitely signing the deal with DigiSly. He thought of making his programmer Dev the head of the project. They would start with a very simple app. It would allow people to see how many "relatives" they had in various parts of the country, then they would expand it for different locations. It was going to be an amazing opportunity. Regina found it hard to concentrate on his words. "I'm sorry, honey," she said, "I'm just still out of it."

That night Regina woke up at 3:00 A.M.—10 A.M. Moscow time—nauseous with anxiety and went to check her e-mail right away. There was no reply from Aunt Masha. She checked her sent folder to confirm that e-mail was sent. It was. She wrote another e-mail to Aunt Masha asking her to confirm that she had received the first one. Regina spent the rest of the night pacing between the living room and the kitchen, switching between the sofa and their three armchairs, trying to relax. Aunt Masha was a compulsive e-mail checker and she usually answered right away. Regina must have offended her when she offered her money. Well, the hell with her, Regina thought, even as she was physically hurting with mortification. She understood now why she couldn't tell Bob about it last night. He would be ashamed for her if she told him. "What the hell is wrong with you, Regina?" he would say. "Masha asked you to take that child, to provide her with a family, with love, with protection, and you offered to send her a check instead? Offended her like that? Masha, the closest you yourself have to a family?"

No, no, she couldn't bear to tell Bob. In fact, Regina found that she could hardly look at him when he woke up that morning.

"Do you want to go to Becky's place with me?" he asked. "She wanted to show you how the renovations are going."

Regina declined, saying that she wasn't feeling well, but the true reason was that she didn't think she could stomach a parent-child lovefest now.

Bob left around eleven and Regina went to check her e-mail again. Nothing. She was starting to worry that she would never hear from Aunt Masha again.

She took the suitcase with her mother's things, put it in the middle of the living room floor, and unclasped the lock. There was an old photo album on top. Regina had seen most of the pictures many times before, but there was a thin stack of photos that she didn't remember. Her mother was in her twenties in them. Lounging on the beach. Testing the water with her toes. Splashing. Posing with some mountains in the background. She looked like a prettier version of Regina. Actually, her mother looked like Virginia Woolf a lot. They had the same dark, deeply set eyes.

There was a photo of her mother and Masha together. They stood on the beach holding hands, laughing, waving to the camera. There was a big white ship in the background. The sign in the corner read: YALTA, 1970. It was strange that her mother never mentioned that trip. Regina picked up the photo, peered at it closer. Her mother was big, dwarfing Aunt Masha, but she looked so happy.

Regina couldn't remember ever seeing her so happy. Were they lovers? Olga Zhilinskaya—straight as an arrow.

She remembered her photograph on Masha's bookshelf. Aunt Masha didn't just keep her mother's photos, she kept hers too. It suddenly occurred to her that Aunt Masha was actually doing this whole adoption thing for her, Regina, not just for Nastya. Aunt Masha cared about Regina, she wanted the best for her, and she believed that the best for her was to have a child. And in return Regina offered her money . . . Regina felt like writing to Aunt Masha and begging her for forgiveness, except that she didn't think she deserved it.

Regina put the album away and reached for the dresses. She recognized her mother's favorite: a simple silk frock with an open neck. Dark brown, almost black, with a pattern of tiny flowers. Her mother had had it for as long as Regina could remember. She had worn it at Regina's sixth birthday party. There were many guests, mostly her mother's friends. Regina thought that her mother was the most beautiful woman in the world. The tallest too. At one point Regina's mother took Aunt Masha's hand and whirled her in a waltz. The material of the dress seemed to move along with her mother's movements, making all those little flowers waltz too. Of course they were lovers. Regina couldn't understand how she hadn't seen it before.

She saw a vivid image of her mother as she stood in front of the mirror putting the dress on. She would always furrow her brow as she adjusted it so that it looked just right. Her mother was around forty in that memory. Strong, healthy. This was the first time since her mother died that Regina was able to conjure up her younger self. She was overcome with emotions that had eluded her during the cemetery visit. This was what people who had lost someone needed instead of stupid cemeteries. Virtual Suitcase. A little nook on the Web where you could store precious memorabilia: letters, photographs, videos, playlists, maps. Where you could visit and imagine the departed at their best.

Regina really needed to talk to someone. To someone who wouldn't be judgmental, who would understand and support her decision, who would be able to relieve her guilt. Who would agree with her that Aunt Masha's actions were crazy and that Regina's letter to her was the natural reaction of a sane person.

Vadik? No, not Vadik. Even if he did listen to her, he wouldn't understand. Sergey? She had been ignoring him for so long that she didn't feel that she had the right to involve him now. And then expecting a sane response from someone like Sergey was kind of crazy.

Her dad? Regina had been longing to talk to him ever since she got back from Russia. But in order to ask him anything, they would have to get reacquainted, really get to know each other. She would have to face some more unpleasant facts about her mother. Regina didn't feel that she had the strength for that.

What she really needed was to talk to a woman. Vica? Vica was a mother. Regina wasn't sure if that made her more or less capable of empathy. Would she take the child's side or Regina's? No, Vica wouldn't take Regina's side in any matter. And she was probably upset with Regina. Vica didn't have anyone in the United States and now she was going through a separation all alone. She should have called to ask her how she was, to offer her support. Several times Regina was about to dial Vica's number, but then changed her mind at the last moment. She was afraid that Vica might think that she was gloating, that their conversation would turn all awkward and wrong. Still she should've called her!

Her phone beeped. There was a message from Vadik. "Are you back? I've missed you like crazy!"

"Coffee?" she texted back.

They met at La Colombe on Lafayette.

"Finally!" Vadik said as soon as he walked into the place.

They settled at a tiny table, too tiny and too low for both of them, neither Vadik nor Regina could comfortably fold their legs. There was barely enough surface area for their coffee cups and their two chocolate croissants.

Vadik looked at her expectantly, obviously waiting for her to tell him about her trip.

What should I start with? Regina thought, pouring sugar into her cappuccino carefully so as not to disturb the beautiful foam heart. Russian politics? Russian TV? The dumb, angry madness that was catching on all over Russia like an infectious disease? But Vadik was so obsessed with trying to fit in as an American that he cared very little about Russia. She could just try to tell him about Nastya.

Vadik took a long sip of his cappuccino. Some foam got stuck in his beard. Regina reached over the table and wiped it off with her napkin. She was about to start talking when he said, "Some crazy shit has happened while you were gone."

"What?" she asked.

"Sergey and I aren't speaking anymore. I threw our precious genius out!"

"You did what? Why?"

Vadik went on a long diatribe listing Sergey's offenses, from dirty milk glasses to toilet paper to butchered Cohen lyrics.

Regina smiled. "He did that when we were dating too."

"Yes, but Sergey and I weren't dating!" Vadik said. "Sergey and I weren't having sex. I had to endure all that for nothing."

Regina shook her head in mock compassion.

It was clear to her now that they would never get to talk about her. That was Vadik for you.

But Regina wasn't angry with him. She was rather relieved that she didn't have to talk about Nastya.

"Was that all?" she asked.

"Pretty much," Vadik said. "And he was Skype-fucking Sejun."

"What?" she asked. "Your Sejun?"

Vadik nodded. He embarked on a long and pretty boring story of how he found out. Regina had to eat her chocolate croissant to keep her focus. Actually, Sergey Skype-fucking Sejun wasn't all that shocking. She remembered how Sergey always said that he liked

Sejun and how Sejun had been impressed with him and his vile Virtual Grave idea at Vadik's housewarming.

"I mean who does that? She's my girlfriend!"

Ex-girlfriend, Regina thought, but she hurried to agree with Vadik that there was no excuse. And it wasn't like it was the first time! Sergey had stolen Vadik's girlfriend before, of course: Vica. She remembered how it had taken Sergey three weeks to tell her about Vica. Three weeks! He was seeing Vica, fucking Vica, professing his love for her, while Regina, like an idiot, was making arrangements for their summer trip to Karelia!

"So you don't think I'm an asshole, do you?" Vadik asked.

He stared at Regina, expecting an answer. It was difficult for her to talk because her mouth was full of croissant—she had finished hers and had started on Vadik's.

She mumbled something incoherent that Vadik interpreted as "No."

"Okay, but it gets worse. I think I might be interested in Vica a little bit."

For this Regina had to swallow the entire soggy mass in her mouth. "What? No!"

"I know, I know," Vadik said.

"What about Vica?"

"Oh, she doesn't give a damn about me."

"Good!"

He started talking about online dating and how exhausting it was, how after a while the dating pool started to seem really small, because the same women popped up over and over again. And how he imagined that the women reacted to seeing his profile in a similar way: "Oh, that guy's still here." And how much it depressed him.

Then he looked at her expecting words of compassion.

Regina didn't say anything. She did feel sorry for Vadik, but she was annoyed too. What was it about Vica that made all these men crazy about her? And Vadik could've asked her how she was. Out of politeness if not genuine interest!

"I have to get back," she said, standing up.

They were already at the door when Vadik squeezed her in a bear hug and said that just being near her made him feel better.

Regina smiled. She could never stay mad at Vadik for long.

"Vadik," she said.

"Yes?"

"Do you think I could take care of a child?"

Vadik laughed. He reached over and flicked the croissant flakes off her scarf.

"If that involves eating a child—then definitely!" he said.

"Thanks a lot!" she said.

He had helped her without realizing it. He had confirmed that her decision was the right one.

What she did was actually honest, and noble in its honesty, Regina decided on the way back. Buoyed by self-admiration, she continued this train of thought. There were plenty of women who didn't want or need children, but only a few of them were willing to admit it. She had met so many women, both in Russia and in America, who were having children not because they wanted or needed them, but simply because they didn't want to miss out. "It's not that I wanted to have a child, but I just really didn't want to not have one," a heavily pregnant niece of Bob's told her at their Thanksgiving dinner. Well, Regina definitely didn't want a child and refused to worry about missing out. She hated the idea that a woman couldn't lead a fulfilling life unless she had children. She had managed to build an independent and rich life for herself. An enviable life. It was the unfortunate combination of her mother's death, then her marriage and emigration that just derailed it a little bit. But she could always claim it back. No more Eat'n'Watch!

Later that week she wrote to Inga and begged her for an assignment. Something nobody else wanted to translate. Anything at all. She didn't care how boring or difficult it was.

The reply came surprisingly fast. "Sure," Inga wrote without so much as a greeting, "I have just the project for you." It turned out to be a Canadian novel called *Humdrum* that had been published in English about two years earlier, been pronounced a cross between Proust and Munro, genius, and addictive, but had failed to attract enough readers. So Inga's publishing house managed to acquire it for a song. It was the story of a Canadian woman who lived somewhere in the north and had to raise her three children after her husband died of cancer.

Regina felt dizzy. Children and cancer, the two subjects that made Regina sick, and Inga knew this perfectly well. She must still be really pissed at her. Well, she wouldn't give Inga the satisfaction of knowing how much that hurt.

"Perfect!" Regina answered and immediately purchased the book on her tablet.

The narrator's name was Cheyenne. The book started with a description of making porridge that went on for thirty pages. Eight of them were devoted to removing a bug that had gotten into the pot and drowned there. Reading the book, Regina felt as if she were the bug drowning in the pot of oatmeal, but the feeling was oddly pleasant. And then the three kids appeared. With their nasty habits, their constant illnesses, their silly words. They took up so much space, filled it with so much weight and presence, that it felt suffocating. Yet Regina felt that if she abandoned the book, her entire fantasy of a fulfilling life would crumble. She was tempted to give up, bouncing between her desk and the couch in front of the TV, mixing or sometimes supplanting work with Eat'n'Watch, but she always returned to the book.

About three weeks into *Humdrum,* as Regina was finishing an especially complicated passage and was about to reward herself with a new episode of *Spies Are Us* and some leftover chili, an e-mail from Aunt Masha popped up in her in-box. She instantly felt a terrible pressure just above her eye sockets. Her finger hovered over the Enter button, unable to go ahead and press it. Just then her microwave beeped announcing that the chili was ready. She considered going to the kitchen to retrieve her bowl first, then became appalled by her cowardice and pressed the button. The pressure in her head was so bad that she could hardly understand the words. She could see that it wasn't aggressive though. She could tell that the overall tone was polite.

It wasn't warm, far from it, but it was definitely civil. Regina made herself read it.

Aunt Masha appreciated Regina's generous offer, but there was no need for it, because she had just found a very good family for Nastya. The husband was a lawyer and the wife was a high school physics teacher and a gardening nut. They had a beautiful dacha on the lake about two hours away from Moscow. They were smart, kind, wonderful people. They were as crazy about Nastya as she was about them.

What a relief. What a relief, Regina thought. I'm so happy.

The microwave beeped again, demanding her attention, but Regina ignored it. She walked into the bedroom, got into bed, turned to the wall, and started to sob.

She must have dozed off because an urgent buzzing in her pelvic area roused her. She found her phone in the pocket of her cardigan and checked the message. Her calendar app was reminding her that she had a "Dinner with Bob's team" today. They were celebrating the official start of their Dancing Drosophilae project. Regina groaned. She could barely tolerate Bob's team on a normal day, but today it would be torture. And she couldn't possibly skip the dinner. It was really important to Bob that she go to these dinners, much more important than her fitting in with his family. She could kind of understand that. Bob's team was his essence in a way that his family wasn't. His family was a given, but it was he who had picked the team, created the team, lived and breathed with the team. Regina had never felt more alienated from Bob than she did at these dinners. It wasn't just that the team members seemed like aliens to her and she could never find anything to talk to them about; her worst concern was that Bob would inevitably turn into a stranger. He couldn't help but look at her through the eyes of his team, and through the eyes of his team she was a sorry sight. A gawky, homely, expensively but still unflatteringly dressed, gloomy, tongue-tied woman. Bored. That was probably the worst. Bob took it as personal affront if she looked bored when they discussed business.

She sent a quick text to Vadik to ask if he would be there tonight. She needed all the support she could get to survive the dinner. Vadik replied: Yes, of course. He was part of Bob's team, wasn't he?

She took a shower and put on "safe" clothes that weren't striking but never looked awful either. It was her face that was the problem. Her skin was blotchy and creased and her eyes were so puffy that she could barely open them. Cucumber mask. She had heard some women (possibly Vica) mention that it helped reduce swelling. She did a quick Google search and found a video of a Korean woman dressed in a black bra and panties grating a whole cucumber and slapping it onto another woman's face. Regina rushed into the kitchen. Luckily there was a cucumber in the fridge. She grated it, but since there was nobody to slap it onto her face, she simply held her breath and pressed her face against the cold green mound on her cutting board. She ate the couple of cucumber shavings that got into her mouth and decided that she felt better, far from great but ready to face the team.

The restaurant that Bob chose, Borghese, was everything that Regina hated about New York restaurants. The decor resembled a library/dining room/wine cellar in a medieval castle. There were cavernous hallways, antique wine barrels, and shelves filled with old books. While Regina had to admit that it did evoke the life of medieval nobility, why would a medieval nobleman eat in a library or read in his wine cellar? The hostess led Regina through the labyrinth of tables all the way to the back. The place was nearly empty. There were just a few couples here and there, looking bored and cold. They were clearly outnumbered by the army of snotty-looking and impeccably attired waiters, eyes trained on their unprotected customers. They reminded Regina of the birds in the Hitchcock movie.

She saw Bob in the very back presiding over a long table aligned

212 · LARA VAPNYAR

with benches rather than chairs. Across the table from him were three ethnically diverse men. Bob had told Regina that he liked to hire immigrants because they were both brave enough and naive enough to tackle impossible tasks.

Bob's men were sitting with their backs to Regina, but it was easy to recognize them. The widest and most relaxed back with a lush silk-clad muffin top belonged to Laszlo Zelahy, Bob's CEO, the man with whom Bob went "way back." He didn't have a perfect athletic body like Bob's, but he seemed just as comfortable in his own skin. The shortest, skinniest, and tensest back belonged to Nguyen Tan, Bob's director of marketing, who was very much into martial arts and claimed that he could break a TV with his little finger— Regina planned to take him at his word one of these days. Not now though, not while she still cherished her TV so much. The longest, slightly awkward back belonged to Dev Mazoomdar, the most brilliant of Bob's programmers. Vadik disagreed that Dev was all that brilliant, saying that all he had was an incredible ability to focus. He burrowed into his work as if it were a tunnel. But perhaps that was what brilliant meant, Regina thought. Back when she worked in Russia, she had to have a truly amazing ability to burrow. Did that make her brilliant too?

Vadik wasn't there yet. Regina sighed.

Bob waved her over. Regina waved back and put on a bright smile. Laszlo, Nguyen, and Dev all made an honest attempt to stand up and greet her, but since that involved moving the bench back, which required excellent coordination from the three of them, they decided not to bother. They greeted her by raising and twisting their bodies. "Hi, guys," Regina said, making her way to Bob's side of the table.

"Honey," she said, but Bob raised his finger to shush her. Bob was deep in a wine list that looked as thick as *Infinite Jest,* and he was not to be disturbed. Bob had taken not one but three different wine classes, so he knew his wine. One of the waiters brought over the bread. Regina took a piece, dunked it into the tiny dish of olive oil, and started to chew. The bread was good, but Regina found that she couldn't enjoy it. Something was missing and she knew exactly what that was. The TV screen. She looked around, hoping to spot ESPN at the bar—no such luck. Instead, there was a gloomy-looking pianist in the corner tapping his finger against the closed top of his instrument. Regina was itching to be entertained. She raised her eyes to the three men across the table from her. All were hopeless at conversation. Dev never spoke. She could possibly prod Nguyen to talk about martial arts, but why would she want to do that? And Laszlo was studying her himself, at a loss as to what to talk to her about. A gloomy Russian woman like her.

"Some day, huh?" he finally said. "Freezing!"

"Yeah," Regina answered with a too-wide smile. She had had to learn how to smile when she got to the U.S., but she couldn't calibrate her smiles yet.

Bob was now talking to the sommelier, and she knew better than to disturb him. She knew his main goal was not to pick the perfect wine for his dinner but to impress the sommelier, to make him realize that this squarely built bald man knew his wine better than most people, and definitely better than the sommelier himself. The sommelier answered with a respectful smile, but Regina couldn't help but see some disgust underneath it. "You think I care, buddy?" he seemed to be saying from behind that mask of politeness. Regina turned away, embarrassed for Bob. The desire to watch TV was getting overwhelming.

"Taste it!" Bob said when the sommelier poured a trial splash into Bob's glass.

"Why?" Regina asked.

"Just taste it," Bob insisted.

"I can't even tell white from red with my eyes closed! Why would I taste it?" Regina asked.

The sommelier snickered and quickly covered it with a cough.

Now it was Bob's turn to be embarrassed. He nodded to the sommelier to fill everyone's glasses and gave Regina a long, displeased look.

"You have something on your face," he whispered. "On your cheek, closer to your right ear."

Regina touched her face and found a few damp slivers of cucumber. She removed them with a furtive glance at the men. Fortunately, they were too polite to show that they'd noticed anything.

"Well, for what it's worth, I think the wine is really good," Laszlo said and drained his entire glass. And just then the hostess appeared at the table followed by a sweaty, rumpled Vadik. Regina could never understand why seeing Vadik—simply catching a sight of him—never failed to make her feel more cheerful and relaxed.

"Vadik!" Regina exclaimed, and Bob winced. It was not that he didn't trust Vadik and her together—it was Sergey who worried him, because Bob knew that they used to date in Russia. It was just that Regina's friendship with Vadik made him feel left out. Bob was especially offended by the fact that Vadik and Regina couldn't help whispering in Russian whenever they sat together at team dinner parties. "You don't have to whisper, you know," Bob said to her once, "I don't understand Russian anyway."

Vadik knew that, so he squeezed in and sat on the back bench next to Bob, not Regina.

"Sorry I'm late," Vadik said, "I had to take care of something."

"Girl troubles?" Bob asked.

"Something like that," Vadik said.

The four other men sighed in support.

The food at Borghese was really exquisite—a salad of chanterelles and lamb tongues, veal brains in pistachio crust—but Regina found that she couldn't enjoy any of it. And most of the conversation at the table was too technical for her to understand.

They had all tested their genomes with Dancing Drosophilae just to see how it worked. The results provided them with fun facts about their genetic diseases and heritages. Bob had tried to persuade Regina to get tested too, but she'd refused.

"Why do I need an app to find people with the same genome? I can just look around for people with the same nose," Regina had said to Bob then. Now she felt compelled to repeat it for everybody at the table.

Laszlo chuckled, but Bob looked at her with displeasure.

"Regina, not everybody has a prominent nose like yours," Vadik said.

Now it was Bob's turn to chuckle. He slapped Vadik on the back and said, "That's true, my friend, that's true."

What the hell, Vadik? Regina thought. Apparently he chose to pick his boss's side over hers.

"Look at my forehead though," Laszlo said. "I have an unusually low forehead, don't you think?"

They all looked. He did have a pretty low forehead as well as a pretty heavy brow ridge that hung over his face like an awning over a terrace.

"That's because I'm 3.1 percent Neanderthal, which is a very high percentage."

"I'm 2.6 Neanderthal," Bob said.

"We're 2.8," Nguyen and Dev chimed in.

"I'm 2.1," Vadik said.

"So little? It's because you're Russian. Russians are descended from bears, not Neanderthals," Laszlo joked.

Everybody laughed immoderately and then they turned to stare at Regina. It was her turn to share her Neanderthal percentage.

"I didn't take the test," she said.

"She didn't take the test," Bob confirmed.

"But why?" Laszlo asked.

"I didn't want to know the results. Definitely not the medical ones."

"Even though her mother died from a genetic disease," Bob said.

Thank you so much, Bob! Regina thought. Let's share my family's medical history with your goddamn team. She had a momentary urge to get back at Bob by telling everyone about his obsession with his supposedly Tudor lineage, but she decided that that would be too mean.

They were all still looking at her expectantly.

"First of all, we are not sure if my mother's cancer was genetic," Regina said, her voice rising, "and even if it's confirmed that I do carry that gene, there is only a fifty percent chance that I'll develop that type of cancer and die. If I test positive, fifty percent is not enough to do grueling preemptive surgery, and I don't want to walk around with the knowledge that there is a very good chance I will die the same death that my mother did. And if I test negative, imagine my shock when at some point some other horrible cancer gets me anyway. Or even the same cancer, just not the genetic form."

The word *cancer* made Laszlo and Dev put their forks down and listen to her. Regina hated that. Hated the attention. She wished she had done the stupid test and could just share the amount of bear or Neanderthal in her blood so that they could move on.

"You have a dark mind, don't you?" Laszlo asked. Bob nodded eagerly as if to say "Didn't I tell you?"

"My father was from Eastern Europe too. Boy, was he dark!" Laszlo said.

"I guess we have to blame the bear gene for that!" Vadik said. Everybody laughed. Regina felt grateful for a moment, but Bob wasn't giving up.

"This is not a question of darkness!" Bob said. "It's about whether you're willing to take charge of your life or not. By refusing the test, you're refusing responsibility."

"But my point is that we can't be in charge of our lives anyway," Regina said.

Bob just shook his head, and everybody else decided that it was wiser to leave Regina alone.

They brought in the second course. But now Regina was simultaneously too rattled and too bored to even attempt to eat. The silverware was too heavy. The act of cutting bits of food and lifting them to her mouth was exhausting.

Bob's team continued discussing their genomes. Apparently, the shape and position of your earlobes could point to some genetic diseases. A large percentage of people with attached earlobes suffered from diabetes, while "danglers" tended to be stronger and healthier.

"I have one of each," Nguyen said. They took turns examining his earlobes.

Regina fought the urge to yawn.

Bob gave her a look. He wasn't stupid or insensitive. He could see how bored Regina was. So bored that she hated him a little bit. He was hurt. He was sad. He was disappointed. And not just momentarily disappointed—he was getting disappointed in their marriage. Why on earth had they ever thought that they could be happy together?

"Immortality!" Bob said suddenly. "Exactly! That's exactly what I was talking about."

Immortality? Regina must have missed the moment when they switched to that topic. If Vadik had been sitting next to her, she would have just asked him what was going on in a Russian whisper. She couldn't possibly ask Bob and let him know she wasn't listening.

Dev, who caught her puzzled expression, leaned over to explain: "We are talking about your friend's app idea."

"Acting from beyond the grave is bullshit," Bob was saying. "True immortality is all about passing on your genetic material."

Regina nodded absently, but then the meaning of his words dawned on her. She wouldn't be able to pass on her genetic material, so according to Bob, she would be denied immortality. Now that was horribly unfair! Regina realized that she was the only one at the table who didn't have children. Bob had his wonderful daughter. Laszlo had four children. Dev had two little boys. Nguyen's wife was pregnant. Even Vadik had a biological child in Russia, even if he had no contact with him or her.

Regina thought of her mother sitting her at the table and showing her all those family photographs, telling her stories, teaching her how to read, teaching her to understand what she read, to feel what she read. And little Regina touching those buttons, each of which used to belong to someone in her family, so every time she pressed her finger to one it was as if she had made a momentary connection with a long-dead family member. It wasn't her inability to pass on her genetic material that was devastating; it was her inability to pass on who she was. Then Regina thought of Nastya playing with the buttons and felt a sharp-edged lump in her throat. She had to make an effort not to cry.

Finally the dinner ended, the bill was paid, good-byes were said, and everybody was headed home. Laszlo had ordered Uber, and the car appeared instantly out of nowhere and whisked him away as if this were a spy movie. Nguyen unshackled his bike and rode off, looking small and defiant with his genetically different ears and powerful little finger. Dev and Vadik descended the steps of the nearby subway entrance. Dev was taller than Vadik, but that could've been because Vadik's back was stooped. Regina thought Vadik would kiss her good-bye, but he didn't. So now Regina and Bob were on their own.

"Shall we walk home?" Bob asked. Regina nodded. It was cold but not freezing like Laszlo said. February in New York was actually warmer than November in Moscow. They were walking in silence, but not in peace. Regina could almost hear Bob's thoughts brewing in his head. He was mentally listing the offenses she'd made through the dinner, sorting through them, choosing which one to call up first. The indelicate pants that didn't fit? The fact that she screamed with delight when she saw Vadik? Her yawning? Her refusal to take the test? Her haughtiness when she explained why she didn't want to take it? Her being on the verge of tears for no reason? She walked, looking down, listening to the ringing sound her high-heeled boots made against the cobblestones, waiting to be chastised like a child.

"Regina," Bob finally said. That alone showed how pissed he was, because he never, ever addressed her by her name unless he was really angry. "Have you ever asked yourself why I take you to these dinners?"

"Yes, I have. Actually, I was just asking myself that earlier tonight," Regina replied.

"And what was your conclusion?"

"I don't know why."

They stopped walking and were standing in the middle of the sidewalk facing each other.

"So you think this is some sort of punishment, right? Making you sit through a boring dinner like this?"

"Punishment? I'm not a child."

"Then stop behaving like one! You kept rolling your eyes like an angry teenager. My daughter used to do that when she was fourteen. Fourteen, Regina! You're thirty-nine."

"I'm aware of how old I am, but thank you."

They both looked and sounded like actors in a play. Standing in the middle of this clean dark street. In the light of the streetlamp. Fighting. Regina imagined Bob wearing a beard and a hat à la Henry the Eighth. She snickered.

"Yeah, that's right," Bob said. "You roll your eyes and you laugh! I take you to these dinners to bring us closer, damn it! To help you understand what I do, to get you excited by what I do. I'm clearly failing to excite you. I thought maybe if my guys talked about our projects, you would find it more stimulating."

Bob did sound like an actor onstage, but he was also sincere; Regina knew that he was. And he was right on a lot of counts.

He did try to bring them closer. He did try to understand her friends, to read her favorite books. He even took some Russian lessons. He stopped with his Russian though, because Regina kept laughing every time he said *spasibo*. She couldn't help it. He pronounced it as "spasybo," which came out strangely soft and touchingly funny.

"You know my therapist tells me to bury my father," Bob said.

Regina groaned.

"Yes, I know, I know. You hate therapy. Therapy is self-indulgent. It's for dumb Americans, right? Russians are so far above it, right?"

"I just don't see the use. How can anybody know me better than I know myself?"

"The point of therapy is to make you do the job of knowing yourself. It's your responsibility to know yourself, but you do have to work at that."

"And I don't?"

"You don't. You're still wallowing in your mother's death. Look at you, Regina. Ever since you came back from Russia, you spend your days looking through your mother's things. You started working, that's great. Let's hope it lasts. But you barely pay attention to anything else. Your mother died two years ago! It's time to get over it. Regina, you need to bury your mother. Bury your mother and get on with your life."

Regina looked up, imagining huge billboards in front of them, rising up, getting closer, all with the words: BURY YOUR MOTHER!

Something in her expression seemed to alarm Bob.

"Honey, I'm sorry," he said. "I didn't mean to hurt you."

He put his arms around her as if shielding her from pain. It always amazed Regina how much physical touch mattered. Bob felt warm, Bob felt big, Bob felt kind. Perhaps she did love him after all.

"BOBCAT," SHE SAID LATER, when they were getting ready for bed.

"Yes, baby."

"I need to tell you something. It's about Russia."

Bob tensed. He asked her to wait, then went to the living room. He returned wearing his eyeglasses and carrying two tumblers of whiskey. He didn't get into bed but sat down in an armchair and handed one of the tumblers to her. Regina had to sit up and cover herself too.

"Go on," he said, staring into his drink.

Shit! Regina thought. The way she said it must have made him think that she had had an affair.

"No, no, it's not that!" she hurried to say. "It's about this little girl I met there."

Bob took a big swig and looked at her curiously.

Regina told him the whole story about Aunt Masha and Nastya.

Bob listened patiently, not uttering a word except to exclaim "Oh, Regina!" when she told him that she had offered Aunt Masha money.

"But she is bluffing, right?" he asked after Regina finished the story.

"What do you mean?"

He swirled his empty glass, making the remaining ice cubes clink. Regina took a long sip of hers.

"Your Aunt Masha. She couldn't have possibly found another family that fast."

This hadn't even occurred to Regina.

"She couldn't?" she asked. She felt insanely relieved.

"Of course not," Bob said. "Let's go to sleep now. We can talk about it tomorrow."

"Honey," she whispered.

"Yes, baby."

"Could you please say 'spasibo'?"

Bob sighed.

"Please?"

"Spa-sy-bo."

And Regina laughed, kissed Bob on the neck, and turned to her side of the bed.

Chapter 10

FIGHT IT! BEAT IT!

"GET UP," VICA SAID AND PATTED ERIC ON HIS WARM, sticky shoulder.

He moaned and turned away from her. It had become such a pain to wake him up in the morning. There was a Three Musketeers wrapper stuck in his blanket and a Nintendo DS under his pillow. He must have been up half the night playing and munching. Vica suspected that it was Sergey's mom, Mira, who had supplied the candy. It used to be Sergey's job to control his mother's whimsical grandparenting. Now Vica couldn't complain to Sergey anymore. She couldn't say anything to Mira either, because she relied so heavily on her help.

Mira would arrive at 7:00 A.M. every day so that she could feed Eric breakfast and walk him to the school bus, then she would wait for him to come home to feed him her elaborate meals. Mira wasn't very good at being neat. There would be a small pile of dirty dishes in the sink, puddles of compote on the floor, and grease splattered on the stove. Mira wasn't very good at overseeing homework either—Vica would come home and find none of Eric's assignments completed. She was almost grateful now that Eric hadn't taken the test to get into the Castle—he barely managed the workload of his public school.

"Get up!" Vica repeated, and this time Eric raised his head off the pillow and opened his eyes. Light brown and perfectly round. The eyes of a frightened cat.

"Grandma here?" he asked.

"Any minute now."

Vica learned to time her departure with Mira's arrival to avoid her mother-in-law's incredulous look, meant to convey that Vica's decision to separate from Sergey was shocking at best, criminal at worst.

So as soon as Mira entered, Vica was at the door and rushing to the express bus stop. She had exactly one second to say hello and not a second more to hear Mira's reply.

Vica made it to the stop just as the bus was pulling in with its wheezing, groaning, and farting noises. She paid her fare and went straight to the middle to take her favorite seat on the right side by the window. Vica loved the hour-long bus ride. The seats were high and stately. The microclimate was always perfect, it was never too hot or too cold, even in the worst weather. And this was the place where Vica could have her precious alone time, where she could work on Virtual Grave and dream and plan her life undisturbed.

So much has changed in these last few months, Vica thought while applying mascara. She had to acquire the skill of putting on her makeup on the bus to save time. First of all, she had finally stopped thinking about Sergey all the time. She no longer had recurring dreams about him. She no longer mistook strange men on a street for Sergey. She no longer tortured herself with regret. She still wasn't one hundred percent sure that separation was the right thing to do, but what was done was done. She had consulted with a mediator about their separation agreement. The mediator had advised her to just get it over with. She had accepted her upcoming divorce as a fact. And she had made a profile for herself on Hello, Love!

Online dating was interesting, very different from what she used to know. Back when Vica last dated, the process was dreamily slow, like a Victorian novel. Vica would fantasize meeting a romantic stranger, she would wait and hope and look for him at a party, on a street, on a subway, in a cafeteria, in a college library. Then just as she stopped dreaming and waiting she would meet somebody. And then there would be a hopeful anxiety, and anticipation, and more dreams now centered around that particular man. And then her favorite part—trying to solve the puzzle of that man's feelings and thoughts, reading letters, analyzing words, interpreting stares, reliving touches.

Now the slow Victorian-novel part was out. If anything, dating resembled a TV series, the stupid kind that Regina liked to watch. The plot was fast-paced but predictable; there wasn't enough time to explore interesting situations or to properly develop the characters.

Online men came in packs of three or four or more. She would plan a date with one of them, while answering a message from another, while browsing to find somebody better. There always was somebody who seemed better even though Vica wouldn't have been able to explain what "better" even meant. A better human being? A better lover? A better fit? It was the seeming endlessness of choices that filled Vica with panic. Thankfully, she had her two dating coaches: Vadik and pretty Liliana from work. When she found a guy she thought she liked, she ran his profile by her coaches. Both Liliana and Vadik warned her not to get too attached. "Because, you know," Liliana said, "he's on Hello, Love!, so he is seeing other women too."

The most recent guy's name was Franc. He was thin, wiry, French Canadian, with those European movie-star features that Vica liked so much. He said that he worked as a freelance architect, but he wouldn't tell Vica what his current project was. That was okay—she didn't tell him where she worked either. The mention of a cancer hospital wouldn't put anybody in the mood for love. Franc's only apparent flaw was that he was deaf in one ear—the effect of a mysterious autoimmune disease triggered by stress. But that was just a charming detail, not a real problem, especially in light of how attractive he was. They went to bed after the first date. Well, actually, Vica wasn't sure that it had been the right thing to do.

"How soon should I sleep with a guy?" she had asked Liliana.

"If you like him?" Liliana asked.

"Of course, if I like him! Why would I sleep with him if I didn't?"

"Oh, many reasons, many reasons," Liliana said.

"So when is it okay to sleep with a guy I like?" Vica asked again.

"Third date, I guess. If you do it on the second date, you would seem too eager. On the first date, you'd be a huge slut. And if you wait past the third date, there won't be a fourth one."

Vadik had a conflicting opinion. "If there is anything that guys hate it's when women are too calculating. I want a woman to come to bed with me because we're crazy about each other, because we both are dying to fuck, not because today happens to be the right date. And another thing that guys hate is when women present sex as this favor to a guy. There is nothing more off-putting."

So Vica decided to go with her own intuition. She went to bed with Franc on their first date. It was awkward, but it was fun. She didn't find seeing and touching a strange dick as repulsive as she'd feared. And soon she and Franc started seeing each other a couple of times a week, usually on weekends, sometimes after work, usually at his place.

Vica let out a little moan thinking of the weight of Franc's body on hers, of going under, disappearing beneath him. A woman who sat across the aisle from her eyed her suspiciously. Vica straightened her back and turned away toward the window.

Vica even told her mother about the really nice man she was seeing. He gave her a La Perla slip for her birthday. She'd been dreaming of a La Perla slip for ages! It must have cost at least two hundred dollars, unless he had gotten it on sale. He said he wanted their relationship to be serious. He was eager to meet Eric. Vica meant to reassure her mother, she meant to show her that she was okay, that her life was good and only getting better, but her mother, usually so tough, started to cry.

As if to banish her mother from her thoughts, Vica took a small leather notebook out of her bag and started to work on her Virtual

Grave proposal. She had so many ideas. If only she could have some real time to work on them. Vica did wonder if what she was doing was wrong. Virtual Grave was Sergey's idea after all. It belonged to him even if he wasn't doing anything about it. She had tried to talk to Vadik about it, but Vadik had tensed and said that Sergey had moved out and they weren't speaking. He refused to tell her why. She decided that she'd talk to Sergey once the proposal was ready.

"BETTER PROTECTION FOR your social media accounts after you die," she wrote. "Nobody should be allowed to post anything under your name."

Her approach to this app was so much better than Sergey's. In her version, customers would work on their own posthumous online presence while they were still here. They would be able to prepare for the time when they no longer would be. Having to work on that would actually help to prepare them for death itself. Alleviate some of the fear. She wondered what Ethan would think about that. Perhaps she could ask him that when he stopped to chat with her next time. Vica wondered if he had an appointment today. Last week he'd tweeted:

> ethan grail @etgrail · Mar 12
> I'm so tired of these f——g tests! But at least I get to chat with my favorite green-eyed nurse. #PerksOfCancer
> 343 retweets 879 favorites

"Ultrasound technician," Vica mentally corrected him.

She really wanted to talk to him about Virtual Grave. Her app was supposed to help people prepare. That was exactly what Ethan wanted. A thought about Ethan's money crept through Vica's mind like an ugly slug. What if he liked the idea so much that he offered to invest in it? He would be the ideal investor. He was both wealthy and high profile. Vica imagined the headline: Ethan Grail Invests in an App That Grants You Virtual Immortality on the Brink of His Own Death.

The shame of having thought about that made Vica wince. She put her notebook down and looked out the window.

Staten Island seen from the bridge was at its most beautiful. Gone from view were the car dealerships, run-down storefronts, and stretches of cemeteries; all you could see were the magnificent green hills, the stretches of sand, the ocean, and the gentle contours of the Manhattan skyline on the horizon. The city looked pale, ethereal, and seemingly unreachable, yet Vica knew that in a mere forty minutes the bus would be right in the middle of it, squeezing down the loud, jam-packed streets between the looming robust buildings that were actually anything but ethereal.

The Bing Ruskin Cancer Center took up several blocks and was growing with impressive speed. There were three new construction sites visible from the bus stop. There were several hotels for patients and their families who came for treatments. There was a huge medical-supply store that sold everything from wheelchairs to chemo hats. There was even a grocery store that specialized in whatever items were touted as cancer fighting at the moment. This rampant capitalist ingenuity filled Vica with both disgust and awe. No commercial possibilities of sickness and death were overlooked there. The only thing that was missing was posthumous care. She thought that if she ever succeeded in creating her version of Virtual Grave, Bing Ruskin would be the very place to market it. Right now its services ended when its patients' lives did, but it didn't have to stop there. Why not keep making money off patients even after they were dead?

The building that housed the radiology department of BR was two blocks away from the bus's second stop in midtown. It took Vica exactly six minutes and twenty seconds to get there. As always, there was a line of large gray vans by the entrance. They belonged to a company that brought in Medicaid patients from Brooklyn and Queens. All the drivers were Russian and they knew that Vica was too, so they liked to chat her up whenever she passed them. One of them, Tolik, always offered her a treat—a Russian candy or a handful of sunflower seeds, or once even a dill pickle.

There he was in the driver's seat of his van. Fat, sweaty, with a wide smile half hidden behind his long bushy mustache.

"Hey, Vicusha!" he yelled, blowing a raspberry in her direction. Tolik liked to behave like an idiot, but at times he would say something that made Vica think of it for days. He had once shown her the route map for his bus with the stops where he was supposed to pick up patients marked with black asterisks. "See what I got?" he had asked. "The cancer map of Brooklyn."

This time he just gave her a candy called Belochka, Vica's favorite, chocolate and nuts with a little squirrel on the wrapper.

The lobby of BR radiology was enormous and filled with light. There was a fountain in the middle with a few little fish in it. In the corner behind the fountain was a small group of teenage girls in green cheerleader outfits practicing their routine.

Fight it,
Beat it,
Go all out to Defeat it!

Christine had told Vica that the girls were juniors from expensive private schools who thought that volunteering at a cancer hospital would look good on their college applications. They were part of the new emotional health program.

Vica winced at the girls and walked down the long hall to the elevator. Once inside she was greeted by the words BING RUSKIN #1! And her own smiling face. Last year, Vica had been picked as one of the eight employees to represent the diverse population of Bing Ruskin on a poster. Vadik said that they picked her because she was the prettiest one. But Vica thought it was because she was one of the few radiology technicians who was white. The administration didn't want to support the cliché that most of the doctors at Bing

Ruskin were white, most of the nurses Hispanic, and most of the technicians black (even though this was certainly true), so for the poster they had decided to include one black and one Indian doctor, two Asian nurses, and Vica—a white radiology technician. They were all holding something that looked like a blown-up business card that said BING RUSKIN RATED #1! Vica had to reach for the card from behind the substantial shoulder of Dr. Gupta, so it appeared as if she was pinching rather than holding it. Her smile didn't come out that great either. "You look rather menacing here," Vadik said when she showed him the photo. "Vica Morozova—the face of cancer!" But then he asked her for a copy so that he could hang it up in his bedroom. Vica didn't know whether he was joking or not. Vadik had been acting weird lately. Reluctant to help her with Virtual Grave, annoyed when she asked him for dating advice, vague on the subject of Sergey. Not that she cared. Sergey was on his own now.

Sometimes the center's personnel or even patients riding the elevator with her would recognize her from the poster.

"That's you, isn't it?" they'd ask, excited, as if they had just encountered a celebrity. "Bing Ruskin number 1!" she'd respond and pump her fist in the air, and they would laugh with delight. Vica hated when that happened, so she tried to stand in the darkest corner of the elevator. But from there her stare would be inevitably drawn to the elevator's board where the passing floors were being lit with a soft neon glow, as if illuminating everything that might go wrong with a person. Cancers of the digestive system, urological cancers, gynecological cancers, and the scariest of them all— pediatric cancers. The radiology department was on the ninth floor, with medical radiology offices on the right side and diagnostic radiology on the left. The walls of the entire hallway were covered with inspirational quotes. Her least favorite was by Willa Cather: "Where there is great love, there are always miracles." The quote itself was okay, but it struck Vica as cruel and unfair in this setting. What about terminal patients? There weren't any miracles for them. Did that mean that the love in their lives wasn't great enough?

Her favorite quote belonged to John Cheever: "My veins are filled, once a week with a Neapolitan carpet cleaner distilled from the Adriatic and I am as bald as an egg. However I still get around and am mean to cats." Vica thought that if she ever got cancer she would find this sort of quote uplifting. She would make sure to be mean to cats.

It was hard not to become morbid at her job. Just the other day one of her patients said to her: "I used to think cancer was this singular tragedy, something exclusive, something shameful, like an embarrassing curse. Now I think it's kind of inevitable, like one of the expected phases in your life. You get born, you go to school, you get a job, you get married, you get cancer, you die."

Vica shared it with Christine. "Well," Christine said, "if that's how it is, then at least we're better off than most people, because we know what to expect."

There weren't any patients yet. Early mornings were usually slow, but Vica knew that the hallways would get crowded by ten thirty and overcrowded right after the lunch break.

Liliana was sitting in an armchair in the waiting room, leaning over a stack of postcards.

"Hey, Vica, do you know how to spell *condolences, c-e-s* or *s-e-s?*"

"With the *c,* I think," Vica said. "Why?"

"I'm writing Dr. Jewell's notes. To the families of the dead ones. They have to be handwritten. You know how people like a personal touch."

"So she picked you to do her personal touch for her?"

"I have the best handwriting!" Liliana bit on the tip of the pen. "You know what, I don't trust *condolences,* I better stick with 'Sorry for your loss.' "

Vica reached over to pour herself some coffee, but Liliana stopped her. "That one's empty. They have fresh coffee in the treatment lounge."

The adjacent lounge was reserved for the patients waiting for radiotherapy. Vica peeked in hoping to see Ethan. It was mostly empty too, save for a Pakistani family and a thin young woman in a blue cancer hat slumped in a corner chair.

Vica finally found coffee at the machine right outside of Eden's beautiful office. She could see Eden at her desk going through some papers, taking tiny bites of something that looked like an almond croissant. Vica tried to pour her coffee as quickly as possible so Eden wouldn't notice her. It was important not to let Eden see her, because she might have yet another interpreter's job for Vica. They never had enough official interpreters, and the first place they looked for help was in radiology with its multi-ethnic, mostly immigrant staff. Vica was usually eager to be useful, always volunteered her services, but the last incident about five months ago was just too hard to bear.

Dr. MacEarchern from the fourth floor had been looking for a Russian speaker. A stately, patrician woman with the features and demeanor of a purebred horse, she was looming over her desk, casting shadows on the papers in front of her. She was also heavily pregnant. For some reason, Vica found this disturbing.

The two people sitting across from the doctor in the narrow armchairs moved very close together; they looked the very opposite of patrician. They were both in their late seventies, small, round-faced, dressed in clothes that seemed to be a mix of things they had brought with them from Russia and bought at discount stores here. The husband was squeezing a checked umbrella, the wife was holding a patent leather bag decorated with rhinestones—Vica's grandmother used to have a bag just like that. Both looked tired and frail, so Vica couldn't tell right away which one was the patient. Then she saw the purple chain of injection bruises on the wife's arm.

"Please introduce yourself," Dr. MacEarchern said.

Vica told the couple that she was Vica Morozova from the hospital's staff and she would serve as the interpreter.

Both the husband and the wife seemed relieved to the point of tears to hear her accentless Russian. Here was a nice Russian girl. She was there to guide and protect them in this doubly foreign and incomprehensible world of America and medicine. The husband took Vica's hand, squeezed her fingers, and called her "daughter." And the wife simply smiled and smiled at her.

"Let's start, then," Dr. MacEarchern said and shuffled a thick heap of medical reports in front of her.

"Doesn't she look like a horse?" the wife whispered, pointing to the doctor. Vica couldn't help but snicker. "She speaks like a horse too. We know some English, but we don't understand her at all," the old man added.

"Don't worry, I will translate every word," Vica reassured him.

Dr. MacEarchern started to talk. She spoke in long but perfectly precise sentences, pausing at even intervals to let Vica translate. She looked directly at her patient while she spoke and only occasionally glanced at Vica to make sure she was following her. But the patient and her husband kept their intense gaze on Vica the whole time. Vica translated everything with diligence and precision, trying to copy Dr. MacEarchern's empathetic but businesslike tone. She listed all the tests and procedures the woman had undergone and waited until Dr. MacEarchern finished describing the clinical picture. Stage IV. Inoperable. Distant lymph nodes. Metastasis in the lungs. Metastasis in the liver. Secondary tumors.

"In the doctor's opinion," Vica started to say when she suddenly stopped. She was about to deliver what was essentially a death verdict. She hadn't expected this. She'd thought it would be a routine appointment. Nobody had warned her about this! She couldn't. She couldn't do this to these people who looked like her grandparents, who were counting on her to protect them. They clearly hadn't expected anything like it or they wouldn't have made that stupid joke about the horse. Vica stared at Dr. MacEarchern as if willing her to say something else. She didn't.

Vica felt a painful constriction in her throat. She was afraid that if she opened her mouth she would start sobbing. And the old people were staring at her so intently. They must have noticed her shock. The old man put his arm over his wife's shoulders. They exchanged a long look.

"I think we understood," he said to Vica. His wife nodded. "Metastasis is the same in Russian," she said.

"She didn't say it was hopeless though," Vica said. "They have very good chemo here."

Good chemo? What was she saying? Quality carboplatin as opposed to subpar carboplatin around the corner?

"I know," the old woman said. "I understand."

Dr. MacEarchern saw that the verdict had been delivered. She put her hand on the box of tissues on her desk and gently moved it in the direction of her patient. The old woman's lips quivered, but she squeezed them into a thin white line and shook her head. Her husband moved the box back. They were too proud to cry in Dr. MacEarchern's presence.

There was more information that Vica was required to translate, but she saw that the couple had stopped paying attention. The wife was staring down, fondling the stupid rhinestones on her bag, and the husband was stroking her arm with one hand while continuing to squeeze his umbrella with the other.

They exited the office together. The old man shook Vica's hand and the old woman said, "Thank you, daughter." Vica gave them her card and said that they could call her anytime with questions.

She never heard from them again.

It was only later that day, on the bus back to Staten Island, that Vica realized that it was the old people who had protected her, not vice versa. They had protected her from having to deliver the verdict.

By the time Vica made it home, she was shaking with sobs. Sergey sent Eric to play in the basement, walked her to the bedroom, then went to fix her some tea. He brought it in on a tray with some salami sandwiches. When she told him how they had called her "daughter," he started to cry too. They had been fighting for weeks before that, but in that moment Vica felt that she had never felt as close to anybody and she never would.

And now Sergey was gone.

Patients started to flock to radiology around ten o'clock. There were so many of them that Vica stopped making distinctions. She glided and glided and glided her magic stick over their body parts, as if they were the same endless body. By the lunch break it was especially hard. Vica was physically tired, and her back started to ache, and she couldn't help but imagine herself trembling on that table while a cold slippery wand slid over her cancer-ridden stomach or chest.

As it always happened before lunch, some of the patients were getting hysterical.

"Don't you have, like, a shred of a soul?" one woman asked after she had begged Vica to let her husband cut the line.

"We need to see the liver doctor at one thirty. If we miss the appointment, they will reschedule and we will have to come again. From Scranton. Do you know where Scranton is? Do you realize what it's like for Peter to be in a car for two and a half hours?"

Peter was sitting right there, painfully thin, with a yellow tint to his skin and a permanent grimace of pain, ghostlike, and perfectly oblivious to the scene.

"I'm sorry, ma'am, but I don't make the rules," Vica said.

And then the woman broke down sobbing and she kept saying through her sniffles and hiccups: "I understand that he has to suffer chemo, radiation, but why does he have to suffer these endless lines? Couldn't he be spared that at least? He has less than a year to live!"

No, he couldn't be spared that. When Vica had first started working at Bing Ruskin, Christine had explained to her the necessity for the lines. Everything at Bing Ruskin was designed to make the machinery of the hospital run most efficiently. Doctors and technicians were moving swiftly from one appointment to the next, the expensive equipment was working at its full capacity. The interns worked their endless shifts. The precise number of personnel was determined by the cost efficiency. And if that meant less efficiency and longer waits for the patients, so be it. The patients were thought of not as important clients to whom you were supposed to suck up for the benefit of your business, but as faceless insignificant consumers who should be grateful for the services provided.

Vica got very angry at Christine back then. She had just started working there and she wanted to think of herself as part of a team concerned with saving lives, helping people, rather than making money off their pain. But the longer she worked at Bing Ruskin, the more she saw the truth of Christine's words. In a couple of years, Vica started to see the hospital as a huge chemical processing plant, where the patients were treated like the chemical matter to be processed, as quickly and efficiently as possible.

What a relief it was to finally exit the hospital at her lunch break. Vica never ate her lunch in the hospital's cafeteria; it was important for her to leave the place even if only for fifteen minutes or so. To go out onto the street, even if their block was always teeming with ambulances, people on stretchers, people in wheelchairs. This time there was an unusual commotion by the ER wing. There was a lineup of news vans and a small crowd by the entrance. She saw Tolik sitting on the stoop of his van and walked up to him. He was drinking coffee from a paper cup and munching on a meat pie. "Want a pie, little nurse?" he asked Vica. "Still warm. I got them in Brighton Beach on my last run to Brooklyn."

"What's all that about?" she asked, pointing to the ER wing.

"You didn't hear? Some famous actor died this morning. It's all over the news."

"Who?" Vica cried.

"Ivan Grail," Tolik said. "I think that's his name."

"Ethan!"

Vica took out her phone and checked her news feeds. There was the obituary.

Ethan Grail, the former TV actor who made his breakthrough in the *Legends of the Dorm* series and who evolved into the richly nuanced, award-winning film star, infusing his performances with deep empathy, staggering emotional power, and brilliant wit, died this morning in the emergency room of the Bing Ruskin Cancer Center, following a heroic battle with a non-small-cell lung cancer. He was thirty-two.

Vica's hands started to shake so hard that she couldn't finish reading. She'd seen Ethan only last week. He'd said to her "See you soon." The doctors had given him a year and that was just a few months ago. He wasn't ready! This wasn't fair!

"Did you know him?" Tolik asked.

Vica nodded, unable to speak.

"I'm not a big fan of the movies myself," Tolik said. "Natasha and the kids love that shit, but I just fall asleep right in the middle."

Vica nodded again and started to walk away.

"Take your pie!" Tolik said.

Vica took a pie and hurried away from the hospital to the nearest coffee place. She ordered a hot tea and sat down at a corner table.

All her social media was abuzz with the news of Ethan's death. Twitter and Facebook were bursting with stills and movie clips all featuring a handsome, lively Ethan, even as his ravaged, exhausted body was lying in the depths of Bing Ruskin's morgue.

Vica found it insulting. But what she really hated was the speed with which some of Ethan's fans appropriated his death. Fellow actors shared news of upcoming films featuring Ethan and themselves. Journalists jumped at the opportunity to rehash their old profiles on Ethan. Ordinary individuals dug up and posted their selfies with him. Those who didn't have a photo to share just described their devastating sadness, all-consuming grief, and shattering despair. Come on! Vica thought. He was just an actor you saw a couple of times a year on a screen—you can't be despairing! I actually knew him! Still, the worst was a huge portrait of a sad German shepherd with the byline: "Ethan's costar Brunhilde mourns his death." She wondered who had broken the news to Brunhilde. And how. Did they show her a photo of Ethan Grail and then tear it to pieces? Or did they use sign language? Vica heard that some monkeys knew how to sign, but she wasn't so sure about dogs. If they did, they must have signed: "Guess, what, Brunhilde, your old pal Ethan just kicked the bucket." And the dog signed back: "Fuck. This makes me sad."

Vica felt that this absurd public outpouring stole her grief from her, cheapened it somehow, cheapened the memory of someone she might have considered a friend. She had a momentary urge to share this with Sergey. He would've been just as appalled at she was.

She really had to stop thinking about Sergey! He was gone. Gone, gone, gone!

Perhaps she could share this with Franc.

Vica looked at her watch—it was time to go back. She finished her meat pie, threw away her empty cup, and rushed back to Bing Ruskin.

In the elevator, everybody was discussing Ethan Grail. "Have you heard?" "Right here in the hospital!" "In this hospital? I might have seen him?" "What a loss!" "Such a talent!" "Such a handsome man!"

On the radiology floor, all the staff was talking about Ethan as well. Vica saw Santiago and Liliana by the coffee machine, both staring at their phones. Sharing the news with each other that their friends had shared on Facebook. Vica rushed past them to her room.

Eric texted her just as she was finishing with the last patient. His fat friend Gavin, whom Sergey used to call Sir Eatalot, invited him for a sleepover. Their homework was very light and there was no school the next day. "Okay," Vica texted back, "but no junk food." "Sure, Mom," Eric wrote, "we'll have a carrots 'n' broccoli night." She couldn't tell if he was being sarcastic. Her evening was suddenly free. She could spend some time with Franc. Maybe even have dinner in one of those East Village cafés near where he lived? She dialed his number. He wasn't picking up. Perhaps he couldn't hear the ring because of his hearing problem. She texted him. Waited for the reply.

None came. She finished up at the office. Changed back into her street clothes. Poured herself some tepid coffee. Texted Franc again to see if he'd gotten her previous text. Franc hated spontaneity. He liked to arrange their dates well in advance, which made Vica a little suspicious. Made her wonder if he was seeing other women as well. Or if he wasn't as available as he claimed to be.

Christine peeked into Vica's room and said that Sam, a nurse from the endocrine cancers floor, was inviting everybody to her place for a makeshift Ethan Grail party. "We'll just drink beer and watch Ethan's comedies on Netflix."

Getting drunk and laughing at Ethan's antics on the very day he died?

Vica said that she had to rush home.

Soon everybody from her shift had left, but there was still no word from Franc. Vica checked her phone again. Nothing. It was stupid to hang out in the hospital waiting for him. Vica exited the building and walked toward her bus stop. The X5 bus arrived within minutes. A thin line of people formed for boarding. But what if Franc called when she was on the bus? She wouldn't be able to get off. Vica decided to walk toward the East Village. It would take her half an hour or so. If Franc called, she would meet him; if he didn't, she would just take the X1 bus to Staten Island, the one that stopped downtown. It was unfair that Vica worked in the city but so rarely got to enjoy it. The light had changed to that deep golden color that only came up an hour before sunset on a very bright day. The buildings were lit up as if by an invisible lamp. She had forgotten how much she loved New York, what a pleasure it was just to walk down the street, looking up, savoring the sights.

Vica got to the East Village in no time, but there was still no reply from Franc. Now she was in the midst of all those cafés with outside tables and chairs that seemed too small for the happy people occupying them. This was one of the first days of the season when it was warm enough to sit outside. The waiters hurried with their trays of steaming food. Vica was overwhelmed by all the different aromas coming at her from different directions: basil pasta, French fries, roasted meat. But it wasn't just the smell of the food, there was also the sense of fullfillment and well-being that was emanating from the restaurants. Her stomach rumbled and she remembered that she hadn't eaten anything today except for Tolik's pie. Vica checked her phone again, saw that there were no messages, and decided that she didn't need Franc to have a nice dinner in the East Village. She walked up to the hostess of the place that had the most delicious smell and asked if there was an available table. The place was crowded, so Vica expected to be turned down, but the hostess said, "Just you? I think I can squeeze you in." Vica thought she caught the warmth of single-woman camaraderie in her expression. There was a tiny row of tables facing the sidewalk, each meant for one person. One of them was empty, and the waiter led Vica right to it, saying, "We're having a sangria special tonight. A glass of sangria and two tapas for twenty dollars." Vica asked for a white sangria, baked shrimp, and croquettes with ham. The waiter put a tiny plate with olives in front of her, but no bread. She ate the olives right away, then dipped her finger into the dish and licked the oil off it. Then the sangria arrived. The first sip made Vica feel fantastic. A man passing on the sidewalk smiled at her. She thought that she must have made a pretty picture right then. A young, beautiful woman enjoying a glass of sangria in this elegant, lively place. Vica pulled out her phone and took a couple of selfies, making sure to smile and get rid of that tense critical expression she so often wore. She picked the best photo and posted it on Facebook with the caption: "Enjoying sangria in the East Village. Could be worse ☺." Let both Franc and Sergey know that she didn't need their company. She paused, thinking of the people from Bing Ruskin. Would they get mad that she had blown them off to hang out by herself? Should she delete the post? Vica weighed the risk of pissing off her colleagues against the pleasure of showing the world how great her life was. She decided to let the post stay.

Vica leaned back in her chair and looked out on the street as if it were TV. She had forgotten how much fun it was to people watch. There walked an old man with a mane of white hair reaching to his waist. There walked a young woman in a bright pink leather coat. There walked a woman with a double stroller with two kids who were feeding each other their toys. There was a woman in her forties standing next to a pet store across the street struggling with her cat. She had it in her arms wrapped in a sweater. The cat was wet, shivering, and trying to escape, but as soon as it was about to slip out of her grasp, the woman would push its wiggly butt up. Vica laughed so hard that she splashed her sangria. Then a man came out from the pet store, took the cat, and secured it in his arms. The man looked like Sergey. Vica sighed—she'd thought she was past mistaking strange men for Sergey. Still, she couldn't help but look again. Could it be? Yes, it actually was Sergey. There was Sergey, and he was with a woman, and they had a cat. After the first shock of recognition, Vica felt numb. She was aware of two things though: that she shouldn't let Sergey see her no matter what and that she should capture every detail about him and the woman so that she could come up with a clinical picture of their relationship. Vica hid her face behind the umbrella stand near her table and peered at them. Sergey was talking to the cat. Vica couldn't hear what he was saying, but his expression was similar to the one he always wore when he reprimanded Eric. The woman was laughing while patting Sergey's back with one hand and stroking the cat with the other. She was a tanned, husky blonde with wide shoulders and thick legs. She had long frizzy hair. She was wearing leggings and Uggs. She was taller than Sergey. She was older than Vica. She was unmistakably American. Too comfortable in her own skin, in her hideous Uggs, to be Russian. Did they live together? They must live together. They had a cat together! Did Vadik know about this? Then she remembered that Vadik and Sergey weren't speaking. The woman looked happy. And Sergey? What about Sergey? He appeared to be perfectly at ease with her. He said something with that ironic smile on his face, and the woman laughed and kissed him on the cheek. The pain of seeing that was so great that Vica thought she might lose consciousness. She closed her eyes and grabbed onto the edge of the table to steady herself. When she opened her eyes in what seemed like a second later, Sergey and the woman were gone. She thought that maybe this had been a hallucination, but she knew that it wasn't. The smiling waiter brought her food, but the smell of garlic made her want to vomit.

Vica put twenty-five dollars under her plate, then left the restaurant and started to walk away. It was hard not to run. After a few blocks, she realized that she was going in the opposite direction from the bus stop. She was drained of strength. She couldn't walk anymore. She stopped at the nearest town house and sat down on the stoop. Her phone beeped. For a second, Vica was terrified that it was Sergey, that he had seen her after all and had seen her run, but it was only Franc. He just got her message and would be happy to meet up. Vica thought that she had never been more uninterested in a man than she was in Franc at that moment. She texted that she was already at home. She thought about taking a taxi to the bus stop, then taking the bus home, but she couldn't bear the thought of spending the night on her own. A man and a woman passed her by. They didn't even look in her direction. She was completely alone here. On this stoop, in this city, in this country. Her phone beeped again. She thought it was another text from Franc and was briefly annoyed, but it was an activity Facebook notification. Vadim Kalugin commented on her photo: "Could be worse indeed!"

Vadik! she thought. She dialed his number. He answered right away. "Vadik, are you alone?" she asked. He said that he was. She made him promise that there wouldn't be any questions, then asked if she could spend the night. A long pause ensued. Vica worried that he'd turn her down, but he said, "Of course! Absolutely!" Vica got up from the stoop to look for a taxi.

Half an hour later, she knocked on Vadik's door. "Come on in, it's open," he yelled, and she entered an empty apartment. She walked in and stopped in the middle of Vadik's elegant living room, not knowing what to do. There was a collection of bottles on the top shelf by the window and she went to inspect it: whiskey, brandy, vodka, a strange little jar whose handmade label read "For a broken heart." How perfect, Vica thought and tried to unscrew the lid. Vadik emerged from the bathroom, wearing a nice shirt, his hair damp and freshly combed. He saw the jar in Vica's hands and said, "No, not that! That's some shit left over from DJ Toma."

He took the jar away from her and poured her some brandy. Vica drank it in thirsty gulps as if it was a glass of juice. She suddenly thought about Ethan Grail. Ethan Grail died today! Seeing Sergey made her forget about it. She put her glass down and started to cry.

Vadik walked closer and took her in his arms. He had an erection. How stupid the human body is, Vica thought and moved away.

"Are you hungry?" Vadik asked. "Should we order something?"

Vica shook her head. She said she wanted to watch TV.

Doctor Who? Vadik asked.

Vica said she didn't care.

They watched a couple of episodes of *Doctor Who,* then went to bed, Vadik in his room, and Vica in what used to be Sergey's room.

She woke up in the middle of the night burning with the worst panic she had ever experienced. She was in desperate need of comfort; she felt that if she wasn't comforted right then, she would die. She got up and walked the short distance to Vadik's room. His door was ajar, and the room was half lit by some feeble streetlights from the outside. Vadik was lying on his back, his mouth half open. Vica slipped under the covers and moved closer to him. He was so warm and so tall. His body took up a lot of space in bed. She hugged him and he hugged her back. They rolled over together so that she was underneath him now. He felt like the warmest, largest, most wonderful blanket. And so what if the blanket had a stiff dick, and so what if that dick was entering her? They were done in minutes, and Vica fell back to sleep immediately.

In the morning she felt much better, but nauseous with hunger. She went into the kitchen, cut herself a piece of cantaloupe, ate it, and went to shower. As she lathered herself with Vadik's stinging body wash, she had a perfect Scarlett O'Hara moment. Tomorrow was another day, and today was tomorrow, and her goal was simple and clear—she had to get Sergey back.

Chapter II

BYE BYE LOVE

N O, VADIK WASN'T ALARMED WHEN HE WOKE UP AND didn't find Vica there. He was disappointed but not alarmed; he knew that she had to leave early to make it to work on time. The bathroom was still misty and fragrant after her shower and he found her freshly washed underpants hanging on the edge of the sink. The mere sight of them gave him a huge hard-on.

The kitchen had some traces of Vica's presence as well. Some coffee left for him in the coffeemaker, a recently washed coffee mug and a spoon in the rack, a dollop of yogurt on the floor by the counter. He texted her: "How are you?" She replied almost right away: "Great! Thank you so much!"

Was she thanking him for fucking her? Or choosing to ignore the fucking and thanking him for letting her spend the night?

Both versions were disconcerting and painful.

He asked if he could see her. She texted that it was crazy at work, sending him into an agony of frustration. But then an hour later she offered to see him at lunch if he could come up there. He drank his coffee and went to his office in Dumbo, which seemed especially hideous that day.

Bob's idea had been to furnish the office in an anti-Google way. He wanted conspicuously adult furniture with a cool modern feel.

He adored Herman Miller pieces, which were elegant, sturdy, and expensive to the sight and touch.

Vadik sat down in his Aeron chair, thinking how much his ass hated the subtle curves of its seat, put his elbows on his glass-top desk, and started massaging his head. When he raised his eyes, he saw two flies moving across his computer screen. He made an instinctive movement to swat at them, but then remembered that they were part of the beautiful graphic design for their new project. They were deep into their work on the Dancing Drosophilae app. The new designer they hired offered to use the images of mating drosophilae just for fun. "Or, you know, whenever you find your genetic match, there would be a fly 'hovering' over your profile." Both Bob and Laszlo thought this was brilliant. Now Vadik was in charge of embedding the flies' movements into his script. The designer, whose name was Kieran, loved to make his life difficult. "Here, I made this little animation with the two flies tap-dancing together, let's make sure it fits." Making flies dance meant two more days of pointless idiotic work.

"Giddy-up, kids!" Laszlo yelled from his office. With Bob gone for a few weeks, Laszlo was in charge. Actually, Bob's sudden departure was bizarre. He said that he had some urgent family business in Russia, that he was going there with his wife. Vadik had called and texted Regina several times, but she wouldn't respond save for a brief note to let him know she was okay. They had never had a break in communication before. Regina'd acted so strangely at that team dinner back in February. He hoped she wasn't having a nervous breakdown.

"Time to buckle down, pal!" Laszlo yelled to Vadik from his desk. Vadik made an effort to smile and peered into his screen with an expression of great concentration. Laszlo's idea of leadership was to shower his employees with American idioms on the subject of hard work and devotion like "buckle down" or "dig in your heels" or "paddle your own canoe" that seemed to have been lifted from some out-of-date management manual. Vadik found himself unable to buckle down and just sat there staring into his screen and counting the minutes until he had to go meet Vica at a coffee shop on Fifty-third Street.

He arrived early and sat down on one of the squishy, slippery bar stools by the window. There she was, walking fast, almost running, crossing the street on the yellow light, waving to him, then opening the heavy door of the coffee shop. Panting, puffy-eyed, but radiant.

Vadik slid off the stool to give her a proper hug, but she squeezed past him and was up on her stool before he had a chance. They did kiss, and it was her kiss that told Vadik everything. Hurried and tense and trying so hard to pass for something friendly. He found everything about her embarrassingly stirring—her damp forehead, her forced smile, her sharp hospital smell—while she obviously didn't want him at all, not even a little bit, and that was stirring too. It was over, whatever romantic history they had had together was over now, and it was as clear as day to Vadik, although not yet as clear to his dick. Oh, give up, will you! Vadik thought, addressing his inapt erection.

"So, how are you?" Vadik asked after they got their coffee and sandwiches.

"Much, much better!" Vica answered with her mouth full, then said that she had left her panties in Vadik's bathroom. They hadn't been dry and she had planned to stuff them into her bag, but she'd forgotten. She gave him an embarrassed smile that made him squirm.

She must have noticed his disappointment, so she started talking very fast, how she had been distraught last night and acting crazy, how she hoped that he wasn't upset with her and that what had happened wouldn't spoil their friendship.

Vadik rushed to assure her that he wasn't upset in the least.

"Really?" Vica asked. "Good!"

She soon swerved to her favorite conversation topic: Sergey. Now she said that she had a plan to get him back and implored Vadik to listen carefully, because it was important for her to get a male perspective.

Is she really that insensitive? Vadik wondered. Or is this her way of telling me that we are back in the depths of the friend zone? This can't be her revenge, can it? Because back then after their tryst on her Staten Island couch, it was Vadik who said that this was clearly a mistake. But no, he didn't think so. Vica was tough, but she wasn't malicious. It looked like she truly didn't realize how much she was hurting him. He remembered how Sergey used to complain that Vica was emotionally obtuse.

"So I'm thinking something like this," she was saying. "He comes to drop off Eric, right? And here I am, in my hottest outfit, but not like party-hot, more like casual-hot, or better yet homey-hot. A T-shirt and yoga pants? And I'll have something on the stove, right? Warm, pleasant, homey atmosphere. And I'll be kind and attentive to him. And hot. Like the best version of me, right?"

There was nothing Vadik could do but nod his head in support. Nod and nod and nod.

Luckily, Vica had only twenty minutes before she had to get back to the clinic.

Vadik endured the rest of the day in the office. Did all that was required of him. Fixed some lines of code. Wrote some new ones. Answered an e-mail from Bob. Discussed a few issues with Dev. Discussed a few issues with Laszlo. Said "Yes, sir!" to yet another "Buckle up." Fixed some more lines of code. So what was he to do now? He didn't know, but, fuck, how he wanted to swat those stupid flies on his screen! And God help them, if they started to dance, God help them then!

It took an eternity for the working day to be over. Vadik went home to his empty apartment, He was looking forward to a few ammonia-soaked seconds of inner peace that the act of peeing never failed to grant him, but the first thing he saw in his bathroom were Vica's underpants hanging on the shower curtain rod. They were dry and stiff. He shoved them behind his large laundry hamper and peed quickly and without any pleasure.

He made himself a light dinner and ate it while browsing through Hello, Love! offerings.

There were some very attractive new faces. He went ahead and scheduled four dates in the next three days.

His best date was with a woman named Serena who worked as an adjunct professor at NYU. "What do you teach?" Vadik asked. "English," she said with a shy smile, as if this was a frivolous and slightly embarrassing choice of profession. That smile made Vadik like her right away. He wasn't that attracted to Serena, but she was nice and she seemed to get his jokes.

Later at home he studied her profile once more. Yep, it was witty and smart and brief, a bit too brief. He wanted to know more about her. He looked her up on Facebook. Her posts were mostly shares of op-eds from the *New York Times, Salon,* and *Slate.* She rarely commented on them, only if one of her friends asked her a specific question. Vadik looked at her photos. There were countless cityscapes, autumn leaves, and spring flowers. He skipped over them, hunting for actual photos of Serena. There she was in bulky skiing garb, red cheeks, wet bangs. And there she was at a party, adorably drunk. Serena in a Halloween costume—fake dark braids, short black dress with a white collar, chalk-white face. Vadik tried to guess who she was supposed to be. A schoolgirl with cancer? A schoolgirl who studied too hard? Nope, no clue. Not getting cultural references was his secret shame. You could pretend to fit in all you wanted, but you couldn't truly fit in unless you understood Halloween costumes.

There was a nice photo from five years ago—Serena and two more girls posing on a white cliff overlooking a bright blue lake: "Lake Minnewaska reunion." It was the same Lake Minnewaska where the sane Sofia had a membership to swim laps. Vadik smiled at the coincidence. All three girls in the photograph wore knitted hats and Windbreakers. Nice colors. Serena was in a yellow Windbreaker and a blue hat, the girl next to her all in green, and the last girl in a red Windbreaker and an orange hat—her light brown hair was sticking out from under the hat. There was something vaguely familiar about her face. He moved the mouse closer to her face to read the Facebook name tag. Rachel Meer. No, that didn't ring a bell, he decided. Until suddenly it did. It rang a deafening bell. Rachel! The girl in the picture was Rachel. His Rachel. The one and only Rachel I.

He wanted to switch to Rachel's page but was terrified to let go of that photo as if it were a mirage about to disappear. Rachel Meer. After years of searching, to stumble upon her just like that. It couldn't be real, could it? He had to force himself to go to her page; his heart was beating wildly and his hands shook so badly that he missed the Enter button.

And finally there she was. Rachel Meer. Big black-and-white profile photo. Still so lovely. He braced himself before looking at her About page. He was almost sure she'd be married, but there was nothing about her relationship status. Well, that didn't confirm or disprove his fears—not everyone shared details of their private lives on Facebook. She'd graduated from the CUNY Graduate Center and was working at Our City Books as a senior editor. How old was she now? Thirty? Thirty-two? Senior editor was impressive. Other than that her Facebook page told him nothing about Rachel's life. Apparently, she only used it to push the books by Our City's authors. She posted good reviews, press releases, and invitations to readings. There was a reading scheduled for this coming Friday. John Garmash would present his deeply haunting novel *The Frozen Train*. Rachel insisted that this would be a fun event—780 people were invited, 23 had confirmed that they would attend. The invite was public, which meant that she was inviting everybody, absolutely everybody, everybody including him. That's how easy it was. All Vadik had to do was go to KGB Bar on the corner of Second Avenue and East Fourth Street at 7:00 P.M. this Friday, and he would see Rachel.

In the following days more and more reasons for anxiety accumulated, legitimate and not (Rachel could be married, her husband could be there, Rachel could be mad at him, he might not be able to summon up the courage to talk to her), until all of them were drowned out by his biggest fear—that Rachel wouldn't recognize him, wouldn't remember who he was. She would look at him and give him a blank stare, a polite, uncomprehending smile that would demolish the entire myth of the great love of his life. He wouldn't be able to bear that. All Vadik's efforts became focused on making it impossible for her not to recognize him. He would do his best to look exactly like he had that day. He found some photos of his first months in the U.S. There were a couple that Angie had taken, a waitress in Avenel. In most of them, he was wearing that horrible pretentious tweed jacket over ill-fitting jeans that he had bought in Istanbul. He had been wearing that jacket when he met Rachel, he was sure of it. The problem was that he no longer owned it. It was Sejun's fault, because she had made fun of that jacket every time she had seen him in it. When he thought about it, Sejun had robbed him of many things dear to his heart—to name just a few: his jacket, his futon, and his best friend. The hell with Sejun! He went and bought himself a very similar tweed jacket in a great secondhand store on Bedford Avenue. He tried it on—it looked perfect, just as ridiculous as in that photo. His body and his face hadn't changed that much in eight years. He hadn't gained much weight. He was starting to calm down when a new panicky thought hit him. His beard! He went through so many beard/no-beard periods that he couldn't re-member if he had had one back when he first came to the U.S. In that Avenel picture he had had a beard, but a very closely trimmed one. It could have been a new one that he'd decided to grow, or it could have been the mutilated remains of an old one. He looked in the mirror—he had a nice lush beard now, but it might make him unrecognizable. Vadik sat down and closed his eyes, trying to focus and remember if he had had a beard on his first day in the United States. For the life of him, he couldn't remember. There were only two people who would possibly remember that: Sergey and Vica.

Well, he wasn't speaking to Sergey and he really didn't want to ask Vica. He finally decided that he would have a compromise beard. He went to a barber and asked him to trim his beard as closely as possible. The nudity of the face that met Vadik in the mirror after the barber was done filled him with a new wave of anxiety, but what was done was done.

On Friday, he began dressing about two hours earlier than necessary. He just wanted to make sure that his second-time-around jacket went well with his compromise beard. They looked okay. He took the L train to Fourteenth Street and Second Avenue, then walked down ten blocks to Fourth, turned west toward the blue neon letters spelling out KGB, and walked the one flight up to the bar. It was only six forty-five. The bar was nearly empty. He ordered a beer and sat down at a dark slippery table in the corner. There were numerous portraits of Lenin staring at him from the red walls. Red Soviet flags. A wartime poster with the angry red woman raising her arm in the air to demand that he give his life for the Motherland. This poster had been in a museum in his hometown. It had been displayed next to a glass case with empty shells in it. The red woman was supposed to be the Motherland or EveryMother. He remembered being scared shitless when he saw the poster for the first time when he was a child. And yet somebody found it cool enough to display in a bar. Vadik was on his second beer when the writer, a tall, pudgy man in a sweat-stained shirt, squeezed behind the podium and cleared his throat into the mike to signal that he was about to start. There were a few more people there now. But no Rachel. Vadik tried to listen to the writer. He couldn't understand a single word. The writer was sweating even more profusely. He had to wipe his forehead and his nose with the back of his hand. His hands were shaking, making the typewritten pages he was holding quiver and rustle. There were times when he had trouble understanding his own text and had to apologize and reread a sentence. He couldn't have been a good writer, could he? But what if he was?

What if he was an unrecognized genius who couldn't bear reading aloud in public?

Vadik picked up one of the books stacked on the adjacent table for sale and signing. *The Frozen Train*. Vadik opened it to page one and read a couple of sentences. He hadn't had that much experience reading fiction in English, so he knew that he wouldn't be able to form a trustworthy opinion, but he liked what he read. The prose was dense, with a thorough absence of clarity, no clearings, no cracks that would allow even the thinnest ray of light, no loopholes, no compromises. You had to respect the guy. Vadik raised his eyes from the book and met Rachel's quizzical stare. She was sitting just two tables away from him. She must have walked in while he was reading and taken a seat somebody had saved for her. She looked away as soon as their eyes met and fixed her gaze on the writer. There was no way to tell if she recognized him or not. She looked plainer than in her photographs, much plainer than he had remembered. But he experienced a shock of recognition so great that his whole body contracted in a painful spasm. There was Rachel. His own Rachel. And the whole bar started to crumple. The writer's voice turned to a distorted drone. The Communist posters blended with the walls. The people turned into blurry figures. There was only Rachel. Sitting as if in a vacuum. Excruciatingly real, unbearably close. So close that he thought he could see her heart beat under her thin white sweater with some sort of ridiculous leather appliqué across the front.

She didn't look at him once. The reading ended and she stood up, raised her hands above her head, and gave the writer tensely enthusiastic applause. Other people started to clap too. The writer inched from behind the podium to the table where he was supposed to sign books. A young red-headed girl arranged the books in a beautiful pyramid, then put a pen and a glass of water next to it. She looked over at Vadik and saw that he was holding a copy of *The Frozen Train*. "Do you want to purchase the book, sir?" she asked. "It's twenty-five dollars."

Vadik reached for his wallet, gave the girl two crumpled twenties, and turned to search for Rachel. She was still at the same table talking to a whole bunch of people, nodding eagerly. "Do you want me to sign it?" the writer asked. He was drinking water from the glass and it was dripping down his neck into the opening of his shirt. "Yes, please," Vadik said.

"Your name?" the writer asked.

"Vadim."

"Spelling?"

Vadik paused. He couldn't remember.

"Just sign it, please," he said to the writer, and the writer shrugged and made a fat, ugly doodle in the middle of the title page.

"Here's your change, sir," the bookseller said, handing Sergey a wad of bills.

Rachel was still talking to those people. Vadik decided that it would be best if he approached her outside. He would come up to her as she exited the bar and introduce himself. It was unlikely that she would be alone. He would still go and talk to her. He would ask her for a drink. There was no plan B.

People were exiting the bar in groups. Chatting, laughing, discussing plans for the evening. They had no idea how irrelevant they all were. Vadik kept looking at the door.

He expected to see her in about twenty minutes or so. She appeared in three. Alone. Wearing a blue raincoat. She stopped on the top step, took a beret out of her bag, put it on, and headed down the steps.

"Rachel," he said, stepping forward. It sounded too coarse and was barely audible. "Rachel," he said again. She stopped and looked at him. She was a few steps above the ground, so their eyes were on the same level. She reacted with the polite uncomprehending smile that he had anticipated and feared. But then almost immediately she gasped and said, "Oh!" She walked the few steps down and looked up at him. "Vladimir, isn't it?"

He hadn't expected this. He had expected her not to remember his name at all, but to use another name? And a Russian name at that. Like he was just some random Russian guy with some random Russian name.

"Vadik," Vadik said.

She crinkled her nose in embarrassment. "Right! I'm sorry!"

That bulky beret looked ugly on her. He could see that she had aged a little bit. She wasn't wearing any makeup, which made her look strangely exposed, unprotected. There were sharp lines as if separating her mouth from her cheeks. And her beautiful amber eyes looked even brighter, highlighted by the dark circles underneath. She kept touching her lips, kneading them with the knuckles of her fingers. He couldn't remember if that was something she had done back then.

"I enjoyed the reading," Vadik said, pointing to the book under his arm.

"Thank you! I thought it went very well too. And thank you for buying the book! I'm John's editor, you know. Do you like his work?"

Vadik said that even though he hadn't read that much of Garmash's work, he admired how there weren't any compromises, no deference to public demands. Not a lot of people were brave enough to write like that anymore.

Rachel was nodding eagerly. She seemed to warm to Vadik a little bit. Now was his chance to ask her for a drink. He made a huge effort to quiet his twitchy heart and did just that.

"Well, it would have to be a very quick drink, then," she said. "I have to be home by ten."

Vadik didn't know any nice places in the neighborhood. He was kicking himself for not having done any research on the neighborhood before the reading.

"This one looks okay," Rachel said, pointing to a bar next door.

They went in, winced at the loud fifties music, and walked to a table in the quietest corner. Rachel ordered a glass of wine, Vadik a beer, and by the time they finished them, they managed to exchange all the important facts about their lives. Rachel was lucky to get an internship at Random House right after she graduated, and even luckier to get a permanent position in a year. Then one of the senior editors left to open her own house and took Rachel with her. She was paid next to nothing, but she loved her job. His own job was too materialistic, Bob's applications too silly. There wasn't any existential meaning in Dancing Drosophilae whatsoever. Its main purpose was to advertise more genetic testing for medical companies. And, anyway, his position at Bob's company was too low.

He said that he was a partner in a start-up that was developing an amazing application. It would allow you to keep your online voice after you died. And not just an online voice, but the very essence of a person. Because where else could we find our essence nowadays? Social media.

Rachel seemed to be impressed. She said that it must be very challenging.

"It is challenging," Vadik said, "but if you get some excellent programmers and team them up with some excellent linguists, it's very doable."

He wondered if he should mention Fyodorov, then thought better of it. He said that it had been Shakespeare's *Hamlet* that had given him the idea.

"*Hamlet*?" she asked.

"Yes," he said. " 'The rest is silence.' "

"Oh, yeah, yeah," she said, "*Hamlet*. You probably know the whole thing by heart too."

Vadik detected a mocking note in her tone, but that could have been his paranoia. As a matter of fact, he did remember quite a few passages from *Hamlet* in Pasternak's translation.

To change the subject, he said that he lived in Williamsburg now. He loved the neighborhood.

Rachel lived in Greenpoint. With her fiancé, Peter, a journalist. They were getting married in May. This bit of news didn't shock Vadik. Rachel's demeanor had already told Vadik that she was either

STILL HERE · 257

married or in a serious relationship. It was as if she was wearing a T-shirt with huge letters on it spelling out TAKEN on the front. Vadik felt a desperate need to lie that he used to have a fiancée as well.

He mentioned Sejun and said that she had left him for his best friend.

"That sucks," Rachel said, but she didn't appear to be as moved as he'd hoped she'd be.

Vadik recognized the song that was playing now: "Bye Bye Love." How fitting, he thought. How cheesy, but how fitting.

Rachel checked her messages and said that they had time for another drink.

It was only then that they started talking about that day. Both remembered it well, but they differed on the details. Rachel didn't remember the smell of chlorine in the diner or that there was a homeless man sleeping in the corner. She didn't remember that it was snowing. She didn't remember her angry rant about Leonard Cohen. She laughed when Vadik quoted some of it. Vadik didn't remember that there was some change jiggling in his pocket all the way to Rachel's place. She found two quarters on the bedroom floor after he left. He didn't remember the dog (Kibbles was his name) who came and sniffed him by the entrance to Rachel's building. "You said something in Russian to the dog." He didn't remember that Rachel wasn't asleep when he left. She heard him moving in the other room and called for him. He didn't answer. He said that he couldn't hear her.

He asked her to forgive him.

She said, "No! There was nothing to forgive!" Her protest was so violent that she almost knocked her wineglass over.

She said that their encounter had been wonderful for her in every sense. She had had just one boyfriend all through college. He had dumped her a few months before she came to New York City to study. She was still reeling from her breakup, and everybody told her that dating in New York was brutal. She was a quiet bookish girl from the Midwest—she didn't know if she could handle it. Her roommate told her: "Just have your first horrible one-night stand, so everything that comes after will seem better."

Is that what I was? Vadik thought. Her first horrible one-night stand?

"And I thought no, I can't possibly do that. To be naked with a complete stranger? To touch a stranger's private parts? To let him touch mine? But then I decided that it was something I had to do. To prove myself or something. It was like going down a double-diamond trail. Or like skydiving."

He could see how that second drink was affecting her, making her looser or, as a Russian expression had it, "untying her tongue."

"And there you were. Tall. Foreign. In your ridiculous professor's jacket. With your Sartre! I couldn't believe somebody would be reading Sartre in a diner. With your English poetry in Russian. The fact that you were so bizarre made the whole thing much easier. It was like having sex with some eccentric literary character, not with a person. I wasn't scared or intimidated."

Okay, Vadik thought.

"And then the sex turned out to be surprisingly good. Tense, awkward, of course, but also so much better than I'd expected."

She reached for her wineglass, but it was empty, so she finished her water in a couple of gulps.

"I mean, it was a bit hurtful when you left without saying good-bye, but I thought that this was a necessary part of the experience. A one-night stand is called that for a reason. You need that moment of pain in order to feel really free and unencumbered."

There was no need to explain himself now. Still, Vadik felt that he had to say something.

"It was my first day in America. I didn't know what I was doing. I really didn't."

Rachel nodded and looked at her phone again.

"Where are you going?" Vadik asked when they exited the bar.

"Home. Greenpoint," she said.

"Let's share a cab," he said. "I'll get out in Williamsburg, and you'll continue to Greenpoint."

She nodded.

In the cab, Vadik immediately felt carsick, and he knew from experience that it was best not to talk when you felt nauseous, but he had to tell Rachel the truth. He thought it was crucial that somebody besides him knew what she had really meant to him.

"I've been looking for you," he said. "All these years. I didn't know your last name. I didn't know your address. I couldn't even remember where that diner was. I would come to the city every weekend and just go to the corner of Fifty-ninth Street and Sixth Avenue and walk downtown, swerving down the side streets hoping to find that diner."

She was now looking right at him and it was hard to take, he had to turn away.

"It was only years later that I discovered Missed Connections, and I posted hundreds of inquiries about you. And then I found you on Facebook. By pure accident. I was browsing through a friend's photos and saw you in one of them. Her name is Serena Geller."

"Yes," Rachel said, "Serena. We were in grad school together."

All this talking was making Vadik's nausea unbearable.

"Do you mind if I crack open the window?" he asked.

She shook her head. He might have been mistaken, but he thought he saw tears in her eyes.

They were approaching the bridge. The wind from the river whooshed right into his ear. He fought a painful spasm in his chest and continued.

"I went and stalked you on Facebook. That's how I knew about the reading. So I just went there, hoping to see you. I'd never heard of John Garmash before. I'm glad I bought the book though." He pointed to it in his lap.

Rachel reached over and stroked the cover with her fingers. "I had no idea," she said.

They didn't speak for the rest of the trip, but as the cab was approaching Williamsburg, Rachel tapped Vadik on the hand and said, "You know that name I called you, Vladimir? I had thought of it years ago. I thought that if I ever saw you again I would call you by some Russian name. A different Russian name. As if you were some random Russian dude who didn't matter. I was so proud of myself that I didn't lose my cool at the last moment, that I did call you Vladimir."

Her voice kept breaking as she talked.

"I mean, how stupid we all are!"

And then it was Vadik's stop.

"Can I ride with you to Greenpoint?" he asked.

She shook her head.

Vadik paid the full fare plus twenty bucks extra for Rachel, then got out of the car.

The cab started to pull away. Rachel was looking at him through the window, then as the car sped up, she abruptly turned away.

Vadik followed the car with his eyes for as long as he could, until it merged with the other bright yellow spots on the road and disappeared behind the buildings. He kept staring ahead until it seemed that the streets and the buildings were moving too, moving away from him, getting smaller and smaller, merging with the horizon.

He had come to this city in pursuit of happiness, and the city had in fact offered him happiness on his very first day here, but he had been too stupid and too blind to recognize it.

Vadik was desperate to share this revelation with his friends, but did he even have friends anymore? Sergey wasn't speaking to him, Vica had just dumped him, and Regina wasn't answering his messages. Even the virtual friends he had on social media tended to ignore his posts. He imagined telling the Rachel story to some brand-new friends in some new city and perhaps even a new country, because, boy, was he done with this one!

He went home and shot a message to his headhunter asking her to find him a position in some faraway place.

Chapter 12

CHEAT IT! SCREW IT!

ERGEY IMAGINED THAT GOEBBELS WOULD BE FAT, but he turned out to be skinny, mean, and half-blind. "No, no, Goering was the fat one," his new neighbor, Helen, explained. Helen had a history degree but worked as a receptionist at a beauty salon. Her apartment was on the fifth floor too, and just as tiny as Goebbels's. Helen was a divorcée who shared a one-bedroom apartment with her fourteen-year-old daughter, Teena. Teena, a pale, pudgy girl, was always there, mostly hiding out in the bedroom. Helen slept on the sofa separated from the rest of the living room by tall bookshelves. She took a liking to Sergey and often invited him over for a drink. She confessed that she hated Goebbels's owner because he was so rude to her and Teena. But she loved, loved, loved the cat! She also said that she didn't get the concept of online dating and would have loved to just meet a guy on the street and go home with him. Sergey had the sense that she would have liked for their relationship to be more romantic or at least more sexual, and he was attracted to her, but he couldn't bring himself to act. Helen was a robust Nibelungen blonde who spoke in a low voice and smelled of artisanal soaps she kept in a basket in her bathroom—Sergey's favorite were lavender harvest and lemon tea. She would invite him to watch Netflix and sit next to him on the couch, leaning closer and closer, tickling his neck with her hair, making his penis all but bounce in his pants, causing him to perspire from desire and panic. For all these years, having sex had meant having sex with Vica. He had had just two relationships since his separation, one was with an electronic voice of the GPS and the other was via Skype. The idea of touching, let alone penetrating, a real live woman terrified him. He confided this to Vadik back when they were still talking, but Vadik just shook his head. "It's not supposed to be like that, man! A new woman is exciting, with her new smell, and all these unexplored little nooks on her body." Sergey knew that he should just take the plunge and have sex with Helen, but something stopped him every single time.

They did become friends though, a friendship mostly based on cat-care help and oversharing of their marital troubles. Helen once saw a huge Facebook photo of Vica open on Sergey's laptop. The caption read: "Enjoying sangria in the East Village. Could be worse ☺."

"That's my wife," Sergey explained, blushing. "Ex-wife. We're separated."

"She's pretty, but kind of angry looking," Helen said. Sergey proceeded to spill out all his grievances with Vadik and Vica and his suspicion that they might have slept together some years back. Helen said that the suspicion was probably well-founded, because she too had cheated on her ex-husband with his best friend. Teena knew about it and hated her for it.

"This is the guy who takes care of Goebbels." Helen introduced him to Teena.

"Sergey," Sergey said.

"Sir what?" Teena asked. "Sir Gay?" And she curtsied, laughing.

A few minutes later Sergey overheard some hushed parenting in the kitchen.

"What did we talk about, Teena? Huh? What did we talk about? We don't make homophobic jokes in this household!"

"I wasn't being homophobic. It's just that his accent is super-funny."

"Teena! We don't make immigrant jokes either."

It took Teena about two weeks to stop rolling her eyes every time she passed Sergey on the stairs. In three weeks she warmed up to him enough to start calling him "Sergio."

It took Goebbels about the same amount of time to stop attacking Sergey in dark corners and biting him on the ankles. It was then that Sergey decided that he loved the apartment. Technically it was a one-bedroom, but the living room was used mostly for storage. The guy must have had a thing for antiques—the room was crammed with old musical instruments, mostly string, with the addition of a few brasses. Sergey had to spend most of the time in the dark bedroom, where the only window was half blocked by the A/C and which he had to share with Goebbels and his enormous cat tree. He learned to appreciate the apartment though, once he realized how nice it was to live by himself for a change. He could do whatever he wanted without worrying that he would upset, annoy, or disappoint someone.

Within three weeks Sergey finished his prototype and started revising his pitch. He debated whether to include Vica's "prehumous" option and finally decided to do it. All the marketing manuals advised making his potential customer base as wide as possible, and considering the growing number of people concerned about their online legacy, Vica's idea served that purpose really well. The next step was to learn how to submit it to investors. He shelled out a hefty sum of money for a three-hour online class and followed the teacher's suggestions to the letter. His pitch turned out to be quite good: accessible, persuasive, detailed but not overly specific, peppered with power verbs and appealing visual images. He e-mailed it to the teacher, and he seemed to be impressed. "Yep, that's pretty solid," he wrote back. Sergey did wonder if this was an automatic reply that he sent to all his students.

Then Sergey proceeded to submit his application and the written pitch to ARC Angel Fund NYC, Life Sciences Angel Network, New York Angels, Astia Angels, SNK Investments, Tribeca Angels, Golden Seeds, and Gaingels Syndicate.

He got no replies.

"Are you kidding me?" Helen said when Sergey wondered why he hadn't heard anything yet. "I don't have a fancy MBA like you do, but even I know that blind submissions never work! You have to use your personal contacts."

That was what his online teacher kept saying too. Use personal contacts, networking, and crowdfunding. But he warned his students that crowdfunding wouldn't work unless you had a very strong online presence. Sergey's online presence was virtually nonexistent. And he didn't have any personal contacts.

"Oh, come on! One of your friends from your business school?" Helen asked. Sergey shook his head. He didn't keep in touch with any of his business-school classmates.

Later, in bed, with Goebbels curled up at his feet, Sergey considered what other personal contacts he might have. He had worked for large banks and investment firms for many years, yet his only contacts were his bosses, the bosses who had fired him, the bosses who had thought that he lacked "skills, spirit, drive." He could've used Vadik's help, but they weren't talking. Then there were Bob and Regina, but Bob had never liked him, and Sergey couldn't endure yet another humiliation from Regina, who kept avoiding him after his separation from Vica as if he had the plague.

There was Sejun. She had offered to introduce him to a great investor, but asking Sejun would be awkward to the point of revulsion. He was still very angry with himself for starting that stupid, pathetic Skype affair with her. He didn't miss Sejun, but he did miss Vadik. They had never gone without talking to each other for more than a couple of days before. Every so often, while Sergey browsed through Facebook, he would look at the right side of his page and see the green light next to Vadik's name and be tempted to shoot him a brief message. He would stop short of that every time.

His remaining business contact was his former schoolmate from his university, Alexey Kuzmin. According to Facebook, he had recently moved to New Jersey and was involved in some kind of shady entrepreneurial scheme. They hadn't seen each other more than a few times since they graduated, but Kuzmin liked to engage Sergey in Facebook chats, the sole purpose of which was to brag about his superrich friends in Russia and the United States.

Sergey started with Kuzmin. Called him up, endured chitchat about health and family. Kuzmin inquired about "that very pretty wife of yours," said that he was so sorry that they had separated! Then he said that he was still married to his first wife, even though he could afford a younger and much prettier woman now. "I guess that's called love, man," he said. "I guess," Sergey replied. He then told Kuzmin about his app. Vica had told him to be careful when pitching—she was afraid that somebody would steal his idea. Helen said the same thing. He thought they were both paranoid, but this Kuzmin was definitely sketchy, so Sergey tried to be as vague as possible.

"Hmm," Kuzmin said, "virtual immortality, huh? So you're looking for investors?" Sergey confirmed that he was. "I'll have to think about it and call you back. You'll definitely hear from me, man. I can promise you that." They hung up. Sergey thought that it was pretty clear that he'd never hear from Kuzmin again.

He made an enormous effort and e-mailed Sejun. He received a swift, brief, businesslike reply. Yes, she would be happy to introduce him to her good friend, James Kisco.

Sergey googled the name and found out that James Kisco was one of the original investors in Vine, Airbnb, and Eat'n'Watch. He also turned out to be thirty-two, good-looking, and surprisingly easy to reach. James's assistant sounded cordial, said that they had been expecting his call, and scheduled a "breakfast meeting" at their New York office within a week.

Sergey asked Helen and Teena to listen while he read his pitch aloud, because he wasn't sure how to pronounce certain words like *radial, infatuated,* or *neither.*

"You look very handsome when you pitch," Helen said after Sergey's first attempt. "Doesn't he look just like Gregory Peck, Teena?"

"Who?" Teena asked.

"Gregory Peck? *To Kill a Mockingbird?*"

"Oh, right!" Teena said. "He does. Like a short and Jewish Gregory Peck."

"Teena!"

Sergey half expected Teena to call him "Gregory Pecker," but she didn't.

He ended up reciting his pitch four times, until Helen and Teena finally said that he "got it." Could it be that they were simply sick of listening to it over and over again? And even if he did "get it," what if the whole idea for this app was foolish? Now that his idea was about to enter the real world, Sergey started to doubt it more and more.

Teena said that she liked it. She said it was creepy but kind of cool. Helen was more skeptical. In her opinion dead people shouldn't be granted either virtual presence or control over it.

"Would you rather that all traces of a person be erased?" Sergey asked, thinking of Vadik's revolting suggestion.

"Not necessarily," Helen said. "You could just mark dead people's profiles to show that they were dead. A simple mark. A black frame over the photo or a cross over the profile, the way they marked plague sufferers' houses. We could browse through the 'friends' rosters and see how many of them were dead."

"But, Mom, Sergio's app lets dead people talk!" Teena said.

"I don't think dead people are supposed to talk, honey," Helen replied.

On the day of the meeting with Kisko, Sergey woke up nauseous with anxiety. Helen's simple words pulsed in his brain like an alarm. Dead people were not supposed to talk. Period. End of conversation.

He showered and dressed, but barely managed to eat his usual piece of bread with butter and cheese. The meeting was set for 7:45 A.M., so on the subway Sergey found himself surrounded by the midtown rush-hour crowd. All these people, surly, sleepy, smelling of acidic coffee, burned toast, and fresh aftershave, sitting down, getting up, squeezing to the exit, resigned yet purposeful, because they were going to their serious adult jobs. Just like Sergey had a mere few months ago. And here he was, a foolish man on his way to sell his foolish, foolish idea. He felt as if he had no business taking up precious rush-hour subway car space.

James Kisco's office looked like a construction site. There were boxes, assembly tools, buckets with paint, furniture in various stages of completeness, and purposeful people in overalls moving among them. In the middle of the room, two large men were busy erecting some very complicated bookshelves.

Sergey tried to ask them if they knew where he could find James Kisco, but they couldn't hear him because of the working drill. Finally, a young girl with a doll face and curly pitch-black hair that reached just below her shoulders appeared from behind a mirrored cube. She asked if he was Sergey. Or at least he thought that was what she asked, because he couldn't hear a thing. He nodded. She was very thin and very pretty in a slightly threatening way. Sergey thought that she would've been perfect for a lead in a horror movie. She must be James's assistant. The girl picked up one of the smaller boxes and motioned for him to follow her. She was wearing ribbed tights and a short gray skirt.

James Kisco's office was all white and had no windows. The only furniture was four large white leather ottomans set around a glass coffee table with a large takeout bag in the center. James was sitting on one of the ottomans drinking tea from a paper cup and eating something that looked like a crepe and smelled like Indian food. He was a large guy, dressed in jeans and a plaid shirt. Shaggy-haired, with bushy eyebrows and a bushy beard the color of pumpkin pie.

Sergey felt very stupid in his wrinkled business suit.

James stood up and reached out his hand for a handshake. Sergey's clammy fingers disappeared in his grip, then reappeared whitened.

"Very nice to meet you!"

"Likewise," Sergey said and lowered himself onto one of the ottomans.

"Tea? Dosa?" James's assistant offered, but Sergey shook his head. He really didn't want to leave a stain on this white leather.

"My favorite food," James said, dipping his crepe into a puddle of bright green sauce on his plate. "I spend a lot of time in India. Love that country!"

Here was Sergey's chance to insert some bit of knowledge about India, show some appreciation of Indian culture, but his memory wouldn't cooperate.

James's assistant walked up to the wall behind James's back, opened her box, and took out something that looked like long strips of colored paper.

"So you're Sejun's friend," James said.

Sergey nodded.

"Sejun and I go way back," James said. Sergey wondered if they had been lovers, then he thought about Sejun's partiality to losers and decided that they couldn't have been.

James's assistant spread a strip of paper against the wall. It looked like a slightly crooked vertical line. Sergey wondered what it was.

"And Sejun tells me that you have a mind-blowing idea for an app," James said.

He's urging me to talk, Sergey thought. He'll throw me out if I don't start right away. It occurred to him that he had barely said a word since he entered James's office. He had a painful spasm in his stomach and a rush of blood to his head. There was no way out. He had to speak.

"Well, I don't know if it's mind-blowing, but I'm certain that nobody else is doing it," Sergey started.

It took Sergey about ten sweaty, stuttering minutes to recite the pitch for James and arrive at his punch line:

"The rest is silence, but does it have to be?"

James met the punch line with an approving chuckle. He swallowed a mouthful of dosa and said: "No, it doesn't have to be! And, in fact, it isn't. Let me tell you a story, Sergey. I used to have a good friend, Jeff Ufberg. We called him Jeff the Squirrel, because he kind of looked like one—I don't know, something about his face. He died about six months ago. Skiing accident in Alaska. He was into extreme skiing, you know, like where you jump off cliffs."

Now that the pitch was over Sergey could afford to relax, but he was still feeling shaky. There was a puddle of green sauce right on the gleaming surface of the coffee table. He put his finger in it, swirled some around the table, and without realizing what he was doing licked the sauce off his finger. The taste was sweet, fresh, and surprisingly sharp, just as the mortification that hit Sergey right after. He hoped James hadn't noticed.

"So, yeah, Jeff died." James continued his story. "The funeral was in Taos, near where his house was. Beautiful ceremony. We all skied down the mountain. After dark, holding torches, in a single file. It was really moving. I can only hope to have a beautiful funeral like that. But a month later? I post a photo of my dog, Gandhi, on Facebook, and guess who 'likes' it? Jeff Ufberg. I was, like, 'what the fuck?' I thought maybe it was some other Jeff Ufberg. But no, it was the very same. He liked two more of my posts, and our friend Marcia's post."

James turned to his assistant. "Cleo."

"Yes?"

"Remember Ufberg?"

"Oh, yeah. My little brother posted a picture once, and the dead Jeff liked it. That was really creepy."

"Creepy, yes!" James said. "And then Jeff's comments started to pop up. Except they weren't in Jeff's voice at all. The man was a fucking Viking; he would never say 'so cute!' or 'lol!' or 'delish!' The worst happened when Jeff posted on my wall on my birthday. 'Happy birthday, darling! Stay smart and stay cute!' Turned out it was his girlfriend, Amanda. She kept posting from his account to keep his memory alive, so to speak. All of us, including Jeff, thought that Amanda was an idiot. And here she was, speaking through his Facebook like the devil through a possessed person. The ironic thing is that Jeff had planned to dump her right after his trip to Alaska, and now she owns him forever. How about that, huh?"

Sergey had no idea what to say to that. He wasn't sure if James told this story to imply that he liked Sergey's pitch or that he hated it.

"That's scary," he said.

"Yes!" James agreed. "That's fucking terrifying. You know what my shrink once said to me? 'Death is not what it used to be.' He's a funny guy, my shrink is. His specialty is tech entrepreneurs."

Cleo cleared her throat. Both James and Sergey turned to look. The wall now had large prints of dandelions with seeds flying away toward the corner.

"I'm sorry, James," she said. "Do you want me to put up the flowers on the other wall too?"

"Not right now, Cleo. I want to see how I feel about the dandelions first."

Cleo shrugged and went to sit on the ottoman next to James. She took a half-eaten dosa out of the bag and took a small bite.

"We just wanted something fun and uplifting for the office," she explained to Sergey.

Sergey doubted that dying dandelions were uplifting, but then he never claimed to understand visual art.

"So back to your app," James said. "What exactly do you want from me?"

"M-money," Sergey said.

James and Cleo laughed.

"I get that. How much?" James asked.

Everybody said that you should be very specific about the amount of money you were asking for, and Sergey had prepared financial information to go along with his pitch, but asking for a specific amount still struck Sergey as rude. He dove in anyway.

"Well, I need a million to develop it properly, but, I guess, not right away. Maybe three or four hundred grand to start?"

There was another communal chuckle, to which Sergey reacted with another painful spasm in his stomach.

"No," James said, "that's not how you do it. You have to ask for an exact amount. And you have to sound confident, even arrogant. Even if you're shitting your pants—act like a dick!"

Sergey stared at him in confusion.

"That was the problem with your entire pitch," James said. "Lack of confidence. Didn't you think so, Cleo?"

"Totally," she said and took another delicate bite.

"You're this brilliant guy with a brilliant idea, right?"

Am I? Sergey thought.

"You have to learn how to sell yourself. You graduated from NYSB, that's good, I guess, but not superimpressive. Then you say that you've been working on Wall Street, but it doesn't get you very far, does it? Who hasn't worked there? And the fact that you've never got promoted past a junior position doesn't sound very good either. But if you say that you're a brilliant Russian linguist who also happens to have an MBA, that sounds much yummier."

It does sound good, Sergey thought. It had been years since he thought of his Ph.D. in linguistics as anything but useless.

"Now that you've interested me in your person, sell me your idea. The best way to do it is to appeal to my FOMO."

Sergey tried to guess what that was. Did he miss this term in business school?

"Look, Cleo, this guy here doesn't know what FOMO is."

"James, Sergey's an immigrant!" Cleo said. "Give him a break!"

"Okay, point taken. FOMO, or the Fear of Missing Out, is the most powerful tool of manipulation right now. Years ago, a guy approached me with this idea for a new social media platform where your posts would be limited to 140 characters. I said no, that's stupid. Why would I want to read people's random shit? Now I feel like an ass!"

"Twitter's stock is up about 133 percent from its IPO price of twenty-six dollars," Cleo said with a pensive expression, a small piece of dosa still in her hand.

"See what I mean?" James asked Sergey.

Sergey pondered FOMO. It did sound like a viable manipulation tool, but his app was so much more than that. He offered to conquer the ultimate fear—the fear of death—not the pathetic anxiety of somebody else making a profit.

"Your next step is to persuade me that people have an urgent need for your app. Cleo? How do we appeal to the need?"

It wasn't clear to Sergey if James was involving her to teach her how to make a successful pitch or to actually ask for her advice.

"Cleo here is a graduate of Wharton. No shit, huh?" he said to Sergey.

Cleo swallowed whatever she still had in her mouth and wiped her lips, looking pensive.

"You say something like this," she started. "Our generation is the first one that has two lives: real and virtual. So far nobody knows what to do about our digital legacy after we die. Do we erase it? Do we allow it to remain active? Do we protect it from being overtaken? We know one thing: We can't just let it fend for itself!"

"Perfect!" James said, staring at Sergey. "You appealed to my Jeff Ufberg situation. I'm hooked. Now you offer me your solution. Cleo?"

"Sure," she said and stared at Sergey too. "Using my unique knowledge of linguistic algorithms, I can build an application that would allow us to preserve and re-create the voice of any Internet user, rendering him or her virtually immortal."

Sergey marveled at how Cleo managed to effortlessly combine his and Vica's ideas.

"Bingo!" James said. "And then after you've shown how huge and exciting this is, you ask me: 'Are you in? Because if you're not, you're going to fucking regret it!'"

Sergey shifted in his seat. He was impressed. He had never felt more enthusiastic about Virtual Grave. He was finally sold on his own idea.

"You're in then?" he managed to ask.

Cleo stood up, picked up the takeout bag from the table, and went to throw it in the garbage.

James looked away and exhaled. "No, Sergey, I'm not. And here's why. Your project is just a little too visionary, too ahead of its time. I'm really impressed with you, man. But to be honest, I don't see how it can make a lot of money. Sorry, pal."

James stood up and offered his hand. Sergey didn't have a choice but to stand up too. They shook hands. Then Cleo appeared at his side and led Sergey through the assembly labyrinth to the exit.

"I'm sorry," she said. She had to shout to be heard over all the construction noise. "I really, really liked your idea!"

On the way back, the subway train was much roomier. Sergey pushed away a crumpled McDonald's bag and stretched in the seat at the back of the train. He realized he wasn't upset. Getting funding from James Kisco would have been too unreal, too good to be true, so it was only natural that Kisco had turned him down. But he seemed to genuinely like his idea. He did! He wouldn't have wasted his time teaching Sergey how to pitch it if he hadn't. And when he said that he didn't see how Virtual Grave could make money, he meant huge money, Twitter, Uber, Eat'n'Watch kind of money, James Kisco money, celebrity money. Sergey didn't need any of that. What he needed was to earn just enough so that he didn't have to feel like a failure, didn't have to work at a job that he did so badly at that it hurt. Just enough money to regain the respect of his family and friends. Nobody said that Virtual Grave couldn't generate that kind of money. And James and Cleo did give him a very good pitch. Sergey took out a notebook and a pen from his pocket and wrote down the lines of the pitch: "Are you in? Because if you're not, you're going to fucking regret it!"

Sergey closed the notebook and smiled. Upset? No. He actually felt pretty good.

He got home, took a shower, and was making lunch for Goebbels and himself when he got a call from Kuzmin.

"I have the perfect guy for you. Perfect!" Kuzmin screamed into the phone. "I can't believe I didn't think of him right away. My good friend Dima Kotov!"

Sergey tried to sound impressed, but since he didn't know who Kotov was, it was hard.

"Oh, come on, man. Kotov? He's rich. Insanely rich. He's been on and off the list of the hundred richest men in Russia. And he's way into the immortality business. He has a good life, so good that it's understandable that he doesn't want for it to end. Kotov is fifty-two and for the last few years he's been looking to invest in whatever will help him live longer. He's built this huge high-tech yoga gym and a chain of health food stores. He's bought a whole fleet of medical-testing equipment along with some Swiss doctors to run the tests. He's invested in cryonics. He shelled out ten million to NYU for a research grant on longevity just a few weeks ago. There's a whole team of scientists working on the longevity formula. As far as I understand it, the secret to the formula is to up the dosage on multivitamins."

Sergey felt as if Kuzmin's lustful spit was flying from the telephone right into his ear. He moved the phone away. Now Kuzmin's screaming reached Goebbels, who didn't seem at all happy about it. Sergey stroked him behind the ears and asked: "So you really think he'd be interested?"

"That I can't promise you, man. Kotov's unpredictable. But we should definitely set up a talk. I got in touch with his assistant. He happens to be on his ranch in Costa Rica now, then before going back to Russia he's going to spend a few days in New York. I guess we should pounce, man."

"Let's pounce," Sergey said.

The meeting with Kotov was to be a "breakfast meeting" too. They set the time—nine—and the place—Kotov's New York apartment on Eighty-sixth and Central Park West. Kuzmin suggested that they meet by the entrance so that they could go up to the apartment together. Sergey arrived five minutes early and had to stand leaning on the blue mailbox across from the building, while Kotov's doorman eyed him suspiciously. Kuzmin arrived in a business suit and Sergey wondered if he had made a huge mistake wearing jeans and a sweater. "What is that?" Kuzmin asked, pointing at Sergey's computer bag.

"My laptop, in case Kotov wants to see how it actually works."

"Trust me, he won't."

The lobby of the building didn't look as grand as he'd imagined. He thought that Bob and Regina's place was more impressive, and the doorman here wasn't nearly as imposing as theirs. Another thing that surprised Sergey was that he wasn't all that anxious. Kuzmin, on the other hand, appeared to be a nervous wreck. He stuttered, he stumbled, he even farted while they were riding the elevator. Sergey pretended that he didn't notice.

A puffy Uzbek woman in her fifties opened the door for them. She was wearing a long bright green tunic and wide pants underneath it.

"Hurry up!" she said when Sergey hesitated before entering—he couldn't decide if he should remove his dirty shoes. "Hurry up! I have kasha on the stove."

She led them into a spacious but drab living room, pointed to the gray sofa, and told them to sit down. "He will see you," she said before retreating to the kitchen. Sergey noted that she didn't add "soon" or "in a moment" to that sentence.

"He doesn't use the place that often," Kuzmin whispered in an attempt to justify the lack of glamour.

The only bright feature of the living room was the magnificent view of Central Park from the window. Sergey stood up to see it better, but Kuzmin hissed at him: "She told us to sit down." His eyes were shiftier than ever, and he was visibly sweating and exuding a barely noticeable stench, as if something inside him had started to rot. Sergey sat down and listened to the faint sounds of the shower.

Finally, the water stopped and they heard the loud bang of the bathroom door, and a few moments later Kotov appeared in the living room.

He was barefoot, wearing loose linen pants and a white cotton sweater, his short light brown hair wet from the shower. He smelled of something very expensive.

Sergey was surprised to find that Kotov was delicately built.

He shook hands and sat down across from them in a low armchair. He had an unusual face with thin lips, pointy ears, sharply defined cheekbones, and slanted gray eyes. The eyes of a bobcat, Sergey thought. He fixed his stare on both of them and seemed to be reading them carefully. His expression was tense, alert, wary. A protruding zigzaggy vein kept throbbing in his right temple.

The Uzbek woman walked in and sidled up to Kotov with a tray that held a single glass filled with thick yellow juice. "Orange mango," she said. Kotov drained the juice, wiped his lips, and kissed her dark swollen hand.

"Thank you, darling," he said with stifled affection in his voice.

She leaned in and kissed him on the top of his head with a fierce proprietary expression.

"Dinara used to be my nanny," Kotov said after she had retreated into the kitchen. "I was ten and she was fifteen."

"Was that your entire breakfast?" Kuzmin said with a stupid chuckle.

"I'll have kasha when it's ready." He turned to the kitchen and yelled, "Dinara, how much longer?"

"Ten minutes," she yelled back.

"Ten minutes," Kotov said. "That should be enough for your pitch."

"Plenty," Sergey said. No, he wasn't nervous. Not even a little bit. Probably because he wasn't hoping to succeed. He was enjoying how calm he was, confident, arrogant. Arrogant was good, wasn't it?

He managed to keep calm throughout the pitch, even though it was getting increasingly obvious that Kotov wasn't and wouldn't be interested. He kept scratching his neck, glancing toward the window, and checking his reflection in the gleaming surface of his Rolex. He wasn't stirred by the beauty of Fyodorov's philosophy. He wasn't even a little impressed by the quote from *Hamlet*. It was clear that the rest would indeed be silence. That is, if Sergey didn't come up with a new explosive punch line.

"Listen," he said to Kotov, "my app won't make you immortal. You will die."

Kotov stopped playing with his Rolex.

Kuzmin audibly drew his breath in.

"But," Sergey continued, "death is not what it used to be. You can actually screw it now. And that's exactly what my app does."

Now Kotov was listening with attention. He squinted, which made him look ruthless, more like the image of a shady Russian billionaire that Sergey had had in mind. He proceeded to give Kotov the details. At some point Kotov jumped out of his armchair and started pacing across the room. "Oh, the sweetness, the sweetness," he moaned, looking out onto Central Park.

"I could arrange that for my wife. She would get a text from me. Every year for her birthday. 'You're a psycho bitch.'"

"Every year?" Sergey asked. "What if you change your mind?"

"Change my mind? I'll be dead, dude!"

And right then Kuzmin squeaked from his seat: "We need two million in initial funding."

Kotov frowned. "Two million? What the fuck are you talking about? You don't need two million. Use programmers from Belarus, they're dirt cheap! I'm giving you a million and a half, and then we'll see."

Sergey could barely register the rest of the talk. Kotov was going back to Russia. Kuzmin was to contact his accountant next week. Kotov would leave him the instructions. He expected to be informed about every aspect of the process. He wished them the best of luck.

"Can we trust him?" Sergey asked when he and Kuzmin exited the building.

"Oh, yes. He would never go back on his word. We got it!"

He made an attempt to embrace Sergey, but Sergey dodged the hug.

"We have to celebrate!" Kuzmin insisted. "Get brunch! Get drunk!"

But Sergey couldn't wait to be alone. "Some other time, okay?" he said.

As soon as Kuzmin was out of sight, Sergey crossed the road into the park and started walking along the path toward the reservoir. He passed the field where dogs jumped wildly around performing their morning rituals. He felt a momentary urge to join them. He passed a few benches where old people sat with their old blankets spread over their laps. He felt like kissing each and every one of them. He rustled through a pile of dry leaves on the path. He kicked an old acorn with his foot and sent it flying into the air. He ran his hand along the sharp edge of the bushes framing the path. He stopped by a food cart and bought himself a bag of roasted peanuts. They were still hot and Sergey pressed the bag to his face to savor its warmth for a moment. He popped a few peanuts into his mouth and walked up to the black metal fence guarding the water. There were almost no people on the path, just one or two joggers. Sergey decided to ignore them. The water was perfectly still, the reflections on it very bright, so it was as if he were seeing two cities at once: one standing up on the other side, the other turned upside down and submerged in the water. He hadn't been there in ages, he didn't remember how shockingly beautiful the view was. He remembered that feeling he had had when crossing the Brooklyn Bridge, that he could fit the entire city onto his palm. What he felt now was different. He felt that it was the city that could fit him, Sergey Levin, onto its palm. That he finally belonged there. He ate the rest of the peanuts and put the empty bag into a pocket of his pants. He placed both his feet onto the little step at the bottom of the fence and grabbed the upper spikes with both hands. He rocked back and forth and right and left, while singing Cohen's "Hallelujah."

I've heard there was a secret chord
That David played, and it pleased the Lord

He sang and sang until he felt that he was David the baffled king, and it was he composing "Hallelujah," and it was he who finally struck that secret chord.

FOR THE NEXT couple of days as Sergey was busy preparing a detailed business plan, he was burning to tell somebody. Eric, his mother, Vadik, Regina, Bob, Sejun, Vica. Especially Vica. The idea was partly hers after all. And Vica was the only who could truly share his joy. Vica could get deeply angry and profoundly sad—no grown person cried as much as she did, but she could get insanely happy too. She would've screamed. She would've been jumping up and down. That was what she did when he announced that they had accepted him to New York School of Business.

And there was Helen waiting to hear how the meeting went. Sergey was about to tell her the good news, but something prevented him from doing it. Kuzmin assured Sergey that the deal was solid, that Kotov rarely promised things, but when he did, he never, ever backed out on his word. But Sergey was afraid to jinx it. He told Helen that he wouldn't know Kotov's decision for a while. He decided not to say a word to anybody until the check was safely in his bank account.

That decision proved to be very wise, because a week after their meeting with Kotov, the bad news came.

"I'm afraid I have a bit of bad news," Kuzmin said on the phone. "Kotov was shot and killed last night. He was in his car on the outskirts of Moscow."

Sergey was in the kitchen, making yet another meal for Goebbels, scraping some brown gunk off the sides of the cat food can into a bowl. He put the bowl down and leaned against the fridge. Kotov was dead. Just a few days ago Sergey was sitting across from the man, so close that he could smell his cologne. He thought of

Kotov's eyes, of the throbbing vein in his temple. He wondered how exactly he'd been shot. In his chest? In his head? He thought of how he looked Kotov in the eye and said: "You will die." Embarrassment and revulsion at the memory of these words made him cringe.

And only then did Sergey realize that Kotov's death meant the end of Virtual Grave. He had just a few weeks left of unemployment— he needed to look for another job. He had no other investment contacts. But, more important, he didn't have the stamina anymore. That short-lived euphoria over the deal with Kotov had exhausted him more than all the time he had spent working on the app.

You've got to hand it to Death though, he thought. Just as he and Kotov were planning to screw it, it went ahead and screwed them.

SERGEY SPENT THE following days browsing the job ads, barely eating, hardly registering Helen's attempts to cheer him up. "I'll tell you what," she said at the end of the week. "Teena will be at her dad's all weekend, so let's have a little party at my place Saturday night. Order some nice food, watch a movie. How about *9½ Weeks*? Haven't seen that in a while."

9½ Weeks? Sergey thought. Wasn't that the old soft-porn movie where Mickey Rourke fed the blindfolded Kim Basinger a chili pepper? He hated that movie! But he said yes simply because he didn't have the energy to say no.

On Saturday morning he drove to Staten Island to spend his usual time with Eric. It was a long, long drive. There was traffic on the BQE. More traffic on the Verrazano Bridge. Traffic on Father Capodanno, where traffic was extremely rare. The ocean was a sickly grayish-brown, as if it hadn't yet quite recovered after Sandy. Some houses along the shore still stood covered with plywood. There wasn't much traffic on Hylan, which was surprising, but, God, how ugly Hylan looked! Those car dealerships, those disgusting storefronts, those billboards for doctors, MRIs, and funeral homes.

Sergey had to admit that the neighborhood where his house stood was actually quite beautiful. Neat houses, sycamores, lilac bushes, streets leading up and down the hills and into the woods. Yet the prettiness of his former neighborhood made Sergey even more depressed than the ugliness of Hylan Boulevard had. He didn't belong there anymore.

He was finally in the driveway of his house. And, yes, legally, this was still his house. He still owned the rusted mailbox. The ugly porch with the scuffed column. The plastic bat hanging off the awning since three Halloweens ago. He still had the key. He felt it would be wrong to open the door with his own key, even though he knew that Vica wasn't there. He pressed the button of the doorbell. There was a wheezing half-choked ring followed by some commotion in the house.

"Eric, open the door!" his mother yelled. "Eric, now! Eric, my hands are all covered in meat!"

Then there was the clicking of the locks. Mira insisted on locking all of them even though both Vica and Sergey tried to persuade her that the neighborhood was very safe.

"Who is this?" she asked from behind the door in her strained and thus a little rude-sounding English.

"Mom, it's me," Sergey said.

Mira opened the door and moved to the side to let him pass. She stood wiping her hands on her little apron printed with cat paws. Complicated jewelry dangled off her hands, ears, and neck. She had stopped dyeing her hair since Sergey's father died, and there was something intensely sad about the combination of her childish frame, her fancy jewelry, and her sparse white hair.

"I'm making *ezhiki*," she announced.

"Great, Mom," he said and leaned in to kiss her. Her skin felt dry and brittle under his lips, which it did more and more so each time they saw each other. His father's death was abrupt, Sergey thought, but he was being forced to witness his mother's demise unraveling in slow motion.

Mira went back into the kitchen, and Sergey walked up the stairs to the top floor. He took great care not to touch or see anything that would remind him of Vica, so he was grateful that the door to their former bedroom was shut, but the door of the hallway closet was gaping open and he caught a glimpse of the pink towels that he had seen wrapped around Vica's body so many times. Eric's door was half open too. Inside, he saw the usual picture: Eric sitting cross-legged on the floor in front of the TV, one sock on, the other sock for some reason lying in the middle of the room. He was flushed and sweaty, clutching his Xbox controller, his thumbs jerking as if on their own, his entire body swaying right and left with the characters on-screen. And what characters they were! Nasty, vicious, dressed in full military garb, loaded with various weapons, screaming, jumping, bursting into flames. Sergey had always said that they shouldn't let Eric play those games, but he never found enough support from Vica to carry it through. "This is normal," she would say, getting angrier as she talked, "this is what boys do. You don't want Eric not to do what other boys do, do you? To grow up weird and alone?"

"Eric!" he called.

"Not now, Dad!" The characters on the screen started screaming in what sounded like Mandarin to Sergey.

"Hey!" Sergey called again.

Eric bit on his lower lip and made several jerky movements with his hands. There was a series of explosions that left a lonely mutilated corpse on the smoke-clouded field.

"Dad! You distracted me! Now I'm dead!" Eric said and dropped his controller on the floor.

"Is that supposed to be you?" Sergey asked, pointing to the corpse.

"Yep," Eric said.

A husky Asian man, bent under his excessive weaponry, sprinted over to the mutilated corpse, squatted over his face, and proceeded to push his pelvis up and down.

"What in hell was that?" Sergey asked.

"Tea-bagging. The winner is supposed to do that to humiliate the dead guy."

Sergey's face contorted with disgust, but Eric must have misinterpreted his expression, because he proceeded to reassure him.

"It's okay, Dad. I won't stay dead forever. All I have to do is to choose a safe place to respawn and then I'll go back to the battle."

"Respawn?" Sergey asked.

"Yeah, when you die, you just follow the spawning process and then you're alive again. It takes no time."

"Boys, lunch!" Mira called from the kitchen.

Eric put his second sock on and they headed to the kitchen.

Sergey loathed these weekly lunches that he had there since the separation. Being a guest in his own house, having his mother cook for him as if he were still a child, straining to fit some parental influence into the little time he now spent with Eric.

Their small kitchen table was crowded with little plates and bowls and tiny serving dishes overflowing with chopped, minced, and sautéed vegetables. Sergey had always marveled at how elaborately his mother set the table, even for a simple lunch, even for just the three of them. He remembered this from childhood: her pretty serving dishes, her layered salads, the mushrooms made from tomatoes and eggs, the palm trees made from franks, the farmer's cheese snowmen.

"*Ezhiki*, cool!" Eric said and piled some onto his plate, ignoring the salad with strawberries and tiny shrimp, the minced eggplant, and the mushroom-stuffed zucchini. Mira took a piece of bread, generously spread it with butter, and gave it to Eric. He accepted it with great enthusiasm.

"Mom, I don't think he needs that much butter," Sergey said, watching Eric take a great big bite out of the bread slice. He immediately regretted it. Mira's lips trembled as she tried to put on the defensive expression that made her appear all the more vulnerable.

"Butter helps digest vitamins," she said.

"That's right," Sergey said, "but we don't see him eating vitamin-rich food, do we?"

"She gives me baby carrots all the time!" Eric said. "They're, like, chock-full of A and C."

"And iron," Mira whispered.

Sergey doubted that Eric was actually eating those carrots, but he wasn't going to pick a fight with his mother in front of his child. Once, about a year ago, Eric had asked him "to be nicer to Grandma." "I'm very nice to her," Sergey had said. "No, Dad, you're not nice, you're polite." Sergey couldn't help but feel that Eric might have been right. He had never loved his mother as much as he loved his father. What he felt for her was pity rather than affection. And the more aware he was of that, the more pity and the less affection he felt.

After lunch, he took Eric for a walk.

"Great Kills or Mount Moses?" Sergey asked, starting the car.

"Mount Moses," Eric answered from the backseat. He was already furiously pressing buttons on his Nintendo DS.

They drove up to the woodsy part of Staten Island and parked the car off a tiny street overgrown with tall blueberry bushes. They made their way through the bushes, into the large clearing that held the remains of the foundation of some old stone structure, deeper into the woods between the large rocks and the tall trees the names of which Sergey didn't know. Mount Moses wasn't that tall and wasn't really a mountain, just a large hill. They climbed up the slope panting and cursing and trying to hold on to the brittle tree branches along the way. "Ooooh," Eric said when they reached the top. He was sweaty and winded—they really should make him exercise more.

"Hey, Eric," he said, "let's start jogging in Great Kills on weekends."

Eric scrunched his nose. He was probably weighing the physical hardships of weekly jogging against the emotional rewards of spending time with his dad.

"Okay," he finally said.

They went to sit down on the cluster of rocks that presented a panoramic view of Staten Island.

"Look, Dad," Eric said, still breathing hard. "The ocean!"

Yes, they could see a narrow line of ocean on the horizon. Blindingly white in the sun, like a sliver of ice.

They could just sit there enjoying the view or Sergey could attempt some parental guidance.

"I didn't really like that game you were playing," Sergey said.

Eric picked up a little rock from the ground and started scratching the surface of the boulder they were sitting on. His expression was one of resigned boredom. He knew that he had to suffer through this conversation, but he also knew that the conversation wouldn't change anything. None of the previous ones had.

"What game? Battlefield? I like it."

"Isn't it a tad too violent?"

"Yeah. But I'm in a battle, battles are violent. That's normal."

"Isn't it tiresome though? You have those guys killing one another over and over again? You dying over and over again?"

"Maybe. But no, not really. I die only because I'm not very good at the game. If I get better at it, I can avoid dying. I can kill all the other guys and not die."

"Doesn't it make you sad when all the other guys kill you?" Sergey asked.

"No, Dad! I told you—I don't stay dead for long. I respawn and go into the battle again."

Respawning—what an addictive concept, Sergey thought.

"Does it work like that in all video games?"

"What? Respawning? Pretty much. In Skyrim, if something kills me—a robot sentry, or a dragon, or even my wife—I just restart the game, and it starts from the point where I last saved. And I can restart from anywhere, like, even if I'm halfway up the dragon's mouth."

Eric could sense his father's sincere interest and was getting more and more animated. He even stood up so that he could face Sergey.

"In Pokemon, if you faint in the battle, you just have to go to a Pokemon center to restore your health. Are you getting this, Dad?"

Sergey nodded.

Eric smiled and continued. "And in Destiny respawns are weirder. Basically when you die, your Ghost, which is this alien robot pal, gathers up all your particles and slowly brings you back to life, while you're watching everything from a deathcam, which is like a pair of floating eyes."

"You're dead, but you're watching everything. You know, I've actually been working on something very similar," Sergey said.

"Virtual Grave, I know," Eric said. "An app that would allow dead people to keep talking. Mom told me about it."

"She did?"

"Yeah. It sounds a little weird. Could be kind of cool though."

Sergey smiled and squeezed Eric's shoulder.

It was starting to get dark. The clouds above the ocean took on a dirty pink color.

"Let's head back," Sergey said.

They were just a hundred feet from the car when they saw a deer. She was standing on the clearing between two birch trees looking at them with calm attention.

"Too bad we don't have any food," Sergey said.

Eric reached into his pockets and pulled out a bunch of baby carrots in various stages of decay.

"I wonder if they are still chock-full of A and C," Sergey said.

Eric threw a few toward the deer.

The deer jolted back.

"Don't throw them! Offer her some," Sergey said.

Eric took a few steps forward and extended his hand as far as he could.

The deer looked away and headed back into the woods.

"She doesn't understand the concept of the carrot," Eric said.

Sergey's heart tightened with an overwhelming mix of tenderness, worry, and guilt. But then wasn't this what parental love was supposed to feel like?

"Will you have time to come into the house?" Eric asked when they got into the car. "I could show you how deathcams work and other stuff."

"Sure," Sergey said.

He would play with Eric, then he would go home and send out his résumé to all those banks he had marked and answer all his LinkedIn inquiries. And tonight, after they watched that stupid movie, he would finally man up and make love with Helen.

It was almost dark by the time they made it back to the house. The first thing he saw was Vica's car, parked a mere inch away from the garage door. Vica never slowed down when she drove into the driveway. She took pride in making her turns sharp and precise.

"I'm sorry, Eric," Sergey said, "I think we'd better look at your games some other time."

Eric tried to hide his disappointment under a mask of male camaraderie. "Sure, Dad," he said, "or if you install a console at your place, we could play each other."

"I'll think about it," Sergey said.

He waited until Eric entered the house and started to pull away. Just then the front door opened with a bang and Vica came running toward the car, barefoot.

Sergey stopped the car and rolled down the window. "What is it?" he asked, hoping that his voice wouldn't tremble.

"Could you come out for a second?" she said.

Sergey got out of the car, bracing himself for a very unpleasant conversation.

But Vica wasn't saying anything. She just stood in the driveway, in her ridiculous too-tight yoga pants, her bare feet pressing into the gravel. There was that hungry, pleading look on her face that he hadn't seen in such a long time that it took him a while to recognize it.

"Do you want me to come in?" he asked.

She nodded and started to cry.

THE LAST CHAPTER

 Regina Mandel   4:18PM

What's the address?

Vadim Kalugin   4:19PM

21 skyth st

Apt 1b

 Regina Mandel   4:19PM

Does bob know?

Vadim Kalugin   4:20PM

Text him just in case

 Regina Mandel   4:20PM

6:30, right

Yep

Vadim Kalugin   4:21PM

Who said yep?

 Regina Mandel   4:21PM

I answered for you

Sergey winced at Vica's stupid emoji and checked the time before putting the phone back into the pocket of his jeans. He still had about four hours before he had to head to Williamsburg for Vadik's going-away party. He had called Sergey two weeks ago to tell him that he was leaving for Singapore. Sergey's heart leaped with joy when he first heard Vadik's voice, then he thought about him and Vica, and the joy got mired in anger and pain. They met for a drink and talked about what was happening with Virtual Grave, and Regina's decision to adopt a child (Can you believe it!), and Vadik's plans. They were both careful not to mention Vica. It turned out that Vadik didn't really have plans. His headhunter had offered him a two-year contract overseas, and he had jumped at the opportunity. Singapore!

"Perhaps this was for the better," Sergey said to Vica when he got home that night. Better for Vadik and for their friendship too. Perhaps what they needed was some distance in order to salvage what they had. Vica just nodded in agreement.

A bicycle bell made Sergey jump. He was walking down the narrow East Ninth Street on his way to Goebbels's place. Even though he was officially back together with Vica, Sergey still had to feed Goebbels and spend some nights with him. He wondered if he was going to miss the cat. His owner was coming back in two weeks. Sergey would definitely miss this apartment, having a room of his own, getting to spend some time by himself. The idea of having a room of his own had supported him all through the turbulent process of reconciliation. He and Vica would be in the midst of yet another screaming fight and he would remind himself that there was a dark, quiet, cat-smelling retreat just thirty minutes away.

"But it's getting better, isn't it?" his mother asked. It was. He had to admit that it was.

The moment of clarity came after the call from Cleo. Bank of America had just offered him a junior financial analyst position. He had given up on Virtual Grave and was ready to accept it. He went ahead and took the drug test and filled out all the forms for the background check.

Then the call came just as he, Vica, and Eric were walking along the beach in Great Kills. Eric was crouching nearby trying to revive a horseshoe crab. The number was unfamiliar and Sergey hesitated before picking up.

"Sergey? This is Cleo Triantafyllides." Sweet female voice. He had no idea who that was. He walked away from the surf to hear her better.

"We met a few weeks ago," Cleo said. "I used to work as James Kisco's assistant."

Cleo! The doll-faced, slightly frightening girl.

"Yes, I remember," Sergey said. He was pacing back and forth, barefoot, on the cold lumpy sand, while Vica sat down on a driftwood log.

Cleo told him that she had decided to branch out and set up her own start-up with her friend Mischa, another Wharton grad who was "amazingly savvy." They were looking to develop a project that would truly stand out. And they thought that Virtual Grave would be an ideal start. Both she and Mischa loved how dark and edgy it was. They didn't have a lot of money, so they couldn't offer him much, but they were willing to pay him a modest salary while the project was in development stage. And a share of the profits later on. They had a wonderful team of very hot young programmers and designers. She knew that they could build something truly beautiful together. She hoped to meet and discuss the details in the next few days.

Sergey's first thought was No, let me be. He was so tired of that roller coaster. Bob, Kisco, Kotov. Hopes up, hopes down. It was so much easier to give up. Sergey was almost hoping that Vica would tell him to do just that when he told her about Cleo's call.

He walked over her and sat down next to her on that driftwood log. He described Cleo's offer, expecting her to say: "Forget about it! You have a nice offer from Bank of America."

But instead Vica hopped off the log and started to jump up and down. "I knew it! I knew it!" she was screaming. "I always thought that Virtual Grave was a brilliant idea! Brilliant!"

Then she leaped at him, making him fall off the log, and fell on top of him. They toppled and tumbled around on the sand, laughing like crazy, until the worried Eric left his crab alone and ran up to them.

"What happened?" he asked.

"Eric! We just sold our app!" Vica screamed. "It's gonna work. People are gonna use it!"

"Yeah!" Eric yelled and hurled himself down onto the sand too.

"There is no way of knowing if it will be successful," Sergey said when they got up and were cleaning the sand off themselves.

"It doesn't matter," Vica said. "We need to see it through, up until the very end."

"Is that the one where you're respawning people?" Eric asked.

"Yep," Sergey said.

"That's seriously cool!"

Afterward, the three of them sat down at a picnic table and had a celebratory picnic of My Europe offerings. They kept talking and laughing, eating like pigs, protecting the food from the seagulls, protecting their napkins from the wind, smearing the sauces around. And all Sergey could think of was Vica. Here she was with her wild hair in the wind, sand all over her clothes, smiling at him, smiling at Eric, smiling at that stupid salami sandwich in her hand. Buoyant, victorious, half delirious with happiness.

I love her, he thought then. I really do.

He did love her, that much was clear. Whether they would be able to be happy together was a different question.

The staircase was dark as always and Sergey had trouble finding the keys to Goebbels's door.

"Hey, there, Sergio," Teena said, sticking her head out of her apartment. "Where's my pal Enrico?"

"Eric," Sergey said. "I promise to bring him next time."

Eric loved feeding Goebbels, and Sergey would bring the boy with him from time to time. Teena had struck up a surprising friendship with Eric. They would play videogames in her room, building castles together, burning bridges, killing their enemies, and respawning their friends.

"Where's your mom?" Sergey asked.

"On a date," Teena said smugly.

"Oh."

"Yeah, good for her. I made her sign up for Hello, Love! It's not like she cares that you went back to your wife or anything."

Goebbels meowed from behind the door and Sergey said good-bye to Teena and walked in. There he was, lying in the middle of the kitchen floor, flapping his tail against the tiles.

Sergey opened a can of minced duck delight, shaped the meat into tiny meatballs, and hid the anti-inflammatory pill inside one of them. That was Eric's idea. He said that he did it all the time when he had to give medicine to Gavin's cats. Then he confided to Sergey that his dream was to be a vet someday.

"But that's so—" Sergey started to say "unambitious." He stopped himself just in time. Let Eric figure out what he wants, he thought.

"Yeah, it's tough, I know," Eric said. "You have to have all As in biology, and Ms. Zeh keeps giving me Bs."

Sergey put the meatballs into the bowl. Goebbels limped over to his food with great fervor. The medicinal piece was down (thank God) and now Goebbels was working on the remaining meatballs. He always turned his head sideways when he ate and that gave him a vicious expression, as if he was eating a live bird rather than the thoroughly processed minced duck delight.

Sergey's phone beeped. There was a text message from Regina: "Is Vica with you?"

"No, why? Aren't you meeting her at IKEA?" he typed.

"She's not here and she's not answering."

"Must be on the subway," Sergey texted back.

Regina sighed. She'd been waiting for Vica for twenty minutes on the crowded first floor of Brooklyn's IKEA and she was getting restless. The place was awful, unbearable, loud, inspiring both agoraphobia because of its size and claustrophobia because of its crowded little pretend rooms. There were all these families moving in all directions half hidden behind the enormous boxes sticking out of their shopping carts. Angry, screaming, exhausted.

It was Vica's idea to meet there. Regina had asked her if she knew a good place where she could look at children's furniture and Vica said: "Are you kidding me? IKEA!" She offered to take Regina there and help her shop.

"Where are you?" Regina texted her again. Still no reply.

Ever since she returned to New York after three months in Moscow, Regina had been plagued by bouts of panic. She realized that during her time in Russia she was simply too busy—taking care of Nastya, handling the grueling adoption process—to feel anxious.

Back home, between meetings with immigration lawyers, she had more free time to doubt the wisdom of her decision.

Regina had to rent an apartment in Moscow so that she could spend time with Nastya free of Aunt Masha's supervision, but, of course, Aunt Masha dropped in for tea almost every day. Bob had spent the first three weeks with them. He was so good with Nastya that it intimidated Regina. Even though Nastya and he didn't speak a common language, they seemed to communicate with ease, or at least with more ease than Nastya and Regina. Bob would play silly games with Nastya, take her on piggyback rides, or just run around a room on all fours and make animal sounds, making Nastya laugh and charming Aunt Masha. It got to the point where Regina was jealous. "She likes me better," Bob said, "but I bet she'll love you more."

Still, she would have preferred it if Bob was as terrified as she was.

Then Bob went back to New York and Regina was left to figure out parenting on her own.

The amount of things she didn't know about children was overwhelming. She had always been a serious reader, so in this situation too she turned to various self-help books on parenting and adoption. None of them helped; if anything, the books managed to intimidate her even further. There was only one book Regina could tolerate, and that was the Canadian novel *Humdrum,* the one she had just finished translating. Regina had reread it and was now hungrily waiting for the second one, which was supposed to come out later in the year. She found solace in the descriptions of the humdrum routine of caring for a child. There were so many urgent tasks described in the book that the reader didn't have time to ponder the philosophy of mother's love. Perhaps that was the philosophy of mother's love—being so busy and concerned the whole time that you couldn't possibly analyze it. Regina shared this thought with Inga, when Inga came over to meet Nastya, and Inga seemed to agree. She supported Regina's decision to adopt, but Regina couldn't help but notice that Inga thought there was something whimsical in it. As if Regina, who had always had such a charmed life, managed to find a fun and easy way to have a child too. Unlike Inga, who had her son in her sophomore year while in the university and had to work and study and care for the baby all at the same time!

As soon as Regina got back to the United States, she was attacked by swarms of people congratulating her on her "noble deed" or pushing their vague child-rearing ideas on her.

There was Becky, Bob's daughter, hugging Regina and saying, "You can't imagine how much I admire you for this."

There was Regina's dad, who said exactly the same thing and then started to cry.

There was Bob's family, who insisted that she should baptize Nastya right away.

There were Laszlo and his wife, the proud parents of four children, who thought that she should model her parenting on their style.

There were Bob's friends, who kept sending her links to books and articles on adoption and child-rearing.

There were distant acquaintances, who wouldn't answer her very specific questions but would say instead that she had to listen to her heart and that her heart held all the answers. Well, guess what, her heart didn't hold the answer to the question of whether American schools accepted Russian immunization records.

Sergey would just tell her an occasional useless fact like: "Eric used to drink from the bottle until he was four."

And Vadik preferred to keep mum on the subject altogether.

Even Bob scared her! Regina couldn't help but feel that he was expecting too much. "You're gonna be a spectacular mother," he would say, and she would panic and think: What if I fall short of spectacular?

Vica turned out to be the only one with whom it was easy to talk about motherhood. She was eager to share her parenting experience, but she never made Regina feel like an idiot. Her best advice came in the form of this sentence: "No matter what you do, you can be sure that you're doing something wrong." That actually made Regina feel relieved. Every parent was bound to screw up in one way or another. She would screw up too. But it would be okay.

Yet another shopping cart bumped into Regina. Where the hell was Vica?

"This place is awful!" Regina texted her. "I don't think I can wait here for much longer."

"Five more minutes. I'm on the boat," Vica texted back, shaking her head in disbelief. She was no more than fifteen minutes late. There had been this amazing sale at Century 21 downtown that Vica couldn't miss. And IKEA was awful? IKEA! She couldn't believe how spoiled Regina had become. IKEA was Vica's favorite store! The store that let the customers ride these beautiful yellow boats! Free on weekends! Free on this warm and beautiful Saturday in May.

Vica was standing on the upper deck clutching the railing, swinging back and forth on her toes, listening to the slosh of the waves, letting the wind pummel her face. Thinking how unimaginable it was that if she died everything around her would have to stop. There would be no sounds, no images, no sensations. Nothing. Nothing at all. It was strange, but ever since she got back with Sergey, Vica had started to think about death more often and more intensely. It wasn't that she was scared, she just really, really didn't want to die. Not ever. She took so much pleasure in her life right now that it felt like it would be incredibly unfair if it would have to end.

Even though things with Sergey weren't exactly smooth. Far from it. She'd told him about Vadik. She felt that she had to—she wasn't sure why.

"You're crazy!" Vica's mother had screamed at her via Skype. "He will never forgive you!"

And so far he hadn't. "Vica, please, try to understand, it's not that I can't forgive you. I don't exactly have the right to forgive or not forgive you. We were separated. But I can't forgive the fact that it happened."

Vica felt a strange satisfaction when he told her that. Perhaps she'd been compelled to confess to him because she wanted to test his love in some perverse way. If her confession hurt that badly, it must mean he really loved her, didn't it?

When the ferry finally docked, there was Regina, tall, stooped, and so stricken with panic that Vica felt sorry for her.

"Don't worry," Vica said to her. "I invented a very efficient way of shopping here, so we'll be done in no time."

She dragged Regina onto the escalator and headed straight to the kids' department. "We'll only look for what you need and then you'll just scan the barcode with your phone and you can take another look at each piece online."

"I like the castle bed over there. And the tent bed," Regina said to Vica. "Wouldn't it be cool to wake up as if you were in the woods?"

Vica shook her head. "No, Regina, no! Don't look for 'cool' things. Look for comfortable and familiar. That's what this girl needs. You don't want to make her life even weirder."

Regina nodded. She looked very intimidated, the poor thing.

"Look at this storage system," Vica said. "Now this is superconvenient."

She wished she had the money to buy all this stuff for Eric. Perhaps one day she would. There was no guarantee that Virtual Grave would make any money at all, but she was hopeful. They were hopeful.

"You definitely want this desk! Look, there's so much space for random crap underneath," she said to Regina.

Regina went ahead and scanned the barcodes.

Later when they were drinking excellent Swedish coffee in the IKEA café, Vica asked Regina about Nastya.

"You know," Regina said, taking a hesitant sip, "I think I miss her."

"Already?" Vica asked. "That's a good sign!"

"We had two couches close together in that rental apartment. And she would jump from one to the other and scream 'Egina, look!' She calls me Egina; she has this little problem with her *r*'s. Her jumping used to annoy me, because she wouldn't let me read in peace, but now I miss that."

"Egina?" Vica asked. "That's funny! Does she listen to you?"

Regina blushed as if Vica had caught her on some parental incompetence.

"Not always, no. And she often lies."

"Oh, that's normal. Kids lie all the time. I would find all these candy wrappers in Eric's schoolbag and he would insist that they weren't his. 'They're Gavin's. Gavin put them there.' And I would say: 'What about that fat on your stomach? Huh? Did Gavin put it there too?'"

They both laughed, then Regina asked how things were going with Sergey.

Vica tensed. She had never trusted Regina and she suspected that she was secretly happy when she and Sergey had split up. Her first impulse was to lie, to say that yes, they were back together and happier than ever.

"Good," she said, forcing a bright smile. "Really good. Especially since he sold Virtual Grave. He promised that if everything goes as planned I can quit my job and go to graduate school within a year."

"Medical school?" Regina asked.

"Probably not. I'm fed up with medicine. I was thinking about a degree in marketing or business. You know that girl Cleo, the one who is developing our app, she says that I have some terrific business ideas. She actually likes my ideas better than Sergey's."

Regina nodded thoughtfully. She didn't appear haughty or patronizing. On the contrary, she seemed as lost and insecure as a person could be. She was looking at Vica with kind attention, urging her to tell the truth. "Regina knows how to listen," Vadik had told Vica once. "She has pulled me through a lot of shit by just listening to my rants. I've never met anybody as capable of empathy as her."

Vica was hungry for empathy. She decided to be honest.

"Actually, it's been really hard with Sergey," she said. "We're back together, yes, but he's still struggling to forgive me."

"Forgive you for what?" Regina asked.

Vica took a long sip of coffee and cleared her throat.

"I slept with Vadik and I told Sergey about it," she said.

Regina put her mug down and stared at Vica.

"We were separated and I thought that Sergey was sleeping with somebody else." She tensed, expecting something like incredulous judgment from Regina. What she got instead was a strained silence followed by hysterical laughter.

"I'm sorry, I'm sorry," Regina kept saying, choking with laughter, which turned out to be rather contagious.

Honestly, Vica couldn't think of a more fitting reaction to the story of her love troubles.

"So how did it happen?" Regina asked.

"Do you want to hear the whole story?" Vica said.

"Of course!"

"Let's go out for drinks sometime soon. I know this perfect little place in the East Village with the best happy hour. Twenty bucks for two tapas and a glass of sangria!"

"I'd love to!" Regina said. "Let's do it soon, before I leave for Moscow."

And they got up and went to the exit.

"Listen," Vica said when they got on that little IKEA ferry that would carry them back to Manhattan, "you can't let Vadik and Sergey know that I told you, okay?"

"Of course not!" Regina said with a new spurt of laughter.

"And don't you giggle!"

"I'll mask it with a cough."

Vica rolled her eyes in a joking way and took out her phone. "Reg and I are on our way," she texted to Vadik.

"Cool," he texted back.

Vadik thought that it was Regina he would miss the most. She was the only one who ever offered him true friendship. Vica and Sergey hadn't. They were so eager to pull him into that vile complicated mess of their marriage only to spew him back out when he wasn't needed anymore. Regina was different. She did care about him. Fuck, he had been such an asshole when he said to her that the only way she could take care of a child was to eat it. How could he possibly have known that she was actually considering becoming a mother? But even if he stayed in the U.S., he doubted that they could remain true friends now that she had a child. It was already clear that the child dominated most of her faculties. Well, he could understand that. There were so many ways to screw up a kid, you had to be in a state of constant alert. Vadik had always wondered why people even wanted kids. He didn't. He had passed on his good sturdy genes, but no kid in the world needed him to pass on his doubts, restlessness, and insecurity as well.

He walked into the living room and surveyed the place. Most of his furniture was already gone. There were just a few pieces left along with a few items of his sports equipment. There was a sense of bareness and open space to the apartment that Vadik hadn't had a chance to enjoy before. In two days, he would be gone to start his life anew in another foreign, unlived, perfectly clean space. He had never been to Singapore and he knew very little about it, which would make his fresh start even fresher. He had made the mistake of trying so hard to fit in, first in Moscow, then in Istanbul, then in New York. He would make no such claim on Singapore. He would just try to enjoy the foreignness of the place for as long as it was enjoyable.

Vadik counted his bottles of booze again. One, two, three, the fourth, the fifth, the minor fall, the major lift.

He went to the kitchen, defrosted the dumplings and the edamame, put them on a tray, and carried the tray back into the living room. He put it right in the middle of the rug.

There was a forceful ring of the doorbell.

Bob, Vadik thought. Nobody else rang the doorbell with such poise.

"Am I the first to arrive?" Bob asked.

"Yep," Vadik said.

It had been a little awkward between them since Vadik announced his decision to leave DigiSly.

"Of course, man, I get it," Bob had said to him. "You need a change of atmosphere." But there was hurt and incomprehension in his eyes. It was clear that he struggled to understand how anybody could want to leave such a cool job under such a wonderful boss. They shared a common pain though, and that was Sergey's success. Bob was suffering from a bad case of FOMO, even though he kept saying that he stood by his word that Virtual Grave didn't have a chance to become hugely successful.

"It's not a success yet, far from it," Sergey said to Vadik when they were having drinks. "There is no way of knowing if there will be any revenue."

But what had happened was better than financial success, and they both knew it. Sergey had created something from scratch, something he was passionate about; he had fought for it with all his might and he had won. While Vadik was back to square one, starting his life anew yet again.

"This looks nice and airy," Bob said, walking into the living room and taking in the emptiness.

"Vodka?" Vadik asked.

"Sure!" Bob said.

"Is a coffee mug okay? I sold all my glasses."

"A coffee mug of vodka would be very welcome!" Bob said. "With ice, please."

Vadik handed him a mug with the words #1 BOYFRIEND. He couldn't remember whether it was a gift from Rachel II, the sane Sofia, or Abby. He poured a generous portion for himself into a mug with a picture of the Empire State Building on it.

They sat down right on the rug and took a few sips in silence. Bob picked up a dumpling on a fork and bit off about half of it.

Both Bob and Vadik were visibly struggling to find a conversation topic.

"Did you find an apartment in Singapore?" Bob asked.

"The company found one for me."

Vadik's fortieth birthday was coming up a week after he was supposed to arrive in Singapore. He would have to celebrate it on his own. Fuck, that was depressing. He needed Bob to change the topic.

"So what's the process now with that little girl?"

"Nastya? We're working on her immigration papers. I have pretty solid connections, so everything should go smoothly on this side. Especially compared to the Russian bureaucratic nightmare. Regina is going back there in a week, and if all goes well, I'd say we could bring Nastya over in a couple of months."

"Great!" Vadik said. "You must be excited."

Bob swirled the ice in his mug and looked Vadik in the eye.

"To tell you the truth, man, I'm fucking terrified. Raising your own kid is tough. But a kid from an orphanage . . ."

"Regina said you've been very chipper throughout the whole thing."

"Well, I had to put on a brave face for her sake."

"But you are really sure this adoption is the right thing to do?" Vadik asked. He remembered Regina's telling him that Bob strongly believed in doing the "right things."

"The right thing?" Bob asked. "Do you think there is the right thing to do for every situation? I don't! No, I'm not sure. Not at all! But that little girl, Vadik! My heart just goes out to her. And I think it's what Regina really wants too."

"It'll be okay, Bob. I can feel that it will," Vadik said, and they clinked their mugs.

The vulnerable, terrified Bob was somebody Vadik didn't have the chance to know. They could've been closer. Vadik felt a momentary regret, which was interrupted by the sharp ringing of the doorbell.

Vadik got up to let in Regina and Vica.

"Vadik!" Vica said. "Look how thin you are!"

They hadn't seen each other in months. Vica had felt that it was important not to aggravate things with Sergey.

"She's right," Regina confirmed. "Let's hope they'll fatten you up in Singapore."

Vadik went to retrieve two more mugs: one that had the figure of a jazz musician leaning back with his sax, and the other that simply said MoMA. He poured some vodka into each and handed the mugs to Regina and Vica.

"Isn't your birthday coming up?" Regina asked.

"Yep," Vadik said. "I'll be in Singapore."

"We'll make a virtual party for you!" Vica said. "We'll go to a resturant together and you'll be with us via Skype."

Great, I'll be like a ghost, Vadik thought. Fortunately, Vica found a diversion.

"What's in there?" she asked, pointing to the huge plastic container in the corner.

"Random junk that didn't sell. Take anything you want."

Vadik dragged the container closer and put it in the middle of the rug next to the food.

"What's that?" Bob asked, pointing to the wooden handle sticking out of the container.

"My first tennis racket," Vadik said.

"It can't be!"

Bob reached for the racket and took his time examining it.

"My father used to have one exactly like that. I've seen it among his things." He stroked the rough surface with his fingers.

Regina leaned into Bob and kissed him on the cheek. "You should take it, honey. It will be a nice memento."

"Can I?" Bob asked.

"Sure," Vadik said.

"Thank you, Vadik," Bob said and put the racket in his lap.

"And I'll take these pretty dishes and this pot and—what is this, a vase?" Vica said.

"It's yours."

By the time Sergey arrived, they were all digging through Vadik's stuff, getting a little tipsy and laughing.

"Drinking and pillaging, huh?" Sergey said. "I want in!"

Vadik handed him a mug with Warhol's Marilyn on it.

"Hey," Sergey said, pointing to the tennis racket, "isn't it your first racket?"

"Is it? I thought Vadik was kidding," Bob said.

Vadik picked the racket up and ran his fingers over the rough surface of the head. He bought it a few weeks after he had arrived in the country. Vica had explained to him that all middle-class Americans enjoyed playing tennis, and if he wanted to fit in, he would have to learn. Sergey had offered to teach him. "Rackets are expensive, buy one on eBay," Vica had said. Vadik had had no idea what a tennis racket looked like. He had bought that one because it was the cheapest. Only twenty dollars.

"Oh, yeah, I remember," Vica said. "He brought it to our court on Staten Island so that Sergey could teach him. Here we are, all ready to play, and Vadik produces this monstrosity! I mean, he was really going to play with it!" Vica was laughing so hard that she almost spilled her drink.

"That's right," Sergey said, "I remember. And what about his first attempt to ski?"

Yeah, yeah, very funny, Vadik thought.

Downhill skiing was the other thing all middle-class Americans were supposed to enjoy. Vadik thought that he knew how to ski, because he had been an expert cross-country skier since he was a child and he could manage the steepest hills. So one day he just went to Shawnee Mountain (it was the cheapest and the closest), presented a half-off coupon, paid for his "after dusk" lift ticket, put on his rented boots, strapped on his rented skis, and took the lift to the top. This is spectacular! he thought, taking in the view of pink clouds at sunset. Within seconds, he made the rather painful discovery that he had no idea how to slow down or control his direction. He was zipping downward, gaining terrifying speed, sure that he would die and horrified that he would die a stupid, embarrassing death like this. Fortunately, he soon crashed into a snowboarder and managed to fall on the icy snow with most of his bones intact. He did break his wrist though. He had to abandon the skis and hobble all the way down in his ski boots, howling from the pain like some wounded wolf.

"Adaptation is a painstaking process," Sergey had told him as he drove him to the hospital. "You keep trying to fit in right away and end up breaking your bones."

And now Sergey was laughing at his haplessness. He could afford to laugh. He was a man who had finally made it.

The party went on for a while, each of them taking one of his things, stroking it, fondling it, telling yet another episode from the life of poor dear Vadik.

Am I the only one who thinks that this sounds like a memorial service? Vadik wondered. All these speeches, all these fond memories, all these jokes, as if he weren't there. It was a relief when they all finally left. Drunk, wobbly, carrying their loot. Bob with his racket. Regina cradling a small potted orchid. Vica and Sergey hauling the rug and two garbage bags filled with everything from kitchen utensils to half-used shampoos.

I might be a loser in their eyes, Vadik thought, but none of the winners could resist my free offerings.

He didn't feel sad though. Not at all. He felt better than he had felt in years. He thought about how much he had always liked leaving. Fitting in was humiliating and painful, but leaving was great, leaving was liberating. Perhaps he was really made for the road, perhaps it was a mistake to try to stop, to try to fit in. Perhaps what he was was a perpetual nomad.

He closed the door behind them and found himself alone in his thoroughly empty apartment. With the curtains gone, his denuded place was fully exposed to the passersby, their legs and feet fully exposed to him. Vadik took out his laptop and sat down in the middle of the bare floor. There was one more thing he needed to do before his departure. He had decided to delete all of his social media accounts. What he needed was to pull himself together, and how could you possibly do that if you had pieces of your soul scattered all over virtual space?

The first account he had ever created was on LiveJournal. He was surprised to find that it still existed. Reading his old entries was as embarrassing as listening to stories of his immigrant mishaps, like the one with the tennis racket. His entries were mostly about his adventures, some real, but most made up. There was the story of his meeting Rachel, told with light self-deprecating humor. It generated plenty of comments. Most of them from people eager to boast that the same thing had happen to them. Then there were his dating profiles on Match4U and Hello, Love! He actually had four different profiles on Hello, Love! He would tweak and change his profile every couple of months, when the existing ones failed to attract the women he thought he deserved. It made his skin crawl when he saw what a fake, cutesy mask he chose to present to the world.

He was equally disgusted with his tweets. Quotes from Sartre? Was he fucking kidding?

Still, his Facebook was the worst. When he first started Facebook, he browsed through the posts of his friends and acquaintances and came to the conclusion that the main purpose of Facebook was to boast of nonexistent happiness and barely existent achievements. Just look at the photos of Vica and Sergey's 2010 ski trip to Vermont. All beaming smiles, bursting with happiness. Vadik happened to know that this was a particularly miserable trip, because the weather was awful, Eric had an ear infection, Sergey had the stomach flu, and he and Vica had fought the whole time. And so Vadik followed suit and started covering up his own misery, only posting optimistic photos. It was only when he was going through an especially hard breakup that he realized how cruel this strategy was. He would turn to Facebook in search of some friendly warmth and be hit with this obnoxious parade of happiness that only made his pain stronger by contrast.

Yep, he had to delete all of that shit!

All the social media giants reacted to Vadik's decision with displeasure.

"Hopefully this is just hypothetical!" Tumblr responded, when Vadik typed in "how to remove my account." They tried to be good sports and sound humorous, but Vadik felt the pleading desperation as he followed the necessary steps, all boasting countless warnings about how much he would lose.

"You must have found your soul mate," Hello, Love! said in a mocking tone.

Twitter refused to use the words *remove, or cancel,* or *delete.* What you could do was to *deactivate,* which sounded less permanent and less scary.

Facebook's tactic was to hide the instructions. Vadik had to browse for a long time until he finally found a way. Apparently you couldn't delete your account, but you could ask nicely, and the Facebook team was willing to do it for you. The tone was slightly threatening:

"If you don't think you'll use Facebook again, you can request to have your account permanently deleted. Please keep in mind that you won't be able to reactivate your account or retrieve anything you've added."

Vadik shook his head at Facebook's self-importance and proceeded to follow the suggested steps for all of the sites.

When all of that was done, Vadik shut his laptop and got off the floor.

Now that his virtual self was in the virtual grave, he was ready to go on living.

ACKNOWLEDGMENTS

I WANT TO EXPRESS MY HEARTFELT GRATITUDE TO LYNN Nesbit, a super-agent and super-woman, who inspires borderline-crazy admiration in me. To Lynn's wonderful assistant, Hannah Davey, whose very voice gives me hope and whose edits are very much appreciated.

To my fantastic editor, Alexis Washam. I still can't believe how lucky I got with her.

To the entire terrific team at Hogarth, Lindsay Sagnette, Rachel Rokicki, Kevin Callahan, Sarah Grimm, Annsley Rosner, Kayleigh George, and Sarah Bedingfield.

To the brilliant Deborah Treisman, whose support has helped sustain me through my entire career.

To my supremely talented colleagues at Columbia's MFA department, whose mere presence at the same program inspires me. Special thanks to Binnie Kirshenbaum, Victor LaValle, June Folley, Stacy Pies, Steven Hutkins, and Mark Mirsky for their support and encouragement.

To my amazing students, who made me discover so many unexpected aspects of writing.

To my extraordinary American professors, Nancy Miller, Louis Menand, Andre Aciman, Lawrence Weschler, Mary Ann Caws, and

Elizabeth Beaujour, whose insights I still remember and shamelessly use.

To my excellent Russian linguistics professors, who taught me how speech recognition works.

To the MacDowell, Yaddo, and Ledig House residencies for providing me with such divine escapes and inspiration.

To the John Simon Guggenheim Memorial Foundation and the National Foundation of Jewish Culture for providing me with their invaluable support.

To all the brilliant artists and academics I befriended at residencies and panels. Especially Chloe Aridjis, Jennifer Gilmore, Olga Gershenson, Jonathan Wilson, Josip Novakovich, David Means, Mary Gaitskill, Chris Sullivan, Anya Ulinich, Kathleen Tolan, Valerie Hegarty, Rebecca Schiff, Vadym Neselovsky, Mikhail Shishkin, and my beautiful "swim team" (Shelly Silver, Meredith Maran, Kirstin Valdez Quade, and Sarah Woolner).

To Andre Yanpolsky, Stepan Pachikov, and Alex Fridlyand, who supplied me with priceless infomation about the tech and investment businesses. To the friends who gave me insights into the world of online dating.

To David Gelber for being the first person to suggest that I should try writing.

To my kids, who were patient with my questionable writer-style parenting and provided me with warmth and support. To David for his lecture on video games and the sticker of a sheep. To Stephanie for her astute literary criticism, insights into the dark workings of a teenage mind, and sounding sincere when she said that *Still Here* was one of the best novels she has ever read.

To my husband for being the best husband and the best literary critic ever.

And finally, to Vadym Tyemirov for coming up with the idea of the Virtual Cemetery.